Praise for *Whores of Lost Atlantis*

"There are two major pleasures in *Whores of Lost Atlantis*. The first is Mr. Busch's right-on satirical picture of the East Village theater scene. . . . Mr. Busch describes his characters' antics in a comic tone that is so right and so entertaining it becomes the novel's second important virtue. It is a tone that owes much to that way drag queens have of telling a story—which, in turn, owes much to the movie queens of the '30s and '40s. Imagine something narrated by Mae West or Joan Blondell, or Rosalind Russell at her most caustic."
—*The New York Times Book Review*

"The humanity, exuberance, and comic inventiveness that distinguish Charles Busch's stagecraft can be found in every part of this, his first novel. It's also surprisingly sexy. *Whores of Lost Atlantis* reads like an inspired collaboration between Patrick Dennis and the editors of *Inches* magazine."
—Armistead Maupin

"Camp playwright and drag actor Busch debuts with a fictional re-creation of his off-Broadway career—a success story that's part middle-brow Oscar Wilde and very much a gay soap opera. . . . There's much here to amuse anyone, regardless of orientation: the perfect crossover formula that's worked so well for Busch on stage."
—*Kirkus Reviews*

"This book is wicked, loving, *and* hysterically funny—quite a combination!"
—Joan Rivers

"Well known as the author of the play *Vampire Lesbians of Sodom*, Busch displays the same outrageous imagination and wacky humor in his first novel. . . . Busch is a natural storyteller and he spins a highly amusing—and at times highly erotic—tale."
—*Publishers Weekly*

"One does not become a Charles Busch fan; one is enslaved. *Whores of Lost Atlantis* displays the full Busch signature: fiendish wit and universal compassion, found in the unlikeliest places. The novel is also extremely moving, as an exploration of theater, gender, and the joys and terrors of inventing oneself in a Lower East Side tenement, using equal parts sequins, eyeliner, and ambition. *Whores of Lost Atlantis* is a celebration—of friendship, wigs, and a kind of wicked innocence. Watching Charles Busch on stage is always bliss, and now at last we can take him home."
        —Paul Rudnick

"Though Busch's comic timing moves the story swiftly, his ability to couch the larger conundrums of life in compact space is lasting. . . . Much of the conflict in *Whores of Lost Atlantis* is about roles, those forced upon us by society, and those we force upon ourselves. . . . Comedy is often the best elixir for such dilemmas, and Busch's sense of humor never wears thin. With *Whores of Lost Atlantis*, he successfully makes the transition from the stage to the page."
        —L.A. *Reader Book Supplement*

"Charles Busch is a brilliant satirist. His aim is as accurate as it is hilarious. He is his own best target in this, his first (and I hope not last) hilarious novel. Ours would be a drab planet without Charles Busch to make it seem new and wonderful and fabulous all over again."
        —Terrence McNally

"Julian goes through a bedlamite bildungsroman's worth of comic upheavals and identity crises. . . . His colleagues . . . come off as an adorably screwed-up bunch, blending equal parts of *La Bohème, The Three Musketeers*, and a traveling carny show."
        —The *Village Voice*

"*Whores of Lost Atlantis* has all the exuberance and good humor of those movies where a bunch of plucky kids find themselves a barn and determine to put on a show—except in this case, Judy and Mickey cross-dress, and the barn is a loft in lower Manhattan. Terrifically funny!"
        —Michael Dorris

"Busch tells this story as if it were an extravagant version of a stage-door movie from the '30s. There is a collection of adorable misfit characters; in most of their breasts beat hearts of gold. . . . What you wouldn't find in a film from the '30s is Busch's inclusiveness and compassion; Busch has a lively curiosity about all the permutations of human sexuality and identity, and he takes a wholesomely lubricious delight in most of them. Fortunately, he doesn't go out of his way to be politically correct, so he makes affectionate fun of everyone, including himself. . . . Busch knows how to write a poignant deathbed scene, and to crown it with a laugh; he has a heart of gold, but his saber-tongue is sharp enough to slice through every platinum platitude."

—*The Boston Globe*

"I'm not sure Charles Busch will take this as a compliment, but *Whores of Lost Atlantis* is one of the most lovable, amiable, wholesome novels I've read in years. Take out the sex scenes and you've got a wonderful children's tale. . . . Julian Young and his creator Charles Busch have stumbled onto what may be the one great truth of American life. We have enough sex (maybe), enough education (sort of), enough freedom (for most folks), but 99 percent of us don't have enough fun. . . . It's about turning the lead of daily life into the 24-carat gold of fun. . . . It's the power of friendship, and the miraculous rescue of society's orphans, that inform the fabric of this gentle novel."

—*The Washington Post*

"*Whores of Lost Atlantis* is often quite funny, peopled with a zany cast, most of them gay. Yet the novel obviously has deeper intentions than simply getting some laughs. It's about finding one's true identity amid the various roles—some sham and some sincere—that we all assume."   —*Library Journal*

"Has the reader rolling in the aisles"

—*The Advocate*

PENGUIN BOOKS

WHORES OF LOST ATLANTIS

Charles Busch is the author and star of the plays *Vampire Lesbians of Sodom*, *Psycho Beach Party*, *The Lady in Question*, *Red Scare on Sunset*, and *You Should Be So Lucky*. He is the preeminent drag actor of the contemporary theater. He lives in New York City.

Whores of Lost Atlantis

A NOVEL BY

Charles Busch

PENGUIN BOOKS

PENGUIN BOOKS
Published by the Penguin Group
Penguin Books USA Inc., 375 Hudson Street, New York, New York 10014, U.S.A.
Penguin Books Ltd, 27 Wrights Lane, London W8 5TZ, England
Penguin Books Australia Ltd, Ringwood, Victoria, Australia
Penguin Books Canada Ltd, 10 Alcorn Avenue, Toronto, Ontario, Canada M4V 3B2
Penguin Books (N.Z.) Ltd, 182–190 Wairau Road, Auckland 10, New Zealand

Penguin Books Ltd, Registered Offices: Harmondsworth, Middlesex, England

First published in the United States of America by Hyperion, 1993
Reprinted by arrangement with Hyperion
Published in Penguin Books 1995

1 3 5 7 9 10 8 6 4 2

PUBLISHER'S NOTE
This is a work of fiction. Names, characters, places, and incidents either are the
product of the author's imagination or are used fictitiously, and any resemblance
to actual persons, living or dead, events, or locales is entirely coincidental.

THE LIBRARY OF CONGRESS HAS CATALOGUED THE HARDCOVER AS FOLLOWS:
Busch, Charles.
Whores of lost Atlantis: a novel/Charles Busch.—1st ed.
p. cm.
ISBN 1-56282-780-4 (hc.)
ISBN 0 14 02.4391 7 (pbk.)
1. East Village (New York, N.Y.)—Fiction.   2. Gay men—New York (N.Y.)—
Fiction.   3. Actors—New York (N.Y.)—Fiction.
I. Title.
PS3552.U813W48   1993
813´.54—dc20   93–1399

Printed in the United States of America
Set in Novarese Book
Designed by Victor Weaver

For three people whose stories
are forever entwined with mine

Lillian Blum
Eric Myers
Katherine Carr

ACKNOWLEDGMENTS

The drama behind the writing of this first novel has provided me with ample material for a second. My family must be thanked as well as my second family, Theatre-in-Limbo, which includes Ken Elliott, Andy Halliday, Julie Halston, Theresa Aceves, Arnie Kolodner, Tom Aulino, Ralph Buckley, Yvonne Singh, B. T. Whitehill, Vivien Leone, John Glaser, Debra Tannenbaum, Sam Rudy, and anyone I may have missed who shared with me those fantastic nights at the Limbo Lounge. I must acknowledge my three unforgettable friends who have died: our choreographer Jeff Veazey, Robert Carey, and Meghan Robinson. Bobby and Meghan's outrageous style and humor inspired this novel as well as the many plays I wrote for them. I was very fortunate to have as my editor Tom Miller, who had the kooky notion that I might be able to write a novel. I'm grateful to Victor Weaver for making me such an integral part of the cover design. Finally, I need to thank all my friends and colleagues who helped me in this effort: my agents Jim Stein and Jeff Melnick, Marc Glick, Robert Benard, Richard Kramer, Steve Beery, Raoul O'Connell, Edward Taussig, David Morgan, Francesco Scavullo, Sean Byrnes, Larry Bullock, Steven Spagnuolo, Bryant Hoven, John Fricke, and Richard Niles.

Whores of
Lost Atlantis

CHAPTER 1

Julian Young is an amazing cross between Sir Laurence Olivier, Helen Hayes, Vanessa Redgrave and Richard Chamberlain. His ability to evoke dozens of characters and weave a complex narrative all alone on an empty stage without the aid of sets or costumes is wondrous. This one-man show is a work of theatrical genius and must be seen by anyone who worships the theatre arts. Go! Yes, by all means go!

> Rena Gruber Shook, critic-at-large
> A & M Supermarket Gazette
> Fort Myers, Florida

Audiences around the country adored my one-man show. I could sell out a hundred-seat theatre on a rainy Thursday in Santa Cruz. I could fill up a seventy-seat cabaret in Pittsburgh on a sweltering Friday in July. This is not idle boasting. I wish merely to show that I was encouraged to pursue my theatrical career.

By my late twenties, I had achieved a certain fame in the bohemian quarters of several of our major cities. Fliers announcing my theatrical engagements were taped to numerous refrigerators in Chicago, Indianapolis, Washington, D.C., Provincetown, and San Francisco, among others.

By the early eighties, I was in the odd position of being urged to continue but at a loss to know what the next step should be. I had developed a circuit of performance spaces around the country, but one by one, all of my bookings fell through. The theatre in New Orleans was closed down due to building code violations following a Zulu interpretation of Plaza Suite. The cabaret theatre in Seattle lost its lease and was split up into a Gap store and a Wendy's. The gay disco in Detroit that paid me such large fees exploded after a Mafia shakedown. I was a theatrical grim reaper.

I was desperate for new venues to book my act. A mailing to over three hundred regional theatres and cabarets yielded one paltry gig in that great old theatre town, Boise, Idaho.

My friend Perry has said I'd schlepp to the third rung of hell if they'd give me star billing and a cut of the drink minimums. An engagement in Hades wouldn't have prepared me for the Way-Off-Broadway Dinner Theatre/Cabaret in Boise.

I'm not sure I can even put the gig on my résumé since the building burned down during my first performance. I had a premonition of disaster when the cab deposited me in front of the former mortuary. I had been told that nearly a million dollars had been spent on the renovation—but why could one still discern the letters "Cutty Funeral Home" over the marquee? Boise was not the place to discover that the manager who'd booked me six months earlier had been fired the following week and the owners and new manager didn't have a clue who I was. A traveling drag revue was currently ensconced in the former chapel, now the cabaret room. The owner, a forty-ish hunk named Bobby, overstuffed into multizippered and fringed designer jeans, tried to make things right.

"Julian, my wife and I are good people. We don't like seeing you stranded. Though we're completely hetero, we like booking gay acts here at the Way-Off-Broadway. It gives the place a New York aura. Besides, my sister's a dyke, so I've got this empathy going with gay people."

I'm very comfortable being gay, but I bristled at this rube's assumption, as if I had FAG tattooed on my arm. He ignored my society lady hauteur.

"You seem like a very nice person, Julian," he continued. "For the next week, you'll borrow some drag from the queens in the show and you'll be part of the revue. Fine?"

This wasn't at all the solution I had in mind. "No 'fine.' I'm not a female impersonator. I'm a performance artist. It is true that in some instances the line is blurry, but not in mine. I don't perform in drag. I play men, women, and children without the aid of costumes or makeup." I realized I was quoting verbatim from my press release.

Bobby's wife, Cyd, also encased in studded denim, snickered. "Get off your high horse, honey, and cake up. You've got a pretty face and you're small boned. Stick your peter between your legs and have a good time."

Her husband gagged on his cigarette and laughed uproariously at her bawdiness. I was less than amused and pulled myself up with great dignity, replying coolly, "If you reimburse me for my plane ticket, I can be on the—"

Cyd grabbed my arm and sat me down. "Hey, hey, hey, cool your jets. Jesus, you're touchy. Look, I'm serious. I wish I had your complexion. I honestly bet you could fit into one of my old Halstons."

Though I had spent my last peso traveling to Boise and was certainly at their mercy, I held my ground. It wasn't that I had anything against drag. I had dressed up en travesti numerous times for Halloween. My friends are still talking about the time I went out as all three stars of *Valley of the Dolls* simultaneously.

I quite enjoy the feminine side of my personality and find the donning of cha-cha heels no threat at all. My one-man show was all about androgyny. Switching from male to female was as simple as crossing my legs in a different way.

My role models have almost always been women. My personality has been shaped much more by Bette Davis than Humphrey Bogart. Holden Caulfield seemed less like me than Isadora Wing, the ballsy heroine of *Fear of Flying*. On a cloudy day, I can't tell if I'm adopting the mannerisms of an effeminate man or a hard-boiled lady. Rather than looking upon this ambivalence as a deep-rooted, tragic psychological disorder, I've always considered myself the luckiest mortal alive. During the day I can strut down the street in a tight pair of jeans and cowboy boots and feel that testosterone pumping inside me. At night onstage, I can rejoice in a glamorous womanly strength and vulnerability.

I just didn't feel like putting on a girdle and sticking my thing between my legs in Boise. I couldn't simply walk out onstage in a dress. I needed a number, and I didn't have anything prepared. I had been hired as the star act. I certainly wasn't going to be demoted to the role of chorus girl in the Boys Will Be Girls Revue. I also felt some lunatic missionary zeal that I could educate the Boise theatregoers in the ways of New York performance art. I imagined the skeptical, hard-bitten Grant Wood faces staring up at me from the cabaret tables. After a scary beginning devoid of laughter, they begin to warm to my one-man play, in which I portray every member of the Algonquin Round Table. I manage to hook their rural, underdeveloped imaginations. By the time I'm finished, the room is filled with admiration for my boyish whimsy.

Despite the eye rolling and general disapproval of everyone connected with the Way-Off-Broadway, I did indeed appear at the top of the second set garbed austerely in black pants and black shirt. My only concession was a trace of mascara on my lashes.

Whether my act was ultimately suitable to the rough-hewn sensibilities of the Way-Off-Broadway, the Boys Will Be Girls Revue, or the citizenry of Boise is rather a moot point. A vengeful hooker named Joy, a former fling of the club owner, decided to get back at him on my opening night. Joy barged into the club during my act and, to everyone's horror, poured a can of lighter fluid along the length of the bar. She then flicked a Benson & Hedges for dramatic effect.

Suddenly, I was spliced into a low-budget 1970s disaster film. A zigzagged line of flames danced across the floor. Noxious smoke billowed as if announcing some old-time magician. The glamorous female impersonators leaped from the stage, instantly transformed into terrified men whose muscular dancers' legs led them to be the first to exit the building. The patrons nearly trampled the poor coat-check girl trying to retrieve their coats. As the star, I felt it my duty to remain at the microphone commanding everyone to stay calm. My exhortations were totally ignored unless you count the Mexican stagehand who aimed the fire extinguisher directly at me and blew me across the stage with its force.

Cut to several hours later and the parking lot of the Farmer's Daughter's Motel, the place of residence of the drag queens on the bill. Unfortunately, I wasn't staying there. There were no vacancies at the Farmer's Daughter's Motel, so I was being put up on the third floor of the Way-Off-Broadway in the former embalming room. My clothes, my coat, my money, and my I.D.s were all burned to a crisp.

The owners of the cabaret were nowhere to be found. Even if I had located them, my problems would have been their lowest priority of the night. What was I to do? Venture into the wilds and seek sanctuary with some frightened blacksmith and his wife? My only recourse was to telephone my Aunt Jennie in Manhattan to bail me out of this situation.

Aunt Jennie is my mother's older sister and, at this point, my only relative who is alive or will speak to me. My nuclear family melted down when I was seven. That's when my mother died suddenly of a heart attack, leaving my father to maintain some semblance of family life for me and my ten-year-old brother, John. It wasn't in my father's nature. He was always something of a free spirit; my mother tried in vain to tame him. He worked as a salesman for a company that manufactured medical prostheses, peddling everything from glass eyes to false limbs and breasts. Gradually his trips on the road grew more and more extended. I became quite desperate in my attempts to detain him. Once, it took my father and brother a full three hours to locate the wooden leg I'd hidden in the doghouse.

By the time I was twelve, my father was away more than he was home. It was inevitable that, during a business trip to Tahoe, he simply disappeared. We made attempts to find him, but he proved elusive as a phantom. Even today, just for the hell of it, sometimes I'll go into a store that sells trusses and false body parts and inquire if they've ever heard of a fellow named Billy Young. They never have. I usually purchase a little something like a hernia belt just to be polite.

After my father's ultimate disappearance, my brother and I moved into Manhattan from the suburbs to live with my mother's sister, Jennie, a widow with no children. I flourished under Aunt Jennie's eccentric care, but John resented her from day one. A kid designed to live in the suburbs, he loved sports and was bored with anything that could possibly tax his imagination. That included Aunt Jennie. One hour with her could exhaust Leonardo da Vinci's imagination. A woman both helpless and indomitable, she can still get lost in her neighborhood after living there four decades, and she makes a shambles out of a checkbook. But she can fix a broken radio, make a matador's costume from scratch, build a kaleidoscope, and she will persevere until she gets the vice-president of Condé Nast on the phone and makes him promise personally to find out what happened to my November issue of *Vanity Fair*.

What she couldn't do was communicate with my brother. She even took a course at the New School called Contemporary History of American Sporting Events in vain hopes of relating to him. It was all for nought. Until then, I had always been the unathletic, peculiar outsider in butch Suburbia. John had been in the "in" crowd. Now he was separated from all he had known, and Aunt Jen and I were like an inseparable vaudeville act that he could never be a part of. When it came time to choose a college, he chose one in Alaska. Upon graduation, he moved straight to the farthest region of New Zealand. John wasn't terribly charitable when we saw him off at the airport. I believe his parting words to us were "I just hope for the rest of my life that I never have to hear another word about Marie Antoinette, Sarah Bernhardt, or Judy Garland."

They just happened to be my three favorite figures in world history.

It disturbs me from time to time that perhaps it was something in *me* that drove my entire nuclear family to the far west, the far east, and heaven. I'm comforted by the knowledge that I've been unconditionally loved by a truly remarkable woman. She's the smartest and most exasperating person I've ever known. Our identities are so merged that sometimes she thinks I went to school with her in Cincinnati in the twenties. Often I can't remember if she dislikes brussels sprouts or I do.

On this desperate night on the outskirts of Boise, I wondered how Aunt Jen would work out her rescue operation. Of course, she wouldn't save me without a lecture. I could hear her crackling old-lady voice saying, "Do you know what your problem is, Julian? You don't anticipate. I told you you should have called that place first before you got on that plane. You assume everything's going to work out just because you fantasize it will. Life isn't an old movie." Oh yeah? Maybe not a feature, but this adventure was most definitely made for TV. It seemed only natural that I should view life as a celluloid fantasy. Hadn't Aunt Jen, the most important person in my life, fashioned herself from one part Lillian Gish, one part Roz Russell, one part Katharine Hepburn, and one part Lucy Ricardo? During my first thirty years, how many times had Aunt Jen saved me from the abyss during the last reel? We'd shared so many adventures, both comic and dramatic, whenever I said good-bye to her, I half-expected credits to roll.

The midnight chill shook me from my reverie. Miss Dixie, one of the queens in the revue, was gabbing on the pay phone. No amount of tapping on the glass or dirty looks would cut short her phone monologue. It was at that point that it occurred to me that I'd hit the end of the road. My obsession with the theatre had left me stranded in the parking lot of a motel thirty miles outside of Boise, Idaho. I was left shivering in my flimsy stage costume, devoid of identification, credit cards, or cash. I was also devoid of hope. I had no future bookings and not even the prospect of a follow-up call. The future lay as open and bleak as the endless vista of highway across from the motel. I wondered if there was some lesson to be gleaned from this experience. Was the fire and my abandonment in this Beckettian landscape some sort of metaphor for my stalled life? In the frigid night, my self-pity escalated to the heights of operatic hysteria. Surely there was a place for me in show business. Hadn't Rena Gruber Shook from the A & M *Supermarket Gazette* called me a genius? Was she crazy? Could her artistic judgment be trusted?

A door to one of the motel cabins opened and out scampered Miss Champagne, a fragile Latino queen who lip-synched to Cher and Shirley Bassey. Before I could utter a word, she draped her purple fun fur coat over my trembling shoulders. "Honey, no need to get pneumonia."

I was very touched that she should care. I hadn't spoken more than five words to her or any of the queens in the show. Now I found myself asking Champagne, "What am I going to do?"

Champagne tightened the belt of her kimono for emphasis and leveled, "You should have done drag, Missy."

I tried to piece together her logic. Was she implying that my insistence on retaining some shred of masculinity had somehow burned the theatre down? Maybe her quip was meant as something deeper. Had she sensed that my career was as finished as an old Yardley lipstick and it was time to rethink? Before I could demand clarification of that Pinteresque statement, she scurried back into the warmth of her bungalow.

Her stage buddy, Miss Dixie, at last hung up the phone and scooted into the manager's office, her beady mascaraed eyes fixed on the soda machine. I ran for shelter in the phone booth. With frozen fingers, I dialed the operator. When a comforting fatherly voice got on the line, I couldn't for a moment remember what I wanted to ask him. The only words I could summon up were "What am I going to do?"

CHAPTER 2

Alone, adrift on this barbaric continent. I, a princess of the blood royal, find myself reduced to the role of slave. In these straits, a girl's gotta find some steel in her girdle."

Milena, *Whores of Lost Atlantis*
Act One, Scene One

After giving me a lengthy phone lecture on my complete ignorance of the mechanics of living, my seventy-eight-year-old aunt arranged at midnight from her aerie on Park Avenue to have a car and driver pick me up at the Farmer's Daughter's Motel with a warm coat (not terribly attractive but fleece lined). With the power of her love, determination, and American Express card, there was a United Airlines ticket waiting for me at the Boise airport and an envelope full of cash.

I was back in my Manhattan garret by late afternoon the following day. I phoned Aunt Jennie to thank her for bailing me out once again. She was sympathetic but kept repeating a very ugly question: "What are you going to do to earn a living?" I had no answer except to pretend that a neighbor was knocking on the door and that I had to hang up.

I could have earned a living as a performance artist if I had found enough bookings for my act. Unfortunately, I could never hook up with any form of management to help me. The pattern of my life was that I'd play an out-of-town engagement and be hailed as "a bright new star." Then I'd have to return home to New York and scrounge around for a day job to pay the rent.

To pay that rent, I've been many things. I can count among my part-time occupations: ice-cream scooper, go-go boy, telephone solicitor of stolen typewriter supplies, sports handicapper, receptionist in a zipper factory, and writer of one-line descriptions of old movies for a now defunct TV guide. Sometimes those gigs were almost as difficult to find as acting jobs.

I was not in the best of spirits, and when I'm feeling melancholy, I make lists to get my mind off my anxieties. Often, I'll just write a list of all the films of a particular star. To give you an inkling of how dismal things were, I had knocked off the films of Bette Davis, Joan Crawford, and Greta Garbo and was down to documenting the filmography of Ruta Lee.

It was a great blessing when the phone rang and it was the office of a movie casting director that specialized in providing extras for movies. I had registered with this office nearly a year before and never heard from them. The casting assistant explained that extras were needed to play gang members for a violent action film about urban gang warfare. The assistant said in her most patronizing voice, "You're kind of a ridiculous choice for such a masculine type, but they need about four hundred bodies so we're emptying out our files."

I was to report to an abandoned public school on the Upper West Side at six o'clock in the evening. A few minutes after I got off the phone with her, the phone rang again. It was my friend Perry. He too had received the call from the casting office and wondered if I'd been cast. Now I certainly didn't say this to Perry, but if I was miscast as a gang member, he'd be better cast as a member of a gang of beauticians. He would of course challenge that, for in the past few years he had been up working out at the gym with almost religious fervor, and his small, compact, wiry body was becoming beautifully rippled with muscles.

We had met at the age of fifteen at an intensely show-bizzy summer camp in New Hampshire. Along with career-driven campers and career-frustrated counselors, Perry and I found ourselves cavorting in camp productions ranging from *Oklahoma* to an overambitious *Marat/Sade*. Our friendship was sealed when I was about to be replaced as a singing/dancing newsboy in *Gypsy*. I just couldn't pick up the seemingly complicated tap routine. The eighteen-year-old choreographer had the volatile temperament of a Jerome Robbins and berated me before the entire cast. I was only fifteen and I was mortified. Perry, a natural dancer, stayed up all night drumming that damn tap combination into me. Due to his patience, I was able to remain in the show. Years later, I reciprocated.

Perry was desperately unhappy and made the radical decision to have extensive plastic surgery on his face. I always felt his long, bony face with its oversized features was beautifully poetic. But nothing could deter him from undergoing the surgeon's scalpel. He had his full lips made smaller, his chin made bigger, his nose upturned, and his eyebrows raised. The final effect was a cross between Perry's original eccentric features and Howdy

Doody. As he did with me in summer camp, I maintained an all-night vigil after his surgery, placing cold compresses on his eyes to avoid swelling.

The abandoned public school where the film was headquartered looked remarkably similar to the insane asylum from which Ronald Colman was sprung in *Random Harvest*. I met Perry outside the building and gasped. Perry, who is very dark Irish-Italian, had frosted the front of his jet black hair so that he looked as if his head had fallen flat into a bowl of peroxide and remained there for a holiday weekend.

"Yes, I've gone blond," he said with exasperation.

"It's just . . . um . . . startling, that's all. It's definitely a fashion statement. It says, 'I'm bold. I'm fearless. I'm—' "

"It says I'm in a horrible depression. And I've learned the hard way never to have peroxide in the house when I feel one of my mood swings coming on."

"Well, can't you dye it black again?" I could see he was bored by my ignorance of hair-coloring processes.

"No, I can't. I've dyed it so many times this year, it's disintegrating. No, I'm just going to have to shave my head."

We entered the building. I offered, "Have you ever discussed with your therapist the connection between manic depression and blonding? I mean, they're both chemically based. And think of all the famous suicide blondes. I bet I'm on to something."

"Julian, cool it. My brain does not crave hydrogen peroxide. I just love blondes."

It really was true. Perry is obsessed with blondes, and not your obvious Harlow or Marilyn, but the hothouse variety, dirt cheap blondes on the order of Sheree North, Marian Marlowe, and Barbara Nichols. I honestly think his solution to world peace would be to make the entire population blond. The slightest word out of your mouth expressing ennui or a lack of plans for the evening and Perry whips out the blonding kit. I once made that error and emerged from his building with a mane of tortured white blond frizz.

"Perry, may I inquire as to the source of your depression?"

He leaned against the tall iron grating. "Oh, let's see. Why am I depressed? Um . . . well, my answering machine broke, which I suppose doesn't matter since I don't have an agent and never go to auditions, and even if I did, I never get cast because they think I'm too gay and too weird looking. My VCR is jammed, which maybe is a good thing since my addiction to old movies has reached such proportions that I can't even leave the apartment for days if there's a Betty Grable film festival. The security door on my building is broken, but what does it matter, I've been robbed four times and I'm sure it's my landlord who's breaking in and I can't afford to move to a better neighborhood. Yes, I'm depressed."

Part of my relationship with Perry since adolescence has been as his part-time therapist. I don't mind at all. In fact, I welcome the position. I share certain of Perry's neuroses and anxieties, and when I help him confront his problems, it helps me sort things out for myself.

"Perry, what you're saying is, you don't have a life."

"Is that what I'm saying?"

"That's what I'm hearing. You are going through a premature midlife crisis, a turning point, and you need to rethink your goals."

"But I've been neurotic since I was born. I went to my first therapist when I was four years old. Before I even learned to talk, I was having trouble expressing my feelings about being adopted." Perry held on to the bars of the fence as if he were in a prison picture. Despite the loving efforts of his adopted parents, Perry has never been able to accept his abandonment in infancy by his birth mother. "Julian, I've never really been in control of my emotions. They control me. Believe me, it's not fun being Perry Cole, or whatever my real name is."

I felt for him. Just one look at his ugly/beautiful clownlike face revealed the tensions within. "Perry darling, you may be in a permanent state of distress, but you've always been the most amusing depressive I've ever known and when you're in a manic phase, you're positively delicious." I gave him a quick hug.

He smiled fleetingly. "You know, Julian, I've always been jealous of your ambition and big personality. People have always liked you."

That observation struck me as rather odd. I've always viewed myself as the eternal loner. If I close my eyes, my self-image is always of sitting alone at a coffee shop counter, or browsing alone in a bookstore, or battling the elements alone on a windy street. As far as that big personality, wasn't that simply an elaborate smoke screen that masked a kind of cipher, a disturbing blankness that often made me feel invisible? A few years earlier, I'd questioned even my ability to choose how well done I liked my steak or whether it was me or my brother who had the heart murmur. My whole identity was one big question mark. However, my friend Perry was right, I did have ambition. My need to carve a niche for myself in American show business no matter how offbeat my talents frightened even me. It wasn't for nothing that I had recurring dreams of having Joan Crawford and Evita Perón over for dinner; only I was able to understand and forgive them.

Perry and I entered the forbidding gates of the abandoned school and were instructed to congregate in the gymnasium to be divided into assorted gangs and issued costumes. The halls were teeming with activity, and it was fun to be suddenly immersed in moviemaking. It didn't take too much of a stretch of the imagination to feel as if we were on the old MGM lot shooting a *Blackboard Jungle*–type message picture. I had heard tales of extras who made an impression on the director and were upgraded to bit parts and sometimes even principal roles. I could see myself being plucked out of the mass of extras to portray the sensitive, tormented member of the youth gang. Perhaps I could be the first one to be knifed during the rumble. There were about a dozen different fictional gangs represented in the film, and each gang had its homogenous physicality and its own uniform. There were gangs of skinheads, tall husky guys, an Asian gang, and a Rastafarian gang. All of them color coordinated. Perry and I were put in a gang of skinny white boys under five eight. Actually, I was an inch too tall, but I slouched so Perry and I wouldn't be separated. Our fierce urban street garb were rather effete mustard-colored jumpsuits out of I *Was a Teenage Delinquent from Mars*. We soon realized that the producers had cast not only members of the Screen Actors Guild but real street gangs as well. Just when we were feeling part of the motion picture community, a coterie of battle-scarred teenagers would snicker at us.

We were herded out of the building and into Riverside Park, where a band shell was the setting for a gathering of the city's youth gangs. In the scene, one of the principal actors is shot and a violent riot breaks out. The second unit director announced via loudspeaker that when he shouted, "Action," we were not to actually riot but simply move about at a natural pace. Music and editing would make us appear to be running rampant.

At the sound of "Action," all hell broke loose. Kids jumped over barricades, knocking everyone out of their way. Actors playing cops grabbed at them and got slugged for their efforts. Perry and I were terrified that we'd be trampled in the melee. Take after take, we ran for our lives—for ten dollars an hour. During one endless chase, I noticed someone hiding beneath the bleachers. I motioned to Perry, and we slipped under them. What we saw was a strange creature. Bundled up in layers of fraying rags was an ageless being, her face peering suspiciously through the fringe of her babushka. She waved us away, but we ignored her admonition and moved closer. Anything to get away from the violence of the movie set.

At last, the director announced, "Cut!" I turned to our companion-in-hiding and said, "Sorry for butting in, but we couldn't take it any longer."

In a low, husky, slightly accented voice, she asked if I had a match. I told her I didn't smoke. "Damn Lila for sending me to this shoot. I don't need this shit. One of those prick bastards stole my lighter. It was a fucking antique."

Getting a closer look, I saw that she was Japanese and not much older than I. Her decadent appearance was enhanced by eyes smeared with black kohl and a bony face streaked with white rice powder.

I said, "I've never seen a gang member like you, dear."

She raised her pencil-thin brows several inches. "I could say the same about you, girls." I could sense Perry bristling. He may play fast and loose with the Clairol, but he hates when anyone disputes his masculinity. She added in an irritatingly superior tone, "I don't imagine you're a member of SAG."

Perry piped up, "Yes, we are. Lila uses us frequently."

She sniffed. "Funny, I haven't seen you two around. Lila uses me on most

New York shoots. Whenever they need bizarre bag people, she calls me. Of course, it's all so ridiculous. Why should she think of me like that? I'm a sophisticated woman."

Indeed, if we didn't look like gang members, she didn't look like any known bag person outside of old Kyoto. I introduced Perry and myself.

"My name is Kiko. Simply Kiko."

I said, "I take it you're from Japan."

"Yes, that is from where I was born, although I have in me the blood of many nations, some Greek, some Mongolian, some French, a good lot of Gypsy."

Frankly, I didn't see it. She looked as Japanese as Miyoshi Umeki. But she sure as hell was exotic. She made me feel like the blander side of Florence Henderson. She spoke in a flat, bored voice that suggested a liberal arts education at a fine women's college and too many nights on the town. "It's been simply hell waiting for my grant money to come in. I hate this time of year. That's why I'm forced to humiliate myself like this."

"At least it's show biz," I chirped.

"I loathe show biz," she growled. "I could have a successful traditional acting career if I chose, but I prefer to create my own work, my own universe."

"You're a performance artist?"

"Must you label everything? I'm surprised you haven't heard of me. I'm rather a legend in the East Village."

I could feel Perry tighten beside me. He has an extremely low tolerance for sham. At this moment, I could envision the sham antennae springing out of his head. As for performance art, if Virginia Mayo didn't play it, he wasn't impressed.

Kiko rummaged through her satchel and found a dirty, ripped manila envelope. I couldn't believe she'd be so tacky as to show us her newspaper clippings. Thank God they were from reputable publications such as *The Village Voice*, *The Drama Review*, and *Downtown*. The photos accompanying the reviews were striking. Kiko nude in a primal scream, Kiko bathed in a tub full of stage blood, and Kiko sprawled nude on a tangled pile of skeletons. She didn't let the clippings out of her hands but rapidly read us yellow underlined highlights. "You see, it says here, 'Kiko is superb,' 'A miraculous artist,' 'A Hirohito of High Performance Art.' " That last quote was a mite ambiguous. I wondered if indeed it was meant to be complimentary and if it was given by critic or management. She shook her head wearily. "So you see, darlings, how absurd is my life, how degrading, playing a bit as this movie bag lady when I'm an acclaimed artist with an enormous following."

Kiko dug out another piece of paper, and sure enough it was a flier for her next show. "Friday I'm premiering a new piece, *Labia Impressions*."

I was confused. "Impressions? Impersonations? You mean of famous women's vaginas?"

"No, they are impressions of a white male–inspired global catastrophe. I

have no interest in linear narrative. My life is after all one of emotional fragments, images, essences."

She thrust a flier at me. She tried to palm one off on Perry, but he said
he'd take the information off mine.

"You both should come, although I should warn you, it will be a mad
scene."

I looked at the flier. The performance was being held at a club called Golgotha, deep in the East Village, between Avenues C and D. Although I'd
lived in Manhattan most of my life, I had never ventured that far east. The
prospect seemed as perilous as traveling to the center of the Amazon.

A twenty-minute break was announced, and Perry asked me if I'd escort
him to the rest room. We left Kiko rummaging through her satchel for some
hand moisturizer. When we were barely five feet from her, Perry snapped,
"She's such a phony, and if you believe a word she said or actually want to
attend that stupid show of hers, you really are a jerk."

"It's only three dollars and no drink minimum."

We arrived at the Port-o-san, and fortunately there was no line. Perry
went inside the booth, and I began a long, tedious wait. He takes more time
to pee than anyone I've ever known. Proust could have typed out another
volume waiting for Perry to return from the loo.

Bopping along the path was a group of about six hoodlums. The costume
designer had garbed them surprisingly in turquoise, knee-length kimonos.
But even dressed in diapers, these kids would have looked terrifying. One of
them with scars crisscrossing his face grunted at me, "Anyone in there?"

I nodded, completely intimidated. The kids laughed and spoke to one
another in a dense, indecipherable street patois. Without warning, they
grabbed all four sides of the Port-o-san and began shaking it like a carton of
fresh orange juice. They found this excruciatingly funny. I pleaded with
them. "Hey, c'mon, my friend's in there, stop it!" With one hand, the small-
est of the group effortlessly knocked me to the ground. They lifted the Port-
o-san and attempted to turn the whole thing upside-down. I could only
imagine poor Perry sitting on the pot being shaken up like an early astro-
naut. I ran around frantically looking for a cop and could only find actors
playing cops "who wouldn't dream, darling, of interfering."

Kiko wandered by, and I explained that poor Perry was trapped inside.
With the studied intensity of a Kabuki Medea, Kiko leveled a finger at the
boys and bellowed, "Stop this at once! Enough!"

To my astonishment, they laughed and bopped away, wiping their eyes
with laughter.

I stared at Kiko with wonder. "You really are good. I better catch those
labia impersonations." I opened the door to the Port-o-san, and Perry staggered out, dazed and ashen, his pants drenched in urine.

What could one say? "Oh, honey . . ."

Kiko examined him up and down. "Look at you, your pants are filthy."

I added, "Perry, these kids tried to turn the whole thing upside-down, but

you should have seen how Kiko stopped them. She really was magnificent."
Perry was too shaken up to reply or thank her for her intervention. I answered for him. "Thank you so much, Kiko. We'd love to see your show
Thursday. Wouldn't we, Perry?" I thought it was the least he could do, but
instead he stumbled a few steps and threw up.

CHAPTER
3

Slave girl, sing for your supper or be slaughtered. Perform for the court
some musical number to soothe our ragged nerves.

Emperor Zenith, *Whores of Lost Atlantis*
Act One, Scene One

Call me manipulative, but I have to confess, I am one of the world's
great convincers. Given half a chance, I can summon up enough enthusiasm to persuade most people to go anywhere. With this special gift, I convinced Perry and our friends Joel and Camille to attend the glamorous *Labia
Impressions* preem at Golgotha. We decided to make a night of it, with Joel
making dinner for us at his place before we trekked to the East Village.

That particular Thursday I was working as a temp receptionist for a small
factory that manufactured armpit sweat pads. The loft was very near where
Joel was employed as the assistant to the very successful Broadway librett-
tist Howard Fuller. We arranged for me to pick him up at work, Howard's
sprawling Central Park West apartment, so we could subway downtown together.

I met Joel Finley during my first week at Northwestern University. He was
in my freshman acting class and made quite an impression on me. I had
pictured myself as a highly sophisticated New Yorker plunked into an arid
landscape peopled with Midwestern rubes. Nothing prepared me for an exotic hothouse flower such as Joel. Over six feet tall, with legs that appeared

to sprout only a few inches below his sternum, he walked with the bored slouch of a 1950s Parisian fashion model. Add to this a dark Prince Valiant bob and delicate features any debutante would envy.

The first day of class we had to sit in a circle, and each of us had to tell our name, where we were from, and state two of our favorite films, plays, or books. The acting class was composed of a fairly dreary assortment of vapid sorority and fraternity types. Their greatest cultural influences tended toward 2001: A Space Odyssey and The Lion in Winter. I was always terribly shy in classroom situations. Rather hesitantly I said, "My name is Julian Young. I'm from New York City, and I'm simply gaga over I Could Go On Singing starring Judy Garland and the 1938 Marie Antoinette with Norma Shearer and, really, anything with Ida Lupino." The teacher and the class had such perplexed expressions on their faces. To this date, I've been trying to analyze it. I was anxious to hear what Joel would say. In a languid, British-accented voice that would have made Lord Alfred Douglas sound butch, Joel drawled, "My name is Joel Finley. I hail from Indianapolis, and I'm absolutely mad about Mary Poppins and The Duchess of Malfi." I adored him from that very moment.

Later in the semester, we had to choose partners to perform a scene from a play. Joel was the only boy in class I could induce to play Doc to my Lola in Come Back, Little Sheba. We spent hours rehearsing the scene, and we established the working rapport that has kept us collaborators in the theatre ever since. Joel was very helpful in editing out of my performance any trace of Mrs. Norman Maine. No amount of coaching from me could keep Joel from turning Inge's alcoholic Midwestern doctor into a soignée Noël Coward playboy. The Ph.D. candidate who taught our freshman class was once again oddly silent after our performance, but one girl, Martha Lee Fuchs, said the sight of me as Lola wearing a tattered bathrobe and curlers in my hair honestly made her want to cry.

A few years after graduation, Joel moved to New York. I was just beginning my career as a solo performer, and without much discussion, Joel became my director. He had matured quite a bit. In fact, physically he was almost unrecognizable from that languid youth. He had broadened considerably and gained dignity. The Prince Valiant pageboy was cropped very short, but he still retained that lovely choirboy face. He now dressed in the casually elegant and conservative Brooks Brothers style of his wealthy father and grandfather. The only traces of his adolescent flamboyance were revealed when he opened his mouth. His speech was still pure British royal family.

In Howard Fuller's foyer, one was apt to bump into all sorts of show biz luminaries. Once, I even shared an elevator with Katharine Hepburn. Underneath my tough shop girl veneer, I'll admit it, I'm hopelessly star struck. I'm not at all discriminating. Anyone who's ever set foot on a stage retains an otherworldly glow in my eyes.

I'll also admit that in the back of my mind, I did have a fantasy that Howard would be racking his brain trying to cast the lead of his latest show, the male equivalent to *Funny Girl*. I'd be waiting for Joel to get his coat when Howard would suddenly have a brainstorm.

"You! You! What's your name again? Jeffrey?"

"Julian."

"Julian, can you sing?" I stutter for a moment and then laugh.

"Can I sing? Can I sing?" I chortle again at the absurdity of the question. I suggest we stroll over to the grand piano in the living room. Joel sits down at the Steinway, and I proceed to launch into a driving medley of Harold Arlen songs that builds to a dynamic, belting finish. Lawyers are notified. Contracts quickly drawn up. Press releases go out proclaiming Broadway's newest Cinderella tale. Once the shock of my good fortune subsides, I get to work. I begin demanding rewrites and a new number to end the first act. I may be a newcomer, but I astonish everyone with my tough professionalism.

"Howard, boys, don't settle. Go that extra mile. I'm a new star, exploit my potential. Give me a showstopper!"

Joel answered the door, waking me abruptly from my daydream. His face was taut, and he had his finger over his lips miming me to be silent. I tiptoed into Howard's apartment as Joel quietly closed the door behind me. I could hear Howard screeching at the top of his lungs on the telephone in the next room. Joel was finishing some filing, so I sat on a stool in the office listening to Howard's tirade. He was screaming at someone named Murray. I whispered to Joel.

"Is he talking to Murray Ashland?" Joel nodded and again put his finger over his lips. Murray Ashland was a legendary Broadway composer who had collaborated with Howard on several long-running shows. I suppose it was no surprise that Howard was nearly hoarse from shouting at Murray Ashland. Howard Fuller was almost as famous for his feuds as he was for his movie-inspired librettos. Three times he had tempestuously announced his retirement from the theatre. I heard him say a final "Screw you!" and then slam down the receiver.

I asked Joel, "Has this been going on all day?"

"And not just with Murray, but with his brother in Miami, his lawyer, his publisher, and Phyllis Newman. For the last hour, I've been dreaming about the perfect martini. I do hope the show we're seeing tonight is a relaxing drawing room comedy." I couldn't remember if I'd told him the name of the show was *Labia Impressions*. I decided to say nothing. Joel was nearly finished with his filing.

"Julian, do you think I talk funny?"

"Funny? What do you mean 'funny'?"

Joel looked pensive. "This afternoon Howard offered me comps to a preview of the new Meryl Streep film, and I said, 'That would be pleasant.'

Howard considered that immensely amusing and said I was too young to be so affected. Am I really affected?"

I wasn't sure how to reply. In truth, Joel's accent is one step haughtier than that of a Mayfair dowager. I answered, "I don't see anything so odd about 'That would be pleasant.'"

"Well, actually I said, 'That would be most pleasant indeed.'"

"Joel, that *is* a bit Ina Claire for regular folk."

"Howard says it's affected for me to employ the words 'alas and alack.'"

"Joel, how did you *get* so stylized?"

Joel thought for a moment. "Well, Julian, when I was a child, I was an absolute devotee of *The Avengers*. I was a raging Anglophile by the age of ten."

"Hmmmm. Therein lies the difference between us, Joel. You wanted to be Patrick MacNee and I wanted to be Patty Duke."

Howard Fuller entered the office.

"Joel, under no circumstances are you to take any phone calls from Murray Ashland. I'm at the dentist's, I'm touring the sewers, I'm excavating mummies. Say whatever you want, but I'm not taking his calls."

Joel had told me Howard digested fistfuls of vitamins every morning. I wondered if that accounted for his hyperactive volatility. He drummed his fingers on the copy machine.

"Murray Ashland is out of his fucking mind. We're casting the lead in a Broadway show, and he's trying to push on me some fag he's boffing whose only credit is a road company of *Woman of the Year*." For the first time he became aware of me sitting in the corner. "I didn't even know you were here, Jeffrey."

"Julian." His eyes lingered on me. For a moment, I wondered if he was imagining me as the star of his musical. My earlier fantasy sprang to mind, but unfortunately Joel can't play the piano and, worse, I can't sing. Actually, it's not that I can't sing. I mean, I'm not Pavarotti, but I can certainly sell a song. Goddammit, I can sing!

Howard continued to stare at me. "Julian, where did you get that sweater?"

I sank back in disappointment. "You gave it to Joel when you were giving away old clothes."

"You know, it was a Christmas present from that son of a bitch, Murray Ashland. Mark these words. Never work with your college roommate. I met Murray at Yale two hundred years ago, and he thinks that's reason enough for him to screw me." I knew Howard wasn't really conversing with us, merely venting his anger, but I decided to toss the ball back.

"Actually, Joel and I went to Northwestern together, and he's been directing my one-man show."

"I feel very sorry for you kids starting out today. The theatre was dying when I started out, and it's as dead as King Tut today. Our friend Joel here is smart to get out of it and go to law school."

Could I be hearing this? Joel? Law school? I felt I was in the wrong play. Before I could say my next line, demanding an explanation of that bizarre statement, the other players in the scene were exiting into the wings. Howard ran to pick up a ringing phone, and Joel grabbed his jacket and headed for the door, carefully averting his eyes from me.

The vocal coach who lived across the hall and a pizza delivery boy were waiting for the elevator, so I had to wait till we reached the street before I could ask, "What's this about law school?"

Joel, still not looking me in the eye, walked ahead. "It's true. I applied to several law schools, and I was accepted by Columbia. I'll be starting classes in September."

"Wh . . . wh . . . when did you decide all this?" I was both astonished and hurt.

"Well, I suppose about six months ago. It takes a while to get applications and so forth."

"Why didn't you tell me? I can't believe you'd keep this such a big secret from me."

"Frankly, I didn't think you'd understand. You're so obsessed with the theatre. I didn't imagine you could fathom someone abdicating from the cause."

"Well, you do me a disservice. I have enormous powers of empathy."

By the time we had reached his apartment, I was hysterical. "How can you abandon me like this?" I flung myself across his bed in agony.

Joel's apartment was even tinier than mine. It was a studio so compact that it was possible to make a bed, have one arm stirring spaghetti sauce on the stove, and sit on the toilet at the same time. While Joel was preparing dinner, I was writhing on his bed moaning, to little effect.

I pleaded, "You're too young to admit defeat. I'm sure you'll make a lovely living as a lawyer, although knowing you, you won't go into corporate law, where the money is. You're not the type for criminal law, and while I think you'd be a natural for civil liberties law, there ain't no cash in that. You might as well stick to show business."

Joel wasn't to be persuaded. Indeed, he continued preparing the ratatouille without missing a beat. "No," he said calmly. "I am tired of being humiliated. I have an M.F.A. degree. I'm more intelligent than most of the people I know who make a decent living. It's time I used my brain for a change."

"What are you talking about, Joel? True, you haven't made any money as a director, but you've certainly used your brain. I think we've done wonderful things together with my act."

"You are your act. It's all you."

"Of course it is. The theatre is my life."

Joel turned away from the stove and looked me square in the face. "Julian, you are the theatre."

I expected our faces to be lit up by a bolt of lightning. What a remark! It was as if he had said, "I'm passionately in love with you." I was nearly speechless. "Why . . . Joel . . ."

"Julian, stop acting."

"I'm not. . . . Maybe I am. I guess I can't help it. I *am* the theatre." It sounded so right.

"I suppose that was like something out of *Wuthering Heights*, but I'll stick to it. You are the living embodiment of the theatre. Think about it. You're flamboyant, outrageous, emotional, obsessed with artifice but also tough, gritty, totally self-absorbed, a survivor, and very seductive."

This sort of emotional epiphany was very uncharacteristic of Joel. He was always maddeningly restrained. Once when we were desperately trying to round up an audience for my one-man show, I heard Joel telling a friend, "Julian's really quite good." Later, I screamed in frustration, "Joel, I know you think I'm talented. Couldn't you have said, 'Julian's fucking fantabulous!' " Therefore, I was amazed to hear him now speak so eloquently. I was enraptured by the portrait he was painting of me.

He continued, "You identify with no religion, no political ideology. Even your identification with your family is negligible. You have no identity but that of a person in show business."

"Joel, is that really so bad?"

"Who am I to judge? But I've come to believe it's not me. There are other joys in the human experience, and I'm willing to find them. I'm asking you to try to see my point of view and not see this as a melodramatic betrayal and, well, just be happy for me."

I could do nothing but bury my face in his bed pillows and groan.

Joel continued to stir the vegetables. "Even Howard told me I was too intelligent to waste my life like this. I tried rather feebly to defend my ridiculous theatrical career, but then I looked down at my current mind-challenging task, and what was I doing? Picking the lint off of Howard's jogging suit."

"Many young people starting out in the theatre would love to be Howard Fuller's personal assistant. You're too close to appreciate it, but he's introduced you to a very glamorous world."

"Well, then *you* can buy his suppositories."

A short while later, Perry and Camille arrived. I'd known Camille less than a year. The manner of our meeting was strictly screwball. Though I'd attempted nearly every occupation other than teamster in my search for a tolerable day job, I tried to steer away from the obvious one—waitering. In my heart I knew I was temperamentally unsuited to hash slinging.

I met Camille during my one pathetic stab at it. The morning shift at Schrafft's was every bit as harrowing as I'd imagined. None of the waitresses showed up on my first day, and the nearly hysterical woman manager informed me that I'd have to handle all the tables, the counter, and the take-out orders. My mouth was still agape when she ordered me to make coffee. How? My application had been a tissue of lies. I had no idea what to do with all that brown powdery stuff. My complete and total incompetence was exposed within five minutes. The joint was soon packed with customers who were in a rush to get to work and needed to be serviced with English muffins, ham and eggs, French toast, yogurt, and that damn coffee. I never even drank the stuff. Despite my nearly tearful lectures that caffeine was deadly for the heart, the customers still insisted on having it. Over the din, I screamed my orders to the old black gentleman cooking, but they always emerged from the kitchen vastly different. The cook kept shaking his head and bellowing cryptically, "You ain't talking my language, boy." I could only recall one short-order phrase from an old movie. How many times could I get away with "Adam and Eve on a raft"? The cacophony of angry voices reached such a pitch that I was intimidated into near paralysis. One face at the counter was sweetly sympathetic. A round-faced olive-skinned girl with a halo of dark curls looked at me with eyes full of pity. I leaned in to her and asked, "Was your corn muffin at all edible?"

She smiled and replied, "Not really, but I should be dieting. You've obviously never done this before."

"And never will again. Nobody will tell me what to do. How the fuck do you make coffee?"

The girl tried to talk me through the various orders from her perch at the counter. When the turnover became fast and furious, she snuck around and began writing out checks. She introduced herself as Camille Falluci and demonstrated how incredibly simple it was to use the coffee machine. I knew she was going to be late for her job, but she shrugged that she was the best word processor in her office and they could go fuck themselves if they didn't like it. She spent the morning teaching me how to stack plates on my arm and eventually took over the take-out orders. Surprisingly, the manager didn't say a word.

At eleven o'clock, two of the waitresses sidled into the coffee shop. At eleven-ten I was fired. I knew how the hostages in the Middle East felt upon liberation. I walked wobbly legged and shaking from Schrafft's. The early-afternoon sun never seemed so welcoming.

The previous two hours had forged an immediate bond between Camille and me. She stopped by a pay phone and called in sick at work. By noon, we were huddled inside the Loews Tower East movie theatre watching a showing of E.T.

We spent the entire day together, and I was very surprised to learn that the very girlish Camille was ten years older than I and pushing forty. Part of her youthful image derived from her being barely over five feet tall, even in spiky heeled boots. She filled me in on her emotion-packed life while sharing a souvlaki in Central Park. Born into a lower-middle-class Italian family with an abusive alcoholic father, Camille was married at seventeen. A few years later, her somewhat moronic young husband was sent up the river for forgery. She developed her typing skills and became an efficient office manager. Camille's first brush with show business was in the seventies, when she became a champion disco dancer. She and her partner Vinnie found Balanchine-like variations of the hustle. A gay temp in her office convinced her to try her hand at stage managing. When I met Camille, she was word processing by day and stage managing off-off-Broadway at night, her brief marriage and disco fame long behind her.

I could always depend on Camille for sympathy. While I was lying prostrate on Joel's bed, it was a relief to hear Camille's bubbling laugh as Joel welcomed her and Perry into his apartment. Camille removed her jacket and quipped, "What gives with the diva?"

Joel replied, "I told him I was accepted into law school."

Perry and Camille both murmured, "Ohhhhhhhhh."

I lifted my head. "Then you both knew about it? Am I such an hysteric that only I have been deprived of this knowledge?"

Perry shot back, "Well, look at you. I'm the one who told him to keep you in the dark."

"Thank you very much. I hope you tried to talk him out of it."

Perry sat on the bed beside me. "Of course I did. I told Joel that he's only been in New York four years. Look at me, I've been pursuing my acting career for nearly a decade, and I haven't given up."

That was hardly a strategic move. In ten years, Perry has not found a single day's employment in show business save the occasional bit of extra work. What sustained Perry was a bottomless capacity for hope and a small but tidy family trust fund.

Joel served everyone drinks. Perry and I had dainty wine spritzers; Joel drank a Tanqueray martini up with a twist, while Camille preferred a butch glass of bourbon. "Personally, Joel, I respect your decision," she said. "We all have to make choices in life. Every once in a while, you've got to evaluate where you're going. I mean, if I hadn't shaken things up, I'd never have become a stage manager. I'd still be married, living in Brooklyn, and being beat up every Saturday night when my husband got back from playing pool."

Perry shuddered. "Did he really beat you?"

"Yes. Of course I slugged him back and broke his jaw, but in my heart, I knew I couldn't go on being his victim."

Joel refilled his elegant martini glass. "How ghastly."

Perry asked Joel, "Didn't *your* parents ever fight?"

"Oh dear no. I only saw my mother lose her temper once in my life. She took one of the andirons and smashed my grandmother's most prized porcelain figurine, but she apologized for it within the hour."

Camille continued her train of thought. "In some ways, it would have been easy staying where I was."

"In grinding poverty?" Joel asked.

"We weren't poor. My husband sometimes made a lot of money as a forger before he got sent up the river. All of you have the wrong idea about me. We were not slum dwellers. My husband and I were part of the elite of Rego Park. I mean, I played poker every Tuesday night with the comptroller's wife, Marie."

Joel nodded without a trace of snootiness. "Rather the equivalent of being invited to the royal pavilion at Ascot."

We got off the crosstown bus from Joel's West Village apartment a block too early. Our walk to Golgotha confirmed every misgiving I had about going to Alphabet City. It resembled photos I'd seen of the ruins of Berlin: burnt-out abandoned buildings, broken up sidewalks, empty lots filled with rubble, and stoned derelicts warming their hands over a trash can full of fire. However, if one looked a little closer, every streetlamp and building was plastered with fliers advertising rock groups with names like The Butthole Surfers and performance pieces such as *Squeaky Fromme, a mock opera*.

As far as we could see, there didn't appear to be a club down the block. The four of us huddled together like spinsters from Boston. A skinny young girl, perhaps twelve years old, zoomed down the street on roller skates, with an aureole of pink hair, the shade one usually sees on bathroom rugs. She appeared to be wearing her father's enormous Bermuda shorts gathered around her waist by a rope. As she weaved figure eights around the startled drug-dealing street people, she was blowing bubbles out of a jar.

Farther down the block, we noticed people going inside a storefront and, sure enough, that was Golgotha. When we entered, we were confronted by a pretty girl with porcelain white skin taking money at the door. Her head was shaved smooth save three little purple tufts of hair above her ears and her forehead. When we went inside, we couldn't figure out what sort of establishment Golgotha was. It seemed to be an art gallery. The badly plastered walls were painted a lurid jungle green and covered with massive paintings in the style of the eighteenth-century painter Fragonard, only the nymphs and satyrs had alarmingly large genitalia. The room was decorated to suit the paintings, with yards of lime green and pink tulle netting draping the gilded frames and rather grotesque papier-mâché putti perched in the corners with blood dripping from their mouths. We weren't sure where to sit because there were only four ripped-up red plastic banquettes, and they were stuffed full of people. We decided to join the bulk of the audience sitting on the cobblestone floor. I searched for the stage, and looking up I saw that a few clamped-on lighting instruments pointed to a space on the floor before us. The room was rapidly filling up, and nearly everyone was dressed totally in black, with something pierced besides their ears, and something shaved besides their faces. They spoke in an indigenous East Village accent that was vaguely Rumanian.

When not one more person could be squeezed in, a young man appeared in the space reserved for the stage. He was exceptionally handsome, with a finely chiseled bone structure and a dazzling smile. His hair was dyed fire-engine red and was shaved back to the middle of his head rather like Daniel Day-Lewis playing Elizabeth R. In a clear, charming voice, he welcomed us to Golgotha. "We're so honored to have our new art installation by Mizer Pashkin coincide with the premiere of Kiko's new piece." He puffed on his cigarette and announced, "We've got a lot of great shit coming up, a performance piece by Voilà about St. Sebastian and next month Miss Thirteen is going to be doing a new show called *Cambodia a Go Go*. If you want to know more about all this, sign our mailing list as you leave, and sign it so I can read it, assholes. Now, everybody shut up. Here's the fabulous Kiko!" He dropped his cigarette on the floor and exited, leaving the butt burning and trailing a fine line of smoke upward into the stage lights.

The performance began. To describe in detail what exactly Kiko did would still fall short. She was brilliant and she was awful. She was also naked and screeched and wailed in a vocal range that would make a dog reach for an ear trumpet.

It didn't matter. Her rapt audience was delirious with pleasure and remained with her through a dizzying variety of moods. At the climax of her show, two men covered head to toe in scarlet and reminiscent of Tudor executioners held her upside-down, her bare legs wide apart. To the beat of a drum, they began breaking raw eggs on her exposed beaver. It made a helluva finale.

Then the magic was over, and Kiko was given a thunderous ovation. But her kind of performer doesn't condescend to take curtain calls. The audience stomped and hooted and applauded till they just plain wore themselves out. The evening was a triumph. Eventually Kiko emerged from the makeshift backstage area and was nearly trampled by admirers.

I turned to Joel in rapture. "Call me crazy, but I think she's the real thing."

"She's real something."

I looked at Camille and Perry, both of them as astonished and wide-eyed as children who've just heard their first ghost story. I was completely energized. Golgotha seemed to be the most perfect place in the world to do a show. Forget Carnegie Hall. *This* was it. One could do anything and not feel judged or threatened. At that moment, Kiko exuded fatal glamour. More than life itself, I longed to be nude and on that stage. Hold the eggs.

The crowd didn't disperse but transformed itself into a party. Kiko floated through the throng of acolytes serene as a goddess. When she was close to us, I moved toward her and said breathlessly, "I'm Julian. I met you the other night doing extra work."

"Oh yes, I remember you."

"Well, you were incredible, thrilling. I'm so glad we came."

If it is possible to smile without moving a single facial muscle, she did it. "Then you must sign my mailing list at the door." Her mellifluous Goddess voice dropped an octave, and she added, "And make sure it's mine and not Golgotha's."

"Oh, I'll sign both. What a terrific space. I'd love to do a show here."

She shrugged. "There is Rupert, the owner. Talk to him." She pointed to the emcee, and then, confident that she had unloaded me, quickly immersed herself in yet another circle of admirers.

There was such a magical electricity in the room. Each member of the audience looked as though he was about to launch into a bizarre performance piece on the spot. I wanted to be part of this wonderful feeling. It seemed so long since I'd felt any real joy in my work. The turgid grind of promoting my minimalist solo act had drained away so much of the basic thrill of performing. I loved the theatre. I loved to act. I loved the danger and giddiness of seducing an audience. So much effort went into booking my act and then fighting for the barest essentials to give the show a veneer of professionalism. By the time I'd hit the spotlight, I could only manage to grimly go through my paces. I needed something to jolt me into a new vitality.

The male characters I played seemed dull and cardboard, as if their interpreter included them only to advance his narrative. The concept of one performer dressed in black inventing stories on an empty stage seemed like an avant-garde cliché. It would have been easy simply to mount my one-man show in this empty room, but that wouldn't have been enough of a jolt. I could hear the whispery voice of the fragile Latino queen in Boise who advised, "You should have done drag, Missy." Maybe I should do drag, I mused. It would be fun to actually look like one of my female characters instead of merely evoking her through voice and gesture.

I wondered if I could return to the innocence of putting on a play the way children do. Wasn't part of that exhilaration derived from "dressing up"? I'd had enough of going onstage wearing a prison uniform of black pants and shirt. I longed to drape myself in the robes of a temptress. I wanted to lay on about a ton of makeup and be an erotic vampiress. For so long I had been trying to simplify my rather rococo imagination in some misguided notion of being more accessible. Fuck accessibility! Like a glutton who'd been on Weight Watchers for years, I was starved for the exotic, the melodramatic, the outlandish, outrageous, vulgar glitter of the theatre!

I squeezed my way through the crowd till I reached Rupert. He was chatting with a striking young woman who unfortunately was missing several front teeth in a jack-o'-lantern fashion. I got his attention and introduced myself. I was shocked and delighted that he'd actually heard of me.

"Yes, you're a solo performer. I've never seen you, but my ex-lover saw your show. Wasn't it like last fall? He said you had six people in the audience but you were fabulous."

"Yep, that must have been me. We had sort of a limited budget for publicity." I was apprehensive about committing myself to my next statement but then just dived right in. "Rupert, I'd . . . I'd love to do a show here. This place is so . . ." Before I could finish the sentence, Rupert squashed a large water bug with his heavy black shoe. He smiled and said with no trace of irony, "glamorous."

"It is. It really is. I want to be in on it."

He raised an eyebrow. "I hope you can bring in more than six people."

"Oh, I will. I'll fill up the joint."

"Would you be doing your one-man show?"

"I don't think so. I want to do something more colorful. Maybe with other actors. They could invite their friends and I'd be sure of getting a crowd."

Rupert looked concerned. "You mean, you haven't even written it yet?" At that moment, despite his flame-colored tresses, Rupert didn't seem so vastly different from the more conventional club owners I'd dealt with. I laughed. "Hey, Rupert. Loosen up. It'll be great."

He pretended to bite his nails. "Who's worried?" He introduced the toothless girl as his partner, Ruby, and picked up a large, heavily marked-up calendar. "Jesus, I'm really getting booked up. Do you want to wait till after the summer?"

"Oh no. I wouldn't want to do that." I needed instant gratification, an insulin shot of attention. He flipped the calendar back to the present month.

"I've got a cancellation in two weeks. I forgot about that. I can give you Friday and Saturday at eleven o'clock. Want it?"

Two weeks. That was cutting it close.

Ruby interjected in a harsh New York voice, "He's being very generous, darling."

"I know. I'm very flattered. Prime time."

They both stared at me, almost daring me to tell them to forget it.

"No, no, I'll take it. Yeah, sign me up."

And there you have it. Life's odd little gifts. I wandered back to my friends, slightly dazed. They had been ready to leave for quite some time. Camille asked where I'd been.

"I've just arranged to put on a show here in two weeks. We've got a lot of work to do."

In sitcom fashion, all three piped up. "We?"

I decided to play it tough. "Yeah, 'we,' and I don't want to hear any belly-achin'. We're going to have a great time." I paused for dramatic effect but could read no expression on my three friends' faces. "We are going to put on a show for no other reason than the pure joy of it. When was the last time any of us did that? There will be no attempt to get critics or agents here, not that any would dream of entering these portals anyway. This production will not be thought of as a career move. Just fun. Perry, you're going to be in it. Camille, you're going to be the stage manager, and, Joel, I can't think of a jazzier way to end your directing career. So are you all going to groan and think I've flipped my artistic lid?" Surprisingly, there was no beefing, but Joel did have one interesting question. "What play are we doing?"

I thought for a moment. I sensed that it should be a comedy and it had to be on the bawdy side and it had to be done for absolutely no money at all. Otherwise, I didn't have a clue.

"Joel, I really can't think about that now. More importantly, what will I wear?" I headed for the door. The others followed.

CHAPTER 4

There is an oracle who resides in the Ivory Tower, but no mortal has ever seen her.

Folio, *Whores of Lost Atlantis*
Act One, Scene Two

I desperately needed inspiration. I had to write us a vehicle within the next forty-eight hours. Artistic inspiration can spring from a chance meeting, rereading a classic novel, or a visit to a foreign culture. I didn't have time or cash for any of those. A costume could inspire me. I needed free access to a warehouse full of old costumes and props. I had to go no farther than my own Aunt Jennie's.

My aunt had lived in the same Park Avenue apartment for forty years, a raffish accumulation of good antiques, kitschy Orientalia, and my paintings. She also has several double-decker closets packed with a veritable history of the past six decades of women's fashion. Her wardrobe could provide costumes for an entire season of network miniseries. Entering her home can be a disorienting experience. Every object in it has grown in either number or size. Her plants are older than the members of most rock bands and have mutated into botanical monsters, decaying, gigantic, and extending into the rooms like leafy octopi. The disorientation also stems from the bizarre murals that cover every square inch of her high ceilings. When I was in high school in the sixties, Aunt Jen encouraged me in my desire to paint allegorical frescoes on her ceilings. Today, they are in worse shape than the Sistine Chapel ever was. It's not unusual to find a cerulean blue paint chip in your teacup. The frescoes portray Aunt Jennie and me floating through a decadently pop-art nouveau universe of bordellos, music halls, and magic forests.

I rang her doorbell to give her a two-second warning that I was coming in, then unlocked the door with my key. Sitting in the tiny room that she lives in within her rather large apartment, Aunt Jennie was in the midst of sewing a skirt. I kissed her on the cheek, took off my jacket, and sat on the daybed opposite her.

"Aunt Jennie, you look pretty today." A scarlet slash of lipstick and her silky silver-gray hair in a tumbling-down Gibson girl hairdo gave her the appearance of a Toulouse-Lautrec model a half century older.

She sighed. "It's terrible, I'm getting big as a house. I have to take out all my skirts."

"Have you been gaining weight?"

"No, I'm shrinking, I'm withering away, but at the same time my waist is thickening. Believe me, the whole thing stinks."

"Compared to most old dames, you do pretty well."

"I suppose, Julian. I suppose. Most of the old bags in this building are paralyzed and can't go out without their keepers. Let's not even discuss it. I don't want to be like those women, always obsessing about their bowel movements. Promise me, if I ever become incapacitated, you'll help me knock myself off. I keep sixteen pills in the medicine cabinet for just that possibility. I heard that's all you need."

I could see she was in a melancholy mood. I would have to don the cap and bells and become court jester to cheer her up. It wasn't hard. Aunt Jen may appear to be the essence of fey elegance, but her sense of humor is strictly scatological. In fact, I stock up on every fart and bathroom joke I hear, for just this sort of occasion. Several years earlier, Aunt Jen was terribly hurt when she heard from an outside source that my brother, John, had married and hadn't wanted either of us at the wedding. I searched high and low for something to break her depression. One day I found her sitting in her parlor, the shades drawn, her reddened eyes closed. I gently took Edith Piaf off the Victrola and played a recording of the world's longest fart. It was fifteen minutes of virtuosic flatulence in every variety of sound possible. Fortunately, it shook her out of her sadness and gave her back some of her old sizzle.

This particular afternoon, I launched into a dizzying tour de force of dumb bathroom jokes with a capper of one about a fat man and a rectal thermometer that left her wiping tears of laughter from her eyes.

I was hungry and decided to make myself something for lunch. I went into the kitchen and checked out Aunt Jennie's pantry—it was a mind-boggling collection of canned goods and drugstore items. She had at least two dozen tubes of toothpaste, more bottles of shampoos and conditioner than

Walgreens would ever stock, stacks of tins of sardines, can after can of Dinty Moore beef stew, canned peaches, peas, creamed corn, artichoke hearts, baked beans, mushroom soup, and quite a few food substances that ordinary folk usually shun in the supermarket.

"Aunt Jen, what are you planning for? A nuclear attack?"

"A pantry is a very private place. Keep out of there. I'll fix you something to eat. I was in a thrift shop last week, and they were having a party, and they gave me a bag with all the leftovers. Would you like a nice chicken sandwich?"

"No, thank you." I found some peanut butter and jelly and then opened her refrigerator in search of bread.

"Honestly, Aunt Jen, you've got some weird diet. Don't you eat anything that doesn't have a shelf life of thirty years? Haven't you ever heard of a fresh vegetable?"

Aunt Jennie hovered over me as I put the bread into the toaster oven.

"Julian, take that book off the toaster. You'll burn the whole joint down. And you know, you're all wet with that fresh vegetable jazz. Nowadays they freeze and can food so it's airtight. It's much better for you than some piece of broccoli that's been sitting outside on the street corner for days. I don't see you eating so well. You cook worse than I do."

"You're the one who taught me. If it doesn't come in a boiling bag, I don't make it."

"What did you do for dinner last night?"

I removed the bread from the toaster. "I had dinner with Joel."

"What's he up to?"

"He's going to law school. Dropping out of the theatre." The words stuck in my throat like dry cereal.

"Well, that ought to make his parents happy. His father is a lawyer, isn't he?"

I laid on the peanut butter. "Yeah, everybody's happy. I'm so happy they're happy." I opened the jar of raspberry jelly and wondered if it was the same jar I'd opened when I stayed home with the flu in the ninth grade.

Aunt Jen cleaned up as I made the sandwich. "Julian, I'm not surprised. Joel's not kooky like you are. He's got dignity and elegance. I think he'd be a good lawyer. I wish you'd have something to fall back on." This was a subject I loathed with violent intensity.

"Please don't bring this up while I'm eating. I am having a hard enough time trying to carve a niche for myself in the theatre without attempting to open a chain of men's stores as well."

We left the kitchen and returned to her room. I sat down on the daybed, balancing the plate on my lap.

"All I'm saying, Julian, is show business is so unstable. Even if you become successful, you may have periods when you're not working."

"No career is completely stable. You could work for a big corporation and the next day get laid off. I understand surgeons are all filing for bankruptcy these days." We had had this conversation before.

She was relentless. "I just think if you had another skill, you could always earn a living. I wish you'd develop your artwork. I always thought you could become a great painter."

I was aghast at her peculiar wavelength. "Aunt Jen, you think I should sell paintings as something to fall back on?"

She picked up her needle and thread. "Well, many stars sell their paintings. Frank Sinatra, Henry Fonda, Katharine Hepburn, Tony Bennett."

"They don't sell them to pay their rent. This is the silliest conversation."

"I never tire of looking up at these murals. I wish you could get the scaffolding out of the storage room and do some touch-ups. People are always picking paint chips out of my hair." Her mind was flipping around like a pinball machine. "Maybe *you* could become a lawyer. They say it's very similar to acting."

"Aunt Jen, you really are full of shit."

"Shame on you, Julian, talking to me that way."

"You really are. You're more stage struck than I. You just have some weird notion that occasionally you need to act like a traditional parent and spout obnoxious platitudes. You'd hate it if I gave up my dreams and became a salesman like John."

She closed her eyes and took a deep breath. "Poor John. That's a wound that never heals. You know, Julian, I've been reflecting on the pattern of my life, and you know when I think we lost him? When you and I read all seven volumes of *Remembrance of Things Past*. John felt left out."

"Oh, Aunt Jen, no use dwelling on it. John simply belongs to another species than us."

She put down her sewing and leaned back into her chair. The light from the window illuminated her face as perfectly as a 1930s Hurrell glamour photo. It occurred to me that she was prettier in old age than she ever was in her youth or maturity. "Julian, I have many regrets. I regret I didn't entertain more. I shouldn't have been such a recluse, but after Uncle Max died, I realized that all of our friends were his business associates. I had no friends. I've never had friends. What kind of life was that for a big, athletic kid like John? He hated living with a peculiar widow with strange ideas."

"And don't forget, a peculiar younger brother with even stranger notions. Well, even if the whole world shuns you, I like you, Aunt Jen."

"Two lost souls." Like a quick-change artist, she dropped her romantic Lady of Shalott pose and became a drill sergeant. "Don't be an asshole, Julian. You're dropping crumbs all over the goddam rug!"

After lunch, I helped her put away some of her winter clothes. This was the perfect opportunity to raid her costume collection. Her closets are two stories tall, so I had to use a long pole with a hook on it to hang a winter coat on the upper tier. While I was putting away her wardrobe, I noticed something velvet and scarlet. "Oooh, what's this?" I took it down. It was an evening cloak from the 1940s. "What else do you have up here?" There were so many things jammed tightly together, it was hard to see exactly what she had stored away. I thought I spied something in pale blue satin.

Fidgety, Aunt Jennie said, "What are you doing? You're screwing everything up."

I took down what appeared to be a satin 1930s evening gown in very good condition. I held the velvet cloak next to my cheek, feeling the plush smoothness and ignoring the trace odor of mothballs. "Where did these come from?"

"I don't know. They've been up there for a million years. I want to give all this shit away."

"Well, then give it to me."

"What are you going to do with it?"

"I'm putting on a play, and I need costumes."

"What's the play about?"

I was finding that question tiresome. "I don't know. It could be about this dress." Holding the satin gown next to me, I could see that I could probably slither into it with no trouble.

Aunt Jennie examined the stitching. "This is a very good dress. It's almost museum quality. I don't want you messing it up. Who's going to wear it?"

"An actress I know. I don't think you've met her."

"What size is she?"

"What size? Hmmmm. She's about my size."

CHAPTER 5

I was born with the gift of prophecy. I see things not as they are but as they will be. I feel the sensation first in my sinuses.

Weena, *Whores of Lost Atlantis*
Act One, Scene Two

Aunt Jen was a little slow on the uptake, but after a half hour watching me make a complete shambles of her hall closet, she threw herself into the fray. This was usually the case with her. I'd toss into her lap some enormous undertaking that totally overwhelmed me. After an obligatory lecture on my lack of organization and discipline, she'd grudgingly roll up her sleeves. Not long afterward, she'd focus on the task like a laser beam. She'd force me to remain involved, but sometimes I had to sit back and marvel at her brilliance.

This scenario has been played out in everything from building a model race car during my brief and disastrous tenure in the Cub Scouts to writing high school book reports and college term papers. One might question the good of this approach. I know that some people around us felt that it would have more instructive had she let me fail and learn some cockamamie life lesson. During my first twelve years living with my absent father and dismissive brother, I learned a lot about failure. Had Aunt Jen allowed me to keep failing, I would have remained a failure. With her as both teacher and collaborator, I've managed to keep up with the pack and even given them a run for their money. Let's just say that Aunt Jen and I have had a wonderful time living my life.

I left Aunt Jennie's armed with two large shopping bags full of potential costumes for my unknown play. Along with the satin gown and velvet cape, Aunt Jennie unearthed a 1920s bed jacket, a Haitian peasant skirt, a pair of castanets, a molting pink ostrich feather boa, and a plastic bag full of broken costume jewelry. I walked down Fifth Avenue wondering what kind of play could be fashioned around this collection of paraphernalia. I thought it might help if I knew who was in it. Kiko certainly seemed to be a big draw. Would she deign to appear in a play of mine? It didn't hurt to ask. What kind of role would bring out her best qualities? Some sort of courtesan. Perhaps the whole play could take place in Japan. Where the fuck would I find all those kimonos? I'd counted three and one Happy coat in my aunt's closet. That wouldn't be enough. This entire epic could only cost at most thirty dollars. I needed to choose a historical period that I could costume for literally nothing. That canceled out the fifteenth, sixteenth, seventeenth, eighteenth, and nineteenth centuries.

Then I thought if it took place in ancient times we could be basically nude and merely drape ourselves with some of the costume jewelry and a few strategically placed scarves. To hell with the scarves, this was the East Village. I would do total frontal nudity! Then I remembered that I was going to play a woman. An audience's imagination can go only so far.

I really did want to play a female role. In my solo shows, I'd always felt that the female characters were my most vivid. Some of the men I played were present simply to forward the narrative. In this ensemble piece, I could saddle the other actors with those roles. In my heart, I'd always seen myself as a leading lady in the grand tradition.

My greatest fantasy has always been to be Sarah Bernhardt. From early adolescence I've read every book and article about her phenomenal theatrical career, which spanned from the mid–nineteenth century to the 1920s. She's as vivid a figure to me as if I saw her in a movie last week. Her name evokes to me the decadent paintings of Doré and the lush melodies of Debussy.

My upcoming gig at Golgotha was most likely the only opportunity I'd ever have to indulge myself in this particular theatrical dream. I couldn't wait to extend my arms in the grand, sculptural gestures I'd studied so long from her photographs. I was aware that most audience members wouldn't recognize that my dramatic rising inflections were based on hours spent listening to her scratchy early recordings at the Library of the Performing Arts. I couldn't care less. We were creating this modest theatrical event for the sheer fun of it. For two precious nights, I could be a faux Bernhardt.

I couldn't just "be" Sarah Bernhardt. I wanted to be a Bernhardtian actress in a romantic role. Perhaps, I pondered, Kiko and I could be rival divas on the order of such classics as Old Acquaintance, The Great Lie, or Aïda.

I passed by an occult book shop, and as I paused to gaze in the display window, my eyes fell upon a volume with the title In Search of Lost Atlantis. Lost Atlantis. Those words certainly conjured dramatic images. Cataclysmic destruction, temples falling, hermaphrodites, evil emperors, high priests, and two bitchy courtesans battling it out as the entire continent sinks into myth.

I wondered if I could tell this tale in forty-five minutes. No matter how compelling, it would be difficult holding the attention of an audience that would be either standing in the back drinking beer or sitting cross-legged on the hard stone floor. I saw my reflection in the bookstore window and envisioned myself adorned with cascading jewels and my eyes rimmed with kohl. I could play a young princess from a foreign land, maybe Gaul. She's taken prisoner but escapes death by becoming a concubine of the sexually perverted emperor, played naturally by Joel. Kiko could portray the head courtesan, who resents my presence at court. As I rise to power and influence, she plots to destroy me. Perry could be my confidant, an intensely neurotic eunuch.

I was already mapping out dialogue when I heard my name called. Crossing the street to greet me was Zoe Gomez. I had met her the previous summer when I was working at the New York Renaissance Faire. Always eager for a buck, I was hired by a neighbor to peddle her homemade apple dolls. I received quite a generous commission, but nothing was worth sitting in a tiny makeshift booth, garbed in a sweltering velvet doublet and tights through a succession of murderously hot weekends. The dolls themselves disturbed me. Representing the denizens of a quaint mythical village, their heads were carved out of decaying apples which were then glazed with lacquer. I did not find them cute. They all uncannily resembled my eighth-grade math teacher, Evelyn LaRock, a heavyset, middle-aged woman with a Javert-like obsession to flunk me. All day I'd sit in that Renaissance lean-to pondering the images of Miss LaRock as ye olde village seamstress, Miss LaRock as ye olde village cobbler, and Miss LaRock as a multitude of olde village brats. I'm afraid I didn't throw myself into the lusty Chaucerian spirit. I rarely socialized with any of the craftspeople who sold candles, leather crafts, or woodwork. My mission was to squirrel away as much dough as I could to give myself a winter nest egg to pursue my theatrical career. I had little interest in cultivating any of the large cast of young actors hired to populate this mock Olde English village.

The most hard-boiled intentions are shot, though, when one comes across an original such as Zoe Gomez. A tiny, fragile handful of a girl teetering on four-inch wedgies, Zoe looked both German and Spanish, with jet black hair, a stark white face, and large, dark eyes that darted about furtively. She was something of a mystery. Zoe never divulged a single fact of biographical information, but five minutes in her presence revealed a girl riding a worrisome seesaw of sexual conflict. Severely prudish about the slightest verbal profanity, Zoe dressed in an often overtly sexual manner. Her small frame was perfectly proportioned, and she chose clothes that drove attention to her pale, heart-shaped face and Playboy bunny–perfect bosom. This afternoon on Fifth Avenue, Zoe was sporting black tights, a convent schoolgirl's plaid pleated skirt, and a 1940s beaded black cashmere sweater opened dangerously to the fourth button.

"Zoe, what rabbit hole did you pop out of?"

She giggled and replied in her breathy virgin-in-a-porno-film voice, "Barnes and Noble. I wasn't sure it was you, so I just called your name and took the chance. I was prepared to run away."

"Well, your hunch proved correct. You look great." I suppose, if being painted up like a Comanche in midday constituted looking great. "Are you in a show?"

She looked downcast, her white powdered face tensing. "No, I've been auditioning like mad, but I always seem to lose out. Sometimes I wonder if I'll ever act again. My acting muscles are in desperate need of stimulation."

I chose not to comment. A little boy walking with his mother pointed at Zoe and shrieked, "Mommy, is that girl supposed to be a clown?" Indeed Zoe did resemble a wistful Pierrette in a forties burlesque show. Her eyes glazed over as she pretended not to have heard the child's remark. I tried to keep the conversation moving.

"Will you be performing at the Renaissance Faire again this summer?"

"Oh no, I could never go back. They think I'm a troublemaker."

"I can't imagine why they would think that." I knew perfectly well why they thought that. Her role at the Faire had been of a Gypsy wench. She was hired to roam the fairground asking patrons if they wanted their fortunes told. Zoe was so shy, one couldn't even contemplate what she'd have done if someone had taken her up on her suggestion. Most of the time she hid away from the sun in the back of my apple-doll booth. That's how we met. On one oppressive day, well over a hundred degrees, I was sitting in my booth watching the sixteenth-century parade pass by. I was doing everything possible to lure in a customer save exposing myself. Zoe tilted by, costumed in peasant garb but still perched on her stiltlike pumps. She looked around her like Bonnie Parker on the lam.

We were all supposed to speak only Renaissance parlance, but it was so frigging hot that instead of shouting forth, "Prithee, wench, come hither," I hollered, "Hey you, come here!"

She quickly ducked inside and in a little voice remarkably similar to that of the young Elizabeth Taylor said, "Kind sirrah, couldst thou provide me with shelter whilst I—"

I was sweating profusely and interjected, "Honey, wouldst thou cool it with the old-time jargon, please?"

She giggled and whispered conspiratorially, "I really shouldn't break character. They dock you, you know, if they find out. I'm supposed to participate in the wench-dunking contest at two o'clock. I'm looking for a place to hide."

"What will they do if you don't show up?"

Her eyes welled with tears, and her voice shook. "I don't care. The two girls who usually do it came down with bad colds, and the stage manager is forcing me to take their place. It's just because she hates me." I said it might be a relief being dunked in the water in all this heat and humidity. Zoe shuddered delicately. "Sweetie, it's so common." She took a lipstick out of her small gathered purse and, with one gesture and no mirror, drew on an even bigger bright red, shiny mouth.

I agreed to provide the wench shelter, and she sat in back of the tiny booth where I stored the unfortunate dolls who had lost a finger or nose in transit. I saw her take out of her bag a paperback biography of Glenda Jackson and asked if she was a fan of Miss Jackson.

"Oh, I just adore her. But then all I read are biographies of great actresses. Inspiration." Then in a surprisingly low, hard-edged voice, she said with intensity, "I am determined to make it in this business. Do you understand me? Determined." At that moment, I felt like I was sheltering Eichmann. She'd remained in my booth for about twenty minutes when a big bruiser of a wench marched down the lane and, with an eagle eye, spotted Zoe's petite foot sticking out. Roughly, she reached past me, grabbed poor Zoe by the arm, and dragged her down the road, Zoe's feet barely touching the ground.

About an hour later, I took a break and wandered about the Faire. I came across a large, raucous crowd. I couldn't immediately see what event they were watching. I heard the sound of splashing water amid their shouting and applause. I poked my head in just in time to catch the end of the wench-dunking contest. I couldn't see much, but floating on the edge of the pool was a tiny, spiked-heeled shoe and Glenda Jackson's soggy face.

Now, standing outside the occult bookstore, I suddenly received a psychic flash. Zoe should be in my play at Golgotha.

"Zoe darling, I'm doing a play in two weeks at a club in the East Village, and I'd love if you'd be in it. There wouldn't be any pay involved, but we'd only rehearse a couple of times. It should be a lot of fun. What do you think?"

"What kind of part would I play?"

Good question. Index cards of biblical types passed before my eyes. "Un . . . uh . . . a terrorized vestal virgin. She's uh . . . clairvoyant. A Cassandra-like figure. It takes place during ancient times."

Her eyes misted with tears. "I'm so honored that you'd ask me. Do you really think I could do it? To fulfill your vision?"

"Yeah, sure. You'll be swell."

Zoe removed from her bag a postcard photo of herself and on the back of it wrote down a whole slew of phone numbers where she received messages, ranging from her answering service to the phone booth outside the bodega on her corner.

Joel had only briefly met Zoe after an off-off-Broadway performance of *Macbeth* in which Zoe Gomez gave a highly original interpretation of Witch Number Three with a thick French accent. Nevertheless, I had faith that my director would ultimately understand my choice of ingenue. I wasn't sure I did.

CHAPTER 6

Andreas, you're a conceited, arrogant, faithless swine but I'm a pushover for ya.

Milena, *Whores of Lost Atlantis*
Act One, Scene Three

If I was to be the leading lady of the production, Joel the villain, Perry the character man, and Zoe the ingenue, I knew we had to have a romantic leading man. Greenwich Village is peopled with any number of hot gym trainers and go-go boys, but I needed someone who could also speak. He not only needed basic language skills but also had to act and move with the panache of a swashbuckler. The only person I knew who fit the bill and could be conned into this escapade was my friend Guy Miller.

Guy was an exceptionally handsome young man, twenty-three years old, who lived around the block from me. We met by chance in a neighborhood men's clothing boutique. Guy's thick auburn hair and chiseled features immediately distracted me from the table of discounted T-shirts. He began trying on very revealing bikini bathing suits, and he seemed to enjoy my running commentary on his spontaneous swimwear fashion show. Guy is a compulsive flirt. He's not particularly promiscuous, but for the fun of it, he'd bat his eyes at the Elephant Man's uglier twin brother. Guy and I are always practicing our seductive wiles on each other and then getting into meaningless spats like lovers in an old MGM musical. We've never had a sexual relationship, and I doubt we ever will. For one thing, we've never both been single at the same time. When I was lonely and unattached, Guy was living with a gorgeous though alcoholic soap opera writer. By the time Guy gave him the heave-ho, I was involved with a hunky Navajo brave who was the keeper of the monkey house at the Bronx Zoo.

It's just as well. If Guy and I were lovers, I'm afraid the third act would end in murder.

I stopped by Guy's apartment with the excuse of retrieving several video-tapes I had lent him. Guy was a theatre major at NYU, and I was appalled that their training program didn't include a word about some divine practi-tioners of the dramatic art, such as Claire Trevor and Gladys George. I felt it my duty to educate Guy in my own rather specialized course in Tough Dame Acting.

I knocked on Guy's door. He quickly opened it. "Hi, Guy, it's been so long. I used to bump into you on the street all the time but now—"

Before I could finish my sentence, Guy thrust a plastic bag full of videos at me.

"Thanks a lot for the tapes, Julian. Kay Francis is great. I really liked *Mandalay*, but *Confession* was a little boring. Thanks again. I'll give you a call."

He was about to shut the door in my face when I pushed my shoulder in to stop it. "Guy, what are you hiding in there? Are you doing naughty things with a goat? I'll be open-minded."

"No, but I do have a date arriving very soon. I thought you just wanted to pick up the cassettes."

"Yes, but a polite little visit might be pleasant."

Guy opened the door a few inches more but looked apprehensive.

"Julian, I'll let you in and even give you a cup of tea, but will you promise to leave before my date arrives?"

"I promise."

He ushered me into the apartment, a small studio designed every inch in chilly high-tech black and white and chrome. The lighting fixtures were out of Dr. Frankenstein's lab, and even the Japanese flower arrangement looked as if it could stab you. It was not a setting conducive to slap-your-thigh-with-laughter evenings. I sat down in an uncomfortable leather armchair that also served as a piece of sculpture. I asked my host, "What's wrong with your date? Why can't he be seen? Bad skin, B.O.?" I had a sudden brainstorm. "Hey, is he a closeted movie star? Have I recently paid seven fifty to see this person?"

Guy was preparing the Japanese green tea. "I'm not playing that game. I've just started seeing this person, and I don't want any critique. I don't want anything to color my own impressions."

I was taken aback. "Guy, I am hardly the Michelin guide of New York fags. I don't have an instant rating system. 'I'll give him a rating of four swizzle sticks.' "

"You have very strong opinions and like to give them." That was a new one for me. I didn't think I had any opinions on any subject. "Guy, I am not a judgmental person. I can find amusement and companionship with the most humble of laborers. I was even married to a sweeper of monkey shit in the zoo."

Guy handed me my tea. "I didn't say you were a snob, Julian. It's just that you have a way of turning every encounter into an anecdote. People usually end up believing your exaggerated version of the truth."

"Guy, next to first-class liars like that cross-eyed bartender at Uncle Charlie's, I'm a rank amateur. I never invent facts. I embellish the truth for dramatic value. Who was it that said, 'The only way a writer can tell the truth is through fiction'?"

"Oh cool it, will ya? Don't spill your tea on my rug."

We sat holding our teacups like society matrons. I asked Guy delicately, "May I query where his people are from?"

"I'd rather not discuss it."

I heard the strange, hollow cooing of Guy's white doves. Like most of my friends, Guy is an aspiring actor. Unlike most of my friends, Guy has the ability to make hard, cold cash and plenty of it. Guy has never worked as a waiter. Guy is a magician and has cornered the market in the high-society children's birthday party racket. He has an extensive repertoire of shows where he plays Peter Pan or Robin Hood or Merlin, all featuring the same five tricks. The supreme illusion is that the kids aren't on to him and he gets booked with the same families year after year. Guy saw me eyeballing the doves in their gilded cage.

"My girls worked hard today. We did three magic shows. The last one was in this incredible duplex penthouse on Central Park South. Mary and Ethel were a big hit." Anticipating the frenzied show biz existence of the birds, I'd named them after the first ladies of the musical theatre, Mary Martin and Ethel Merman. How right I was. By the age of two, they'd racked up more performances than any current dues-paying member of Actors' Equity.

"Guy, you've got to give those girls a rest. Ethel's looking downright hard-boiled."

"Don't laugh, but I've got an agent now that books the doves for print work. Mary and Ethel can get two hundred dollars an hour." I wasn't laughing. Even the lousy pigeons had an agent and not me.

"Dammit, Guy, I knew I shouldn't have given up those hamsters. They could have been my annuity. Why didn't I develop some marketable skill like magic?" I grabbed my hair with both hands in agony. "Why must I be obsessed with stardom? It's a fucking curse."

Guy had a smug look on his face and said benignly, "If you visualize your goal, it will be yours."

"Oh fuck you with your visualization." He was getting on my nerves.

Guy was knee-deep into every aspect of New Age philosophy. He was particularly hooked on the teachings of a channeled entity named Adonijah—he had more cassettes of Adonijah's ravings than I had Garland records. As usual, Guy had worked out an angle of profiting from his spiritual concerns.

"Guy, have you been doing much healing lately?"

"I've been really busy. A lot of massage and even past life regression. I've been learning so much. I've been getting incredible results without even touching."

"Do you charge less if you don't touch?"

Guy rose from the couch, irritated by my cynicism.

"You know, Julian, I don't talk about this with everyone. I never proselytize. If you're not into it, let's not discuss it." I hadn't meant to be so harsh in my teasing.

"I'm really sorry, Guy. That sounded tacky. Really, I discount nothing. I mean, please, I recently went to see this guy who for thirty bucks gave me a massage, a psychic reading, and a hand job. No, I'm very open-minded. I believe in your powers as a healer. I remember when I threw my neck out and you placed your hands on me and I honestly felt the heat emanating."

"You're being sarcastic. You didn't feel the heat."

"No, I did, I did. When you left, I was so scalded, I had to put butter on my neck. My only quibble is why, Guy, why do all you New Age gurus have to attach a buck to everything? I mean, you charge to do a magic show, you charge to have your rabbit shot for *Vogue*, you charge to heal someone's sciatica. I don't think Moses or Jesus or Buddha took credit cards or a personal check with the proper I.D."

Guy refused to lose his cool. "Why shouldn't I? If I have a gift and still have to exist in this material world, why shouldn't I allow my gifts to support me as well as help others?"

I didn't have an answer. I guess to my way of thinking, a true visionary should do it gratis and get pierced by arrows for his troubles. Guy then added, "As a matter of fact, I am donating my time to work with AIDS patients at the Healing Center."

I was impressed and contrite. "Well, I think that's great. Sincerely. I apologize for being so flip." We sat in silence sipping our tea. The birds cooed tauntingly in their luxurious caged loft space. How I envied their life-style. They were coddled, supported, worked constantly, and had artist representation. I wondered if I cast them in the play whether their agent might come and discover me. It was time to pitch the show to Guy.

"Guy darling, how would you like to entertain a group older than six years old?"

"What have you in mind?" He sounded suspicious.

"Well, I'm putting on a little play at a very hip and chic East Village club. It's about the fall of the lost continent of Atlantis, and it's going to be a wild sort of play, very decadent and erotic. I'd love you to be in it."

Guy looked at me as if trying to read my mind. "I'm flattered to be asked, but I have tickets to the opera that night."

"But I haven't even told you what night it is."

"It doesn't matter. I'll call my ticket broker."

I wasn't prepared for such a rebuff, particularly from someone a good eight years younger than me. "You're too cruel, Guy."

"I just haven't forgotten my humiliation when I was your opening act at SNAFU. That was one of the worst nights of my life."

It seems that a few years earlier, I had asked Guy to be my opening act at a club called SNAFU. We did two shows that night. Guy did his first twenty-minute set to dismal audience response. He was so accustomed to performing for toddlers, the adult audience thought he was slightly gaga. He finished his act to almost zero applause, and then I came out and, all modesty aside, scored a personal triumph. In my curtain speech, I exhorted the crowd to stick around for the late show because I was premiering completely new material. Guy was furious because he didn't know that had been my plan and had only one act. So for the ten o'clock show, poor Guy and the animals had to return before the exact same audience that had nearly booed them before and repeat the exact same act. It was nearly six months before he'd speak to me again. The lesson to be gleaned was that, be it show business or life in general, one must develop an extensive repertoire.

"No, no, no, no, Guy, this is a very different situation. This is a play that I'm going to write—I mean that I've written. And it'll take a very little time commitment from you, just a handful of rehearsals, and we'll play it only twice. Friday and Saturday, two weeks from now. There will be no pay, but and I say *but*, it will be a lot of fun and, correct me if I'm wrong, despite all your activities in the realm of magic and healing, is not your first ambition to be on the stage as an actor? Therefore, this is your chance to act and with me!"

He still looked dubious. "I don't know. Whenever I get involved with you, I end up being totally degraded. What about when you assisted me in my act and you couldn't even—"

"Must we go into that? For a young person, you spend an awful lot of time rehashing the past." Guy was referring to an unfortunate incident when we were performing Houdini's metamorphosis trick where Guy tied me up in a sack, threw me in a trunk, locked it, and then, with a curtain covering us momentarily, I suddenly appeared on top of the trunk with Guy locked inside within three seconds. Unfortunately, I left the key inside the trunk, and we never could get Guy out. I had to finish the act alone, performing a somewhat underrehearsed but nonetheless well-received comedy routine.

"Look, Guy, do this for me. I think you'll have a joyous experience, and I promise you, you won't lose your dignity." Actors have a peculiar need to ask what sort of character they're going to play, so I decided to beat him to the punch. My improvisational skills were about to be tested. "You're going to play . . . um . . . you're going to play a handsome soldier of fortune who falls in love with the emperor's concubine, exquisite, elusive, but with a sharp way with a wisecrack, played of course by me, and in the play we—" I was hitting a patch of dead brain cells. I didn't have a clue to this part of the plot. "Guy, it's a beautiful love story, almost Shakespearean. I need someone with your charisma and classical training to give the show weight."

His intercom buzzed, announcing the arrival of his mystery date. He led me to the door.

"Julian, I have to think about this one."

I protested. "No, you can't think. If you think about it, you'll say no. C'mon, give me an answer right now. We've got to start rehearsing in a day or two. If you hem and haw, you'll screw me up, and I won't be able to find anyone else. Please, darling."

He pushed me toward the door.

"Julian, did you have trouble with the elevator coming up?"

"No, why?"

"It's very undependable. I got trapped in it for twenty minutes earlier today. You better take the stairs down at the other end of the hall. You better get going."

Guy's improvisational skills are even worse than mine. Something fishy was going on. One didn't need to be J. Edgar Hoover to figure out that he didn't want me to run into his date coming up in the elevator. If I hadn't really needed Guy's participation in my show, I would have been rather annoyed at his assumption that I cared anything about his date. Instead, I proceeded relentlessly with my hard-sell campaign.

"Guy, I'll go down the stairs. I'll fly out the window, just do the show. Don't you get a great vibration about this? Isn't Atlantis a New Age buzzword like pinto bean? It's destiny, darling. You and me as Atlantean lovers."

"Julian, something tells me I'm going to be your stooge again, but all right. I'm in. Just leave."

"You won't regret this."

The doorbell rang. Guy sighed. It was too late. I was going to have to meet the mystery man.

"Julian, I should tell you. My date . . . it's someone you know."

That was certainly intriguing. "Oh?" I opened the door, and standing before us was my ex-boyfriend Bruce, the Navajo zookeeper. Never remotely articulate, he stood there with his mouth agape, with long black hair, bandana, deep tan, and slack-jawed expression. Frankly, I wasn't sure what my reaction should be. I had broken up with Bruce many months before, and it was hardly the romance of the century. His silent manner and permanently puzzled expression had fooled me into reading all sorts of complex, abstract thoughts behind his every labored utterance. It took me a good four months to arrive at Perry's instant diagnosis that my stalwart, beautiful Indian brave was bone dumb.

Bruce was incredibly stupid. When I finally pinned him down on some hard, cold facts, it turned out that he thought the Civil War was fought only a few years prior to World War II. He thought the star of *Raiders of the Lost Ark* was Clark Gable. He thought the continent of South America was one of the

United States. His common sense was even more negligible than his history and geography skills. However, he had the most gorgeous rippled abdominal muscles and the most powerful thighs and those biceps with the veins and, oh my God, he had the most wonderful manly smell even when he sweated. Without getting too graphic, let me just say that while nothing worthwhile ever came out of his mouth, he had certain oral skills that were fairly devastating. There were reasons why I tried to make this marriage work. Our breakup was more of a slow fade to black. That's been the scenario of most of my relationships. I've never been the confrontational type. Not for me the grand emotional scene, the tears, the bitter, lancing accusations. No, I prefer the bittersweet tone of resignation, the wistful smile that speaks volumes, and a brief but beautifully worded farewell that says, Perhaps if the world were different, well . . . With Bruce, it was a case of each of us saying, "I'll call ya," and we didn't.

I had to approach this new situation between Guy and Bruce with tact. I don't think Ann Landers would say that Guy was in any way wrong to sleep with my ex-beau. I had no strings on Bruce. Still, with all the beautiful and stupid young men available, it seemed a little tacky for Guy to pick this one. What did it really matter? The important thing was for Guy to be in my play. I couldn't think of any other leading man type who would work for free. It was up to me to make a diplomatic gesture.

"Hello, Bruce. Guy told me you were coming over. I think it's great that you two are getting together. Is this the first time?" Bruce nodded as if he had to translate my words from the Cantonese. I didn't wait for a verbal response. "It's been a long time, Bruce. You look great. I really have got to get going. Guy, we'll probably start rehearsing on Thursday. Bruce, um . . . I'll call ya." I headed out the door and then remembered to add, "Guy, pick yourself up a gold lamé G-string. See ya!"

Guy shut the door behind me. Almost immediately I heard Bruce making the grotesque monkey sounds that always gave me the creeps. I wondered if Guy would find that erotic. I was rather amused by the thought of this pairing. For one thing, Guy would feel so embarrassed that he'd have to do my show. For another, now I could phone Bruce and find out exactly what Guy was like in bed and save myself the trouble.

Once out on the street, I tried to imagine what stage of disrobing they were up to. Were they already kissing? Precoital conversation wasn't the best idea with Bruce. He lost some of his smoldering mystery when you discovered he didn't know that we also voted for senators and governors. It was dark out, and everyone was rushing home from work or embarking on a night on the town. Were their clothes off yet? Had Guy found the small tattoo of Sitting Bull on Bruce's left ass cheek? Perhaps the Cheetah-in-heat sound effects weren't so ridiculous. Perhaps they were rather endearingly childlike. For a moment, I thought of dashing back into Guy's building, racing up the stairs, forcing my way into the apartment, tossing off my clothes, jumping into bed with them, and coercing them into a ménage à trois. Then I'd really know the meaning of loneliness. Guy and Bruce would probably have a lot of fun in bed together. Guy prided himself on his technical prowess in the sex department, and Bruce was quite adept in an instinctual Cro-Magnon sort of way. I passed by a Baskin-Robbins and decided to splurge on a small cup of coffee ice cream. The dead white fluorescent lighting made all of us gluttons look hideous. I took the dish and ate it while walking home.

I didn't need to be wedged between Guy and Bruce to feel lonely. I felt the sharp knife of undesired solitude like a hunger pang. It was as if a wild storm were brewing and I had no shelter to hide in. I tried to blot out this growing surge of sadness by concentrating on my new play. It would be so much fun to dress up in outrageous costumes and throw together a little show with a group of sympathetic friends. It might divert my attention for a week or two from awful moments like this; awful, wrenching moments when everything from the polluted acid green sunset over the Hudson to the sight of a young couple scooting into a taxi reminded me that I had always been alone.

CHAPTER 7

I'd like to see that bitch boiled in oil, but dammit, she's got connections in this town.

Milena, *Whores of Lost Atlantis*
Act One, Scene Three

My cast was nearly complete. Joel, Perry, Zoe, Guy, and . . . hmmmm, the big question was my costar, Her Divinity Herself, Lady Kiko. I really needed her to lend the show some credibility in the performance art racket. I screwed up my courage and decided to phone her at once. It was nearly eight o'clock in the evening. Perhaps she was dressing for a sepulchral night on the town. You may wonder how one locates a cult figure. I let my fingers do the walking in the Manhattan phone book. I wasn't sure this was she, but there was a listing under K; one Kiko, Terry Sue, 640 First Street. I dialed the number. After ten rings, I was connected to a very groggy cult figure.

"Kiko, I'm sorry. Did I wake you? Were you napping?"

"Yes. Who is this?"

I thought for a moment of hanging up and trying again the next day. Kiko then barked out, "Is this that fucking crank caller? I'm gonna have your psychotic balls on a plate if you—"

"No, no, Kiko, this is Julian. We met doing extra work in Riverside Park, and I attended your fabulous opening night."

Her voice betrayed no enthusiasm. "Oh yes, I remember you."

"Your performance piece was so fascinating. Will you be performing it again soon?"

"I'm doing a women's festival in Oregon in May. Is there something on your mind?"

"Well, yes, there is. I'm doing a play at Golgotha. Rupert booked me a week from Friday. Friday and Saturday night, and I'd love for you to star in it with me." The word "star" has a magical ring in any stratum of show business.

Kiko hesitated a moment and then responded, "Julian, I receive many offers to do plays, but I prefer to create my own universe."

"I certainly can understand that. It occurred to me that since I rarely perform in New York, you're not familiar with my work."

"You're right. I'm not."

"Well, I hate to toot my own horn, but I'm quite successful as a solo performer. I book myself across the country, and I play at some very prestigious theatres. I suppose I could bring you over some of my reviews. I've got raves from San Francisco, Indianapolis, Washington, D.C., Chicago. I'm not just another asshole who wants to exploit your reputation."

"I can see that. No, I understand." Hmmm. She sounded much nicer. I wondered what I had said to get this change in attitude. She continued in a chatty tone. "But you can understand my hesitancy to get involved with someone I don't know. One only has so much energy to expend. Where do you play in San Francisco?"

Oh, that was it. I divulged, "A marvelous place called the Black Box. It's sort of a cabaret–theatre arts center, very political but not humorless. It would be an excellent place for you to perform. Have you ever worked in San Francisco?"

"I've had numerous opportunities, but it never seemed quite right. But this Black Box sounds promising."

"If you'd like, I'd certainly write them about you or do anything I could to help."

"That would be lovely. I imagine we could be helpful to each other. I'd very much like to pick your brain."

The image of the cadaverous Kiko picking my brain had nightmarish implications.

"Well, Kiko darling, we should get together some afternoon and pick at each other with hammer and tongs. In the meanwhile, what do you think of treading the boards with me?"

"What is the play about?"

"It's called *Whores of Lost Atlantis*." The title suddenly tumbled from my lips. I had no idea how I came up with it. Perhaps Guy's entity, Adonijah, was in a creative mood and was tossing me a few crumbs. I liked the sound of the title. Come to think of it, I loved the sound of it. "Yes, *Whores of Lost Atlantis*, and it's a fantasy about two courtesans battling to conquer the throne of Atlantis and both ultimately losing as the continent sinks into the sea. They realize at the end that all of their rivalry doesn't mean very much when important issues of life and death are at stake." I was on a roll of sorts and realized that I was pitching the show to Kiko in terms of political analogy. "I see it very much commenting on the grave issues that confront all of us, AIDS, the environment, Nicaragua. We must strive to find our common humanity."

Kiko replied sagely, "That is very true."

I wasn't quite sure what we were talking about, but I sensed I was hooking her in. I continued, "It would be a fabulous role for you, imperious but sexual. Very glamorous." After sensing her chomping at the bit for my San Francisco contacts, I wasn't quite so awestruck. Why was I treating this dame like Ellen Terry when only the night before I'd seen her get triple grade-A eggs cracked on her not-so-privates?

Kiko put down the phone to get her date book. When she returned, she continued. "You're in luck. It looks as if I am available that weekend. You say two weeks from this past Friday."

"That's right. Friday and Saturday at eleven o'clock."

Kiko's voice took on a camp edge. "Really? I'm rather surprised Rupert gave you such a prime spot." I decided to let that dig slide. Then Kiko stated, "I'm in the midst of rehearsing a new piece myself, so my time is limited."

"Oh, we'll only be rehearsing a handful of times, and we'll work around your schedule. I'd like to have the first read-through Tuesday night. How's that?" She thought that would be fine. That gave me about thirty-six hours to pen the epic. I thought I'd speak to her in her own lingo. "Although the text will be written, it will be fascinating seeing the piece evolve out of our collective consciousness." To which she coldly replied, "But I am the star."

"Yeah, you're the star all right . . . with me, of course."

Kiko was mine, in all of her crabby magnificence. At that moment, though, I wondered if perhaps we might have done better with a stagestruck and sappy NYU undergrad.

CHAPTER 8

> Before all the gods, you know in your heart that the shame is yours.
>
> Ultima, *Whores of Lost Atlantis*
> Act One, Scene Four

Monday morning, I reported to my one-day temp assignment as a receptionist for the very conservative Wall Street investment firm of Fletcher, Kimbrough and Moss. For this job, I was told to dress appropriately in a jacket and tie. Considering the shabby state of my dress-up wardrobe, I would have cut a far more corporate image had I worn a simple skirt, sweater, and scatter pins. As it was, I was sporting a tie that was too wide, pants that were too short, and a jacket that was too tight.

I was the first to arrive and sat for what seemed an eternity in the small area between the elevators and the glass doors protecting the reception area from terrorist activity. At last, the elevator door opened, and a tall, gangly, comic-looking blonde came off. She was rather pretty despite having not much of a chin and alarmingly big blue eyes. She looked me over and said, "You the temp?"

"Yes, I'm the temp. I have a name too, Julian. Julian Young."

"You also have an attitude. My name's Roxie. Roxie Flood."

Once inside, Roxie flicked on the lights, and the white noise peculiar to windowless offices began to purr. The reception area was very elegant, wood paneled with fine moldings, brass fixtures, and marble floors.

Roxie pointed to the immense receptionist desk. "You sit here. The buzzer under the center drawer is the panic button."

"You mean as in—"

"I mean as in if you have a gun to your head. Don't think about it, it's only happened once, and we got her to the hospital in time to avert a tragedy."

I went behind the desk and noticed the massive space-age switchboard. I felt sick. "Roxie, tell me that isn't the switchboard. Why are there so many buttons? One false move and there goes Moscow."

"It's not so bad," she assured me. "For one thing, here's a directory for which name corresponds to which button. And also, half of the partners are out this week, and their secretaries pick up their lines directly. You only pick up when they're away from their desks. I'm the corporate librarian, and this is my number. You can call me if you've got a problem. The two lines you always pick up belong to Donald Caspar, this one, and Fedora Von Avon on line two."

"Fedora Von Avon, you've got to be kidding. Is she a drag queen?"

Ms. Flood rolled her eyes like a 1930s hard-boiled comedienne. "She should only have the panache of a drag queen. She's not what you call a people person. She relates easier to liquid white out."

Roxie's voice reminded me of someone, and then I hit on it. She sounded amazingly like Audrey Meadows in *The Honeymooners*. It was somewhat incongruous emanating from a girl in her late twenties. "The important thing, dear, is to look busy. Illusion is the keynote on Wall Street."

I didn't tell her that I would be very busy indeed. I had, after all, an entire play to write. Then, remembering I had a flier to run off, I asked, "Oh, where's the copy room?"

Roxie replied, "The second door on the right, but I doubt you'll have to copy anything." She looked at me with a slightly suspicious air.

I sat down at the desk and clasped my hands together. "Well, I think I'm set. I'll call you if I have any questions, Roxie."

"Yeah, you do that." She paused for a moment, scrutinizing me with one eye closed. "Julian Young. . . . You intrigue me." On that investigative note, she loped down the hall.

It turned out to be the perfect temp assignment. I didn't have to do anything. True to Roxie's word, the phones hardly rang at all. Of course, the lights on the board flashed more frequently than Times Square, but, evidently, the lines were picked up by the army of secretaries behind me. The partners themselves seemed like an interchangeable procession of corporate mannequins. Roxie was quite accurate. The exotically christened Fedora Von Avon was revealed to be a dowdy, fortyish, gray-suited executive. Polite, and not the least bit patronizing, Ms. Von Avon refused to look me in the eye. I decided to test her. At eleven forty-six, she emerged from her office perusing a document. She told me to hold all calls for the next half hour. While she spoke, I crossed my eyes like Ben Turpin and pretended to

give my finger a blow job. She thanked me for my cooperation and seques-
tered herself once more.

It was the complete and utter anonymity of tempdom that drove me mad.
I realized that my function was merely to keep things moving on an even
keel until the permanent receptionist returned, but sometimes I wished
that my employers would take just a second to recognize that I was an individual whose particular outlook might either amuse them momentarily or
prove helpful. Faceless and bland as the partners were, my other direct line,
Mr. Caspar, was startlingly vivid. He strode out of the elevator, fixed his
cobalt blue eyes on me like a searchlight, extended an enormous, meaty
hand, and shook mine as if I were the first name on *Forbes*'s list of top
money-makers. Well over six feet, with a mane of silver hair, Mr. Caspar was
probably at the age of fifty-two or thereabouts, at the peak of his virile, yet
elegant perfection. He gave me a good old boy wink, and then he too bar-
ricaded himself in his office.

I put a sheet of paper into the typewriter and began writing *Whores of Lost
Atlantis*. To be honest, I had begun working on it the day before. I'd outlined
each scene in great detail and had even jotted down snippets of dialogue
throughout the play. However, I am now in the act of creating a myth, so I
prefer to imply that I wrote the entire play from scratch during my one day
at Fletcher, Kimbrough and Moss. Once I got going, the lines flew out. The
play really did write itself. I enter in Scene One straight off the slave ship
bound in chains. Being not only of the royal blood but street smart, Milena
(me!) quickly assesses the situation at court. The Emperor Zenith (Joel) is
being manipulated by his chief courtesan, Ultima (Kiko). I contrive to
become a royal courtesan and take her place. I overhear the emperor com-
plaining that he's never had a really successful hairdo, and I leap at my
chance.

MILENA

My Lord, if thou wouldst permit me, I know in my heart, I could provide thee
with a coiffure that would do sublime justice to your royal personage.

ULTIMA
(*scoffing*)
And why, pray tell, should the Emperor allow a common slave girl to cut his
locks? You, a filthy wench, crawling with vermin, reeking of mutton, grease,
and gristle and other meat by-products, and possessing nary an operator's
license.

ZENITH

Enough, Ultima! However, slave girl, my courtesan has a point. Why should
I give you rein to caress my royal tendrils?

MILENA

Because I am not a mere wench, Sire. (proudly and defiantly) I am a princess royal of the tribe of the Mishegossa, the proud daughter of the warrior

king Tuchus. I have learned the arts of beautification from my trusted eunuchs. Those girls could do more in five minutes than this dame could do in a millennium.

I was moving at a clip. I stopped briefly to call Joel, Camille, Guy, Zoe, and Perry and tell them about the read-through on Tuesday night. My only other brief distraction in the first part of the day was when Mr. Caspar called me into his office. And a very grand affair it was. With a magnificent view of lower Manhattan, the office was furnished with antiques and photos of what I assumed was Caspar's family. I sat for a moment while he finished a phone call. It gave me time to give the once-over to his office and study the photos.

"Are these beautiful young people your children?"

He smiled pleasantly. "Yes, the small ones are my grandchildren."

"Well, you have a very photogenic family."

He lifted one of the framed photos on his desk and examined it.

"You will find that the greatest joy in life is having a family. The greatest joy."

I decided to play along with him. I looked wistfully out the window and said, "That's my dream. I just want to wait until I achieve some success in my chosen field. Then I'd like to marry and have children."

"And what is your chosen profession?" He seemed genuinely interested.

"The theatre. I'm a playwright and an actor."

He rose and stretched his long legs. "That's a tough row to hoe, son. When I was very young, I wanted to be an actor. Frankly, I don't think I was very good."

I wanted to tell him that, with his looks, he could have out-Pecked Gregory in Hollywood.

"I'd like you to take this letter. I should have asked you to bring in your steno pad," he said.

"My what?" He had the wrong temp. The only thing I was capable of doing was answering the phone wrong and light typing. "Mr. Caspar, I don't know how to take dictation, but if you have a little patience, I'm one of the world's fastest longhand writers. I can only do my best."

He seemed to appreciate that response. "I can only ask for your best shot. Let's have a go at it."

I was smitten. I fairly skipped out of his office, grabbed my notebook, and returned. I pretended I was Doris Day in an early sixties sex comedy. I was Doris as a spunky but virtuous career girl, and Don Caspar was Cary Grant as her boss, whom she marries in the last reel. I started to cross my legs à la Doris but caught myself and kept them open in a masculine manner. Mr. Caspar began dictating, and I kept up surprisingly well. Occasionally he'd stop and look. "Are you sure you're still with me?" Perky as hell, I'd chirp, "I'm three words ahead of you, Mr. Caspar."

But then my mind began to wander, and I fantasized that soon he'd start making advances and chase me around the office till I grab the photo of his wife (who it turns out isn't really his wife—he isn't even married—so much easier to run off with me, Doris, at the finish), and I bop him over the head and run out. Sometime later, I run into him at a glamorous luncheon where I'm working as the hostess and . . .

"Julian, you want to read that last part back to me?"

"Oh, I'm sorry, I missed that last sentence."

He chuckled. "I thought I detected a blank stare. What were you thinking?"

If only you knew, Mr. Grant—I mean, Mr. Caspar. I told him where I'd left off, and he continued with his dictation until he made reference to a certain enclosed document.

As if a curtain had dropped, his handsome face clouded over and reddened with rage.

"That dumb cow. How many goddam times do I have to ask . . ." He picked up the phone and jabbed his finger along the numbers. "Roxie, Don Caspar. I want you in this office this minute." He said nothing more to me. I wasn't sure if I should leave the room, so I stayed put.

Seconds later, Roxie appeared in the door. I could see she looked both scared and primed for battle. "Yes, Mr. Caspar."

He paced the office, eyes studying the rug. "Dear Ms. Flood." He lingered over the "Ms." as if ridiculing any feminist notions she might entertain. "Am I insane or have I not requested at least six times to have the Logan/ Mere file copied and on my desk?"

Roxie cleared her throat and replied calmly, "I'm training a new assistant, and we must have had a miscommunication. I'm very sorry. I'll have it on your desk immediately."

She began to leave, but my formerly charming Mr. Caspar barked in the ugliest tone imaginable, "I have not dismissed you, young lady." Roxie turned around with a look of embarrassed amazement. He continued, "You have got a lousy attitude, Ms. Roxie Flood. And I'm going to mention this to Walter Kimbrough."

"Mr. Caspar, you're very demanding, and that is your perogative, but there are only two of us in the library, and we have to service this entire company plus work on our own projects."

Caspar grasped hold of the two corners of his desk and leaned in toward her. "I don't give a crap about your projects. You're the most inept, incompetent department head I've ever worked with. You're clearly out of your depth."

"The other partners don't seem to have a problem with me."

He laughed derisively. "I'm glad you feel that way. I've got a temp here who's got more on the ball than you." Roxie looked at me, but I couldn't read her expression. I just wished he'd left me out of it.

I could see it was an effort for her to keep her voice even. "Mr. Caspar, I'm sorry if you—"

He didn't let her finish. He waved his hand, dismissing her. "I don't want your apologies, just get out of here."

I could almost see Roxie dig her feet into the carpet. "Just one minute, Mr. Caspar. Don't you ever, ever speak to me in that manner. Or my assistant." Her accent may have been New York tough, but her attitude was pure Clytemnestra. She was Olive Oyl playing Lucrezia Borgia. "We are not your concubines. We are not your chattel." She was absolutely thrilling.

"You may presume that you can run roughshod over everyone you consider your inferior, but you're not going to do it to me. Get that straight right now."

Caspar looked at me as if I were his costar in the scene. I averted my eyes. He turned to Roxie. "That shouldn't be a problem for you since I doubt you'll be with us much longer."

Roxie elongated her neck even more. "You may have me fired, but if you succeed, if you succeed, Mr. Caspar, *the shame* will be yours." With that grave utterance, Roxie made her exit to my silent applause. "The shame will be yours." Where the hell did she pull that out of? I was crazy about her.

Of course, I was stuck with the villain. Suddenly, Don Caspar wasn't quite as gorgeous as he had been a few minutes earlier. His lips were a bit too thin, the lines in his face a tad cruel. Who was I kidding? He was still stunning. Even this ugly temper tantrum of his gave him some of the volatile moodiness of Mr. Rochester in *Jane Eyre*. From Doris Day, now I was the timid and noble young governess seeking his approval but not bowing to his every mercurial whim. Somehow I finished taking his dictation, even with my mind percolating with sexual images.

I returned to my desk and typed up the letter to his satisfaction. Though I was only there for the day, it felt good pleasing this handsome son of a bitch. I wondered if that implied I was of far weaker character than Roxie Flood. Did I have the soul of a cheap dame who'd give her coozie to any powerful man, no matter how villainous?

I shook off that thought and returned to the important work of finishing my play. I was up to the scene where Milena (me!) and Ultima square off. Milena has risen to the position of concubine, and Ultima's hold on the emperor is threatened.

MILENA

So you see, my dear Ultima, the tables have turned with a vengeance.

ULTIMA

Don't make me laugh, Whore. When the Emperor tires of you, he'll toss you back in the mire from which you've sprung.

MILENA

Not me, Sister. I'm playing hardball. In fact, when you retire to your chambers, you will find my gowns in your closet. Your tacky duds have been stashed in the servants' quarters.

ULTIMA

You evil, conniving bitch. You may have displaced me for the moment. You may have won this particular battle, but before all the gods, you know in your heart, the shame is yours.

A momentum built, and I was racing through the play, enjoying myself immensely. I was giving Kiko a fabulous role. I hoped she'd appreciate it. The only thing that worried me was whether she could be funny. She certainly didn't rack up any weepers in real life, and her own act, while perversely amusing in a scathingly bitter way, didn't demonstrate crack comic timing.

As the clock moved toward five-thirty, I headed toward the homestretch, determined to finish the play by six. Naturally, during that last half hour, I was interrupted by the Federal Express man picking up an envelope, two messengers delivering pouches, Madame Von Avon going to the ladies' room and having me take her messages, and Don Caspar asking me to phone in a reservation for him at the Gotham Bar and Grill. Scoff all you like, but come six o'clock I was composing the last lines:

MILENA
(*looking out the window*)
Ultima, behold our lost world, sinking irrevocably into the sea.

ULTIMA
(*joining her*)
And soon this ivory tower, the highest point in all Atlantis, will tumble. And here we are alone, the Emperor dead, your Andreas dead, every eunuch and courtesan in the joint drowned or crushed, and I ask you, Milena, what does it all mean?

MILENA
That I cannot tell you. Only that throughout all of my trials and travails, the one constant has been your unrelenting bitchiness. And in a strange way, I thank you for it. Our feud provided me with the strength to endure.

ULTIMA
I know exactly what you mean, dear. We've had each other. And if the seers are correct, perhaps we will meet again in another eon.

MILENA
I hope so. Then shall we drink a toast to us, the last survivors? (They raise their goblets as the music swells.)

ULTIMA
To us.

MILENA
To us. (Suddenly a loud crash is heard. Milena throws down her drink.) The

hell with this shit, there's a lifeboat at the end of the pier, I'm making a run for it! Good luck! (She runs off.)

ULTIMA

Move over, bitch, I'm joining ya! (She exits too, as the continent continues to sink.)

CURTAIN

THE END

It needed work, but I could do that in rehearsal. The main thing was, I had lines on paper. A play existed. Once I'd written those words "The End," my whole body began to tremble. It had been quite an effort. I was exhausted yet exhilarated. It was now six o'clock, and the corps de ballet of secretaries was beginning to leave. My replacement who covered the reception desk from six to seven arrived. But I was not through with this particular gig. There was a resource at Fletcher, Kimbrough and Moss too rich to ignore: the copy room. Fortunately, it was empty, and I frantically tried to figure out how the machine worked. I needed ten copies of the script. It all looked fairly simple, but just as I was about to push the start button, a very pert redheaded secretary with enormous glasses waltzed in with a sheaf of papers to be copied. I decided to let her go ahead of me so she wouldn't see what I was doing. As she progressed, I looked at my watch. There was no way I could stay there past seven, and I couldn't afford the services of a professional copy shop. At last she finished, and I proceeded with my undercover activity. It was a very fast machine. I watched in amazement as the pages shot through the various shelves. The script was forty-five pages, and just as page thirty-two sped through, the copy machine ground to a halt. Red and green lights began flashing wildly. I opened the door to the machine to check if the paper supply had been depleted, but there was plenty of paper in there. I began to sweat. Another secretary walked in wanting to use the machine.

She moaned. "Tell me it's not broken."

"I'm afraid it is. There may be some paper stuck."

I heard Roxie's strident voice in the hall. "Something wrong, Kimberly?"

"The temp says the Xerox machine is on the fritz. I can't wait around. I've got an aerobics class."

Kimberly left, and Roxie entered, wearing her coat. "What are you still doing here? Did Don Caspar ask you to stay late? Because, you know, it's not in our budget to—"

"No, this has nothing to do with him. I'm, um . . ." Roxie took a page from the top of the pile and read the title of the play out loud. "*Whores of Lost Atlantis.* This is definitely not an assignment from F, K and M."

I decided to come clean. "Look, I'm a playwright and I'm putting on this play and our budget is so minuscule, it would be an enormous help if I could get it copied for free."

"Just don't let Marilyn catch you. She's in charge of office supply acquisitions, and she's a total bitch. So what did you do to the machine? With all those red and green lights blinking, it looks like my father's front lawn at Christmas." She opened up the copy machine, and, sticking her hand into the mechanism as if she were delivering a baby, she located a crumpled page that was clogging up the works. "I think it's one of your originals." With great delicacy, she extricated the page from the machinery without ripping it. As she straightened the page to run it through again, her eyes fell upon a familiar phrase. She read aloud, "Before all the gods, you know in your heart, the shame is yours." She paused for a moment. "You find me grist for comic inspiration?"

I quickly replied, "It was just the phrase. I couldn't resist putting it in. It was an intoxicating moment when you let Caspar have it this morning."

"If he speaks to me again that way, he'll find himself in traction. Look, you're never gonna get this finished at the rate you're going." She threw off her camel's hair coat and took over. Soon, the pages were flying through the machine.

Suddenly, Roxie snapped her fingers and tapped herself on the head. "Oh my God, now I remember. Julian Young. I saw you perform at SNAFU a couple of years ago. You were fantastic. You played all these characters. It was like a murder mystery, and you were this old black jazz singer like Billie Holiday and a prince, and a lady who ran a haunted house . . ."

I nodded enthusiastically. "Yes, that was me."

"Right, that was you. And at the end all the characters were getting killed right and left, and, oh yes, you had the most miserable young magician as your opening act."

"That was my friend Guy. He's really very talented. What made you come see my act?"

The script was finished. Roxie began removing the copies from the shelves. "I was performing there the following week, and I wanted to check out the space. I used to do a comedy act with my friend Lenny. We used to play all those places, the Duplex, Jason's, you name it."

"Are you still together?"

"Oh no. I mean we're still friends. I love Lenny, but he's out in L.A. doing costumes on a soap, and me, well, it's a long story but I'm out of show business. There comes a time in your life, dear, when you ask yourself, 'Regrets? priorities? values?' My marriage fell apart, I made his life miserable, I had an ovary removed, very scary but I'm perfectly fine now, and I was flat broke. And while my mother would love me to be a star—she's the stage mother of all time—I had to find a way to establish a life, and thank God I had a college degree and had studied library science, and I was able to talk my way into this job at F, K and M. That was six years ago, and now I'm like this corporate person. What can I tell you, darling? I've got a life. I've got a life." With that statement, she handed me the stack of finished scripts.

"Roxie, you're gonna kill me, but I was hoping to run off my flier too."

Roxie rolled her eyes. "Your flier! You want me to run off a copy of the NYNEX yellow pages while I'm at it?"

"Nobody's going to notice a little paper missing."

"Oh no? There's a nasty little meter that reads how many copies have been made. That Marilyn's like a hawk. The exploitation of this copier has great emotional resonance for her. Well, let's just do a couple hundred."

I gave her the flier. I'd made a collage of a photo of me in drag taken a few years earlier and a photostat of a photo of Sarah Bernhardt in one of her more exotic roles. It gave the impression that the divine Sarah and I were costarring at Golgotha. Over that I'd scrawled the title, the credits, and the time and place.

Roxie put the flier into the machine and pushed the buttons to get the monster in motion. She sat down on top of several boxes of paper. "I really don't know anything about Sarah Bernhardt except that she had one leg."

"Oh, she's my favorite person in history. I'm sort of an authority on her. But you know, she didn't lose her leg till she was over seventy. There are many stories as to how she injured herself, but I think the truest one is that she had an accident many years earlier when she was playing Tosca on tour in South America. At the end of the play, she leaped off the parapet, but the mattress that was to cushion her fall was badly positioned and she crashed. The South American doctors didn't know how to treat her, so her leg gradually deteriorated. She lived for the next thirty years in progressive agony but still had this amazing career and active life. It was finally at the beginning of World War I, when she was in her seventies, that her leg became gangrenous and it was necessary to amputate it. But then she insisted on entertaining the troops at the front lines, this withered, ancient creature, being carried about in a sedan chair. Contrary to rumor, she never wore a wooden leg, but she retained her golden voice. They say she thrilled the tired, weary soldiers and inspired them with her own courage and indomitability. I think it was Colette who said Bernhardt was in a sense greater at this time than perhaps in the golden height of her youth. Oh, I just adore her."

Roxie listened attentively and said, "Evidently, dear. You should write a piece where you play her."

"I've thought of that, but how could anyone suggest how great and charismatic she must have been? Besides, I don't want to play her. I want to *be* her. I guess I sort of identify with Bernhardt because I've had such a hard time getting a career going. I can't help thinking that if I keep pursuing it with no deviation and continue to learn and improve, I can't believe I won't be successful. I hate being a temp." I wasn't sure why I was telling her all this. Most likely I'd never see her again, but I felt oddly comfortable with Roxie Flood. I wondered if it was because she was uncannily like the warm, wisecracking best friends I'd seen in dozens of old movies. "I've had very discouraging times, Roxie, particularly when I see so many people around me wise up and drop out of the theatre, or even worse when I see kids I went to college with playing on Broadway or on TV. I suppose I identify with Sarah because her career was built very slowly, brick by brick, and she too had been told that she'd never be a success, that she was too weird looking, and too thin and too offbeat. I have to maintain faith that I'm right, that I must create this career in my own unique way." I could tell Roxie was thinking about herself and her own decisions. I said, "I hope I'm not depressing you, right after you told me you'd dropped out of show business."

"Well, frankly you are, a little, but that's okay. I guess part of me will always wish I was on the stage. And I'll wonder what if?" She made a grand, sweeping gesture and looked to the heavens in the Xerox room. "Had I followed the dream!" The fliers were finished.

"Here, take one, Roxie. Come see it. I can't promise it'll be any good."

She folded the flier and slipped it into her purse. "Darling, I may just show up opening night, and I'll bring friends. I'm quite the popular gal, but if the show stinks, can we just say it?" She leveled a finger at me and uttered with dramatic intensity, "The shame will be yours."

CHAPTER 9

This mighty crown does weigh heavy upon my imperial brow.
All I do all day is hear complaints and sit on the throne.

Emperor Zenith, *Whores of Lost Atlantis*
Act One, Scene Three

About two thirds through our first read-through of the script in my apartment, Joel turned to me and casually remarked, "Julian, do you realize that all of these people you've gathered here are mentally disturbed?"

I scanned my living room, where the cast was assembled. I suppose by the psychological layman, the cast of *Whores of Lost Atlantis* could have been described as borderline crazy. Spiraling down to the pits of depression, Perry had dyed his hair a fluorescent shade of orange. He sat on the far end of the sofa daring anyone to speak to him. Zoe entered the apartment carrying a large stack of months old *Vogue* magazines and in her frenzied yet somnambulistic manner insisted on palming them off on us. "It would be a hideous tragedy to throw them away." Zoe's compassionate take on inanimate objects was right out of a Disney cartoon. At one point early in the evening I was gratified to see Perry and Zoe engrossed in conversation. On the pretext of clearing some books off the coffee table, I bent down to eavesdrop. I heard Perry saying in a somber monotone, "I was taking a nap, and I dreamed I was trapped in a den full of goblins. I woke up so suddenly,

I feel disoriented. Do you think you're part of my nightmare?" Zoe tilted her head thoughtfully. "Perhaps I am."

Our leading lady, Madame Kiko, was definitely part of *my* nightmare. She sat in my decaying armchair, a silent statue of condescending benevolence. She'd speak only when spoken to and then in cryptic, haikulike fragments. Joel asked her if she had walked all the way from the East Village. Kiko curled the edges of her lips into a constipated Mona Lisa smile.

"East, west, it's all an odyssey of sameness."

"Hmmmm," Joel replied. "I hear the M13 crosstown bus runs quite frequently."

Guy, who could almost pass as normal, was in a heightened state of exaltation. I remembered that he was going to do a magic show for Donald Trump's children.

"Guy, you look so radiant. Did you just come from Donald Trump's?"

Guy also had that Mona Lisa–needs-an-enema smile. "No, that was yesterday. This morning I received an important message."

"From whom? An agent? A producer?"

"An ancient mystic."

"What did he say? Was it a 'he'?"

Guy's eyes drifted beatifically toward the open window. "I believe he was a male presence, and I'd rather not discuss it."

I was genuinely intrigued. Guy had received a message from an ancient mystic. We were about to do a play set in lost Atlantis. Maybe the mystic could fill us in on some hot gossip. "Guy, where did you meet him?"

Guy casually flipped through the pages of his script. "His silhouette emerged in the bathwater, and that's all I'm going to tell you, Julian. You are not entity friendly." With that, he clammed up. The nerve of him.

Camille bustled around making coffee. She radiated brisk efficiency and yet maternal warmth. Compared with the other kooks in the room, she seemed refreshingly down-to-earth. One had to ignore her dominatrixlike outfit of skintight black leggings, black leather vest, and floor-piercing high-heeled boots. While she performed her stage manager duties, she also drank in every detail of my memorabilia-filled home.

"Julian, I love your apartment. You've done so much to it since I was last here."

"Really? Lord knows I didn't spend any money. If I couldn't afford to buy something, I just painted it on the wall."

"Your bedroom's so cute. I love all the lace and pillows and the antique picture frames. It's so Victorian." She became wistful. "You know, it's exactly the bedroom I always wanted when I was a little girl." I suppose I had deluded myself into thinking that my very feminine boudoir reflected both sides of my androgynous nature. The only masculine touch were my Converse sneakers tossed in the corner.

Camille whispered from the side of her mouth. "Julian, honey, I don't mean to criticize your casting, but the first reading of this play should've taken place in Bellevue." Before I could thank her for her supportive remark, Joel announced that he wanted to begin the reading.

From the first scene, I was very pleased by how the play read aloud. It's a good sign when the cast finds the play amusing. Kiko didn't crack a smile, but Perry, always my best audience despite his emotional state, was consistently laughing. Zoe giggled with her tiny hand covering her mouth. Camille shrieked at some of the bawdier lines, and Joel guffawed in his booming laugh, so in keeping with his overcultivated speech. Guy, seated beside me, was clearly enjoying our scenes together. I was amazed that I had written him such a great part, considering that I had only recently caught him boffing my ex-beau the zookeeper.

Andreas, a prince of the realm, meets the lovely Milena (me!) when she's fresh off the banana boat from Gaul. Milena, a foreign princess taken as a slave, is about to drink poison. Andreas knocks the vial from her hand.

ANDREAS
You little fool, you might have killed yourself.

MILENA
Ay, sir, that was the point. What future have I? To be raped by the Emperor's legion? I choose death before dishonor.

ANDREAS
But of course, you are a virgin princess. I should have known. No man has ever penetrated your sacred mound of Venus.

MILENA
(feisty)
Let 'em try. Upon my birth, the High Priest of Gaul made a covenant that my land would be bountiful if my hymen remained intact before marriage. If it was punctured hitherto, the wrath of the gods would be invoked. I don't feel like testing it.

To ease her misery, Andreas marries her in a quickie secret ceremony, then immediately takes off on a crusade that keeps him away from Atlantis for years. When he returns, he finds that Milena has exploited her beauty and wiles to become the emperor's most desired courtesan and the most powerful woman at court. Milena's chief rival for the emperor's affections is Ultima, the former first courtesan, played by Kiko. With his Indiana-bred English accent and excessive good manners, Joel treated Kiko with the deference a 1920s stage director would have accorded Ethel Barrymore. Miss Barrymore at her peak couldn't have been more condescending than Kiko was to us. Any line that wasn't accompanied by a disgusted roll of the eyes was handed to us as a pearl before swine. One of my favorite scenes in the play is when Milena accomplishes her palace coup, has herself crowned empress, and confronts the astonished old regime. Ultima denounces her in a mounting tirade of fury.

ULTIMA
(*bitterly*)

I beseech thee, Royal Court of Atlantis! Do not worship this rabid she-wolf. Cast her away, condemn her to the vilest of deaths, this creature who has defiled the ancient lineage of our throne. Snatch away her stolen crown and have her dragged nude through the streets, have her disemboweled to the amusement of the mob. Decapitate her and have the strumpet's viperish head stuck on a pike for the rabble to jeer!

Not shaken in the least, I put down my nail file and croak in my toughest Susan Hayward baritone, "Would someone tie a tin can to that broad's tail?"

The entire cast got a good laugh out of that one. Kiko pursed her lips primly and muttered loud enough for only me to hear, "Camp is the funeral pyre of Art."

Much like my character Milena, I shook off her insult. I knew that for all of her artistic pretensions, she was just miffed that I had the punch line.

We rehearsed three times that week, and each rehearsal had enough examples of offstage lunacy to fill several issues of *Psychology Today*. Joel maintained his professional demeanor, although from time to time he'd say to me in the most placid of voices, "This is precisely why I'm going to law school." This statement usually came after Kiko would storm off the set, that is, bolt out of my living room and barricade herself in the bathroom whenever Joel would give her the slightest bit of direction. If Joel told her to slow down, she'd argue that she was building a momentum. If he asked her to pick up the pace, she'd counter that she was attempting to create an elegiac mood. When Joel finally gave up and didn't say anything, Kiko would burst into tears and rant that she couldn't act in a vacuum. Her prima donna tantrums brought the rest of us together. Joel and Camille and Perry were friends, but they knew Guy only as a casual acquaintance, and no one had ever met Zoe before. The only thing they had in common was frustration in their theatrical ambitions and me in their lives. Now, in the form of the baleful witch Kiko, we had a common enemy.

By the second week, all of our performances were beginning to jell. Guy's first impulse was to play the heroic Andreas in a strange, downbeat contemporary manner. Sometimes he murmured his lines so quietly, I didn't have a clue to what he was saying. During a break I found him reading a paperback book of his metaphysical entity Adonijah's most whimsical sayings. I suppose it was unprofessional of me, but I couldn't help quipping, "Guy, during this next run-through, do you think you could stop channeling Max von Sydow and throw in a little Martha Raye?" Guy refused to dignify my criticism with a rebuff and retreated into a cocoon of serenity. It was a damn shame that Joel was giving up the theatre, because with his excellent coaching, Guy began eliminating the snorts, grunts, and sniffs that he mistook for gritty naturalism and soon was playing the romantic Andreas with an appealing swashbuckling panache.

Perry's depression lifted but was replaced with a zany, manic high. Ignoring his severe hypoglycemia, he devoured a box of chocolate donuts hidden in my kitchen and slid into madcap euphoria. He shocked Kiko out of her dragon lady inscrutability by slapping her on the ass and wisecracking, "Fishcake, you may be a mean-spirited hussy, but you're one of a kind." He shocked us all by playing Folio the Hermaphrodite with such comic grotesquerie we wondered how it was possible that every casting director in town had failed to recognize his potential. Joel and I crossed our fingers and hoped that his virtuosity wouldn't vanish once his blood sugar stabilized.

Joel was having trouble with his characterization of the perverted emperor until I suggested he imitate his gay high school drama teacher from Indianapolis. Braying in a tight Midwestern accent, he really let the royal hermaphrodite have it. "Lissen, Folio, I don't give a good goddam whether you have a penis and/or vagina, I simply demand good service!"

I was having a marvelous time playing Milena, the ambitious courtesan. Every moment came so easily, I discovered a vocal range I didn't know I possessed. Playing a female role seemed to liberate me from the self-consciousness that had often plagued my performances. No longer did I ever question what to do with my hands. They simply responded naturally to the demands of the situation. I was also enjoying interacting with other people onstage. There is a marvelous satisfaction to being a solo performer who is responsible for every second of the evening. However, there was also a kick to really listening to another actor and spontaneously reacting to the reality of his playing.

The other actors in our play struck sparks off me that Joel was the first to observe. "It's funny, Julian, but I've never seen you so loose and imaginative. It's sort of a pity only a handful of people will ever see you play this role."

It didn't matter. I wasn't playing an Atlantean hooker to further my career.

The true dramatic high point of our brief rehearsal period was delivered by Zoe. We were all disappointed hearing her recite her lines in a numbing little girl's singsong. None of us could decide whether she was intentionally throwing away her performance or she was simply the world's worst actress. I had written her a fiercely emotional scene where she confronts the court with their unbridled decadence. Cassandra-like, she reveals her dire predictions of the future of Atlantis.

After the tenth time watching her walk through the scene, Joel stopped her. "Zoe, this scene is not working, and I've instructed Julian to do a rewrite and have you impaled on a burning poker after Scene Three." Zoe's round eyes flashed with defiance.

"You mean, you want me to ham it up?"

"That could prove fascinating." We ran the scene again, but this time, tiny Zoe lashed out at us with the guttural ferocity not of Glenda Jackson but of Wallace Beery. Her entire body seemed to change shape. She grew squat, and her face took on the pugnacity of a prizefighter. She growled out her curses, and then tears streamed down her face, causing rivulets of black mascara to stain her stark white complexion. She pounded her chest with her fists and implored the gods to strike down the royal house that had enslaved her family. She was terrifying and hysterically funny. When she finished, we burst into applause. She blinked her eyes as if coming out of a hypnotic trance. She giggled nervously and fled the room. We knew we were in the presence of genius.

Camille and I had decided to design the costumes together. "Design" wasn't, I suppose, the most accurate term. "Cull" might have been more appropriate, perhaps "salvage." In addition to Aunt Jennie's duds, over the years I had collected a large box full of theatrical paraphernalia in case I ever tired of my minimalist solo act and desired to go full-tilt drag queen. Camille and I dug into the trunk and found among my artifacts a red velvet bustier, an Elizabethan doublet, lace garters, an African tribal headdress, gold brocaded 1950s toreador pants, a green sequined prom gown, three rhinestone tiaras, a cat-o'-nine-tails, four pairs of spats, a collapsible top hat, and numerous packets of jokester's itching powder. Camille and I thought if we stretched the historical period somewhat, we could utilize most of the more exotic items of my collection. I also had a plastic bag full of tangled Dynel wigs in assorted brassy colors.

We laid them out on my bed like the remains of a dead animal act. There was a waist-length auburn wig that we thought had possibilities for me to wear in the first scene. Pulling apart another matted mess of auburn hair, we discovered several "switches" that could be used to augment the coiffure. I began piling the hairpieces on my head, hoping for an inspiration.

"Julian, wait, wait, let me try something." Camille reached into her bag and pulled out a plastic hair pick and a packet of bobby pins. Fingers flying, she teased the wig until it was a massive Kabuki mane of red hair. She circled me, holding hairpins in her mouth and sculpting the cotton candy–like mass into a hairdo. I couldn't wait to see what she was up to, but she kept shushing me to be patient.

At last, she gave me permission to judge her creation. I ran to the mirror and screamed. There was a suggestion of *Quo Vadis?* but the wig more clearly resembled a 1960s Motown girl group run amuck. It had height, it had length, it was alive! I grabbed Camille and pressed her to me. I couldn't believe she had this perverse talent in her.

She lit a cigarette and studied her creation on my head. "Well, you know, Julian, I did a lot of hair in the sixties." Despite the weight she'd piled on during the last few years, Camille had such a girlish quality, I always forgot that she was nearly ten years older than I. "My girlfriends in Brooklyn and I used to compete to see who'd have the biggest hair. I mean, like we used to copy every hairdo we'd see in the hair magazines you'd pick up in the beauty parlor. You should see my wedding pictures. I had thirty pounds of hair on my head, all teased into Grecian curls. I think I counted four hundred and fifty hairpins."

I loved watching Camille smoke. Although she was exceedingly feminine, with fragile wrists and ankles, she held a cigarette like a gangster. If we were on the street and she'd finished with a cigarette, she'd simply toss it lit with an effortless bravado that I found dazzling. "Yeah, so I had this knack for doing 'big hair.' Well, you know I was working as a typist since I was like sixteen, and whenever one of the girls in the office had to go to a wedding or on a big date, they'd ask me to do their hair. Then in the late sixties, teasing went out of style, and we got geometric Sassoon cuts, and my services were no longer in demand."

We were on a creative roll and decided to do more work on the costumes. I took out of a drawer a number of old bed sheets that we thought could be draped into togalike fashions. Zoe needed something both sexy and ethereal. Camille like Zoe was barely over five feet tall, so we used her as a stand-in. Camille was self-conscious having me see her in her bra and panties.

"Julian, it's not that I'm by nature modest, it's just that I'm so out of shape. I mean, when my ex-lover Mel and I went to Club Med in the seventies, I let them body-paint me in the nude."

"Have you tried dieting?"

"Yes. I just can't seem to lose it. Maybe it's my destiny to turn into a fat old Italian lady."

"Camille, I hope you don't get one of those weird skin tags hanging from your eyelids."

"And if you ever see long black hairs hanging off a mole, cut 'em offa me. I just don't know why I can't lose the weight. I hardly eat a thing. Maybe it's a hormonal imbalance."

I had personally witnessed Camille "total" a sixteen-inch anchovy and pepperoni pizza, so I was silently dubious about the hormonal diagnosis. We squeezed her into the velvet bustier and draped a striped sheet around her hips. The effect was more Sicilian peasant girl than ancient mystic. Camille dressed to conceal, and I enjoyed the novelty of seeing her full breasts overflowing the bustier.

"Camille, it's a pity we live in a society that worships the anorectic, 'cause you look pretty fabulous in this getup. I'd love to paint you as a lusty Italian peasant wench with your boobs hanging out. Maybe holding a pitcher over your head or getting into a bathtub or maybe pulling a boot on." Camille blushed and covered her face with her hands. It was pushing midnight, but I wasn't remotely tired.

"Hey, we can't get a real sense of this costume with your face looking like a nun. Let me make you up." Camille protested that it was too late, but I bullied her into it.

"I never wear much makeup anymore. I used to do big Cleopatra eyes during the sixties."

"It sounds like you had a lot of fun during the sixties. What happened to you in the eighties?"

Camille fluffed up her hair with her fingers. "I've been working on my inner life. After my divorce, I went from one rotten, abusive relationship to another. I mean, this one guy I lived with cut up all my clothes into little pieces like a jigsaw puzzle. I haven't had an easy life."

I pulled her into the bathroom and sat her down on the toilet seat. I took out my theatrical makeup kit, and it was now my turn to transform her. When I finished my glamour makeover, Camille got up and checked herself out in the bathroom mirror. Despite the excess poundage, her high cheekbones were prominent and gave her an exotic air.

"Camille, you look like Gina Lollobrigida."

"I look like a busboy made up like Gina Lollobrigida."

We stared at our reflections in the mirror. Both of us instinctively turned our heads slightly three quarters so that we looked as if we were posing for a record album cover.

"Camille, my face looks so bland next to yours." Her face was now a colorful map of reds, oranges, greens, and blues. My face au naturel seemed a pale blur of sallow beige. I sighed. "Isn't it a pity a man doesn't have the option of painting his face without being thought of as a nut or risking being beaten up?" It was this odd fear of blandness that gnawed at me. I was haunted by a feeling of invisibility that was resurrected whenever I was with someone more flamboyant than I. There were times when I'd appear in a benefit variety show and I'd be introduced backstage to a performer more outrageous than myself. They'd be seeking witty badinage from me and I'd find myself losing any trace of campy insouciance and sometimes just plain old sense of humor. I'd be submerged in a pool of niceness. It seemed that the only way I could be sure I existed on the planet was to be separated from the crowd, preferably in a spotlight and wearing the brightest colors.

"Camille, give me some of that lipstick."

She reached for the tube, but I grabbed her by the shoulders and gave her a long, lingering kiss on the lips. It felt good. It had been a long time since I'd kissed anyone. We didn't open our mouths. We were a bit too stunned to part our lips and too stunned to separate. After enough time to develop a photo, we parted. Camille patted her cheek as if reviving herself.

"Oh my, that certainly woke me up. Better than a cup of espresso."

I had no rejoinder. I just looked in the mirror and was delighted that my mouth was perfectly coated with Elizabeth Arden Fire Engine Red.

CHAPTER
10

Who is this callow youth with the sacred mark of Shana on his buttocks?

Emperor Zenith, *Whores of Lost Atlantis*
Act One, Scene Three

Joel's boss, Howard Fuller, was being given a surprise birthday party, and I was thrilled when Joel asked me to accompany him.

The game plan was for all the guests to arrive at Howard's sprawling Central Park West apartment between seven-thirty and eight. Howard was being detained at his sister's across town. By the time Joel and I arrived, Howard's apartment was teeming with a glittering array of Broadway craftsmen and celebrities. Joel and I stood off in a corner and gaped at Gwen Verdon, Jerry Orbach, Comden and Green, and Celeste Holm, to name a few. It was so frustrating to be so close to my idols. It felt presumptuous to sidle up to Gwen Verdon and say, "So, Gwen, what's cookin'?" I had to be content to watch them interact. It was fun wandering around the labyrinthine apartment and ogling Howard's Tony awards and the Hirschfeld caricatures from his many shows. Entire walls were covered with autographed photos of Howard hugging the likes of Carol Channing, Ethel Merman, Lena Horne, and Mayor Koch. Insignificant wallflower that I was, I was introduced to lesser lights such as Howard's accountant's secretary's sister, Bonita.

I sipped my wine spritzer slowly. When you have limited funds, it's imperative to master the technique of nursing a drink. I can keep a vodka and tonic going for a good two hours. Of course, it wasn't necessary in this situation, where the drinks were on the house, but old skills are hard to forget.

At about twenty after eight, the doorman buzzed and said Howard was on his way up. The guests were herded into the main living room. We heard the front door open and several voices gabbing in the foyer. Howard turned the corner, and we yelled, "Surprise!"

Howard stood there in his old jogging suit, meticulously depilled by Joel, and surrounded by what I recognized from the family photos as his ancient blond mother and his attractive gray-haired sister. Howard's face registered many emotions, the chief one being abject horror. For one thing, he had on an old baseball cap, which meant he wasn't wearing his toupee. He was immediately engulfed by friends. He comically raised his fist to the party organizer, Jerry Moss, a longtime friend and press agent.

When Joel and I finally reached Howard to wish him a happy birthday, he was still red-faced and fuming. Howard is obsessively neat, and one of his compulsions is never to let anyone set foot in his living room. All entertaining is done in the kitchen, his office, or his small den, where he has his forty-six-inch TV. Just before Phyllis Newman whisked him away, he whispered to me, "Darling, do me a favor, and make sure no one burns a hole in the furniture." Would he have said this to Celeste Holm? I ask you.

About a half hour later, I was standing on the outskirts of the crowd near the door when I noticed Jerry greeting an extraordinarily beautiful young man carrying a large ghetto blaster. He had dark hair and large, dark eyes with thick, black lashes. His features were almost a parody of beauty. His black eyebrows were too lush, his nose too straight, his lips too full. I couldn't hear what Jerry was whispering to him, but soon the young man flicked on the ghetto blaster, and the sophisticated crowd was startled out of their cocktail chatter by the blaring disco music. The young man began dancing and working his way through the party. As in a movie musical, everyone moved aside and left the young man a large space to dance in the middle of the room. He unzipped his black leather jacket and flung it into Howard's arms. Soon his shirt came off; he had a magnificent, smoothly muscled chest. The reaction in the room ranged from amused to appalled.

Howard's face was frozen in a deadly smile. He was not happy with this gift, not happy at all. The beautiful young man pulled off his boots, and then, magically, his black leather pants flew apart in several pieces and he was left bumping and grinding in a red jockstrap. When he turned around, he displayed a perfect ass that made the statue of David look like it had secretary's spread. Jerry and a few of the younger gay guests were clapping in rhythm to the music. Miss Holm, looking as if she were rehearsing a revival of *Victoria Regina*, sailed grandly out of the room, followed by a half dozen other offended guests. It was made an even dozen when the young man pulled off his jockstrap. Around his genitalia was a red bow, and hanging below his balls were replicas of Howard's two Tony awards.

Jerry turned down the music, and in a very raspy, New Jersey–accented voice the young man sang "Happy Birthday." We all nervously applauded. Howard, beyond mortification, put his arm around his ninety-year-old mother, who was shaking her head in shame, and escorted her through the throng.

The young stripper suddenly looked very vulnerable bending over to retrieve his clothes, the Tony awards bobbing as he moved. Impulsively, I moved toward him and helped him pick up his socks and shirt. "You move beautifully."

He muttered "Thank you" while continuing to search for his left boot. When he found it, he said, "I get the feelin' our birthday boy didn't dig it."

"He's kind of in the closet, and that old lady next to him was his mother, who's not supposed to know he's gay."

The young man's mouth dropped open in comic amusement. "You gotta be kiddin'. How old is he, sixty-five? And with all his dough? You'd think he could just say, 'Ma, I'm a faggot. If you don't like it, don't cash no more of my checks.'"

Once he'd gathered all his clothes, still nude, the young man walked with dignity to the foyer. He asked if I knew where the bathroom, or rather "the bat-room," was. I led him in what I thought was the right direction. Unfortunately, that direction took us to the master bedroom, where Howard, stammering with rage, was screaming at Jerry Moss. The gist of it was "You fucking asshole, how dare you humiliate me before the entire theatrical community? Not only are you fired but I will see that no one in this business ever uses your faggot agency!"

Drawn as if by a magnet, the young man put down his clothes and boots, walked over to Howard, and extended his hand. "Mister Fullah, it's a real honah dancin' for you."

Howard, purple-faced, narrowed his eyes to nasty slits and hissed, "I just want you out of my home immediately! I don't know how much this schmuck paid you to embarrass me, but I will pay you more to get the fuck out of here!"

The young man was so muscular and a good five inches taller than Howard, I worried he might just haul off and deck him. But instead, as in a Betty Grable picture, the burlesque queen burst into tears. It was awful and fascinating. He stood there sobbing and coughing. I quickly picked up his clothes and pushed him into the bathroom. My eyes filled with tears too. I was so embarrassed for him. The young man, still completely nude, fumbled with the red bow holding the fake Tony awards around his dick. In his hysteria, he pulled at it wrong and knotted it tight.

"Oh fuck, I'll never get it off." He kept yanking at the knot until finally he threw up his hands helplessly. I said, "Don't despair. I'm great with knots." I got on my knees and tried to pull the ribbon through. My Florence Nightingale saintliness fled when I was confronted with the young man's large and very picturesque dick bobbing in my face. I tried to ignore it, but it was like brushing an elephant's teeth and ignoring its trunk. I almost had the knot untied, but the young man howled, "Shit, you're pulling my pubic hair."

I got up and found toenail scissors in Howard's medicine cabinet. The young man winced and said, "Hey, watch out, don't cut into my scrotal sac." Gingerly, I cut through the knot and extricated the relieved young man from the party favor. I sat on the edge of the bathtub and said, "I do think at this point in our relationship I should ask you your name."

He blew his nose and replied, "Buster . . . Buster Campbell, like the soup. And yours?" I told him. In his best Sunday school manner, he shook my hand.

"I can't believe I started crying. I'm a very emotional person. I take after my mom. She's very tough, but she cries a lot."

He seemed totally at ease with his nudity. So at ease that he lifted the lid of the toilet and began to pee, continuing our conversation. "You know, piss is the best cure for a zit. It's true. You dab a little of your pee on a pimple and the next day, Zappo! it's gone. Works every time."

I asked him, "Do you have any other career besides strip telegrams and home remedies?"

He flushed the toilet and put on his underwear. "I guess I don't. I don't know what I want to do. I've got zero ambition. A fatal flaw. I was working for a while behind the desk at the Hilton. But I got bored with that. And I worked at Gucci for a while. You know, I waited on Jackie O once. I even saw her in her panties."

"Really? How did she look?"

"Oh, beautyful. You can tell she works out with a trainer." He opened Howard's medicine cabinet and rifled through Howard's bottles of cologne and after-shave. He sniffed at all of them. "Hmmmm, I don't care for Armani. Are you into fragrance?" I shook my head. He then paused, straightened his spine, and began reciting in his streetwise accent an elaborate poetic quotation about scent and sensuality. When he finished he said, "Baudelaire. Pretty, huh?"

I was very impressed. "Is he your favorite poet?"

Buster sprayed a little cologne on his hands and rubbed it into his groin. "Hmmm, yeah, I like him, and I'm also into Verlaine. You read him?"

"I'm bone dumb about poetry. I'm better read in drama."

"I love poetry. I can recite big chunks by heart."

I studied his perfect profile. A shiny black lock of hair fell casually on his forehead. "Buster . . . I'm putting on a little play next weekend, and I think you'd be fabulous in it."

"Really? A play? I'm not an actor."

"Well, it wouldn't be a hard part. But I could use someone who looks like you."

"Oh, you want me to strip?"

"Not exactly. You'd enter naked. Not really naked. You could wear a

G-string. All right, basically you'd be carrying a spear. But it's a small cast, so I promise you, you'd stand out."

"I don't care about that. Like I say, I'm not an actor. I'd be really scared."

"It can't be any harder than what you did here tonight." He continued to browse through Howard's medicine cabinet. This time he took out a tube of Preparation H. He squeezed out a little on his finger and rubbed it under his eyes.

"What are you doing?" I cried. "That's hemorrhoid medication."

"Baby, if it shrinks hemorrhoids, it'll do the same thing for the loose skin under your eyes."

"Gimme that stuff." I rubbed some of the cream under my eyes. "I hope I don't walk out of here looking like Anna May Wong. So what do you say? You wanna be in the legitimate theatre and get no pay? The cast are all friends of mine. I think you'll like them. And I hope I'm not—I don't know, prying into your emotions, but maybe it would be good for you to be involved in something fun."

He closed the door to the medicine cabinet.

"Buddy, I'm in. Next weekend. It's a date." He then pointed to his genitalia. "But I don't show Pedro unless I'm paid."

I patted him on the ass and quipped, "What about Consuela?"

"You get her services gratis."

We left the bathroom, and Joel immediately found me.

"What happened to you? I thought maybe you'd left."

"No, I made a new friend. Buster, this is Joel, who's directing our play." I realized I'd slipped. I had wanted to tell Joel my new casting idea when we were alone.

Joel smiled and said to Buster, "Are you going to be in our show? How marvelous."

Joel was ready to leave, so we grabbed our coats. As we were totally unknown, there was no need for long good-byes.

While we were waiting for the elevator with Buster, I said, "Joel, I'm sorry I've sprung this on you. But don't you think our version of Atlantis is a bit underpopulated? I think Buster will look fabulous as a temple guard or a slave or something."

"No, I agree. Buster, are you an actor?"

"Nope. I was in a school play once. Brigadoon. We called it 'Grab-a-boob.' "

"You should hear Buster recite Baudelaire."

Buster gave Joel the once-over in a highly provocative manner. He may have lacked ambition, but his come hither look could have landed him a job as the CEO of General Motors. "Joel . . . um . . . , is that your name? Joel, this could be like a really good learning experience for me. I'm completely and totally in your hands."

Joel blushed and pressed the elevator button twice more. Joel said, "Welcome aboard, Buster. The play is a tad underpopulated." Then, looking at me, Joel added, "Perhaps you should go back inside and ask Miss Verdon if she'd like to do a specialty number."

Buster came to our next rehearsal wearing a white shirt and tie and looking like a schoolboy trying out for the drama club. It was a lucky break for him that he was cast without an audition because I had never come across anyone with less aptitude for the stage. His line readings were so stilted, it was as if he had never heard the English language before. But there was also something endearing in his delivery of the florid, pseudoclassical dialogue with his thick New Jersey accent. I was confident that when he removed his clothes, it would be akin to the young Lana Turner walking down that MGM street in a sweater. A star would be born.

Buster was on good behavior, calling Joel "sir" and once accidentally addressing me as "ma'am." I enjoyed watching the various personalities in the room react to this gorgeous new addition. At one point in the rehearsal, I noticed Buster writing down for Perry his recipe for a super-duper vitamin shake for bodybuilders. He took Zoe's nail file and demonstrated the best way to shape her nails into a French manicure. Joel had to pull Buster and Camille apart from their competitive accounts of bloody fights they'd witnessed. It seems both Camille and Buster were frequent witnesses to and participants in bone-crunching car accidents, gang warfare, and domestic violence. They both liked nothing more than to describe in nauseating detail the various contusions, torn limbs, and smashed-up faces they'd come across in their travels. Camille had a favorite, beloved anecdote from adolescence when she got into a fight with the toughest girl from her high school. Camille's fellow debutante from Canarsie pulled out a switchblade, but Camille took the more elegant self-defense option—ripping off the girl's pierced earring, replete with lobe. Her street smarts fascinated me. I asked her "Camille, did you carry a switchblade in your purse?"

She rolled her eyes at my naïveté. "Julian, this was real life. We didn't do that sort of thing in the early sixties."

We were all disappointed.

"No," she continued, "I used to file down my index fingernail to a very sharp point. Joey DiFrazio will never forget that little encounter."

Buster gazed at Camille with the respect due a brigadier general. Camille was cute and tough, all five feet of her. I loved watching her lean back in my kitchen chair, punching the air with her half-smoked cigarette and teaching Perry how to blow smoke rings. I had to laugh. I was beginning to develop a crush on her. I hadn't felt that way since I fell for my seventh-grade French teacher, Miss Rachlin. They shared similar qualities that would appear contradictory, a self-possessed coolness and a sunny girlish enthusiasm.

Buster latched on to Camille immediately. They made an appealing team of boastful Dead End Kids.

One member of our ensemble was less than enchanted with Buster. Guy bore the brunt of Buster's thespian ineptitude, for they played most of their scenes together. During a break, Guy took me aside. "This is really unfair, Julian. He cannot act. I suppose you find it funny seeing this big lunk butchering his lines."

"Well, I do find it a shade whimsical." I attempted to pacify Guy by complimenting him on his personal charm, sex appeal, vocal technique, and even the cleft in his chin, but he was having none of it.

"Julian, he makes me look like an idiot. There's no give-and-take."

"I wonder if perhaps you're just a bit peeved that you're no longer the only beautiful boy on the stage."

Guy scoffed and snorted. "Julian, I'm really not concerned about how I measure up to Buster Campbell."

I was getting fed up with Guy's arrogance and decided to shoot him straight between the eyes.

"Well, while we're on the subject of male beauty, I wish you'd do something about your eyebrows."

"What's wrong with my eyebrows?"

"Make that singular. You've only got one, and it stretches between your eyes." Guy was nearly speechless from the silly pettiness of my attack. I meant it. He was terribly attractive, but he'd let long, curly black hairs sprout in every direction of his handsome brow.

"Well, I've never had any complaints before. In fact, many of my admirers find my eyebrows sexy."

"What do they say about the hairs growing out of your nose?"

"Julian, this discussion over the grooming of my eyebrows and nose hairs is simply a decoy to get off the subject of Buster's lack of talent. The play was fine without him. Just tell him it's not working out."

"I certainly will not." I was getting angry.

"It's not fair making professionals work with—" Guy's arrogance triggered off an emotional response that impelled me to push him against the refrigerator.

"Listen you, you are twenty-three years old, and you are not a professional, not yet. You may be a professional magician and even a professional New Age healer, but you are not a professional actor, not in my book. I have been paying my fucking dues in this business for the greater part of a decade. I have lived in grinding poverty, humiliated myself daily, groveled for whatever pennies I can find to pursue my dream of a theatrical career. You, my darling, have a long way to go. This little 'amateurish' gig in the East Village is the best thing you could possibly do to get you off your high horse." Guy stuttered and tried to break into my rant, but I wouldn't let him.

"Pretension and pomposity are not attractive qualities in anyone and definitely not in a little pisher like you. So you just cool it and go in there and help Buster and don't make him feel more inadequate and intimidated. Get it?"

I was as astonished as Guy by the force of my stern parental lecture. I meant every word of it. I was concerned about that pretentious edge in

Guy's personality, and I'd also taken an instant liking to Buster and considered him my personal protégé. He had a child's face atop that magnificent physique, and his unguarded vulnerability found a soft place in my heart.

Guy returned to the living room, and while he didn't exactly exude fraternal warmth, he refrained from saying anything rude to Buster. I knew Buster could defend himself. He had, after all, boasted of being the victor in any number of violent altercations with ex-lovers. The way he glared at Kiko whenever she'd carp about the stupidity of the script made me worry over her own well-being. Buster reminded me a lot of Wolfie, the German shepherd I'd grown up with.

This little charade of putting on a skit for two nights in an East Village bar was far from the effortless romp I'd envisioned. This was a volatile cocktail of kooky personalities. Perry, a passionate devotee of the mystery genre, said, "Julian, by every rule of Agatha Christie, one of us will murder Kiko before opening night."

I was determined as author and star to improve the climate of the rehearsal period. From now on, I swore that I'd be perky, upbeat, and supportive of everyone, no matter how vile and obnoxious.

CHAPTER
11

I and I alone am the Emperor's favorite. I, who have nursed him through
the pox, cured his gout, and powdered his thighs when chafed.

Ultima, *Whores of Lost Atlantis*
Act One, Scene Four

That Thursday night, we had our dress rehearsal at Golgotha. Camille
and I handed everyone the costumes and wigs. Buster, with his hyperactive
enthusiasm, had become our assistant costume designer. I had given him
some cheap purple satin drapery I'd used for my apple-doll booth at the
Renaissance Faire. From that he'd fashioned a long, flowing cape for Kiko
with a stand-up collar stiffened by a bent wire hanger. He'd also ripped
apart an old leather jacket and stapling the shreds together created sexy
loincloths for himself and Guy. Guy had gone over to Buster's apartment
the night before, and Buster had draped the leather directly on Guy's nude
body. Now our two beautiful boys were as thick as thieves.

It took a few minutes before I noticed the perfect plucking of Guy's eyebrows. Buster admitted he had been the perpetrator of that act.

"Oh, honey, I told Guy that ape-man look was really tired. I worked like an
hour on those brows. And, you know, I don't think he looks overly groomed.
I also gave him a manicure and a pedicure. I told him I'd trim his pubic hair
if he wanted, but he said maybe some other time."

"Buster, did you two sleep together?"

"Nah. Guy's a good-looking guy and all, and I like him when he's not being so, you know, Miss Important, I'm-the-great-enchantress, but he's not my type at all. I like somebody more mature, I dunno, somebody I could learn something from. A great body doesn't mean that much to me. I mean, baby, I got enough to go around." He comically arched his back in a grotesque S-curve to show off his phenomenal ass. Only one truly confident of his beauty could allow himself to look so ridiculous.

Rupert, the young owner of Golgotha, was at the front of the club chatting with what appeared to be a rough longshoreman. I joined them to see if we had any reservations for our show.

"We sure have, sweet thing. Let's see." In a slightly dazed manner, he fumbled through the reservations book, and, sure enough, the page was full of names. Therein lay the secret to a sold-out house. Get six actors together, and if each invites ten people, you're a raging success. Rupert extended his arm in a melodramatic gesture and exclaimed, "I must introduce to you a great legend: Her Divinity, the one and only Thirteen."

The divinity was the flat-faced longshoreman. The coarseness of his features and his spiky haircut could indeed have passed him off as a denizen of the waterfront. On closer inspection, I saw that he had completely shaved off his eyebrows and wore the remnants of the previous night's mascara. I suspected he was some kind of female impersonator. "Girly-girl, you're invading my turf. I told Rupert I didn't want any other drag queens strutting their twats around on my stage."

Rupert laughed and said, "Baby Doll, half of the acts in the East Village are drag queens. Without them, I'd never be able to book the place."

I tried to avoid a confrontation and said sweetly, "We're just doing this show for two nights. I can't imagine I'd be much competition for you." I decided to lie and lay the flattery on thickly. "I've *really* enjoyed your work. You're absolutely fascinating."

A smile broke out on Thirteen's prematurely sagging face. He was only a few years my senior, but heavy drinking and a bitter attitude made him look like one of the more hardened dames in a women's prison picture. He lightly caressed my cheek. "She's sweet. I give my permission. The show may go on. Have you ever seen such smooth skin?" Then he added in a harsh tone, "What do you sleep in, a vat of moisturizer?" After that crack, he picked up his beer and chugged it.

A screech was heard from the back of the club. "TeeTee darling!"

He screeched back, "Kiki darling." Kiko flung herself into his arms, nearly toppling him over onto Rupert and myself. Thirteen gasped. "Are *you* in this thing?"

Kiko dropped her voice an octave. "Precious, I stoop to conquer."

I couldn't believe she'd insult me in such a bald-faced manner. I refused to get into any conflict with her, though, so I laughed along with the others. I asked them, "Have you known each other long?"

Kiko brushed her hand over Thirteen's flattop and said, "We go way back, we're sisters." Immediately I saw them as the wicked stepsisters and me as the gal with the small shoe size.

Thirteen picked up the edge of Kiko's purple cape as if it were crawling with maggots. "What the fuck have you got on your back?"

Kiko shuddered demurely. "I know, dear, it's hardly Balenciaga." I really wanted to belt her. I could only imagine the time and effort Buster had gone to making the damn thing. Buster had wandered over and heard her disparaging remark. He spun around and walked to the back of the club, where the rest of the cast were gathered.

We began the dress rehearsal in a climate of tension and bloodlust. Camille was manning the tape recorder with the sound cues and also turning on and off the lights. Joel was running around madly in his orange toga and African braided wig that was posing as an Atlantean headdress. Thirteen decided to stand in the back and watch. I wouldn't have cared if Kiko hadn't taken to making little grimaces about the quality of the script whenever she fumbled for a line. We had precious little time to rehearse in the space, so I chose to be totally oblivious to Kiko and Thirteen's rudeness. I also didn't want to upset the rest of the cast.

I shouldn't have bothered. They were seething. During one scene, Perry had a long tongue twister of a line and got so screwed up in it he could hardly squeak out a sound. Sitting in the audience with her pal, Thirteen, Kiko snickered over Perry's articulation problem. I was getting tenser by the second. Perry, shaking furiously, refused to look at Kiko, but Buster couldn't refrain from glaring at her with evil intent. Little Zoe, in her innocent, oblivious way, inflicted the most damage when she repeatedly stepped on the train of Kiko's trailing robe, jerking our malevolent diva backward like a puppet.

We were in the midst of the coronation scene, when I'm crowned the new empress. Kiko stopped the rehearsal and projected in a loud, clear voice, "No, this will not do. This will not do."

Joel inquired gently, "Kiko, dear, is there a problem?"

Kiko, mocking Joel's affected manner of speaking, drawled, "Yes, dear, there is a problem." The rest of us were frozen as if in a game of statues. "You have me blocked in the most ridiculous staging. What kind of a director are you?" She looked out to Thirteen and threw up her arms. "TeeTee, am I crazy? Look at this mess."

TeeTee smiled soothingly. "Darling, you look fine. It's just a little skit that no one's gonna see."

Perry was now trembling so fiercely, I thought he'd start spinning like a rotisserie. I placed my hand on his arm, and he brushed me off. He raised his voice and said, "Excuse me, I would like to know what this nut is doing watching our rehearsal. Kiko, you've got some fucking nerve criticizing Joel's staging. You are the most amateurish, ridiculous, pretentious person I've ever met. Even Buster has more talent than you."

Buster had a quizzical expression on his face, not sure if Perry was being flattering or not. Joel took charge and shouted, "Enough, Perry. This is getting us nowhere. We're almost at the end of the show . . ."

Kiko mumbled under her breath, "Thank the Goddess."

Joel continued, "We're going to finish this run-through, and hopefully tomorrow we can enjoy the performance." We began again, with Kiko walking through her scenes in an exaggeratedly bored manner.

What had possessed Kiko to turn on us this way? Was she nervous and insecure? Now that it was down to the wire, did she realize how tacky the enterprise was and regret her involvement? I knew the script wasn't a newly discovered Chekhov masterpiece, but I thought it was amusing enough for a night on the town in the raffish East Village. Nausea overcame me, and I wished I had never set foot in Golgotha.

Horror of horrors, our opening night was upon us.

There was no room in Golgotha to put on makeup, so we agreed to meet at seven-thirty at Zoe's apartment, conveniently located across the street from the club. Camille still had some work to do on the costumes. The plan was for her to meet me at my place at six, and we'd go to Zoe's together.

By six o'clock a large project still loomed ahead: getting the hair off my legs. There are various methods of depilatory, and I debated the pros and cons of each. Just as I settled on a tube of Nair, the intercom buzzed. It was Camille. It seemed forever while she walked up the stairs. When I opened the door, I could see why. She was as pale as overcooked spaghetti and just as energetic. She collapsed on the first chair she could find.

She threw off her coat and wiped her forehead. "I woke up this morning fine, but about three hours ago, I started feeling so sick. I think I'm coming down with the flu. I feel like I'm going to throw up."

I placed my hand on her forehead. It was burning hot. "Let me take your temperature." I got the thermometer out of the bathroom cabinet and stuck it in her mouth. She sat at the kitchen table holding her head, her elbows on the table. Sure enough, her temperature was nearly 102 degrees. Camille then added that her temperature was always a little below normal, which meant she was really pushing 103! "Darling, we've got to get you home. I mean, why did you even bother coming over? You should be in bed. Let's get you in a cab right now."

"No, no," she protested, "I'll be fine. I've got to run the show."

"You can't run the show. Look at you. I've seen zombies in horror quickies that look better than you."

"Maybe if I just lie down for a little while."

I took her to my bedroom, and she lay down with her arms crossed on her chest like a corpse. Then I grabbed the phone and called Aunt Jennie. She had once been a nurse, and I was sure she would tell me what to do. I filled her in on the Camille situation. Her response was "Are you crazy? She can't do a show. She's got to be in bed. Get her home right now."

"She won't go."

"Keep taking her temperature. If it gets any higher, you've got to bring her to the emergency room."

"Emergency room! But I've got a show to do!"

"Call me back if anything changes." She hung up.

I put on a relaxed face and returned to the bedroom. Camille was lying there with her mouth agape like a mackerel on a bed of ice.

"Camille, we've got to get you home."

She struggled to sit up. "No, no, I'm going to be all right. Who's gonna run the show if I don't?"

"Don't worry, Camille, we'll find someone. Do you want to stay here? Get undressed and get in my bed?"

"But I've got to finish sewing straps on your gown."

"I'll safety-pin them. Don't worry." Camille wouldn't give up until I gave her the box of sewing supplies and my red dress. I ran to the kitchen, put some ice in a washcloth, and placed it on her forehead.

By now it was six-thirty, and I still had hairy legs. I took off my pants and put on my dance belt. I went into the bathroom and began smearing the hideous-smelling depilatory cream all over my legs. The instructions were to leave it on for twenty minutes. Camille appeared in the door of the bathroom, this time as green as overcooked spinach fettuccine.

"Julian, I've . . . I've got to throw up." She moved past me to the toilet and sat on the bathroom floor.

The act, the sound, the look, nay the concept of vomiting were so abhorrent to me, I'd lived in dread of the moment I'd have a child or loved one who needed my help. Clad in only a T-shirt and dance belt, legs stiff with Nair, I bent at the waist to hold her head as she began to retch. I tried to avert my eyes but found myself watching in morbid fascination as she vomited a hideous stew, tears streaming down her face. I stroked her sweaty hair away from her cheeks. When it seemed no more was coming up, I took another washcloth and wiped her face with cold water. I put her back to bed, but once more she picked up the needle and thread and began stitching the shoulder straps onto my gown.

The phone rang. It was Joel at Golgotha. Where was Camille? I explained she couldn't possibly run the show. He hung up, desperate to rustle up a stage manager. It was time to wipe off the Nair. I ran the water in the bathtub and stuck one leg in. I wiped the Nair off, but my gam was still as hairy as a caveman. The phone rang again. I ran to the phone, dripping water all over the kitchen floor. It was Joel again, wanting the phone number of a stage manager friend of ours. Just as he was asking about Camille's condition, the patient herself staggered into the kitchen. Before she could utter my name, vomit shot out of her mouth across the room, hitting the front of the kitchen cabinets. She began to sob.

I hollered into the phone, "Joel, I can't talk! Camille is shooting vomit across the room! It's like the fucking *Exorcist*."

I hung up the phone. Camille was on her knees wiping up the vomit. "Get back to bed. I'll clean it up," I said. I couldn't believe I was hearing myself utter those words. She returned to the bedroom, and, after falling flat on my ass on the bathwater on the kitchen floor, I performed the revolting task of cleaning up the vomit. I returned to the bathroom grimly determined to get rid of my leg hair. I grabbed a can of shaving cream and smeared it all over my legs. With great force of character, I took my safety razor and began shaving from my ankles up.

Wherever the fine bones of my ankle jutted out, I cut myself. Both legs were a Mondrian design of scratches, scrapes, and cuts, and they were still far from silky smooth. The phone rang a third time. I hobbled to answer it, and it was once more Joel, this time asking for another phone number. From the bedroom, I heard Camille weakly calling my name. I looked down and saw rivulets of blood trickling along my calves. I gave Joel the number he requested, and he asked how I was. My voice flying wildly out of control, I screamed into the phone, "The fucking hair won't come off!" and hung up. I limped into the bedroom. Camille was lying on the bed like one of Dracula's drained girlfriends with a threaded needle hanging out of her mouth, my dress stretched across her.

"Oh, honey, you're gonna swallow that needle."

"No, I'm almost finished." She noticed my leg. She whispered almost inaudibly, "You're bleeding."

I tried to act nonchalant. "No, darling, that's just the pattern on my panty hose. Now what is it, dear, that you wanted to ask me?"

Camille attempted to sit up and said weakly, "I just wanted to . . ." Her eyes widened and I could see it coming and I wasn't sure whether to flee or duck, but she threw up again, this time in my beautiful bedroom, and it hit me in the chest! When the attack was over, she began to sob. ". . . all over your pretty bedroom, all over your T-shirt. Your hair."

I smiled pleasantly and said in an even, measured tone, "Don't cry, darling. I'll clean it up." While I wiped off myself and my bedroom, I wondered if there was some greater significance to this ghastly moment. Actions spoke louder than words, and here I was wiping up Camille Falluci's throw-up. Perhaps I loved her. I saw some more vomit on one of my boots leaning against the bed. "Love" was perhaps too extreme a word to describe my feelings. I got a real kick out of Camille. She was nurturing. She was fun. She'd be a good person to have with you if you were being mugged. She also had an innocence that was appealing in a forty-year-old ex–disco champion. She looked forward to being surprised and loved laughing at her own sense of wonder. Moving into the warmer recesses of friendship with Camille was as comfortable as slipping into an old pair of bedroom slippers. I wiped some more vomit from the Oriental rug. No, it was too glib to say I was in love with Camille, but I kind of adored her. During my cleanup operation, I only gagged twice. That spoke volumes for our friendship.

Forty-five minutes later, having experienced blood, projectile vomit, and defective depilatory cream, I was ready to face my audience. I threw the completed dress in a bag, along with about fifty pounds of wigs, costumes, and makeup, kissed Camille good-bye, and left her in my apartment. She had passed through the worst of her crisis, was emptied of anything in her system that could possibly be ejected, and was resting peacefully.

With much grunting and cursing, I managed to get everything in a cab and over to Zoe's apartment.

Word was out about Camille's illness. I reassured everyone gathered at Zoe's that all was being taken care of. Of course it was a lie. I hadn't a clue to how Joel was doing at the club, but there was no use getting the children excited. I tried to put it all out of my mind. After all, it was time to put on my face.

I hadn't done drag in at least seven years, not since I dressed up as Audrey Hepburn as Holly Golightly for a Halloween party. Zoe set up a makeup table at her desk with a mirror. I covered my face with a pale pan stick and powdered heavily. No flop sweat could penetrate that plaster. I shaped my brows, lined my eyes, put on the longest pair of false eyelashes obtainable commercially, and drew on a big funny-lady red mouth. I looked at my reflection. The last time I had seen this face, I looked like a young girl. Now, seven years later, I knew in my heart of hearts, I had become a woman!

*Ultima, despite your bitchery, there's a quality about you that hits me on
the raw.*

Milena, *Whores of Lost Atlantis*
Act One, Scene Four

I left Zoe and Perry still wielding their eyebrow pencils and proceeded to
Golgotha. If I had been apprehensive about walking through that bizarre
neighborhood in full drag makeup, I needn't have worried. I was by far the
most normal individual walking the streets that night.

When I arrived at the club, I had to check twice to see if I'd entered the
correct door. In the twenty-four hours since I'd last been there, the entire
decor had been overhauled. A new art exhibit of jungle paintings, Rousseau
with Christmas lights woven through the fronds, inspired a tropical setting.
The walls were covered with hastily painted palm trees and coconuts.

Buster was standing in the area designated for the stage, while Joel was
on top of an eight-foot ladder focusing the lights.

"Joel, did you find a stage manager?" I asked.

A voice behind me said, "Yes, sweetie pie, me." The enthusiastic voice
belonged to Rupert, whose hair now matched the midnight blue of the
walls. "You guys, don't worry about a thing. I used to run the projectors and
stuff in high school." Rupert noticed my makeup. "Look at you, you're gor-

geous. You should always be made up like that. You look like what's her name. The movie star from the thirties. You know, she made all those movies."

"Yeah, I know. Thanks. Did Joel explain the cues to you?"

"Oh yeah, simple as pie. Turn 'em on and turn em off. But, hey, maybe I'll get a little creative and surprise you with something."

I grabbed his arm desperately. "Please don't surprise me."

I carried my shopping bags to the back of the club, where Buster was now sweeping. "Buster, how are you doing on the night of your legitimate stage debut?"

He raised his eyes heavenward and growled. "Honey, I'm so nervous. I'm like petrified. I'm like . . . look at my nipples." He lifted his T-shirt and exposed his muscled chest. "Look, they're like standing straight out like Christmas trees."

Behind Buster, I saw Kiko picking at her teeth in a compact mirror. I told Buster, "We'll get back to this discussion in a minute." Kiko was all made up and in costume. She looked magnificent in her outrageous blond wig and skintight purple gown. At the last minute, she had decided to forage through her own drag collection for a suitably temptresslike costume.

"Kiko, you look gorgeous. You really look great as a blonde. You have so much style. You could wear anything and look fabulous." I tried to kiss her on the cheek. She moved slightly, so my lips missed their mark and landed in the air.

She smiled with cool amiability. She wasn't about to give an inch. I tried again to smoke the peace pipe.

"I really want to thank you for doing the show. I know you've been very busy, and I appreciate the time you've given us. I hope you'll be able to enjoy the performance more than you've enjoyed the rehearsals." I was expecting her to say, "Oh, I know I've been a bitch and I apologize. I really did have fun."

Not a chance. Instead, she smiled painfully and said, "Thank you, Julian. I know now that I must always work alone. It's not fair of me to expect others to have the obsessive emotional commitment that I have. I'm not saying that I'm right and others are wrong. It's just a different process."

Perry and Zoe arrived with enough makeup on between them to stock an entire Woolworth's makeup counter. Zoe had gone too far. Her drawn-on black brows extended all the way past her ears, and her big red mouth made Bozo's seem bee stung.

I turned to Perry. He had on several pairs of false eyelashes, and after he'd blocked out his own brows, he'd drawn two lines for eyebrows that were so large and round, one would have thought he'd traced them around Coke cans. "Did you save a *little* makeup for tomorrow night?" I asked.

Totally serious, Perry replied, "It has to read to the back row."

"Perry, we're not playing Yankee Stadium."

Guy arrived alone, sans bird.

"Where's Ethel?" I inquired. Ethel played an integral part in the performance.

Quiet and drawn, Guy replied, "Ethel's dead."

Zoe, Perry, and Buster overheard this and gathered around. In hushed voices they all repeated, "She's dead?"

Guy took off his coat and, with vague gestures, looked for someplace to hang it. He then related to us the sad tale of the dove's tragic demise. "We were doing a magic show this afternoon for five-year-olds on the Upper East Side. I do this trick where Ethel is hidden in this flat tray. There's a pocket that I put her in, and she lies very flat. It gives the illusion that it's a regular empty tray. Then I push a button on the bottom and the flap lifts up and the dove pops out. Well, Ethel got into an awkward position, and when I pushed the button, she sprang out and broke her spine." All of us gasped. "She was paralyzed. It was the beginning of the act, and I couldn't ruin the birthday party by telling the kids Ethel was hurt, so I kept going as if nothing was wrong. I had to let the kids pet her, and the poor thing was in agony. As soon as the act was over, I rushed her over to the vet, who put her to sleep."

A single tear fell down Zoe's cheek, and she whispered mostly to herself, "Poor girl." I could tell at that moment Zoe and the late Ethel were emotionally bonded and in her mind were one.

Perry asked Guy, "Why didn't you bring Mary to take her place?"

"She's not properly trained. She's still green. We just have to cut the bit. I'm really sorry, Julian. I really am."

"Don't be silly. I feel awful for Ethel. I know I was jealous and envied her success, but I never wished her ill. I respected Ethel as I would any hard-working veteran. It'll be fine. We'll just cut to my line 'You can bet your ass we'll have peace.' Got that everybody? Got that Zoe?" She nodded, deep in thought. I went to the front of the club and told Joel the sad news about Ethel and the suggested cut in the play.

He asked, "Does everyone know the new plan?"

"Yes, I've told everyone. Don't worry. It'll work out fine."

The audience was beginning to arrive, and we soon realized that, with the rest rooms in the front of the club, if we didn't want the public to see us in costume, we'd have to make other arrangements. Buster and Guy had to get into their skimpy leather loincloths. A back door led to the stairway of the tenement building next door, so the boys stripped down behind the stairs. Once again, due to the bohemian and derelict atmosphere of the neighborhood, none of the tenants of that building entering or exiting gave a second thought to the two young men changing in their vestibule. I received more of a shock when Zoe passed by wearing a long, frizzy fall. It looked as if she'd found a rug on the street and glued it to her head. She took such delight in wearing it, I didn't have the heart to stop her.

Rupert nailed a dusty black drape over the archway behind the stage area so the audience couldn't see us. But we were all peeking out to see them. The place was really filling up. All the banquettes were full. People were sitting on the floor and standing by the bar. Suddenly Perry said, "Oh my God, look at that!"

"That" was Thirteen, coiffed and garbed in high drag in a towering pink wig as many-tiered as a wedding cake. He was wearing a glittering hot pink lamé jumpsuit and eight-inch pink platform shoes and swinging a pink fake fur stole. The audience applauded, not out of recognition but out of acknowledgment of his sheer audacity. Thirteen stood at the bar chatting with Rupert and Ruby.

I said to Perry, "I don't know what he's trying to prove. I'm not in competition with him. I'll probably never do drag again."

"Well, he must be mighty insecure. What was that murder mystery we both read? An English one. A *Ditty Called Death*."

"Was that the one where the old music hall star murders the young soubrette? Thank you, I get the analogy. But if I recall correctly, didn't the actual murderer turn out to be the soubrette's buddy from boarding school?"

Perry checked his false lash. "Hmmm, I guess that's not a good example."

Rupert turned on the tape of preshow music, a medley of themes by Rachmaninoff and the Andrews Sisters. The music switched to Hindu chanting, and Rupert, perfectly on cue, faded the lights to black. We were off. I had a delayed entrance, so I listened to Guy and Buster play their first scene. Guy got some solid laughs and Buster some inadvertent ones. His line readings were so endearingly amateurish, he got laughs I hadn't counted on. Joel entered to an enormous laugh in his outlandish emperor's costume. At the very top of his headdress, I'd attached a gold-painted spatula. I was thrilled to hear the audience laughing. When you write comedy, it's only a hunch that others will find the lines amusing. It's a real kick when you hear the play for the first time with an audience and count off which lines hit the bull's-eye.

Rupert pushed the button on the tape recorder again, and a triumphant fanfare was heard. Kiko entered . . . to complete silence. I had assumed she'd get a round of applause on her entrance, but there was nothing. I peeked through the curtains and saw why. This wasn't her audience at all. Most likely she hadn't invited a single person. These were all friends of the rest of us. They didn't know who or what she was.

Kiko didn't help things by intoning her dialogue at a funereal pace. I was so appalled that I forgot my own jitters, and suddenly Guy and Buster were offstage and rolling me up in the rug for my entrance. We had forgotten to shake out the carpet. I could feel the dust rising up my nose. I held my breath and sensed that I was now onstage . . . then they dropped me and I rolled over and was out of the rug and lying on the floor in my G-string and waist-length red wig, a gaminelike slave girl. I didn't get any applause either, but I hadn't anticipated an ovation. Most of the crowd didn't know me. They were friends of Guy, Perry, Zoe, and Buster. Actually, judging from the reservation book, Buster had the biggest claque.

We learned the extent of Buster's personal following when I as Milena, now the powerful courtesan to the emperor, demanded my own sex slave and ripped off Buster's loincloth. At the sight of Buster's spectacular posterior, the audience exploded in hoots, hollers, and foot stamping. It was as if Callas had hit a high note. I never knew asses could blush, but Buster's did. He was a star. I glanced at Kiko, who looked as if she'd just been ravaged by the Mongol hordes. I knew she felt her artistic integrity had been compromised by appearing in a gay strip show. The performance regained its composure as soon as Kiko began droning her lines again. Whenever she exited, you could almost hear the audience breathe a sigh of relief.

The show picked up steam soon enough, and even Kiko got into the melodrama of the plot. We were approaching the big moment when Kiko did her dramatic monologue pleading to the gods for peace, which ended with the white dove magically appearing and me saying, "You can bet your ass we'll have peace" and then a blackout. I couldn't quite remember where the cut went to eliminate poor Ethel's big moment. Unfortunately neither could Rupert. Even worse, I'd forgotten to tell Kiko that Ethel had died. Kiko extended her arms to the heavens, lifted her head in ecstasy, and was about to open her mouth to begin her speech when Rupert blacked out the lights and pumped up the volume. In the blackout, all I could hear was Perry saying ominously, "Oh shit."

As we exited, I reached out blindly for help in finding the exit and knew the large warm hand I touched was Buster's. Just as we found the exit, I could also feel someone else rushing past me, jabbing me fiercely in the ribs. Kiko.

We had one more scene to go, and I was thrilled that nearly every laugh hit its mark. Not bad considering my costar was playing the climactic scene where we become friends with a look of implacable hatred.

Kiko said her last line—"Move over bitch, I'm joining ya!"—and we ran offstage. For a group of sixty, the audience generated thunderous applause. Buster came out for his curtain call to more cheering, hoots, catcalls, and whistling. One by one the cast received a lovely reception. I came out second to last and was thrilled by the swell in applause. Then I extended my arm to the entrance, and Kiko took the final bow to a decidedly less enthusiastic response. We all held hands and took a company bow to renewed applause.

We exited backstage, or rather behind the black drape. Buster was jubilant. "Oh man, did you hear my applauds?!" He grabbed Perry and hugged him tight.

Perry's eyes were shining, and he grasped my hands and said, "This was the maddest idea you've had yet. I'm so happy. I won't need an antidepressant for days!"

Zoe took her lipstick out of her purse and drew on a bigger mouth. "Oh, sweetie, I think they liked it."

Joel pulled off his crown, leaving a deep imprint across his forehead. He was all flushed and sweaty. "Well, we pulled it off!" He then lowered his voice. "Rupert really blew it when he blacked out Kiko's big speech."

"I know. I don't think the First Lady of the Avant-garde is pleased."

Rupert stuck his head through the curtain and smiled broadly.

"Girl, you were divine. I had no idea it would be this good. We've got to talk. You guys have got to do more shows here. We're like from the same place." I looked at his blue hair shaved into the shape of the continent of Africa and wondered what was that place we were both from. Rupert continued, "Oh, by the way, what the fuck happened with the dove? I didn't know when to turn off the lights."

"The dove died, and so will I when I run into Kiko."

I followed him through the curtain and saw a group gathered immediately outside the backstage area.

Rupert's partner, Ruby, grabbed me by the shoulders. "You were a pisser! A pisser! And so beautyful. I'd fuck you if you were a dyke. You were all great. But Kiko—I love her, I really do, but she's not a comedienne."

"I know, that dame's so unfunny, she makes Hiroshima look like a night at the Improv," I said.

Surprisingly Ruby topped me with "She's so unfunny, she should wear a laugh track in her shoulder pads."

From behind I heard a familiar New York–accented female voice say, "That bitch is so unfunny, she thinks Beirut is the comedy capital of the world." Ruby stepped aside, and Roxie, the gal from my Wall Street temp job, appeared in a strange outfit. She looked like an actress playing a TV cop posing as an East Village artist. I was flattered that she'd come. Roxie let her eyelids droop and voiced in her most hushed dramatic tones, "Julian, when you entered in that G-string with your ass hanging out, frankly I was shocked and, may I say, somewhat saddened."

"Oh, that I was no longer garbed in the austere vestments of my art?"

"No, darling. That I was not up there with you, exposing my breasts for the world to see."

Zoe appeared in a tattered trench coat, her hair covered with a dark scarf knotted tightly under her chin. With her head bowed, she attempted to scurry out of the club like a little mouse. Roxie grabbed her arm and stopped her progress. Zoe's dead white face twitched with rabbitlike nervousness. Roxie declaimed, "You! You! Zoe Gomez. You were marvelous! You with the voice. My Gawd, I'd kiss the hem of your coat but I don't know where it's been." Zoe giggled and did a little curtsy. She then excused herself and vanished. Roxie had a sage expression on her face. "The madness of the artist."

The towering pink figure of Thirteen appeared, like a Macy's Thanksgiving Day balloon, his big, flat face encased in heavy pancake makeup. "Darling sweetie honey baby, you were too too too much. Wasn't Kiko fab? She's such a star. You gotta be careful, that Jap bitch can wipe the stage with you. Honey, you didn't look like you were enjoying yourself. Darling, you've got to loosen up."

Roxie interjected, "And you, darling, could have buttoned your lips." Thirteen looked at her, confused. Roxie continued in her toughest New York accent, "Yes, dear, I was the, how did you put it so elegantly, 'cunt' who kept shushing you throughout the performance."

Thirteen was too smashed to really zap her. All he could manage was a belligerent "Why don't you go back to the Bronx, bitch?" and wrap himself in his fun fur stole. Then he spied Kiko, now garbed in her own clothes, which were every bit as flamboyant as her stage wardrobe. "Kiko! you were just toooo fab, darling. You did me in, baby."

Kiko wasn't in the mood for flattery. She was mad as a hornet. I felt like Bette Davis confronting Gale Sondergaard in *The Letter*. I remembered a line of dialogue that described Sondergaard's character as possessing "the eyes of a cobra." It also applied to Kiko at this very moment. In a mean, even, dead-on voice, she spat out, "You are a vicious, evil, manipulative, conniving, opportunistic, no-talent queen."

All I could respond with was a flip "But I'm good company."

She spewed, "It was always your plan to use my name to attract a crowd and then try to humiliate me."

One brief look at the audience split up in groups surrounding each member of the cast disputed the first part of her claim. "I'm so sorry Rupert screwed up the light cue. It was my fault that I forgot to tell you Guy's bird died and we had to cut the bit. But I didn't forget on purpose. I was so nervous. Please accept my apology."

"I wouldn't believe a word you uttered. I'm just mad at myself for degrading myself by appearing in this trash." That sounded like she was quitting. We had one more performance to do the following night! I loathed and despised her, but I needed her.

"Kiko, please believe me that I wasn't trying to humiliate you. I just wanted us all to have a good time. The audience loved the show, loved your performance. Please, let's get over this."

Kiko raised her hands to stop me from continuing. Very grandly, she replied, "I don't have time to waste any more energy conversing with you."

"Does that mean you're not doing the show tomorrow night?"

She expended one more burst of energy, gave me a sharp slap across the face, and left the club.

Thirteen shook his head sadly and said, "Darling, your days at Golgotha are over. See you around, doll." He spun around to exit, and his shedding stole knocked over a beer bottle and sent it crashing to the floor.

I turned to Roxie. "People come and go so quickly around here."

Roxie took a tissue out of her bag and wiped the lipstick that had smeared from Kiko's slap. She said, "Better call Central Casting, it looks like you're out a leading lady."

An enormous wave of exhaustion rushed over me. The events of the past two weeks seemed pointless. We had expended so much energy and emotion, and for what? To entertain sixty people with an hour of camp movie clichés. I should have spent the time searching for a decent-paying day job. I wished I'd never involved everyone in this foolishness. I had been so starved for the mad pleasure of performing. I should have thought twice and stayed home and made faces in the bathroom mirror.

With Kiko walking out, even this silly adventure had the aura of failure. I wondered where I'd gone wrong with Kiko. Had I not deferred to her and treated her with the utmost respect? Perhaps that had been the wrong psychology. I might have had more success with her had I matched her bitchery tooth and claw. If she was best friends with a creature like Thirteen, obviously she enjoyed a battle of egos. That just wasn't my style. I sought affection from my friends, not a competition of insults. There was no point flogging myself. Kiko was gone, and I was too proud to grovel and beg her to do a second night.

I looked at Roxie's odd but attractive face. Each of her features was either too big or too small, but they combined to form a face that one was compelled to notice. She was a tall girl. I hadn't realized she was exactly my height. "The shame is yours"—I had been so tickled when Roxie threw that melodramatic phrase at her boss at the investment firm. The words were amusing in the situation, but what made it funny was Roxie's tough intensity and middle-class Long Island accent. She was a personality. Her voice, gestures, and exaggerated facial expressions combined to make her someone impossible to forget. You wanted to hear more.

Roxie adjusted her scarf and shrugged. "Julian, this has been an evening of theatrical brio, and I must now depart."

As she turned her head, I blurted out, "What are you doing tomorrow night?" All at once Roxie's bravado vanished. She looked ten years old. "Are you serious?"

I'd uttered those fateful words. I couldn't take them back.

"Sure I'm serious. What else am I going to do? I don't want to cancel tomorrow night." I really didn't want to cancel. Despite Kiko's nastiness, I enjoyed being in the fantastic world of the play. I liked being the whore from lost Atlantis, and I wanted to be her again. There were a couple of lines I'd blown that I knew could get laughs. I wanted another chance to get them right. Putting Roxie in the show was my only recourse.

"Roxie, do you think you could learn the role in one day?"

She was still stammering with disbelief. "Is this for real? Me play that part?"

"Yeah. I'm asking you. It's a nutty idea, but you're certainly a big personality." As I was speaking, I was questioning whether I really wanted her in the play or whether I was taken in by the old movie fantasy of a star being discovered in the strangest of circumstances. What did it matter? In a joint like Golgotha, there was an entirely different standard for theatrical excellence and it was called "sheer nerve."

"Roxie, do the role. Before you know it, the whole thing will be over, and you'll have a great story to tell at the office."

"But you don't even know if I can act."

"Can you act?"

Roxie fixed me with an intense look. "I'm Bernhardt and Imogene Coca rolled into one." She then once again became young and vulnerable. "God, I'd love to do it. I understand exactly why you'd want to do a show here. It's as if all things are possible here." It seemed so right that Roxie had been present when Kiko walked out. It was true that I had no idea if she was any good onstage, but then she couldn't have been any worse than our current leading lady and she was far better natured.

"Roxie, wait here. Don't go anywhere. Let me talk to Joel. I think it would be fantastic if you did this. It'll be part of your myth. Wait right here."

Joel was chatting with Rupert by the bar. "Joel, Kiko quit. She won't do tomorrow night. She even slapped me."

"She slapped you?"

"Damned hard. My lipstick was all the way on my ear and moving toward Altoona. I don't want to cancel tomorrow night."

"Well, what are we going to do?"

"I've got a replacement. I think she'll be wonderful."

"Who?"

"Roxie Flood."

"She's an actress?"

"No, a librarian. I know her from one of my temp jobs. She's a wacky comedienne with a big personality. She's standing right over there. Want to meet her?"

I brought Joel to where Roxie was standing and introduced them. Roxie said, "Oh, you're British."

"No, just affected," Joel replied. "I understand Julian has offered you the lead in our show."

Roxie smiled apprehensively. "Yeah, he did. I'll . . . I'll do it if you want me to. I mean, I'll try. But if you'd rather skip it, I will. Whatever you want."

"Don't take this the wrong way, but we're desperate. Have you ever studied acting?"

"Oh yes. I was a theatre major at Hofstra. I was like, this very intense classical actress. Honey, I played Nina in *The Sea Gull.*"

I knew Joel was dubious, but still he said, "It's a lot to learn in one day. I suppose if you had to, you could hold the script."

Roxie screwed up her face, dismissing the thought. "Oh please, you jest. I'll be word perfect. I'm a great study. Darling, you give me the role, and I will give you a performance. Where do I go and what time do you want me?"

CHAPTER 13

*Aw both of youse, quit your beefin'. You're both cut from the same cloth
. . . and it's cheap!*

Folio, *Whores of Lost Atlantis*
Act One, Scene Four

We asked Roxie to be at my place at ten the following morning. She was twenty minutes early. She looked like the quintessential librarian, glasses perched on the tip of her nose, pencils sharpened with a notebook opened to a clean page. I had given her a script before she left Golgotha, and Joel and I were very impressed that she had large chunks of the play already committed to memory.

I would be remiss if I gave the impression that Roxie's performance was a revelation from the first read-through. The hard truth was she was awful. I wasn't sure if she was trying to imitate Kiko or re-create her own performance as Nina in the Hofstra *Sea Gull*.

Joel and I had fixed saccharine smiles of encouragement on our faces. We didn't fool our new star.

"All right, boys, I know I stunk, but in every aspect of my life I always start off poorly and then work harder than anyone. Just tell me what you want. I have no ego as an actress. I'll imitate you. I'll do anything you say. Just be very clear. And another thing, you put me onstage in front of sixty gay men and hold on to your hats, fellas."

We worked all morning, and true to her word, Roxie kept improving. Joel and I gave her precise line readings, and she imitated them perfectly. I also gave her a crash course in grande dame body language. Roxie had a tendency to slump as if she were embarrassed by her gangly long arms and legs and neck. I tied a bedspread around her hips that created the impression of a long train and placed Kiko's headdress on her head.

"Roxie, you have to feel like the most beautiful woman in the world. Whatever you think is weird or ugly about yourself, focus on it and think of it as a jewel, a gift that makes you an original."

"I've got no chin."

"Stop that. You may have no chin, but you have a neck like a swan's. So lift it very high and think up, up, *up*! Now let's walk around the room like a great lady." Joel sat on the sofa suppressing a laugh. I didn't care. It was working. I continued my litany of instruction. "Round arms, always have a curve to the arm. That's right. Like a ballerina. Make all the lines in your face go up, high cheekbones, a lovely curve to the lips, lift your eyebrows, don't wrinkle your forehead, let your head float above your lovely neck like an exquisite balloon."

Roxie paraded around the room like an ostrich playing Margaret Dumont. "But is it funny?"

"Darling, you'll be funny, but you'll also be imposing and glamorous."

Camille took off from work early and arrived at my apartment to see if Roxie's costumes needed altering. Amazingly, Camille had almost completely recovered from her illness. "Guy came over to my apartment and helped me visualize myself healthy and energetic. He led me through an imaginary underground cavern and I unlocked a secret stone door and on the other side was the most beautiful meadow of mossy banks and willow trees."

Roxie handed Camille a safety pin. "Dear, it's called a twenty-four-hour bug."

"You can all laugh," added Camille, "but I worked for doctors for nearly ten years. I saw things you wouldn't believe, such abuses. I was just the secretary, and I used to assist the doctor in medical procedures." She then proceeded to go into excruciating detail about a gallbladder operation she'd witnessed that had gone awry. Camille was as fascinated by colostomies and amputations as I was by nineteenth-century actresses.

All the costumes basically fit except for a sequinned brassiere Kiko had worn in the ceremonial procession. Roxie suggested she go topless. "Why not? I've got the most beautiful breasts in New York. I say that without a trace of arrogance. I have one ovary and no chin but lovely breasts." To prove her point she popped one out. It was rather perfect, firm with a picturesque pink nipple. We all were impressed that she'd bare her breasts for art. "Oh no, you don't understand, this has been my fantasy for years. To be in an avant-garde play in an East Village club. One has to have a nude scene. That's part of the whole trip."

I was carried aloft with enthusiasm. "Well, I think you should be totally nude, and Buster can carry you in on his shoulder. We could just spray glitter over your whole body."

"That's all right, dear. Let me just tell you right now, I will show my tits to anyone, but only the man I make love with sees my beaver." The subject was closed.

Roxie stayed with me in my apartment till we left for Golgotha. We found that we shared many passions. One was a fascination with President Kennedy's assassination. Roxie admitted to visiting the Museum of Broadcasting at least seven times to view the Zapruder assassination footage. We also were obsessed with bringing Nazi war criminals to justice. I suggested as an alternate career to fall back on that we be Nazi hunters.

Roxie sprang to her feet with zeal. "Julian, we must do it! I want to be on the steps of the Supreme Court shouting, 'Never forget! Shame!' "

To put it mildly, we really hit it off. Roxie was such a dynamic presence, I was concerned how she'd blend with the fragile sensibilities of our little troupe. They had all been contacted and told of our change in leading ladies and to meet at Golgotha an hour early. I introduced Roxie, who temporarily lost her bravado and had the air of someone about to be placed before the firing squad.

Buster spoke up first and bellowed in his raspy voice, "Well I say fuck Kiko and her saggy tits. Thank God she's gone. You're gonna be fabulous, I just know it." Everyone applauded, and we began the rehearsal. Roxie was awfully nervous performing for the cast and generally forgot half of what we'd worked on. Whenever they weren't in the scene, the rest of the company sat out front watching. I was touched that they all tried to be encouraging by laughing at everything Roxie did. Still, I knew they couldn't have been terribly impressed.

When we finished the rehearsal, Roxie thanked the cast for their indulgence. "I'm sure you're all thinking I'm lousy. I know that's what I'm thinking, but I have played comedy before and I just need an audience. I promise all of you, I won't let you down."

We all crossed the street to Zoe's to get made up. It was fascinating observing Roxie integrate into the group. Shortly after arriving at Zoe's, she and Buster were comparing surgical scars—his appendix scar and her scar from her ovarian surgery. She got Guy to discuss his bar mitzvah and Hebrew school training.

"It is my great regret that I was not born a Jewess." Roxie groaned. "Mark my words, Guy, before I die, I will marry a Jewish man and convert. I will become a true Daughter of Israel."

She engaged Zoe in the most involved discussion I'd yet witnessed. They were both hovering over a makeup mirror, so I couldn't actually hear what they were saying, though I gathered it was very much girl talk. I overheard snippets of dialogue, such as Roxie confessing, "Zoe, every night I cry into my pillow," and later Zoe sighing, "I really admire you, Roxie. You're such a modern woman."

Roxie refused to allow Perry to give her the cold shoulder, a by-product of his shyness. She checked her roots in the mirror and asked Perry if sometime he'd help her lighten them. He was hooked and from then on worshiped her as a blond goddess.

Once again, the place was packed with our friends and a number of the curious who had come across our flier posted on streetlamps. Rupert and Ruby let in a number of their friends for free; they certainly gave the room local color.

The show was remarkably smooth. True to her word, once Roxie was secure that eighty percent of the room was gay, she found colors and facial expressions I'd never seen before. She was a holy terror. At various points in the show, we all stood back and just watched her with fascination. I don't know if it was good or bad acting, but she certainly made an impression, and I could feel the audience rooting for her. It was as if she was the most popular girl in summer camp and you liked her so much, you imagined she was a great actress.

At the curtain call, I made a little speech welcoming Roxie and letting the audience in on the drama of her taking over the role in twenty-four hours. They cheered, and I was very proud of my latest protégée. The whole cast held hands, and we took a company bow. I had this strange feeling that somehow we were now complete. We were a group. We had only done one other performance and rehearsed a handful of times, but at that moment, there seemed about us a certain perfection. We were meant to be together.

CHAPTER
14

Folio, have the slaves light the torches. Let the Masque begin!

Emperor Zenith, *Whores of Lost Atlantis*
Act One, Scene Four

It seemed so cruel that just as we'd found the perfect leading lady, the gig was over. My gown went back into Aunt Jennie's closet; the wigs were tossed in a plastic bag and stuffed in the back of a drawer. A week went by, and it was as if we'd never done *Whores of Lost Atlantis*. All that was left was picking up the snapshots we'd taken backstage from the drugstore. Alphabet City seemed as far away as . . . well . . . the continent of Atlantis.

I missed my group of vagabond players but didn't phone any of them: I had nothing to say. When I wasn't scrounging around for a temp job, I was mailing press kits for my one-man show to theatres throughout Ohio. Joel threw some work to Perry and me. His boss, Howard Fuller, had a show celebrating its first year. He had Tiffany's create a crystal paperweight engraved with the show's logo, and we helped Joel deliver them to the members of the chorus at half hour, dragging four large boxes to the backstage of the Broadway theatre. I complimented Perry on his week-length growth of beard.

"I had to do something. I was so depressed. Since the show, I didn't dare go near peroxide. It's comforting that men have the option of growing facial hair."

I sighed. "I suppose it is a comfort."

The dancers were onstage warming up. We stood in the wing calling each of their names so they could pick up their presents. Carole Jo, Ty, Skip, Florrie, Suzy, Mitch. A lovely draft blew across the wide expanse of stage. Perry said softly, "I wish we were out there."

"You had a good time at Golgotha?"

Perry closed his eyes as if conjuring forth the mental picture. "Maybe the best time of my entire life."

I tossed a paperweight at a dancer named Kenny, nearly hitting him square on the jaw. "Well, dammit, let's do it again!"

After we handed out the last present, Perry and I took Joel's arms and escorted him to the exit. "I can't take it." I groaned. "I need the applause. Attention must be paid to such a drag queen! We gotta call Rupert and do another show."

Joel threw back his head. "Oh thank god you said so. Let's get the hell out of here. I can't wait to be once more a big fish in a little New Wave pond."

Rupert booked us to open in two weeks. With great haste, I wrote a rather lewd Victorian fantasy entitled I Married a Fairy Queen.

The other cast members of Whores of Lost Atlantis were also suffering from Golgotha withdrawal and were desperate to return. I played the title role, a whimsical fairy princess with a bitchy streak named Chanterelle. She's proclaimed queen of all the sprites who live at the bottom of an English garden and must choose between her crown and the love of a mortal played by Guy. Roxie played my wisecracking best friend, Truffle. Joel was the evil fairy king Morel, Perry a mischievous sprite named Coriander. Buster was an exhibitionist fairy named Shiitake, and Zoe was a blowsy alcoholic nymph named Helen. The choice of subject matter was dictated by my theory that all we'd need for cheap costumes were sequined fig leaves and antennae. I also took into consideration that we were moving into an exceptionally warm late spring and wouldn't catch a chill.

However, nothing prepared us for the thermometer-breaking late-summer heat wave that followed. Golgotha, in the true spirit of the avant-garde, was devoid of air-conditioning. It was soon apparent that a performance could not go on, no matter how nude. Buster opened the back door and noticed that Golgotha shared a backyard with Breughel's Dream, the art gallery next door. The backyard was being used as a sculpture garden filled with rather erotic totem poles. Tippi, the severely Marxist owner of the gallery, begrudgingly gave us permission to frolic amidst the totems. The surrounding tenement buildings created a Shakespearean-like gallery, and we envisioned the space as a kind of urban guerrilla Globe Theatre.

The heat wave broke the afternoon of the show but brought forth torrential rains. Now it appeared that the interior of Golgotha was still too humid for habitation, but the sculpture garden was like something out of *The Rains of Ranchipur*. And, wouldn't you know, this was the night that *People* magazine was sending around a reporter and photographer to snap our picture for possible inclusion in their piece on the burgeoning East Village performance art scene. I languished in my apartment waiting for Joel to phone and tell me if the show was going to go on. By five the rain had stopped, and Manhattan was experiencing that very rare atmosphere of pure radiance that occurs only after intense and sudden rainfall. The phone rang. It was Joel.

"Put on your lashes and get over here. We're going on."

"Inside or outside?"

"Outside. . . . The bad news is, the backyard is flooded, the good news is . . . well, we're working on it."

When I arrived at Golgotha, Ruby blocked my entry into the sculpture garden.

"Sorry, girlfriend, my instructions are not to let you see the backyard till it's presentable."

Really, what did they take me for, some Bankheadish diva with nary a shred of team spirit? I pushed Ruby aside and gasped. The sculpture garden, which had an unfortunate dip in the middle, was as filled with water as a Jacuzzi. Joel and Rupert and Buster were feverishly absorbed in a peculiar activity involving brooms and mops. They looked up and stared at me as if I were a stern governess.

"What are you three doing?"

Rupert, his turquoise hair damp with sweat, grinned. "I found a hole in the cement. We can push all the water through the hole and flood the basement." Joel and Buster enthusiastically agreed and said it would take only a few hours.

"Do you think the audience will stick around that long?" I asked.

Buster struck a bodybuilder pose. "Get real. They'll wait for hours to see these titties. I've got the most famous breasts in the East Village."

It seemed a bit like painting the roses red, but I was very touched that Rupert would flood his basement on our account. Though in full leading lady maquillage, I rolled up my jeans and joined in. It was still such a novelty having other people emotionally involved in one of my projects. During my years as a solo performer, if the theatre had flooded, you could be damn sure I'd be alone pushing the water through that friggin' hole. Here I had Joel and Buster and the management determined to see the show go on. How could I not get down on my knees and pitch in?

The other actors as well as the audience began arriving. The cast was let in, the audience detained outside Golgotha. It was now eight o'clock, and there was still a good deal of work to be done before the show could proceed. Joel ran around to the corner bodega and bought cans of beer for the crowd milling outside the club. Could it be possible that there was word of mouth about *Whores of Lost Atlantis*? The lights still had to be hung and focused. We were worried that the audience outside would grow restless and vamoose. I was struck with a Mickey and Judyesque notion. Why not entertain the waiting crowd with an improvised variety show in the empty lot two doors down from Golgotha? We set up a few clip lights with the help of some superlong extension cords and kept the crowd diverted for nearly an hour. Camille and Perry wowed 'em with an improvised adagio act, lindying and doing the mashed potato to an Elvis Presley tape played on Buster's ghetto blaster.

I knew Perry was a dancer, having hoofed beside him in several summer stock musicals. Camille was the terpsichorean revelation, but then she shouldn't have. Hadn't she told me of her nights competing in hustle contests in the late seventies? Perry danced with the spry lightness of a Peter Pan, but Camille dug her toes into the pavement, making every little twist and turn highly sexual. With her short, bosomy body covered with a black pullover sweater and black tights, she seemed like the toughest girl at the gym dance. Perry spun her around, and she created memorable picture after picture, moving her hips to the rhythm and always with a lit cigarette between her fingers. It would be hard to imagine any guy, gay or straight, who wouldn't have wanted to grab her right there on the spot.

Other acts followed. Guy ran home and returned with two doves and a rabbit and several feats of legerdemain, and Roxie revealed a flair for blue stand-up comedy. She regaled the crowd with stories of her aborted attempt at a lesbian experience years before in San Francisco and how her first gynecologist couldn't find her uterus. Even shy little Zoe joined the bill. Her face painted a ghostly white, her usual daytime makeup, she stood amidst the rubble of the empty lot. A stark, fragile figure lit only by one light, she recited Lady Macbeth's sleepwalking speech. I was worried about how her act would go over following Roxie's vaginal confession. I shouldn't have been. Zoe held us spellbound. She was an actress. Oh, honey, you just had to be there! Plenty were, including the writer and photographer from *People* magazine. They had actually stayed, and the scuttlebutt was that they enjoyed the performance!

About halfway through I *Married a Fairy Queen*, the improbability of the evening finally got to us. While we were changing behind a draped sheet outside, completely exposed to the denizens of the tenement next door, Roxie turned to me, her naked breasts sparkling with glitter. "I keep reassuring myself, 'I'm a normal person, I have credit cards, a job, I have a life.' " I helped her strap on her fairy wings.

Rupert and Ruby were once more thrilled with the show. "You guys are like the greatest thing that's happened to us," panted Rupert. "You gotta be here every week. This could be like your home, your theatre. That's what I always wanted this place to be. I don't care about fucking rock and roll. I wanna be like, you know, what's his name." His eyes rolled up in his head, and he snapped his fingers in search of the correct name. "You know, the

Russian, Diaghilev! That's my trip, man. Art, theatre, music! A synthesis!"

Ruby dug her bony fingers into her mass of turquoise hair and shook it out. She looked at us with heavy-lidded eyes. "You guys really inspire us totally."

Rupert continued, "I tell ya, I think we should be in business together. Julian, Joel, we come creatively from the same place. I completely identify with you guys."

Joel had a painful little smile on his face, like a dowager sitting among terrorists. I could see him staring at Rupert's earring made from an IUD. I sensed Joel didn't identify.

The following Friday, all of us except Zoe were on a ferry bound for Fire Island Pines. Howard Fuller had left for his villa in the south of France and gave Joel the use of his house in the Pines for the week. Spread out majestically on the beachfront, the house had so many levels, it reminded me of a gray, wooden Elsinore complete with pool. I remember that lovely week as if it were an overedited 1960s movie montage of wacky madcap moments, underscored by Henry Mancini. I can see Buster, his magnificent golden body covered by only the tiniest of Speedo bathing suits, teaching us gymnastics on the beach. Camille unveiled for us every day a coordinated resort wardrobe, everything in black, white, and red to go with her Italianate coloring. Another memory of Camille: the two of us searching for a spot along the beach to place our blanket peopled with enough obese sun worshipers so Camille wouldn't feel self-conscious about her less than svelte figure. Neither of us cared much for the ocean, and we gingerly tiptoed in and lightly splashed ourselves like two senior citizens from Miami.

I remember Guy giving us all the most fabulous massages and demonstrating that heat could emanate from his hands. It was hard to believe that Guy with his yuppie materialism could indeed possess the gift of healing. I was a skeptic, but midway through the week, I woke up with a ghastly stiff neck. After an hour of heavy-duty treatment from Guy, I could spin my head like a dreidel. Guy didn't just give a massage. He placed his hands on various parts of my body, and as I began to feel the heat, he led me through a series of images that triggered emotional responses. The theory is that the physical condition is a metaphor for what's bugging you emotionally. For instance, Perry's sinus problems were created by his feelings that his mother was smothering him. I could vividly picture Mrs. Cole sitting inside Perry's nose spreading out mah-jongg tiles. The pain in my neck stemmed from my anxiety that I had the weight of the world on my shoulders. I wasn't sure about the world—but certainly paying my rent was a concern.

Ah, more memories. One afternoon Perry and Roxie and I went for a stroll on the beach. Roxie was rigged up in a turn-of-the-century-style beach outfit, a peppermint-striped sundress, ribbons in her hair, and a bright red mouth. I hadn't shaved since we arrived and looked a bit like Carole Lombard posing as Clark Gable. We approached some older gentlemen reclining on beach chairs. Perry recognized one as a retired 1950s movie chorus boy he knew slightly. Perry knows a number of these veteran male chorines and collects them like model trains. He called out to the gentleman.

"Lance!" He then whispered to us that Lance had been one of the dancers who lifted Marilyn in the "Diamonds Are a Girl's Best Friend" number and that he had seen both of our shows and was a fan. We reached the beach chairs. Perry and Lance embraced. Perry introduced us. "Lance, this is Julian Young and Roxie Flood."

Lance's eerily youthful face lit up, and he made a deep bow before us. Then looking directly at Roxie, he clasped her hands and said, "Julian, I absolutely adore you!"

Roxie raised an eyebrow. "Lance, I may suffer from fertility problems, but I certainly do not possess a male gene pool."

"Oh, oh, oh, oh, do forgive. How dreadful!"

To her credit, Roxie was amused as well as irritated. The encounter, however, led to the highlight of our vacation. Lance's buddy was a silent partner in a parasailing concession and arranged a free flight for us. Perry declined due to his sinus condition, but up, up, up Roxie and I flew.

Perched in a small seat connected by a chord to a motorboat and blown aloft by a parachute, we could see our friends waving to us from the deck of the house. For the first few dizzying minutes, we were so exhilarated to be flying we could only squeal and gasp for breath. Soon one becomes accustomed even to free flight, and Roxie and I were launched into a discussion of a mutual childhood idol, Hayley Mills, or as Roxie with her librarian's flair for detail reminded me, Hayley Mary Rose Vivian Mills.

Aloft I don't know how many feet in the air, it seemed oddly appropriate for Roxie and me to be in serious recollection of Hayley's adolescent perfection, and her disastrous early marriage to producer Roy Boulting. I must explain that our analysis of pop culture celebrities wasn't limited to camp nostalgia. We used these personal icons to illustrate our deeper concerns. Garbo's lonely last years made a starting-off point for an intense reflection on the tragedy of self-absorption and our own fears of suffering from what Roxie's therapist called "a narcissistic disorder." Our in-flight meditation also drifted to the recent dissolution of a famous movie star marriage as reported in the *Star*. Both Roxie and I felt that marriage, gay or straight, was problematic. Roxie wondered if she could ever have a successful marriage, fearing she lacked the nesting instinct. Her monologue cataloging her disappointments on the Rue d'Amour so consumed her, she didn't even notice that we nearly crash-landed atop two nude lesbians playing Scrabble.

I was hardly judgmental. I share with Roxie my utter fascination with myself, but we also love discussing other people's lives. When you get down to it, Roxie and I loved gossip. But our whole group did too, except perhaps Joel. I don't want Joel to come off as prissy or goody-goody, but at times he seemed like a weary camp counselor shepherding an unruly group of preteens. Our favorite activity was gossiping about one another. Perry and I discussed Camille's weight gain and its direct relation to her calamitous history of abusive relationships. We both felt she was removing herself from the possibility of another violent encounter. Roxie voiced her concern to me about Perry's lack of focus and perhaps the disadvantage of having a small trust fund. We both wondered how much of Perry's mood swings were caused by a chemical imbalance and how much by garden variety neurosis. Buster confided to me that he thought Roxie had an eating disorder.

"Of course she has an eating disorder, Buster. Her idea of gorging herself is munching three grapes! Obviously, she equates weight loss with success. So if she loses a pound, she's accomplished something."

Joel took me aside and wondered if I thought Buster had a drinking problem.

"Of course he has a drinking problem, Joel. When someone has five beers and a bottomless glass of wine at dinner and begins talking in a completely different voice and ends the evening with his head in the minestrone, I'd say there may be cause for alarm." We all adored Buster like a rambunctious little brother, but when he stared drinking—*quelle horreur!*—his streetwise Jersey voice took on a pretentious, sophisticated slur and he'd dwell on some inane point till his listeners' nerves were stretched to the breaking point. One night during our Fire Island sojourn, Buster disappeared after dinner, and it wasn't till the following afternoon that we found him passed out on a deck chair a half mile toward Cherry Grove.

Joel's own drinking was a frequent subject. Guy felt that Joel's normalcy was a facade suppressing a deep-rooted resentment of his upper-class WASP family and their rigid system of values. Perry agreed that Joel's family was definitely dysfunctional. I was confused. Joel had often told me that he didn't recall a single incident in his childhood when anyone in his family had an emotional outburst. Perry screamed at me, "That's not normal! Besides they're too plastered from their all-evening cocktail hour to say anything but 'Make me another Bloody, dear.'"

I suppose Zoe was our favorite person to gossip about. I have heard more anecdotes strung about that dame than there were about Tallulah at her peak. It helped that she was so elusive. Zoe almost never socialized with us. After a rehearsal or performance she'd tie a scarf around her head and scoot out of Golgotha still in her clownlike makeup and four-inch spike heels. We concocted all sorts of theories about her and her activities. She had no apparent means of support except for an occasional gig ushering, yet she saw every movie and play in town and had an endless supply of tarantula-length false eyelashes. We never could get her to answer a single query as to her past, her family, what state she was born in, where she went to school, what she ate for breakfast, and definitely not her age. Buster even riffled through her purse to find a wallet with a driver's license to no avail. Her blank vagueness masked a torrid past, an illegal career, or a life spent in a convent. Nothing would have surprised us. We didn't even know why she declined to join us for our beach holiday. We knew from the almost abnormal whiteness of her skin that she harbored a terrible fear of the sun. When she heard of our plans, she pleaded with Roxie to be careful about letting the ultraviolet rays touch her.

Roxie tried to allay her fears. "Zoe darling, I will slather myself with number-thirty sunscreen whenever I walk outside the house."

"That's not enough, Roxie. Please. Use the sunscreen indoors as well. It's even more dangerous. The rays bounce off the water and through the windows. I beg of you."

All you needed was a five-minute encounter and you got an anecdote you could dine out on for a week. You may think that in the gossip sweepstakes, the common denominator was moi. No, no, no, no. You can bet your ass whenever I left the room, there was plenty of jawboning about the diva. It didn't bother me in the least. We were all perfectly aware of what the others were saying about us. We accepted that we were a whimsical bunch of drunks, anorectics, narcissists, and manic-depressives, and we found one another absolutely fascinating.

Besides our collective neuroses, the most frequent conversation topic was the future. Did we want to continue doing shows at Golgotha? On our last night in the house, after an enormous pasta dinner, Joel had us all sit on the deck overlooking the ocean. He related our conversation with Rupert and Ruby and their wish for us to be the resident theatre company of Golgotha. Before he could launch into the negative aspects of the commitment, all of us began shouting, "Yes, yes, yes, yes!"

Joel tried to retain a businesslike composure. "If we're going to do it, I really want to do it right. Spruce up the production values, and, well, it's also a matter of attitude. We'll have to start thinking of ourselves not as a bunch of misfits but as a company like the Royal Shakespeare Company or the Moscow Art Theatre." I glanced around the room. We all looked about twelve years old. Joel continued, "I suppose all my life it's been my dream to run a theatre. This wasn't quite what I had in mind, but here we are." Joel's bank president manner evaporated, and for a moment he looked startlingly vulnerable. "I . . . I . . . I think we're good." Roxie looked down at her lap and surreptitiously wiped a tear from her eye. For all of her tough-tootsie ways, she was achingly sentimental.

I raised my hand. "But, Joel, you're going to law school in September."

"I found out I could get an extension. I can delay it as much as a year." He really was serious. I could only imagine the hell he was going to get from his parents in Indiana, and I could almost hear them blaming me as the evil genius destroying their son's life. Joel laid out for us his plan. We would perform continuously without a break until we lost interest or ran out of an audience. He thought one way to maintain attendance was to change the bill every three weeks. Almost in unison, we all sputtered, "Every three weeks!" Joel countered, "The shows only run forty-five minutes long. Lucy and Desi did it for years, and we have three weeks to rehearse a new show instead of one." He looked at me. "Do you think you could write a new play that quickly and that frequently?"

"I suppose. It would help if we could improve our improvisational skills." I was referring rather pointedly to Joel's own gaffe during the last run. In his fight scene with Perry, Perry accidentally twisted his line around, causing Joel to go completely blank. He could only utter a red-faced "I . . . I hate you . . . um, I could kill you. You, you nut!" Perry didn't help the situation by forgetting his next line and simply walking offstage. I had to run on with half my costume to make some sense of the plot.

By the end of the evening, we had elected officers for our new corporation. Joel was president, I was the vice-president, Roxie, because of her Wall Street experience, was the treasurer, and Camille with her years as an office manager was elected secretary. We also came up with a name for our company. Our acting style definitely wasn't realistic. We were bigger than life. We weren't trying to present life as it was but a fantasy of what it could be. That spun Perry off into a rhapsodic description of his favorite Lana Turner picture, the 1959 *Imitation of Life*.

I cried out, "That's it, *chéries*, that's it! We're the Imitation of Life Theatre!"

CHAPTER
15

My face belongs to all men. My soul belongs to all women.

Milena, *Whores of Lost Atlantis*
Act One, Scene Four

Once back in Manhattan, we began operations immediately. We became marathon runners, performing Thursday through Sunday at nine, and rehearsing a new show the other three nights and in odd moments snatched during the day. Creating a new play every three weeks enabled me to realize my every daydream. I could be Kay Francis in a shipboard melodrama one week, and the next I could be an elegant British noblewoman in a parody of *Lady Chatterley's Lover*. Our only publicity was a mailing list that kept growing—visible proof that we were attracting a devoted following. There were times when I almost resented our popularity. After all, I had tirelessly promoted my solo show for a good six years with nothing near this kind of public enthusiasm. It didn't seem fair that what I considered silly drag movie spoofs should take off with such momentum.

I got over that condescending attitude the first time someone in the audience yelled, "Brava diva!" I couldn't quite believe what I was hearing. It was during the curtain call for our third show, *Murder at the Ballet*. I played Vera Boronova née Daisy Peckham, prima ballerina in a touring ballet troupe where dancers were being knocked off like mosquitoes. "Ah zut!

That mad choreographer and his fifty-eight bourrées. I refuse to perform his
Devil Ballet!"

We had begun to attract faithful regulars, and they treated me like the
grande dame of a raffish theatrical company. I received an ovation on my
entrance and another one during the bows. Almost every performance
someone ran up the aisle to present me with flowers. I was amazed that
others could share my fantasy of being a nineteenth-century leading lady. It
seemed if one believed enough, others would too.

An astute actor friend of mine from college, Tom Aulino, explained it to
me after a show one night. "It's like there's two shows going on. One is the
current play you're performing, but the other show is about this somewhat
faded actress performing a play she doesn't quite approve of with a tacky
repertory company. She can't quite believe she's appearing in such reduced
circumstances. You obviously have that in mind, don't you?"

I was stumped. I was so busy churning out these vehicles, I hadn't had
time to ponder aesthetic choices. I was confused on one point. "But, Tom,
when I get all that applause during the curtain call, isn't it for me, Julian
Young?"

Tom looked thoughtful. "To be perfectly frank, it's for both you and that
old actress."

By this time I was certainly looking every inch the star. We had acquired a
costume designer. Hugh Normand had watched us from afar numerous
times during those early weeks until he finally introduced himself. We were
certainly aware of his presence. Always seated on the aisle in the third row,
he was an enormous black man with a thundering laugh that seemed to cue
the rest of the audience when to join in. He was always seated with a truly
exotic companion, a fragile, diminutive black queen who sat throughout
the whole show poker-faced, smoking through a long Oriental cigarette
holder. Before we knew Hugh Normand, Buster used to refer to him as "the
queenie genie." His sobriquet was Mamacita. Because his last name was
that of the silent film star Mabel Normand, he was called Mabel, which was
abbreviated to Ma, and then, well, this part descends into myth. He made a
mantilla for a Spanish contessa who christened him Mamacita. His tiny
lover's name was Mudge.

I was standing at the bar speaking to Perry after a performance when
Mamacita in all of his flamboyance accosted me. "La Divine! You need me!
You cannot continue to garb yourself in these rags. This cannot go on!"
Mamacita towered over me. On top of his head was a peculiar little beanie
with a plastic propeller on it. His companion said nothing but puffed on his
foot-long cigarette holder. Mamacita launched into a lengthy monologue
cataloging the achievements and personal qualities that made him essen-
tial to my further success. While I was intrigued by their exotic looks, by this
time I was inured to the strange characters who frequented my performances. The East Village was peopled with fake European royalty, phony
sons of politicians, and self-proclaimed great artists who hadn't created

anything since leaving the sandbox at the age of two.

At this point, Joel and I sought out the down-to-earth and definitely not the lunatic fringe. Mamacita and Mudge were certainly decorative—they were both the exact same shade of rich milk chocolate—but with Mamacita gesturing extravagantly and conjuring forth images of the long trains and tiaras he envisioned me wearing, I assessed him to be a nut and graciously removed myself from the two of them.

Several minutes later, when I was leaving the club, tiny Mudge tapped me on the shoulder. His head shaved smooth, he resembled a ten-year-old boy masquerading as a World War I spy. He spoke in a small, quiet voice and enunciated each word at a measured pace. "Mr. Young, do not let Mamacita fool you. He is a genius and a craftsman. I heartily suggest you call this number tomorrow." He handed me Mamacita's business card and vanished.

There was a tough sanity about Mudge that made me call them the next day. I've never regretted it for an instant. Both Mamacita and Mudge worked as drapers for a large costume shop but harbored dreams of being designers, or rather Mamacita as designer and Mudge as his very efficient assistant. I visited them in their loft, and Mudge's faith in Mamacita's abilities was confirmed for me. I was dazzled by the sketches and gowns lying around. They had both worked for years costuming the Ice Capades and had pocketed a glittering array of ornate costume jewelry and trim. Mudge was correct; Mamacita was both mad genius and persnickety craftsman. When he got down to realistically telling me what he could do for me, I totally gave in to his new ideas. I had taken charge of our costumes merely out of necessity. I was more than willing to hand over the responsibility to so able a colleague. Once again, I was worried how this bizarre duo would fit into the odd sensibility of our company and our combination of Broadway professionalism, complete amateurism, and above all the heavily neurotic. Mudge rarely opened his mouth but was remarkable in the speed with which he could drape a large piece of fabric on one of us and pin it into the shape of a ball gown. Buster was positive Mudge was some kind of a witch or warlock and swore that he and Mamacita were part of a satanic cult. I was sure that wasn't true. The cult they worshiped day and night was that of fashion. When they weren't creating costumes for us, they were making clothes for movies and Broadway shows, and when they weren't doing that, they were devising outrageous outfits for themselves to wear in their daily lives. It was rare to speak to either of them on the phone without hearing the constant clatter of the sewing machine in the background.

For such a gargantuan personality, Mamacita was amazingly adaptable to the various members of our company. To Roxie and Zoe, he was a wise-cracking older sister constantly doling out advice on fashion and romance. To Buster and Guy, he was a strict but loving father. Once, after picking up Guy's strewn clothes too many times, he bellowed, "I will accept this mode of behavior from straight men but not from my gay boys. Je ne comprend pas!"

Joel found him to be the perfect professional colleague. He was flexible to change, understood the concept of a play at once, and delivered costumes on time, better than we could have imagined. Perry was his special favorite, and considering his devotion to the tiny Mudge, I often wondered whether Mamacita nursed in his heart a similar infatuation for the small-boned Perry. I first acquired this notion when Mamacita told me he was the only person he knew who was sexually turned on by the Munchkin sequence in The Wizard of Oz.

Our audiences were growing bigger as well as our profits, but all of the proceeds went into the next show's budget. What was left over we split among ourselves. Unfortunately, it barely amounted to the price of a hamburger and milk shake. Mamacita had a small costume budget, which he could stretch like turkish taffy. This was largely because he had a vast network of buddies in costume shops and rental businesses throughout the city. Most of our shows took place in various historical periods, and Mamacita was able to "borrow" dozens of valuable costumes. Thus my lavish nineteenth-century wardrobe as "Kiki, the Rage of Gay Paree" was culled from a summer stock production of Can-Can, and my Catherine the Great wore gowns filched from a bus and truck tour of 1776.

Camille's wigs were also becoming more ambitious. One Dynel confection for Catherine the Great was so towering, the sheer weight of it threw my neck out again, forcing Guy to give me another New Age work over. Camille and I bought all the wigs at Korean wholesale distributors. Soon we had friendly relationships with all sorts of business acquaintances with names like Soon Luk Eng and In Chun Lo. There was one Korean lady who ran a wig business on the fourth floor of a midtown office building who insisted on believing Camille and I were a romantic item. She called Camille Mrs. Young, assuming we were married. It sounded so odd. There hadn't been a Mrs. Young since my mother died in 1962. I told Eng, the proprietress, that we weren't married, and she clucked her tongue in disapproval. I couldn't imagine how we could have given her this impression. I'd try on some flame red wig and Camille would pile it on top of my head. I'd insist on a feather bang and Camille would be adamant on a side part. Meanwhile, Eng would be hovering about questioning us on when we planned to have children. Perhaps we were giving her mixed signals.

Camille and I had become very intimate and rather physical with each other, with lots of hugging and holding hands. Camille was rather maternal, yet also something of a cheap dame—it was a sexy combination. Also she thought I was a genius, and that's a mighty powerful aphrodisiac. I found myself spinning erotic fantasies involving Camille. We'd be in a junky wig store and she'd be bent over rummaging through a box of discounted wigs and I'd suddenly have a wild impulse to grab her and do it right there in the back room on a bed of Dynel wigs. I was shocked at these latent heterosexual feelings.

Some of these perverse emotions may have been aroused by my secret fear that I was losing any sense of my own male sexuality. My drag persona of a flamboyant grande dame actress became so vivid to people that most often I was referred to as "she." I suppose it became too confusing to constantly go back and forth between genders, so they opted for the bigger personality and "she" won. At first I found it rather amusing, but when I too began thinking of myself as "she," the joke wore as thin as an old wig. I noticed myself offstage wearing loose, gender-concealing outfits and blow-drying my long hair out in a style that I liked to think was that of a male rock star but more closely resembled the latter-day Lauren Bacall. I tried not to think about it but instead to concentrate on my current stage role of Anna Karenina.

After rehearsal one night, Perry and Camille and I went to a revival house screening of the Betty Grable musical *Coney Island*. The theatre was packed with gay men. In fact, Camille was the only woman present. During the movie, I kept sneaking glances at her. She looked so cute with her glasses perched on her nose and her large hair clips still pinned to her blouse. I had convinced her to stop perming her hair and to let it grow longer. Her soft, dark hair was now reaching her shoulders, giving her a lovely 1940s look. I reached for her hand and squeezed it. Camille leaned toward me so that our shoulders touched. I felt so comfortable with her. I loved that she was aware of my shortcomings, my self-absorption, my insecurities, and my vanity and not only accepted them but was fascinated by them. We sat holding hands for quite a while until I noticed Perry on my other side watching us. We quickly became disengaged.

Somewhere in the second half of the movie, I surprised myself by putting my arm around Camille's shoulders. Camille was startled but then relaxed and leaned her head against me. I could sense both Perry and the man seated next to Camille stiffening with disapproval.

When the movie ended and the lights came on, Perry rolled his eyes and said, "Really kids, I'd hardly call this a makeout movie." He insisted on staying to see the first twenty minutes of the second feature, *Mother Wore Tights*. Camille and I went into the lounge, where she could smoke while Perry visited the men's room.

We found a sofa in a dark corner of the lounge. Camille blew a smoke ring. "Do you think we're acting silly?"

"Kind of. But I'm enjoying it. You know, Camille, I don't think I've ever been on a date before, I mean, with a girl. I've done just about everything else in every position, but I don't think I've ever necked with a girl in a movie theatre."

"We weren't necking. You didn't kiss me."

"No. I didn't kiss ya." I adored watching her drag on a cigarette. It never ceased to amuse me, particularly when she'd hold it in her mouth while she engaged in some other activity, like combing out a wig or in this case straightening out her black legging. She threw her head back to keep her Veronica Lake peekaboo bang out of her eyes.

"Julian, don't you think I should get my hair cut?"

I brushed her hair away from her face. "No, no, no. You've never looked better." I glanced around the lobby, and it looked as if the coast was clear. No one was looking at us. I stroked my hand through her hair and turned her face toward me. Camille's eyes opened very wide, and we kissed. I wasn't sure what I intended to do. Did I only want a short kiss on the lips? Whatever my intention, we were now going at it full throttle. She was a great kisser, almost masculine in approach. I guessed that this was the way they did it in Brooklyn. I felt as if we were in each other's mouth for at least as long as a feature film when I heard someone loudly clearing his throat.

We pulled apart and saw Perry standing before us like a school principal. He said coolly, "I think the picture is about to begin."

As we walked back into the theatre, I trembled. My sexual attraction to Camille was terribly confusing and couldn't have developed at a more inconvenient time. Why did I have to begin feeling heterosexual desires now, just as I was emerging as a gay cult star? Word of this outlandish behavior could destroy me. I'd be branded in the gay press as a turncoat, a neurotic phony, the enemy. We sat down in our seats. Perry looked at me once more with an expression of annoyance. I leaned back in my seat. Maybe I wasn't a closet heterosexual. Maybe this dalliance with my wig stylist was the next evolution of my gradual loss of male identity. Perhaps I should accept that I was simply becoming a lesbian.

Shortly afterward I had to go to Camille's apartment to have her style a wig on me, and I was thrown when she said her mother would be joining us. At this point, my feelings for Camille were so complex that it was of great importance that I make a good impression on her ma. I mean, who knew, maybe someday I would be her son-in-law. This wasn't the introduction I had in mind. I arrived at Camille's and saw her mother sitting in the corner crocheting. Mrs. Falluci was a tiny woman in her seventies. She wore no makeup and almost faded into the stucco walls. Camille explained to her the task at hand, and before Mrs. Falluci could drop a stitch, Camille placed on my head an enormous tangerine-colored wig the texture of cotton candy. We were in rehearsal for a play set in 1962 Cape Canaveral, in which I was a stripper named Faye who, on the lam from gangsters, hides out in a rocket ship. She accidentally sits on the stick shift and is shot up into outer space. The title of this particular opus—*Sex Kittens Go to Outer Space*.

Mrs. Falluci observed with poker-faced solemnity while Camille teased and tortured the wig. "Mom, I bet you didn't know I had this in me. I'm a real beautician now. Nobody beats my beehives and bubbles." I tried to read her mother's expression, but in this case, I was an illiterate. Camille was also anxious about her very Catholic mother's impression of me. She rattled on like a subway express train. "Julian just started doing drag. You should have seen his one-man show. It was absolutely brilliant. He played this one character of this ninety-year-old Italian prince that was incredible.

And he didn't use any makeup or costume. And he writes all his own material. He's a wonderful playwright." Her large left tit was smashed into my nose as she trimmed the bangs of the wig. Mrs. Falluci continued to stare at me with a thoughtful but slightly disturbed expression. I tried to overcompensate for my expanding hairdo by sitting in a macho way, with the ankle of one leg crossing my opposite knee. I also tried conversing in short, staccato phrases that I hoped would sound butch.

After an endless silence, Mrs. Falluci uttered, "Camille, I think she needs a spit curl over the left cheek for softness."

So much for butchness!

CHAPTER 16

What's come over you, Milena? You've taken on the colors of those mannish half-women from the Isle of Lesbos.''

Andreas, *Whores of Lost Atlantis*
Act Two, Scene One

After the show one night, Camille and I went for a nightcap. We slipped into one bar, but it was so aggressively heterosexual with its sports coverage on TV and violently raucous singles bellowing curses at the televised game that we quickly fled. We ventured into a gay bar, but the mannequin-like gay boys staring transfixed at the video screen showing clips from *Faster Pussycat, Kill, Kill* averted their eyes only long enough to glare at Camille as if she were the Swamp Thing.

Back on the street again, we stumbled across an atmospheric little saloon without any sign on the door. We were warmly ushered in by a bulky, crewcutted bouncer. Edith Piaf singing "Le Vieux Piano" was on the jukebox, and while the joint was not packed, it had a lively clientele of men and women.

We found seats at the bar. On my left was a very cute boy with a long shag haircut and just a trace of peach fuzz above his lip. He looked like a teen-aged rock star. He smiled jauntily at me and winked and resumed his conversation with a tough-looking fat girl.

The bartender was a very butch woman with slicked-back short hair and a leather vest over a T-shirt. She asked us brusquely but with humor, "So, you're tying one on tonight, girls?" I was momentarily at a loss. I felt Camille's fingers clutch my knee, indicating that I should keep my mouth shut. Another glance at the cute rock singer on my left made me realize that he was a pretty lesbian.

I quickly surveyed the room and came to the conclusion that I was the only male on the premises. We were in an old and exclusive lesbian bar. I sheltered my face with my hand and murmured to the bartender that I'd like a Budweiser. When the bartender turned around, Camille whispered, "I think it's best, honey, if we remain lesbians for the duration."

I looked up and caught my reflection in the mirror over the bar, and I could understand why the bouncer and the bartender mistook me for an androgynous girl. I didn't look very different from the young woman next to me. I had on boots, jeans, and a loose-fitting corduroy pullover jacket. My hair was down to my shoulders, and my eyes still had traces of my theatrical makeup. I actually looked like a very jazzy lesbian. The soft lighting couldn't have been more flattering. With the delightful jukebox playing Dinah Washington and Billie Holiday tunes, I felt extremely comfortable.

I overheard the rock star's girlfriend dishing her chauvinist pig landlord. I identified. I certainly had my share of unpleasant experiences with straight men.

Frankly, my history with gay men wasn't exactly one long knee slapper either. My love life was checkered with brief obsessive physical flings, drawn out liaisons based on the convenience of having a steady sex partner, and halfhearted mismatched dating to ease the sting of lonely Manhattan living. The lesbian life-style didn't seem like such an outrageous change of direction. It was all a matter of self-image.

If I thought of Camille and myself as heterosexual lovers, I was awash in self-loathing. I hated the image of myself as a hypocritical closet queen exploiting Camille in a foolhardy attempt at respectability. I couldn't do it. The very act of holding her in my arms seemed stiff and self-conscious. Embarking on a lesbian relationship with Camille was another story. I rather liked viewing Camille and myself as part of the long, illustrious line of enigmatic lesbian couples. Camille could be Colette to my Missy, Una Troubridge to my Radclyffe Hall, Vita Sackville-West to my Virginia Woolf. With my broad, angular shoulders and strong jawline, I saw myself as Garbo playing Queen Christina, passionately kissing my fragile lady-in-waiting. Yes, Camille and I could be lesbian lovers. To the outside world, it would seem a trifle eccentric. We could be regulars on the Donahue/Oprah/Geraldo circuit. "Men Who Think They're Lesbians," today on *Oprah*. After several decades of marital bliss in Santa Fe, raising our sheepdogs, Djuna, Gertrude, and Alice B., I sit down and pen my controversial memoir, A *Finger in the Dyke*. I appear at feminist bookstores across the country, a dignified but roguish figure with graying bobbed hair, riding boots, and monocle. The new generation of lesbians praise my revolutionary ardor and courage in defying sexual definitions. They are all my spiritual daughters.

I would brook no criticism of my penis. The most hard-line lesbian sepa-
ratists would be forced to accept that aspect of my physiology not as a flaw
but as a shining symbol of diversity. I could never look upon my dick as a
problem. At the risk of appearing arrogant, I've always been rather proud of
it. When nearly every aspect of my life has given me reason for insecurity,
my dick has never failed me. Aesthetically it's lovely and works like a charm.
In toto, it's a delightful cock. No, I could never look upon my cock as an
organ to be ashamed of and ignored. I would have to be a radical lesbian
with a big dick and be proud of it.

While I nursed my beer and composed this ode to my prick, Camille was
having a spirited conversation with a very good-looking couple standing
next to her at the bar. They looked over at me occasionally and seemed to
accept Camille's story that I was her girlfriend Julie. I was grateful that the
lighting was dim enough for shadow shows, and I kept my head in my beer.
The taller, blonder, and more gregarious of the couple reached over and
tapped me on the shoulder. "Hey, Jules, you gonna talk to us or what?" She
laughed huskily and held out her hand. "I'm Kate, and this is my lover, J.R."
J.R. was a short redhead with a flattop that extended into a long, thin braid
down her back. I shook their hands and tried to appear shy so they couldn't
examine my features too closely. They'd have none of it. Kate moved closer
to me.

"Camille says you're a writer. So am I. I write poetry. What are you into?"

I had to think fast. "I'm writing a science fiction novel about a lesbian
love affair on the lost continent of Atlantis." The two women were very enthusiastic and began telling us all about their adventures using a Ouija
board and how they had contacted the poetess Sappho herself. Fortunately, they had a self-deprecating sense of humor about this discovery.
Sappho's erotic suggestions had put new steam in their sex lives.

An early Ruth Brown rock and roll single came on the jukebox, and without warning Camille dragged me out onto the postage stamp–size dance
floor. She tore into the hip-twitching lindy that had so enchanted me during our impromptu talent show. Camille was transformed through dance.
Her somewhat squat, top-heavy body became a sexual dessert of curves
and points. Her movements weren't the least bit exhibitionist. What was so
erotic were the small but concentrated twists of her torso and hips. Every
move and spin had a sexual confidence that didn't require a big flourish. It
was the subtlety of her rhythmic rocking that was so exciting. Her virtuosity
wasn't lost on the women in the bar. Suddenly I was nudged out of the way,
and Camille was spun into the arms of a good-natured, big-boned gal who
quickly introduced herself as Marty. Kate's lover, J.R., generously wouldn't
leave me stranded and partnered me beautifully. The next song was another early sixties dance tune, and a rather blowsy but chipper older
woman named Kelly asked me to dance and didn't wait for an answer. She
held me close, and though a good six inches shorter than I, she definitely

considered herself the dominant one in our pairing. She whispered, releasing a powerful whiff of gin, "Baby, I like 'em just like you. You gonna come home with Mama?" I whispered back, "I'd love to, but I'm with my lover, and we've been seeing a counselor trying to get our relationship back on track." Kelly dropped me as if I'd suddenly sprouted a full beard and mustache.

"Baby, I don't steal anybody else's chick. You're cute but I've got my code."

I was having a marvelous time in my lesbian coming out party. Kate bought us a round of beers. All of us had words of praise for Camille's dancing. Camille giggled self-consciously and lowered her eyes. Placing her small hand over her stomach, she said confidentially, "I really have to be careful. I'm not just overweight. I'm . . . I'm expecting." Kate and J.R. nearly whooped with enthusiasm. I had to bite my lip so I wouldn't screech, "You're what?" Camille explained delicately that for years she and I had wanted to have a child. Finally my brother, John, had consented to impregnate her and then get out of the picture. I was flabbergasted at her storytelling skills. She was wasted in the wig department. She was by far the greatest actor in our troupe. I noticed that she didn't once look at me during her epic fibbing. She didn't dare. While Kate and J.R. deluged her with questions and tips, I moved from being appalled to amused to wistful.

Camille was one of the most genuinely maternal people I'd ever known. She laughingly referred to herself as the mom of our company. She worried when Perry had allergy problems. She lectured Roxie about the dangers of anorexia. She made sure that Buster paid his insurance premiums. Everything about her round, cuddly being spelled out M-O-T-H-E-R. She was now approaching forty, with no prospects of ever becoming pregnant. The bartender, now known to us as Casey, listened in on the conversation and refused to serve Camille another alcoholic beverage. This little saloon was definitely what you'd call nurturing. I agreed with Casey and suggested that we head the little mother toward home. Camille took out a cigarette for the road. I said, "Tut tut tut turut. No more of that." I took the cigarette from her fingers and broke it in half. Kate, J.R., and Casey all grinned and roared, "Whoa!"

We really had made a big hit at the bar. As we began to leave, we received an invitation to go white-water rafting with Kate and J.R. and square dancing with Kelly and her friends. The cute rock star–looking girl was indeed a musician, she invited us to a women's fest in Pennsylvania.

When the raffish glow of the bar was behind us, Camille was the first to speak.

"I know, I know. It was a silly thing to do."

I laughed. I had no reason to be critical. Two thirds of the words out of my mouth have usually been for effect. I was touched that she'd have even the slightest fantasy of having a child with me. I don't imagine anyone had ever thought of me in that context before. It was quite flattering. "Camille, I thought it was funny and also sort of sweet. I'm really flattered. In a crazy way, I . . . I sort of wish it were true."

Neither of us spoke, but we instinctively reached for each other's hands. We walked nearly a block in silence before Camille chuckled devilishly and gurgled, "Could you *imagine*?"

CHAPTER
17

It was only a harmless dream, Sire, but in it I saw the total destruction of our world.

Weena, *Whores of Lost Atlantis*
Act Two, Scene One

At our next rehearsal in my apartment, Camille and I regaled the cast with the tale of our social triumph at the women's bar. When we got to the part of the story where Camille said she was pregnant, I was the only one laughing.

"Really, you should have heard her. She was so incredibly specific. All about how my brother was going to impregnate her. Camille, had you been planning that revelation all evening?" I said.

Camille was in the act of creating a new blond wig for Roxie. Without pausing in her teasing and pinning, she said, "No, it just came to me in a flash. The whole story. Although, I mean, I've always wanted to have a child."

Buster stubbed out his cigarette. "Can you imagine Julian as a father? That would be a pisser."

I was taken aback by the slur from my protégé. "I don't think that's such a ludicrous concept. I'm not a drunk or a child abuser. I have a career. What's so impossible to believe?"

Joel had been making a phone call during our rehearsal break and came in on the tail end of my rebuttal. "Julian, are you planning on having a baby? You better tell Mamacita so he can design gowns around your figure."

This time everyone in the room laughed except me. I get testy whenever anyone makes an assumption about my character. "Joel darling, Camille and I were just fantasizing about what would happen if we decided to have a child."

Joel reached for a donut on top of the refrigerator. "It would be a disaster. And your aunt is too old to raise it."

This time Camille took umbrage. "Hey, nobody's raising my kid but me. Julian can have as much or as little responsibility as he wants, although I know that once he sees the little angel, he'll be the most devoted of fathers."

I picked up her defense. "When you really think about it and don't just dismiss me in a hail of clichés and stereotypes, I'd be a very original and very good father. I'm creative, imaginative, and nonjudgmental."

Roxie looked up from her copy of the *Enquirer*. "You'd be a marvelous father to Truman Capote."

I refused to be put down. "I would have been a marvelous father to any of you. Then perhaps you all wouldn't have been a mass of neurotic syndromes." That strong statement was greeted with a burst of laughter from the entire company. I continued despite their ridicule. "We're not saying we're actually going to have a child, we were saying that if we did it could be sort of wonderful. I'd love to have that sort of affection in my life."

Without any sarcasm, Perry interjected, "There's this new bird store on Bleecker Street, and they've got the most beautiful cockatoo in the window."

I replied, "They're very expensive." I'd had enough of the discussion. "None of you understands at all."

Roxie put down the newspaper. "Julian, you are a gay man with a penchant for mascara. Camille, you are a hot-blooded Italian girl with a pretty face and a weight problem. Lose this fantasy immediately. It's worrisome."

I protested. "I am very disappointed in you, Roxie. I would have thought you'd be above fitting people into tight categories."

"Me? Are you kidding? I believe in labels. It's part of the scheme of life. We all have our labels stamped on us from birth, and it's part of our life's journey to expand our horizons within those perimeters. Though I may vilify my mother, I have accepted after much horror that I am indeed her twin, her doppelgänger."

I was astonished by her rigidity. "You really believe that?"

"Julian," she said with comic gravity, "I am a seeker of the truth, and that is the truth as I see it."

I bristled. I was about to delve deeper into this issue but then thought it best not to reveal that I was considering changing my life label from "gay" to "lesbian." That was best kept to myself.

Camille paused in her athletic wig teasing. "I don't get all this yapping about the truth. All I know is I'd be a great mom and I'm running out of time. I make good money doing word processing, and why shouldn't I have Julian father my child? I know the kid would be attractive, bright, and talented."

Perry said rather wistfully, "That sounds like you want to have a boy. Wouldn't you rather have a little girl? I mean, you could dress her in pretty clothes and buy her dolls and have tea parties. What if your little boy grew up to be exactly the kind of bully who made our lives miserable?"

I tried to reassure him all that was a bit premature.

Camille warned us to hold our noses while she sprayed lacquer on her latest creation. Meanwhile she added, "We shouldn't even have brought it up. We should just do it, and I'll wear bigger and bigger overblouses, and one day, I'd surprise all of you with a healthy baby. You'd all be aunts and uncles and we could set up a little playpen backstage at Golgotha."

I continued the fantasy. "Yeah, and I'd write the child into the shows. He'd grow up on the stage. I could do *Madame X* or *Blonde Venus* or any of those mother love dramas."

Camille announced that we'd already thought of names. Jeremy if it was a boy and Sarah Rose if it was a girl. I could see by the prune-faced look on his mug that Joel was both unamused and thought the whole fantasy ridiculous.

Buster was perplexed. "But how would you conceive the baby? Your brother lives in New Zealand. Would you use a turkey baster?"

I was appalled at the slur on my manhood. "No, I'd fuck her."

Zoe blanched. "I really don't care for that kind of talk."

Roxie patted her arm. "Oh honey, it's just the way of the world."

"Well, not my world."

To change the subject, I told the group I had an idea for our next play. It would take place in a French penal colony. With that, Zoe suddenly stood up, her face flushed. "That does it. That *does* it!" She strode to the door. "I will not play a penis!"

Mamacita gave Camille a corner of his loft to work on her wigs, and since I wore so many of them, Camille and I ended up spending quite a bit of time with Mamacita and Mudge at their atelier. M & M, as they called themselves, were superb cooks and could whip up a terribly exotic meal for four in less time than one could hem a skirt. However, gossip was on our lips more often than curry. As usual, Zoe was our favorite subject.

"Zoe is beyond eccentric," I exclaimed while gluing sequins on a pair of gloves.

Mamacita raised his threaded needle to make a point. "Julian, dear heart, she has the divine gift of madness. Anyone who can do what she does on-stage must not be judged by mortal standards."

"But is she for real? I'll never forget when Joel reminded her to turn back her clocks for daylight savings and she replied, 'Watches too?' Do you think she really meant it? And what about this changing her name business?" Zoe loathed her last name, Gomez, but couldn't decide on a stage name. Every three weeks she tried out a new one on the public; only the Zoe remained constant. She was Zoe Leigh, Zoe Hayworth, Zoe Goddard, Zoe Crawford, Zoe Davis, and, yes, inevitably Zoe Garbo. It didn't confuse her cult of admirers, who greeted Zoe Whoever with a stupendous round of applause on her every entrance.

Mamacita swooped his needle into the fabric. "Well, baby, I am determined that one fine day, I, Hugh Normand aka Mamacita, will find out that child's true age. She won't even give out her astrological sign!"

Mamacita was so tall that he found most contemporary furniture uncomfortable and unsuitable to what he referred to as his "personal grandeur." Instead, he filled his atelier with enormous pillows and tuffets covered in magnificent Indian and Oriental fabrics and trimmed in ornate antique tassels and fringe. The two Ms had covered the walls of the loft with their costume sketches, Polaroid snapshots of friends and family, and their unbelievably large collection of massive rhinestone costume jewelry. Whole walls were draped with the glittering jewels once worn by ice skaters in long-past revues. I loved hearing Mamacita recount stories of his childhood in Barbados. Mudge and he were childhood sweethearts whose parents were servants on a large plantation. They were both being groomed as house servants, but the discovery of their illicit love rocked both the gentry and the servants' quarters. Mudge was to be sent away to live with relatives on another island. Mamacita was nearly suicidal at the thought of their separation. In the nick of time, Mamacita had them both stowed away on a banana boat, and eventually they found their way to Manhattan, penniless but possessing a spectacularly beaded evening gown of Mama's own design as their passport to the costume industry. Camille and I questioned the veracity of the tale, but Mudge remained silent and smiled enigmatically.

The one part of the legend that I knew to be true was the spectacular beading. Mudge's delicate fingers were never idle. When he wasn't cooking or sewing, he was stitching beads on some garment. He loved beads of all kinds and wove intricate Escher-like patterns of bugle beads, caviar beads, the tiny rocaille beads, and flashy paillettes.

Buster remained convinced that Mudge was some kind of petite devil worshiper. Buster would stare intently at one of Mudge's finished beaded garments, searching among the pattern for a 666 or a diabolical hexagram. There did seem to be some repeated legend in the complex pattern. I sought Perry's help in breaking the Mudgian code. After a migraine-inducing session, we were prepared to murder Buster, for the satanic symbols were none other than "M & M" repeatedly endlessly in an Art Deco style.

After supper, we'd play cards. Mamacita and Mudge were passionate gin rummy players, but even they were impressed with Camille. After years of being a part of that fabled card game among the elite of Rego Park, Camille knew the book of Hoyle like the gospel. She could shuffle cards with the flamboyant dexterity of a Vegas croupier. She offered up endless variations of solitaire as played differently in all five boroughs. Mamacita was so enraptured by the image of Camille shuffling the deck with a cigarette butt dangling from tightened lips that he made her a green plastic visor and insisted she wear it each time we played. Lending an exotic note to our game was the fact that Mamacita and Mudge only spoke French when they played gin. When Mudge wasn't actually dealing or discarding, he'd be, *naturellement*, sewing on beads.

For a while, it seemed as if we were two married couples. A few times, Camille and I sewed and played cards so late into the night we slept over among the many overstuffed pillows. Mamacita and Mudge became our parents, bustling about in their bugle-beaded nightshirts, providing us with additional afghans and comforters.

When all was silent and dark, I'd cuddle next to Camille and breathe in the lovely coconut scent of her shampoo. It seemed inevitable that soon we would consummate our relationship.

It wouldn't be my first time with a girl. There was a brief period of my life, during my senior year at college, when I indulged in all sorts of unexpected heterosexual activity. I was already the most notorious gay boy on campus. This was during the last gasp of the David Bowie unisex look, and I wouldn't say that I rocked the campus but more puzzled the campus with my dyed hair, mascaraed eyes, and ratty fur coat. I thought I looked like Maria Schneider in *Last Tango in Paris*.

Even then I felt like I was in a vice of public perception. It rankled me that everyone at school had such a clear idea of my sexuality. A mild campy flirtation with a saucy female grad student led to some wild nights in her apartment above the B & G Coffee Shop. She got a real kick out of showing me the ropes. Indeed, one night she tied me spread-eagled to the bed. We got through the evening to her satisfaction, but in my heart I knew that if I was to be dominated, it was not going to be by a Loretta Swit look-alike.

My liaison with the dominatrix grad student led me to one-night stands with a motley group of free-spirited young ladies, all of whom knew I was gay. They enjoyed me as they would an exotic fruit; I was a teenage kiwi. After a few months of this extracurricular activity, I realized that though a good man is hard to find, you can usually find a reasonable facsimile before the bar closes at four.

I never considered myself bisexual, but I've certainly slept with more dames than some fellas who cling to that moniker. Here, years later, I was experiencing a genuine physical affection for a woman, but the word "sham" kept ringing in my ears. I grew angry with myself. I was bored with caring what people said about me behind closed doors. What did it matter? Other than a few dismissive sentences, nobody really gave a damn about what I did in the boudoir. It was my own guilt. Sleeping with Camille wasn't implying that I was straight or that to be gay was some sort of a "choice." On the other hand, hadn't I only recently chosen to be a lesbian? I was confused. All I wanted to do was fuck her. Each time we lay beside each other, there would be that tense moment when I'm sure both of us were thinking, "Well, this is it." Then one of us would glance at the illuminated Art Deco clock on Mamacita's wall and the other would sigh. "Gee, it's awfully late. Better get some sleep." That first boff was becoming the equivalent to swimming the English Channel.

I lay there with my arms folded across my chest desperately hoping sleep would overtake me. My mind was buzzing with thoughts of Camille Falluci's genitalia and whether Mamacita was right that I could get away with wearing a 1950s New Look strapless gown.

I artfully extricated myself from the beaded futon and tiptoed in the dark to the kitchen at the far end of the loft. I found the light and sat down at the counter. It was covered with cookbooks of every nationality. Though I don't cook (I once broiled an apple pie), I enjoy reading recipes, particularly convoluted concoctions that take a week to prepare. To my luck, I found a dog-eared copy of *Frenchmen's Folly: Recipes from the* Ancien Régime. Before I could look up "soufflé," Mamacita appeared in the doorway wiping sleep from his eyes.

"Julian, my love, finding sleep elusive?"

"Like the Loch Ness monster. Did I wake you?"

"Darling, if one of Mudge's beads drop, I awaken." He touched the tip of his tongue with one of his stalactite fingers. "Shall I light up a joint?" I declined. "Hmmmm, then brandies I believe are in order." He searched through the cabinets but could only come up with cooking sherry. After pouring us both some, he sat down beside me at the kitchen counter.

"Julian, you asked before if Zoe was for real. I ask you, are you for real?"

"Hugh, do you think I'm a big phony?"

"Most of the time, no, but sometimes when you are with Camille, your eyes say one thing and your mouth another."

"Oh, Mamacita, you sound like a road company Bloody Mary. Are you saying I'm leading Camille on a wild-goose chase with no intent to goose her?"

Mamacita bugged out his big eyes as if to comment, "Who am I to say?"

I took a sip of the sherry. "Some people would say that I'm being extremely mature and sophisticated, that I'm allowing myself to be open to all human experience. But I'm getting feedback from everyone around me that to be so open-minded, I'm this awful, manipulating, hypocritical person."

"We're all concerned about Camille. She's been awfully scarred by men, and she puts herself in the position to be hurt."

I had to laugh. "Boy, this is a switch. From being a fey, androgynous elf, I'm the latest in a line of sexist mobsters. . . . Oh, Mamacita, I'm just so lonely. I guess I'm just looking for a little intimacy in this cold world."

He asked to look at my hands. He examined them carefully and then placed his palm on the back of my neck. When he removed it, he took another sip of his sherry. "Julian, it has been much too long since you've been laid."

"How the hell did you derive that conclusion?"

"Never you mind. Ancient island method. You need to get laid. When was the last time you had a man?"

"It depends what you mean by that. Real do it in every position kind of sex or just let's go in the back of the bar?"

"Let's spend the night together kind of lovemaking."

I tried to remember and couldn't recall. A Warner Bros. montage of calendar pages turning and newspaper headlines flashed by and no man's face appeared. "Gosh, Mamacita, it's been nearly a year since I divorced my last husband, Bruce."

"You've never even mentioned him before." What was there to say about Bruce except that he was very hunky, was fascinated by his Navajo roots, worked in the monkey house at the Bronx Zoo, and was the stupidest person I'd ever met? Guy told me that after one night with Bruce, he couldn't wait to return him to the animal kingdom.

"Mamacita, it wasn't a real relationship. It was more like an intermission between long acts of being by myself. You're right. I *am* horny. I need it bad. Do you really think that's why I'm giving Camille the fish eye? Just because she's there like Mount Everest? Isn't that awfully simplistic?"

Mamacita leaned over like a wise old woman at her backyard fence. "Darling, men are simplistic, and while you may straddle the fence in fashion and can wear a Givenchy knockoff better than any socialite, you are still a man."

"Thanks for reminding me. I forget sometimes. Even in my dreams, I'm wearing a red wig."

Mamacita downed the rest of his sherry with a grimace. "Sweetheart, if you drink any more of this firewater, you'll be dreaming you're having your stomach pumped."

CHAPTER 18

Inner torment—I find that extremely attractive in a man. It's my curse.
Ultima, *Whores of Lost Atlantis*
Act Two, Scene One

The show set in a penal colony circa 1911 was temporarily derailed when Mamacita and Mudge had to work on a movie with a tight deadline. That prompted us into one of our rare forays into contemporary satire. The new show involved Roxie and me as rival suburban housewives. Frankly, I couldn't wait to return to the grandeur of the distant past. Mamacita suggested that Roxie and I go to the discount shops in the garment center area of New York and buy our dresses off the rack. I found it awkward shopping for women's clothes and particularly having to negotiate with the terrifyingly tough *vendeuses* in the garment district. None of them seemed to appreciate the whimsicality of our shopping needs.

Thus it was with wearing fatalism that Roxie and I entered Fleishman Fashions on Thirty-eighth Street. We flipped through the racks of dresses, and both of us agreed that a black-and-white three-piece suit would be perfect and within our budget. The only problem was that I needed to try it on. The store was filled with shoppers rummaging through the racks. We found a corner obscured by an open door to a back room. I slipped on the jacket. Just as I was getting a good look at myself in the mirror, I saw over my shoulder the disapproving glare of the saleslady, a tight-lipped older woman with fried, triple-processed beige hair.

"Just what do you think you are doing?" she barked. "Take it off immediately."

I tried to reason with her. "We're costuming a show, and I need to try the jacket on before I buy it."

She didn't buy it. "We get a lot of drag queens in here soiling the garments. Take it off."

Roxie leaped into the fray. "My good woman, I don't think you heard us. My colleague has just told you we are from a professional theatre company, and we are not going to purchase this garment without trying it on."

"Young lady, I don't care for your tone. I'm stating our company policy."

I had removed the jacket, and the saleswoman rudely yanked it away from me. Roxie was relentless. "Do you not sell to the theatrical trade?"

"Yes we do, but—"

Roxie pulled out of her bag a copy of the current *People* magazine with our photo in it. Unfortunately, it was a photo of me in a G-string and fright wig from *Whores of Lost Atlantis*. Roxie pointed to the photo. "Madame, this gentleman is Julian Young. This is his photo in *People* magazine. Now we don't have all day."

Another salesgirl came by to see if her supervisor needed assistance. Indeed, the raised voices of Roxie and the saleswoman had attracted the attention of a number of shoppers. It now seemed a matter of principle to the saleswoman. She pointed to a sign above the door. "Young lady, please read that sign: 'We reserve the right to refuse service.' Now I'm asking you both to leave the premises."

Roxie shook her head. I couldn't believe she was being so adamant. "No, no, no, Madame, I will not capitulate to your homophobic bias. I demand that you lead this young man to a try-on room, so he can get an adequate look at this rather shabby piece of goods."

The shabby piece of goods line really frosted the saleswoman, who ordered the younger salesgirl to find a policeman. Then suddenly a man's deep voice commanded, "Hilda, you will do no such thing."

We all looked up, and a large, gray-haired man with a mustache appeared before us. The saleswoman treated him with deference. "Mr. Fleishman, these people are creating a disturbance. They refuse to leave."

"What's the problem?"

I decided to jump in and explain the situation, lest Roxie invoke amendments to the Constitution. I showed him the photo in *People* magazine.

"So, that's what's happened to the Lower East Side." He pointed to Roxie in the photo. "A nice pair of legs. I see no reason why the young man shouldn't be helped. Come with me."

Roxie brushed aside the fuming saleswoman as Mr. Fleishman, the owner of the chain of shops, led us into the storage room. "Here, put on the suit. Let's see if it's your size. All of these garments are marked differently.

Off with your trousers." I took off my clothes and pulled on the camisole top, the skirt, and then the jacket. Mr. Fleishman, who appeared to be a robust man in his late fifties, gave me a professional assessment. "Young man, you've got quite a trim figure. What do you do about a bust?"

"It's kind of hard to explain, but I never use falsies. It's like I'm not trying to totally convince people that I'm a woman, just sort of the impression. It's sort of a postmodernist—"

Fleishman made a dismissing gesture. "All I know is the darts in the jacket fall funny. Here, let me see if I can find you a larger size. We'll mix and match." He went back into the store. Roxie was uncharacteristically silent.

"Penny for your thoughts, Roxie?"

"Am I crazy, but isn't he incredibly attractive?"

"If Ed Asner is your idea of the ultimate in male pulchritude, then yes."

"He's so strong and exudes an ancient Hebraic wisdom. I think he's very sexy."

He returned with the larger suit jacket. It fit perfectly. Mr. Fleishman turned to Roxie. "Young lady, will we be looking for something for you?" Roxie declined in her best-modulated Wall Street lady manner. Fleishman pulled a beaded jacket out of a closet and insisted Roxie try it on. The shimmering fabric reflected her blond hair and pale skin. We were dazzled. Fleishman checked all her angles. "It skims your figure perfectly. Have you ever been a fashion model?"

Roxie looked at him askance. "Oh please, with this punim?"

I had to resist rolling my eyes. I knew Roxie was tossing that Yiddish word to make him think she too was of the Jewish persuasion.

"Are you Jewish? I wouldn't have thought it."

I broke in. "She's not, but it's her life's ambition."

Roxie nodded. "Yes, my two ambitions are to win an Emmy and a lifetime achievement award from the Hadassah."

Roxie and I left the shop armed with enough suits, dresses, and hats for a cruise to the Caribbean. We also left with a promise from "Sam" Fleishman to attend Thursday night's performance. He kept his promise but arrived an hour early, which meant on time. Due to the reliable eccentricity of the management of Golgotha, every show was at least an hour late, with the audiences backed up down the street like planes taxiing on a runway. Roxie, in full makeup and beaded jacket, took Sam to the Life Cafe on the corner for a cup of coffee.

When she returned just in time for the performance, she was flushed with excitement. "Well, I gave him the full Barbara Walters in-depth interview. He's a fascinating man. Fifty-six years old. A widower. His wife, Elaine, died of cancer eight years ago. He has two daughters, both married, and Marcia, the younger, is expecting her first child in August. She decided against knowing the child's sex in advance. Sam's a very successful entrepreneur. He's got a chain of shops in New York, Long Island, and New Jersey. And let's see, what else?" And then her voice dropped to a hush, her face taut. "Julian, he's a Holocaust survivor. They lied about his age so he'd be old enough to work at the camp and not be sent to the gas chamber. He saw his entire family die. I have to tell you, I'm quite infatuated."

And so were we all. After the show, the whole company went for a bite to eat at a neighborhood Chinese restaurant, and Sam picked up the check! Sam was like a visitor from another planet. He couldn't get over the raffishness of the club. "And that boy, that boy with the red and green patches of hair, that's the owner? Don't tell me he can keep books." He found Ruby equally intriguing. "And those paper clips in her nipples, they don't irritate?" He wanted to know everything about our company, so we told him the fairy tale of how we had all been at such low ebb and found each other and become a cult success. I appreciated that Sam understood that our success was measured in the wild enthusiasm we generated from the audience and definitely not by monetary standards. All of us still had our day jobs. That very same day, yours truly, the Bernhardt of the Lower East Side, had been busy stuffing envelopes in a seedy accountant's office in Brooklyn Heights. Zoe, mute as usual throughout dinner, surprised us all by making a toast. We listened rapt, for we had never heard her voice an opinion about any of us or virtually any subject. She stood up and spoke in a quiet, dignified tone, as if she were addressing the East Village Chapter of the D.A.R.

"I'm afraid I must leave shortly. I must get to bed. A good night's sleep is of paramount importance to me as an actress. I require ten hours at least. But I just wanted all of you to know how much being in this company means to me. I'm aware you think I keep secrets. I have no secrets."

Buster, having ingested at least seven Heinekens, bellowed, "Then how old are you, honey?" We all laughed and perked up, but Zoe merely smiled enigmatically and continued her speech.

"I've always felt, well, felt as if we were children who were somehow given the privilege of playing with this very special, gifted, and eccentric young boy."

I had to lower my head to restrain my surging emotion. We were children, no matter how decadent or raffish our costumes. Perhaps it was that innate innocence and our raw glee in "putting on a show" that charmed our jaded audiences. I was still the same abandoned child who was overjoyed to be embraced by a circle of friends who appreciated his originality and the odd gifts he had to offer.

After Zoe's testimonial, the evening was awash in house wine and sentiment. Everyone was toasted individually and collectively, and standing ovations were frequent.

The only damper on our evening was Buster becoming drunk and obnoxious. We were seated in a conglomeration of pushed together tables. Buster and Joel sat at the far end. Buster dominated our trip down memory lane by insisting that Kiko didn't attend the first reading of *Whores of Lost Atlantis* when in truth she was there and Buster wasn't present. Indeed, we hadn't even met him yet! I tried to explain this, but he refused to listen. Roxie cut off his rant with some gossip that she heard Kiko and her crony Thirteen were livid that they weren't included in the *People* magazine spread on the East Village. Soon we were laughing and trying to explain to Sam all about Kiko and Thirteen, when at the end of the table, we heard Buster shout at Joel, "For Christ's sakes, would you stop smothering me!" Buster leaped up from the table, spilling his drink, and stormed out of the restaurant.

Joel looked mortified but immediately followed after him. The rest of us sat in silence. We loved Buster as we would an outrageous little brother, but we worshiped Joel. Joel after all took care of every detail, fought every battle, calmed everyone down. We were shocked to see anyone, particularly one of us, speak rudely to him.

I asked, "What was that all about?"

Perry replied, "It's simply the latest remake of *Of Human Bondage*. Joel in the Leslie Howard role and Buster is Mildred, the cheap waitress he's obsessed with."

I had no idea. "Joel's in love with Buster?"

Roxie rolled her eyes. "Julian, wake up and smell the coffee. They've been having an affair since we went to Fire Island."

I had to keep my mouth from going slack. Zoe turned to me. "If it's any comfort to you, I didn't know either." That was hardly a comfort. Zoe was so vague, she'd only recently figured out what I was doing backstage when I'd take a paper cup, go in a corner, and lift my skirt. The only rest room was in the front of the club, and I couldn't very well let everyone see my costume. That would have been an unforgivable breach of theatre etiquette.

Guy related how Joel had begun walking Buster home early on and he'd caught them holding hands during a rehearsal break. Camille continued the tale by adding that they first spent the night together after the opening of *Murder at the Ballet*.

I asked how I could have missed this, ignored all the signals, misread the signs. "Really, you'd have thought during this time I'd been away on some trip."

To which, Perry, my dear, sweet, oldest friend in the world muttered under his breath, "Yeah, a star trip."

CHAPTER 19

Madame, your face haunts me like a tune. Perhaps we met in Babylonia
during the Festival of Fools.
    Heavenly stars! You're my wife!

Andreas, *Whores of Lost Atlantis*
Act Two, Scene One

Perry was offered free tickets to a six-hour restoration of what had been a
seventy-minute silent film classic. It was a lovely fall evening, so we lingered outside Avery Fisher Hall. We lingered, but we didn't chatter. I was
somewhat miffed by Perry's quip about my being on a star trip. I wasn't
even sure what that really meant. I was never rude or haughty to anyone in
the company. I was very aware that my role as star of the troupe gave me the
responsibility of setting the tone for our backstage life. If I was a bitch or a
bastard (depending upon the garment I was wearing), that could color all
aspects of our productions. The charge of self-absorption is a sensitive one
to me. One of the unfortunate by-products of a solitary childhood is a necessary fascination with one's own company. Later on, when you join the
rest of the world, it's difficult giving up a total preoccupation with your first
love, yourself. I knew I could occasionally be oblivious to the sensitivities of
others, but no one could ever say I had not been a good, solid friend to
Perry Cole. Over the years from adolescence to adulthood, I'd sympathized
with his anxieties, built up his ego, and in this latest phase of our lives,
created roles to showcase his offbeat talents. Watching the crowd gathering

outside the theatre, I was puffing myself up with indignant justification for any possible criticized behavior. Perry broke the growing chill.

"Julian, I can tell you're stewing about that quip I made the other night about the star trip."

I didn't want to cause any kind of scene in public, but at the same time I wanted to get this situation over with. "Well, I have to tell you, I am somewhat baffled by it. Have I been so overbearing? What are my crimes?"

Perry slapped me on the shoulder. "Oh stop it. Maybe I jumped the gun. Maybe I overreacted to a warning sign, the seeds of a star trip."

"What the hell *is* a star trip?" I wished I smoked so I could make a good, sharp Bette Davis gesture to punctuate my question.

Perry dug his hands into his jacket pockets. "It's just that . . . Isn't life sort of perfect right now?"

I'd known Perry for fifteen years and seen him run the gamut of every emotion at every level of intensity, but never had I heard him say life was perfect.

"Julian, I'm just so afraid we'll fuck it up."

"You mean I'll fuck it up."

His dark brown eyes bore into me. "We all could, but you have the power to really blow it. Everything ultimately revolves around you, and that's how it should be, I suppose. Don't let all the flattery get to you."

I was moved by his sincerity but annoyed at the suggestion that I'd have such a clichéd response to my small cult success.

"Julian, sometimes I can't tell the difference between when you're you and when you're improvising your aging star lady character."

I hated to admit it, but sometimes I couldn't tell the difference either. I was increasingly finding myself in situations that demanded I be very tough and in control. I had to find the steel in myself to lay it on the line with an exploitative photographer out to shoot us as tacky street drag queens. There were occasions when I'd surprise myself with my film noir toughness in negotiating with a corrupt club owner on one of our infrequent gigs outside Golgotha. Immediately following one of these scenes, to diffuse the tension, I'd fall into my camp characterization of a hard-boiled aging movie actress. There were times when I wasn't sure where one character ended and the other began. I didn't feel like discussing this with Perry just as we were about to see a six-hour silent film.

"Perry, if you are afraid that I'm sowing the seeds of our destruction, trust me, I will be most careful. I'll try to be . . . I don't know, I'll try to be more aware of how I come off to people. I don't know what else to tell you." I knew I sounded defensive and testy. I tried to soften my response. "This group is the most wonderful thing that's ever happened to me. The last thing I want is to push any of you away. If you ever catch me being highhanded or arrogant, just kick me in the ass. I'm sure you will." I noticed two young men looking in our direction.

"Perry, I think those two cute guys are cruising us." One of the young men pointed to Perry and mouthed the words "You're great."

Perry nudged me. "They're not cruising us. He recognizes me from the shows. It happens all the time. At the gym, it's wild. Sometimes I get surrounded by guys, all telling me how much they love our shows."

"Gee, nobody ever recognizes me. Maybe I should have Camille design me a red wig for street wear."

"Julian, do you think you'll ever play a male role?"

I hated that question and was asked it quite often. "I'm sort of scared. Now that I'm an established leading lady, it would be kind of a comedown to go back to being a juvenile. Frankly, I never thought I was all that hot at playing my own sex."

"You were great as Peter Pan at camp."

"Perry, at fifteen I was already playing Peter Pan as an aging movie actress making a foray into summer stock. Perry darling, let's get off the subject of gender role playing. It's honestly so confusing."

"That's funny. That's one area I thought you'd never be confused about."

"Since we started these shows I am so fucking confused, I don't know if I'm a boy or a fortyish glamour girl. I even wear high heels when I sit on the pot."

"Oh, you've been that way as long as I've known you. I remember even at camp, you were pretending to be Norma Shearer in *Marie Antoinette*. I distinctly remember you running into the dining room saying, 'Oh, Maman, think of it, just think of it, I am to be queen. I am to be queen of France.' "

I dismissed him with a wave of my hand. "Oh, Perry, all teenage boys do that. Of course, in one sense, you're right. It's my gift and my curse. I've always had these opposing pulls in my life. On one hand, I long to be this decadent creature with flaming red hair, wearing bizarre clothes and free to explore my every fantasy. On the other hand, I care what people think. I don't like upsetting my aunt. I still harbor strange notions of commercial success and don't want to be considered a nut. Hell, I want to be sexually attractive to people. Yes, Perry, I'm ashamed to say it, but I do care what people think."

Perry looked at me quizzically. "Julian, I am so surprised to hear you say this. I always think of you as such a free spirit."

"I guess it depends on whose standards. It's sort of relative, isn't it?"

"I had no idea you were this confused. I feel so much better. I'm really glad we're having this conversation."

I was finding it exceedingly maddening. Perry was supposed to be my best friend who knew me longer than anyone besides my family, and he didn't seem to have any insight into me at all. "I suppose we should go inside. Perry, I think what prompted this whole discussion was your fear that we'd allow our personal problems to screw up this strange miracle at Golgotha. We won't let that happen. We'll just have to protect it and nurture it like a child."

I turned to go inside the theatre. Perry stopped me. "Julian, speaking of children, I'm worried about your 'thing' with Camille."

"What do you mean, my 'thing'? That sounds rather provocative."

"Your romance. That's something that could hurt the group."

"It's not a romance. Besides, Joel's boffing Buster, and are the sex police investigating that liaison?"

"They're not planning on having a baby."

"Oh, Perry, we were just joking."

"I don't think she's joking. Women don't joke like that. She means business. I think you're being dishonest pretending it's all a joke."

I was getting really fed up with everyone expressing his opinion about my relationship with Camille. There was absolutely no privacy within the Imitation of Life Theatre. "Perry, this is really getting me mad! I have been lectured and advised and harangued about some little fantasy that Camille and I foolishly shared with a bunch of horny old maids." The audience was now filing into the theatre as I turned back to Perry. "I've a mind to fuck Camille tonight, and, goddammit, I hope we have triplets!"

My eyes left Perry and met the intense stare of a remarkably handsome older man with a mane of thick gray hair. His dark eyes were so penetrating, I gave an involuntary shudder. I was pushed along by the crowd but looked back again and once more connected to the man with the X-ray eyes. He looked familiar. For a moment I thought he was a former TV star. I was flattered that such a handsome man was cruising me but also somewhat frightened by his intensity.

"Perry, if you slowly turn around, you will see a very tall, very handsome middle-aged gentleman. Tell me if he's cruising me or if he's a fan."

"I really shouldn't be speaking to you after what you just called me, but I will turn around." He turned his head none too subtly and replied, "I think you must mean the man who looks like a former TV cowboy star in the tuxedo who's staring at you like you were a cream-filled cupcake. He's with a group of people, one of whom is a woman with lovely white hair who is holding on to his arm."

We gave our tickets to the usher and were instructed to go up to the balcony. I looked back once more, but my admirer was now lost in the crowd.

Despite the live orchestra accompanying the film and the restoration of its hand-tinted color sequences and legendary lost reels, I couldn't concentrate on the film at all. My mind was consumed with the image of the mysterious man in the lobby. He looked so familiar. It wasn't Fess Parker. It wasn't Dale Robertson or Clint Walker or George Montgomery. Intermission finally arrived three hours later, and we went to the rest room. Perry is extremely pee shy and had to go into a stall, so after I visited the urinal I told him I'd meet him back at our seats. I left the men's room and pushed my way past the crush at the mezzanine bar. At last I freed myself from the mass of bodies and heard a deep, mellifluous voice call out to me. "You there."

I swallowed. I knew who it was and spun around. It was he. He smiled and said, "Staying for the second act. You have endurance."

"And you?"

"We're on the benefit committee. We're obligated to stay." He made a point of saying "we," twice.

"I had to notice the lovely lady with the beautiful white hair. Is that your wife?"

"Yes, I'll have to tell her you said that." He studied my face. "You look very familiar."

I decided to play the scene in the grand MGM manner. "Perhaps you've seen me on the stage."

He seemed amused. "Have you been on Broadway?"

The whisper of a smirk around his sexy lips gave me the feeling he was being lightly facetious and had me pegged as a theatrical lightweight. "No, not Broadway. I'm performing at a club on the Lower East Side called Golgotha." I kept a slight tough edge to my voice to let him know I wasn't a pushover.

He smiled and said, "I wish I were there instead of here."

"I can't quite imagine you east of First Avenue."

"I wouldn't underestimate your imagination."

Our brittle, sophisticated badinage petered out. We looked at each other in awkward silence. At that moment, I wished Avery Fisher Hall had a back room for sex. If Sam Fleishman projected mature stability, this guy emanated mature power and sexuality.

It bugged me that he looked so damn familiar. I've always had a terrible time placing faces. It's a real problem. When I was an apprentice in summer stock, we heard there was a hotshot agent in the audience. I was sure I had him picked out at Row C on the aisle. I played the whole show to him and later realized it wasn't the agent at all but my brother, John.

I was sure I'd met this man before. "I have this feeling we've spoken before, or maybe I've just seen you around. You look like a movie star. If you were ever in a movie, chances are I've seen it."

He laughed. "You know, I played a few bit parts in movies when I was very young. Now I'm just a boring Wall Street investment consultant."

That was it! That was it! Wall Street. I'd worked for this man as a temp months before! I work for so many people, their faces are a blur. Suddenly it was all clear. This was the guy who was at the firm where I first met Roxie. I remembered how awful he was to her. Oh but those blue eyes, those huge hands, that mane of tousled gray hair, the square jaw. He was even more striking than I had remembered.

"Now I remember where I've seen you. I was a temp receptionist at your company for one day maybe five months ago. I even took dictation from you."

He crinkled up his eyes in an appealing effort to recall. "Yes . . . yes." The dawn began to break. "That was you. You made an impression on me even then. You were very much on top of things."

I wished he were on top of me. I chose not to mention that I'd become friends with Roxie. I was feeling a bit guilty flirting with someone who had been so nasty to her. Maybe they'd patched things up and he was kinder now. Maybe I could just block that whole episode out. He studied me like a legal brief.

"But your hair, there's something different about your hair. I don't remember you being so blond."

Damn Perry and his highlights. Highlights? Hell, streaking. "The summer sun does this to me." Only a blind man would believe that one. The lights flashed, indicating the intermission was coming to a close.

The big man took my hand as if to shake it but let it linger for a moment. "I'd like to see you again. I'm Don Caspar. Are you in the phone book?"

"Yes, Julian Young on Twelfth Street."

"Young Julian, easy to remember."

Don Caspar was impossible to forget as I discovered during that long sleepless night.

CHAPTER 20

*Milena, my beloved, I am being consumed by this raging fire in my loins.
Touch it!*

Andreas, *Whores of Lost Atlantis*
Act Two, Scene One

Camille and I were wig shopping when I told her how annoyed I was by
the meddling, judgmental attitude of our company.

"Oh, Julian, don't get worked up. They just care about us and are very
opinionated."

"Opinionated! Roxie Flood thinks she's the Voice of America. And Perry
Cole is the unofficial Radio Free Europe." We passed by Bergdorf Good-
man. The windows were already displaying winter fashions, opulent black
velvet evening gowns with a czarist influence.

"Julian, you'd look fabulous in that high-necked one on the right."

She had a valid point, but still I felt compelled to comment, "Camille,
you're screwier than I am. It's one thing for me to envision myself in that
gown, but for you to share my warped fantasy, that's bizarre." I paused for a
moment. "You're not really serious about this baby thing, are you?"

Camille fiddled with the papier-mâché pin I'd made her. "Well . . . serious? . . . Yeah, I'm serious. Sure, I'm serious." We continued to study the
gowns in the display window, but we could also see our reflected faces.

"But, Camille, I'm gay and have absolutely no money. I hope to be a great success one day, but right now, cult figure or no, I'm basically a temp."

"I've told you, darling, I make plenty of money. I get thirty dollars an hour word processing. I'm learning desktop publishing. I can do that at home. I want to have this baby." In the window's glare, Camille's determined chin reminded me of Mussolini.

"This isn't the best place for this conversation, but why? Why do you want to have a baby?" I didn't really want an answer. I wanted her to turn into Tom Cruise.

"I honestly can't tell you. It's a female thing. I want to nurture something. I want . . ." She looked as intense as Don Ameche as Alexander Graham Bell trying to make that stinking telephone ring. "Julian, I want to be a part of something bigger than me."

"We've got our theatre company," I offered up somewhat feebly.

"It's not the same. I love you, Julian, and I want to have your child."

Who was this strange, short, overweight woman? How well did I know her? She seemed oblivious to my silent scream.

"Julian, this will be something that will bind us together forever. Just think of it, our child. Our little adorable Sarah Rose Young."

I hoped Bergdorf's window's reflection didn't expose my look of terror in all of its cold, clammy, stomach-churning hideousness.

I returned to my apartment chilled to the marrow by Camille's demonic maternal bent and Poe-like visions of our shared old age. I sat on my sofa brittle as a mummy. I could see us in fifteen years. Camille, up to two hundred pounds and dotted with hair-sprouting moles, sitting in front of her word processor. I'm prematurely aged, a graying, shriveled failure watching TV game shows with a drink in my shaking hand. Our chunky teenage son, Bruno, crashes through the apartment with his hooligan pals. Several of his terrifying friends are crack babies. Before Bruno turns on his eardrum-blasting stereo, I overhear him snickering. "My dad used to be a drag queen. Once I caught the old fag making a pass at one of my buddies."

Camille had to listen to reason. I enjoyed fantasizing about the beauty, charm, and creativity of our imaginary child, but making that dream a reality was ludicrous. Perry and Mamacita had been right. This wasn't a game to Camille. She was determined to get pregnant. I wondered if I could get a doctor to write a phony diagnosis that my sperm count was zero. For all I knew, it could be true, but this was no time to find out. I was terrified of my own powers of suggestion. Just as I'd inspired Joel to build our company into a cult success, I'd inspired Camille to want to bear my child. I felt like a witch whose magical powers were totally out of control. I had to make it a point in the future to keep all my kooky ideas to myself. One idle remark and I could inspire Buster to assassinate the president!

I tried to ease my anxieties by cleaning my apartment. I was in the midst of some frenzied spray waxing when the phone rang. It took me a few muddled moments before I realized it was Don Caspar calling me from his Wall

Street lair. The conversation was brisk and over in seconds.

After he hung up and I was left holding the receiver, it occurred to me he was on his way over. Within minutes, depending on the traffic, that amazing hulk would be in my apartment. Not long after that he would be nude! Don Caspar was going to be nude in my apartment. That gorgeous man was going to be mine for at least a short while. What would he be like? In the brief time since I saw him at the film, he had taken on mythical dimensions. His gorgeous face could have been one of the gang carved out of Mount Rushmore. I was honored that he was attracted to me. It was like being nominated for an Academy Award. My eyes rested on the paint peeling on my walls and the dark streaks where the pipes in the apartment upstairs had leaked. I wondered when was the last time Don Caspar had been in a dump like this. No doubt he would find it amusing to slum it for an afternoon siesta.

I ran around frantically, tossing stray high heels, sneakers, wigs, and newspapers into closets and under the couch. While only moments before I had convinced myself that I wasn't a slob, now a thick sheet of dust appeared on every surface. I pulled off my T-shirt and wildly wiped over lamps, the stereo, the TV, and the coffee table.

I heard the intercom buzzer.

I let him in the downstairs front door and quickly threw some water on my face. I pulled on another T-shirt just as I heard his firm knock on the apartment door. I took a deep breath to stop my trembling. I opened the door. He filled the doorframe. He was every bit as stunning as I remembered.

I made a feeble attempt at being nonchalant. "Hey there, Don. I'm glad you stopped by. Come on in."

He glanced around the room and chuckled. "I haven't been in a walk-up like this for a long time. I guess I can skip the gym today." He gazed down at the length of my floor-through apartment. "I lived in a railroad flat decades ago. It was a cold-water flat. I think I paid thirty-eight dollars a month for it."

"I pay a lot more than that, but I do have hot water . . . sometimes."

He made an enormous fist and gave me a paternal chuck under the jaw. No man had ever done that to me before. I had the suspicion this was going to be a novel encounter.

We settled in the living room, on either end of the couch. I couldn't believe that my Cary Grant–Doris Day sex fantasy from months ago was coming true.

Don looked around the room and spoke calmly without looking at me. "This morning at the office I kept thinking about our meeting last night. I wanted to see you again. I wanted to see if you were as I remembered." He turned his eyes to me. "You're a good-looking boy." His tone was so matter-of-fact. I felt like a pair of pants that you look at twice before buying. I was sitting with my legs up on the couch. I was wearing cutoff jeans, and

Don lightly stroked my bare thigh. He cocked his head slightly. "Do you shave your legs?"

Hmmm, the jig was up. I'd have to tell him about my notorious career. I wondered if he'd flee in revulsion. "Yes, I do. In the show I'm in, I play a female role. When I'm all caked up, I've gotta tell you, I look pretty good."

He cocked his head again and looked at me quizzically. "Really? You in drag? I can't picture it. There's nothing effeminate about you at all."

I had to restrain myself from rolling my eyes and drawling, "Oh puh-*lease*." I decided to play the scene by his rules. "Sometimes I think I over-compensate by butching it up offstage. It gets a little tiresome being a par-ody diva."

A nasty smile crept onto his face. "Is it difficult remembering to keep your legs together?"

"Don, I'm no angel, but I'm always a lady." I tossed him a saucy smile.

"You don't dress up offstage, do you?"

"No, just professionally."

"I'm glad. I have to tell you, I have trouble with effeminate men. It both-ers me." I was a little confused. Offstage, I'm not always carrying calla lilies, but my wrists could use a splint now and then to keep from limping.

Don continued to stroke my leg. He muttered as much to himself as to me, "I don't feel any need to label or limit myself. Life is too short and too . . . interesting." His fingers moved just above the edge of my cutoffs. "Are you exclusively homosexual?"

The sight of Mr. Caspar in his conservative gray Brooks Brothers suit and tie and the drift of his conversation were decidedly nineteen fifties. Al-though I felt this posturing to justify our imminent lovemaking was rather ludicrous, I opted to play along with him. You must remember I'm a play-wright and can't resist inventing new scenes, no matter how dated or politi-cally incorrect. "Actually, Don, other than a few hetero experiences in col-lege, I have been exclusively gay these past years. But recently I've been involved with a close female friend."

"You're screwing her?"

There was something both terribly elegant and oddly coarse about Don Caspar. I wasn't sure if I was attracted or repulsed by him. "Um . . . yes, we've . . . been having an affair. It's been . . . really wonderful . . . satisfying." He took my hand and placed it on his crotch. I could feel something very big and hard moving under the pinstripe. I continued my monologue.

"Yes. . . . I'd forgotten how unique a sensation heterosexual intercourse can be. She's so soft and voluptuous."

Don's hand was all the way up my shorts and moving closer to the trea-sure in the Cracker Jack box. With his other hand, he swiftly pulled apart his tie and ripped open the top buttons of his shirt. "Do you go down on her?"

"Sure."

"Tell me about it."

I wondered if I could remember what it was like. It had been, after all, at least eleven years since I had performed that particular activity. "Oh yes . . . well . . . I love it. We really get into it. For hours. She, uh . . ."

He was so massive I felt like I was indulging in foreplay with a statue by Rodin. With his free arm he encircled my neck and pushed my head against his broad chest. He smelled divine. It was the combination of his masculine musky body odor and the clean starch of his white shirt. "Julian, describe it to me."

"Uh, well. . . . She's lying there and I put my head down and it looks like a gorgeous peach opened up. So tantalizing. So . . ."

I delved further into the pleasures of my entirely fictitious act of cunnilingus to the purring delight of Mr. Caspar. As I invented details of Camille's orgasmic moans. Don slid off the sofa with me on top of him. Our clothes were flying off in transit. He was beautifully tanned, with dark hair covering his chest and tapering down his stomach. The body must have been rather spectacular ten years before, but even now with the slight paunch, it was riveting. The powerful muscles in his hairy thighs and calves were those of a comic-book superhero in retirement. He wore silk boxer shorts that I knew cost as much as a dinner for two at the Four Seasons. He stood up, and his meticulously styled shaggy head nearly reached the ceiling. I was slightly breathless and remained on the floor. I looked up at him and felt like I was staring up at the Chrysler Building. He was waiting for something. I got up on my knees and put my fingers in the waistband of those exquisite silk shorts. I knew there was something remarkable barely hidden behind the tightening, fragile fabric. Very slowly I pulled down his underwear, watching the black pubic hair get denser. Though he was in perfect proportion, his hips were as wide as my shoulders. I was almost afraid to give that final yank, but I did.

I'm sure my eyes bugged out. Mr. Caspar had one of the biggest pricks I'd ever seen. Magnificent was the only word to describe it. There was a perfection and grandeur to his epic genitalia that evoked a great ocean liner or the cathedral at Chartres. It stood out from him like one of the main branches of a tree. The back of my jaws hurt just looking at it. I felt like a rank amateur. I tried to do it justice but failed. I looked up and saw him wince with pain. It was like the first time I tried to eat an enormous hero sandwich. He got down on the floor with me and cradled me in his arms. We rolled around on the rug kissing and being careful that he didn't crush me. It was heavenly being smothered in his enormous bulk. Gently, he placed me on my back with his two large paws and pinned both of my legs over my head. He licked his finger. I knew exactly what he had in mind.

"Uh . . . uh Don, wait a minute. Whoa . . . Don?" His fingers were smoothing the way for his attack. I tried to pull them out.

"Hey, hey, Don, wait a second."

He stopped abruptly. "You don't want to make love with me?"

It was a simple law of physics. That big thing was not going to get inside of me. "Don, I just don't want to be fucked. I don't really like it. And that thing you've got wouldn't fit in a transom."

He had this rather perverse look on his face. "Julian, it's extremely rare that I indulge in this sort of experience and . . . I thought it would be truly intimate to be inside you."

The rug was itchy under my back. "Don, I don't want to ruin our passion, but is this aspect of our lovemaking strictly de rigueur?"

He rolled over and stroked the large rejected organ. I thought of all the people in the world, women and men, who would think me crazy and would like nothing more than to plunk right down on that amazing maypole. I think I also didn't like the assumption that naturally I was going to spread 'em for this big macho millionaire. We lay there in silence for a moment while I imagined myself a symbol for all of the disenfranchised whom society assumes will get it up the ass, the poor, the downtrodden, the unemployed actor. However, one of my earliest childhood crushes was Fess Parker as Davy Crockett, and here he was lying on my rug naked with his eyes closed.

Playfully, I raised myself and sat down on top of him, just on top of his loins, mind you. He felt so wonderfully warm underneath me. His eyes opened hopefully.

"Don, the other thing is, because I never get fucked, I don't have any condoms around here, and that precaution I would have to insist upon."

"Why? Are you afraid of getting pregnant?"

I wondered if Fess Parker could be this arrogant and obnoxious. "I'm speaking about safe sex." I detected an unfortunately spinsterish tone to my voice. I was no longer a fun-loving, bohemian free spirit but a frigid schoolmarm wagging her finger. I tried to obliterate that quality. "Don, you have heard of AIDS?"

Still lying on his back on my living room rug, he answered matter-of-factly, "Yes, I have. Do you have AIDS?"

His question threw me off guard. "Well no, I don't. I was tested and I'm negative."

"I'm glad to hear that. I've been married to the same women for thirty years. Now are there any other issues we need to discuss?"

"And you've never stepped out before in lo these thirty years?" I lifted his weighty dick in my hand. It was so thick I could barely get my fingers around it. "I find it hard to believe that only one woman has had the pleasure of this prizewinning bratwurst in thirty years."

Don chuckled. "Well . . . I have had a few escapades."

"And you've never used a condom?"

He pursed his generous mouth somewhat petulantly. "You know, they never made them quite . . . well, you know . . ."

I fanned my fingers through his chest hair. "Yeah, yeah, I know. Never quite big enough. Tell it to Sweeney. I've got plastic trash bags that might fit around this thing."

He widened his eyes comically. "I'm game."

I still had another ace up my sleeve. "Sure. If you'll let me fuck you first."

"Me?" I thought he'd choke from shock at that request. "You're joking, right?"

Men! So selfish and smug. Don Caspar was a perfect example of why I almost became an honorary lesbian separatist.

Prone on his back, Don raised his long arms to my shoulders and began lightly stroking the length of my body. He had a remarkable sense of touch for such a bully, and I was compelled to roll my head back and surrender to it. When he wasn't so damn determined to invade an orifice, I could see that he was quite a skilled lover.

He sat up. Our legs were locked around each other, and he held both of our cocks together.

"So, Julian, what do the guidelines say we can do? Hmmmm?" His hands were so adept, I couldn't believe this foray into bisexuality was a once in a blue moon activity for him. He repeated the question. "What can we do?"

He was so good. I found it difficult to speak. I could see he was amused by my lack of poise. I shuddered. When he finally let up, I was able to murmur, "I'll . . . I'll tell you when we get there." I pressed my body so close to his that I felt he was wearing me like a coat.

Our erotic athletics went on for hours, until there was no more sunlight streaming through my living room windows. Our naked bodies still sprawled across the Oriental rug were now edged in the silvery blue of the streetlamp. I felt weightless as he effortlessly lifted and placed me in whatever positions aroused him. Once between bouts, he groaned in pleasure, "It's been a long time since I was with a boy." I was pushing thirty, but clinging to his dark, rugged, oaklike body, I looked like a pale, smooth, and quite unearthly twelve-year-old.

Don Caspar visited me four times the next week for a fast hour of intense sex. When the alarm clock rang and he threw on his suit to return to work, I felt like a whore, but it wasn't such an awful feeling. He made me feel like a fabulous whore. I counted the minutes till he'd appear at the door and I'd have another opportunity to explore every inch and secret of that magnificent, bigger-than-life body. For that hour, every bit of skin and hair was mine to breathe in, lick, caress, and knead.

Although I'd lied to Don that I was having a sexual relationship with Camille, I did have an emotional one. I'm embarrassed to admit that once I was getting laid regularly by Mr. Caspar, my heterosexual fantasies involving Camille abated. I tried not to let it be too obvious. However, twice Camille wanted me to meet her during her lunch hour at work and I had to decline. Both times Don was taxiing up from Wall Street. My string of rendezvous with Don also enabled me to put some cold water on the baby situation. My last encounter with Camille in front of Bergdorf's windows had jolted me back into reality. It was cruel to lead Camille on. It was also cruel to drop her like an old typewriter ribbon. I wanted to strike a happy balance between the high spirits of our past friendship and a cooler, more sensible attitude toward the future. "Cooler" seemed to come easier. At the theatre at night, Camille would see me walk in the door and throw her arms around my shoulders in a warm embrace. I tried to fight off my involuntary reaction to freeze. I kissed her on the forehead and then hurried to put on my makeup. I kept our conversation light and full of campy impersonations. It was better to evoke Tallulah than be myself and risk getting into a serious conversation with her. The following week when she phoned again to meet me for lunch and once again I declined, she asked outright, "What's going on, Julian? Are you having some kind of a problem with me?"

I wasn't prepared for such a direct question. Yes, I had in private improvised numerous versions of this possible moment, but I wasn't satisfied with any of them. I caught my breath and responded, "No, I'm not mad at you or anything. Of course not. I'm feeling under such pressure to churn out these scripts and then performing at night, I need some time to myself." I tried to explain that it had nothing to do with my feelings for her. I was hardly convincing. She said nothing though her steady breathing on the other end of the phone was most eloquent. I stopped speaking. I let my silence offer my point of view. She broke the tension by asking me to pick up several wigs from the wholesale outlet. She was trying to keep her voice cheerful and disguised. I felt horrible hurting her yet paralyzed to honestly tell her I thought that this baby charade had gone too far, and worse, that I'd moved on.

I had a sense of déjà vu. It wasn't hard to figure out why. There were other times when I've had to turn myself off from feeling.

When my older brother, John, was a senior in high school, he was so blocked emotionally that his grades were finally affected. I don't know what took him so long. My grades were always lousy. John in his completely unintellectual way was surprisingly scholastic. His guidance counselor insisted he see a psychiatrist. My aunt was full of hope that therapy might lessen his total dismissal of her. Something happened during his fourth session. John came home and went directly to my room. He opened the door and stood there like the Frankenstein monster with a frightening look of raw, unfocused emotion. I had been almost psychotically immersed in a biography of Jean Harlow. His jolting me out of the MGM back lot and into his ugly butch world made me totally unresponsive. "What is it? What's wrong?" I asked him brusquely. He sat on the floor next to my bed and buried his face in the cover.

"I don't know, I don't know, I don't know," he kept repeating. I heard his voice catch after about the tenth "I don't know," and I saw his muscular back contract. I knew he was crying.

"Julian, I don't want to be hated." He lifted his head, and his inexpressive slab of a face was red and wet. I knew I was supposed to take advantage of this rare emotional breakthrough and hold him. It was in some script somewhere that I was supposed to tell my brother I loved him and that we should always be there for each other. I didn't say anything. For what seemed like an endless moment, I wasn't sure what I was feeling. I waited for my correct attitude to float to the surface like a message in an eight ball. The message was "do nothing." I didn't feel like forgiving him. Why should I comfort him? I thought. He was the enemy. I didn't feel like forgiving him for a child's lifetime of ridicule and coldness. He had never been my ally when other kids taunted me for being different. He was a coward who refused to protect his fragile younger brother.

I was luckier than the other effeminate boys in school. I had a coolness and wit that created a peculiar protective shield about me. The worst monsters in school unconsciously knew they could only go so far in their harassment. What they feared I can't tell you. The real losers, like bucktoothed Phillip Levine or blind as a bat Scotty Schindler, got beat up and regularly humiliated. I was snickered at but ultimately left to pursue my strange solitary interests. I suppose they knew that I had no interest in fitting in, that I found them all impossibly dreary. I couldn't care less if I received an A or a D, and neither did my family. I was just biding my time until I could grow up and become fabulous.

The movies taught me that an embattled heroine, noble but tough, could endure earthquakes, fire, floods, mob hypocrisy, and tragic love affairs and still emerge the victor in a man's world. I would survive junior high school. I seemed to recall one of those Warner Bros. dames sardonically quipping, "Expect nothing and don't be disappointed." I expected nothing anymore from my brother. I expected nothing from my long departed father. I saw John at that moment as my father's true son, something I never was. I didn't feel like forgiving my father for abandoning me. No, I'm afraid it wasn't so easy. A few tears after a cathartic shrink session weren't enough to win me over. John looked at me like a dumb animal seeking a command. I simply stared at him as if he were a test pattern on the TV screen. It was 1968. I was fourteen years old and felt as powerful as President Nixon. I didn't have to say a single word for my brother to comprehend that I was indeed the stronger of the two of us. He understood at that moment that we'd always be strangers. He raised himself off the floor and left the room quietly, gently shutting the door behind him. I didn't feel triumph. I felt sick. I had learned the effective cruelty of passivity. Today, if someone asked me what was the worst thing I've ever done, I would have to say it was hurting my brother that day. He was only seventeen, and he had also suffered the loss of our parents. I've never forgotten the soft closing of that bedroom door

He was afraid of me. I've never forgiven myself. Freezing my affection for Camille brought back a bit of that dull, guilty ache.

Don impressed upon me that we had to be extremely discreet. His professional and social position made our liaison difficult at best. It suited my romantic nature to be the mysterious, elusive mistress, but it killed me I couldn't blab to Roxie that I was having an affair with a senior partner in her firm. There was no way she could keep that a secret. I also decided definitely not to tell Don that I was best friends with his corporate librarian. I shuddered even to think of his reaction. There was something Big Daddyish about him but also slightly sinister. He reminded me of someone who would be on intimate terms with the Kennedys—someone who might have introduced JFK to Marilyn. Just when I was feeling particularly whorish, Don surprised me with a present. I unwrapped the small box to find a lovely antique jeweled bracelet. He put it around my wrist. How many times had I seen this played out in the movies?

I gushed, "It's gorgeous. I know a little about rhinestones, and I can tell these are Austrian rhinestones and they're among the best."

He burst out laughing. I had never seen him exhibit more than a chuckle. He laughed so hard, he even began to cough.

"What did I say that was so funny?"

He took a sip of water. "You may know your rhinestones, but you obviously don't know your diamonds."

My eyes bugged out. "These are diamonds?"

"And fairly good ones. You better keep this one hidden beneath your mattress."

"Is this fabulously expensive?"

He caressed the bracelet lightly. "Not fabulously, but it could keep you in cans of chili for quite a while. Don't get any ideas in your head."

"I'd never hock it. No one's ever given me anything like this before. I feel like Marguerite Gautier."

With his hands on either side of my face, he peered at me intensely. Neither of us said a word.

"Don, where did you find the bracelet? I hope you didn't riffle through your wife's jewelry box."

"No, the bracelet was in my personal collection. I buy pieces at auction occasionally. Definitely not to wear but to cherish. I have a need to surround myself with beautiful things." His fingers moved from my ears and ran gently over my face. I closed my eyes and felt as exquisite as a Lalique figurine.

Bring on my silver-tongued eunuchs!

Emperor Zenith, *Whores of Lost Atlantis*
Act Two, Scene One

We were all amazed at how swiftly our fame grew. By our fourth month at Golgotha, a long line would form at every performance. The queue would include hard-core skinheads, West Village gay men, hip straight couples who sought entertainment that was both dangerous and safe, and then there were the celebrities. We were dazzled when Golgotha would play host to the likes of Calvin Klein, David Bowie, Lee Radziwill, and Rosemary Clooney. I became the drag queen of the moment. I was photographed as Scarlett O'Hara amidst the rubble of Alphabet City for *Interview* magazine. *Details* shot me as Aphrodite emerging from the water at Brighton Beach. I presented a Bessie Award for excellence in avant-garde theatre and judged a Nancy Reagan look-alike contest at an AIDS fund-raiser in the Hamptons.

Mind you, none of this translated into hard-core cash or opportunity in the more legitimate areas of show business. I was an underground cult fig-ure—if not the flavor of the month, perhaps the spice.

After the show, people wanted to meet me. I was so thrilled to be intro-duced to the fashion designers and performers who came to Golgotha that

I'd make the mistake of simply being myself. I could see their disappointment when the grande dame actress would be revealed as a fairly normal, low-key young man. They didn't want normalcy from me or a no-nonsense approach to my work. They wanted the performance to continue and me to be as outrageous and colorful as my stage characterizations. I am at heart a coquette and will do anything to please. Now when Rupert would bring round a visitor, I'd pepper my speech with "darlings" and "it was simply too, too" and "it was totally a madcap caper!" I was Constance Bennett circa 1934, and let me tell you, Connie went over real big at Golgotha. This persona was extremely comfortable to slip on. Like many performers, I am somewhat shy, and this offstage character gave me the strength to confront anyone, no matter how formidable. I became so accustomed to this role that I'd find it confusing when the kids in the company would tell me how often people would ask them, "What's Julian Young really like?" I'd say, "What did you tell them?" And they'd reply, "Oh, that offstage you're very quiet and ordinary, not at all flamboyant." They made me appear so bland, so colorless. If that's what I was really like, perhaps this Constance Bennett act was an improvement. Whatever ambiguity I may have felt in my private life, it was worth it. I adored being a cult star. Perhaps the majority of the population had no idea of my existence, but to a small, hip minority, I was something special.

Of course, as one star rises, another must fall. Miss Thirteen, who had once emceed glamorous benefits at Town Hall, was now reduced to barking out the winners of a Best Buns Contest at a Jersey City disco. Because we played Thursday through Sunday, there wasn't much room at Golgotha for Thirteen or Kiko or the other neighborhood first ladies of the theatre. They didn't lack exposure. New clubs were springing up like wild mushrooms. Zither was a strange, frequently flooding fourth-floor loft space near the highway where occasionally Kiko would crack an egg or two. Thirteen, in desperate need of expanding a dwindling audience, latched on to the old ruse of hosting a variety show every Friday night at midnight at a punk pulverized diner named Once Eddies. There he introduced scads of rough-edged female impersonators whose friends would fill up the joint and provide Thirteen with something resembling a living wage. I could certainly identify with that struggle. Queen of the night I may have been, but during working hours, I was punching a clock selling typewriter ribbons over the phone. I often wondered how my fellow cult figures made ends meet. After pressing several divas for statements regarding their income, I realized that that was a question so personal, they'd rather overdose than divulge. It was important for all of us to preserve an illusion even to ourselves that we were stars.

While I was writing a vehicle for our company that took place during the Middle Ages, it occurred to me that the East Village was a somewhat feudal society. It was divided into little kingdoms ruled by various drag stars and performance artists, each with his or her court of admirers. I was firmly ensconced at Golgotha, Thirteen at Once Eddies, Kiko at Zither, and other starlets grabbing whatever turf could be had.

Golgotha may not have been as elegant as the Rainbow Room, but it had prestige in the neighborhood. We weren't the only aspect that was providing greater visibility. The club was becoming an important art gallery Respected collectors were paying top dollar for the grotesque images displayed on the cracked walls. When Ruby and Rupert weren't being as bizarre as queens from outer space, they were canny promoters. They didn't just hang a painting, they created an environment or installation around it. The place sometimes looked like an erotic version of the Pirates of the Caribbean ride at Disneyland or a cocktail lounge decorated by Nosferatu. Just as I began thinking of our impresarios as savvy professionals, they would destroy that image by suddenly painting the club hot pink. It wasn't the choice of color, mind you, but that they began splashing paint around just as our sold-out crowd was scrambling to leave the club. I can still see those livid faces with their pink-splattered leather jackets.

Golgotha got so successful that when an abandoned garage and body shop became available, within two weeks Ruby and Rupert had moved operations. The new, much bigger Golgotha was a remarkable space. Even more remarkable because there was virtually no renovation work involved. Some of the mechanic's equipment was left behind and employed to display sculpture. The building was two stories high, and the previous owner had removed two thirds of the second floor, leaving a treacherous overhang with only two rickety ladders to reach the bottom floor. In its new incarnation as Golgotha, this was used as a balcony. The most successful artist in the Golgotha stable, Mizar Pashkin, created massive painted tapestries that were hung like banners from the nearly thirty-foot-high industrial ceiling. The general effect was a cross between the Bowery Boys' clubhouse and the great hall of Camelot. We built a small stage with a narrow backstage area. There was still no toilet within fifty feet of the stage. I would have to continue with the paper cups.

The opening night of the new Golgotha was a major event in the East Village that fall. The gala was a big variety show featuring more stars than there were in the heavens above Tompkins Square Park.

Rupert gave Joel a list of the talent and asked him to organize it into a night to remember. Camille was the stage manager and in the enviable position to see that all of the bizarre performers' needs were met. We all wondered whether Kiko and Thirteen would attend. Imagine our surprise when Rupert announced that they would be emceeing the event. It was a long show. On the bill was an underwater ballet performed dry, an excerpt from an atonal opera based on the TV series *Bewitched*, a silent dance of death, more drag queens than you could shake a stick at, comedy and music from a trio called The Uncut Dicks, and a slew of other East Village luminaries. Our company appeared last, performing the closing scene from our signature piece, *Whores of Lost Atlantis*.

There was no way to get the performers together for a rehearsal. The night of the show, all we had was a printed rundown of the acts and a hope for the best. Camille's job was to ease tension, but she created more of it than she soothed. I sensed trouble when I arrived at Golgotha and found her frenetically teasing a wig. She spit out a couple of hairpins and spoke in a high-pitched, clipped voice. "I have just finished my first full week off cigarettes." She furiously brushed out a section of the wig. "I've decided to make a number of changes in my life. I've always lived through other people and I've gotta stop it." I knew she was referring to our relationship. Any statement more direct could precipitate a showdown, and neither of us was prepared for that. A slow fade-out was more our style.

"You're not quitting the group, are you?"

She let out a tense laugh and smiled. "And give up my wigs? Not a chance. I just gotta get myself a life outside of the theatre. Guy's been helping me work things out."

Guy kept his other career as a New Age healer very separate. He felt no need to proselytize and knew that the rest of our group was as New Age as the Theatre Guild. Joel had his spiritual concerns, but they centered around Sunday services at the First Presbyterian Church on Eleventh Street. Whatever, I felt guilty seeing Camille so tense. I hadn't meant to be callous and insensitive, but my sexual obsession with Don Caspar pointed out to me how fragile my fantasy of a romance with Camille really had been. It was unfair to lead her on, but why did I have to be so cold and distant? I hated myself for giving her a phony smile when I still wanted to plant a spontaneous kiss on her cheek. She was so important to me, yet I was systematically pushing her away. I tentatively stroked the back of her neck.

She pulled back and gave me an air kiss.

"Honey, you better get made up before everyone crowds backstage." Good advice, except that I was already in full drag makeup.

Our glamorous emcee Kiko arrived with a gaggle of black-garbed faux European flunkies. Warily, I approached my former leading lady. "Kiko, you look gorgeous."

"Thank you, Julian. You look tired. So tired."

I had a feeling her concern wasn't genuine. "Kiko, I guess it's just the life of the cult figure. Work, work, work." I strived for levity. "And in that outfit, I must say you're a cult figure with a cute figure."

She remained impassive. "Julian, I worry about you. You mustn't burn yourself out, dear . . . or your audience." She slithered away like a cobra who'd drunk too much gin. The club was filling up with performers.

Before I could reach the backstage area, I was tapped on the shoulder by a tiny, compact fellow in a 1920s tuxedo and white makeup. "Julian, we've met before. I'm Gavin Gilbert. I met you after *Sex Kittens Go to Outer Space*."

I had no idea who he was. "Of course. How are you?"

He had an ear-to-ear grin and looked amazingly like Perry, sort of a road company Perry. "I'm fine, darling. I've just gotta tell you, I love you so much.

I've seen all of your shows. You're a fucking genius. You know that of course. I'm so honored to be performing on the same stage as you."

"Do you perform here at Golgotha?"

"No, darling, it's always booked up. *Avec vous*. I'm over at Once Eddies on Friday nights with Thirteen." My eyebrows involuntarily raised. He picked up on it. "Well, it's a gig. We've been getting great houses, packin' 'em in."

"Thirteen is very popular."

Gavin Gilbert looked around furtively. "One has to be careful, doesn't one? Thirteen's wrath can be awesome, and he's really been quite generous to me. I do two numbers in the show, a Fu Manchu thing and a Dietrich number from *The Flame of New Orleans*. God, I'd do anything to work with you. Everything your group does has such class. I'd be perfect for you. I can do any role that Perry Cole does. People are always telling me how much I look like him."

"Yeah, you do. But I've known Perry many years. He's sort of my best friend."

"Loyalty, that's so fabulous. No, he's great. Perry's fabulous. But I can do other things, too, men, women, old, young."

I wondered if he could disappear, like immediately. "Anyway, it sounds like you're doing very well with Thirteen."

Gavin Gilbert sucked his cheeks in in a faintly grotesque manner. "I'd leave Thirteen so fast, his head would spin. She is a vicious cunt. Most of the audience comes to see me, and she takes half of the door." Suddenly, like a ventriloquist, he changed voices. "But don't get me wrong, he's a wonderful performer, very supportive, so giving, so caring." His swift changes in attitude as well as in gender pronouns were getting me dizzy.

There was a sudden hoopla of shouting in the front of Golgotha. I recognized Camille's high-pitched screech and Joel's stentorian boom and Kiko's affected drawl. I imagined it must be fairly ugly because in my memory, I didn't recall ever hearing Joel lose his cool. I could see Camille waving her arms and Joel towering over her, pounding his forehead. Kiko was seemingly posing for a statue in Central Park. Several key phrases leaped out of the shouting match. Kiko declaring, "I will not go on under these circumstances!" Camille whining, "But what about me! My needs! I have needs!" Joel topping her with "Camille, you are supposed to keep things under control! You are driving me crazy!"

I turned away from the fracas, but then two more braying voices, Thirteen's flat monotone and Buster's rasping croak, made it a quintet. I could hear Thirteen hollering, "Kiko and I are stars and must be accorded the respect (burp) due deities in our station. Julian is not in our class." Buster grabbed him by the collar and growled, "Dickhead, you say one more word about Julian and I'll punch your fat face in till it looks normal."

I stormed into the lobby, where everyone was shouting at once. With every bit of theatrical voice training at my command, I topped the chorus of angry voices with "Stop this at once! We have an audience outside!" Nobody listened. Guy floated in, his head encased in headphones, hooked into a relaxation tape. I grabbed him and pleaded, "Guy! Take Camille and cure her! Cure her!" I couldn't break through his mask of serenity, and he moved on. I noticed Perry leaning against the gallery wall.

"Perry, are you all right?"

He was wringing his hands and panting heavily. "I can't breathe. I'm having an asthma attack. I need to stand outside for a while."

I had a cousin who died from an asthma attack, so I was concerned. "Perry, don't you have your inhaler or whatever you call it?"

"I'm all out. It was really stupid. I don't know what happened. There are a lot of cats around here too and I'm so allergic."

"Well, darling, we've got to do something. Obviously, you can't go on. I'm getting you a cab. You're going to the hospital."

He gripped my arm. "No, I'm doing the show. I've got to do the show." He looked like he was going to faint.

Zoe, painted up in her usual silent movie way, arrived with large, dark sunglasses and her hair in a turban. I stopped her at the door. "Zoe, Perry's having an asthma attack and is out of medication. Here's money for a cab. You've got to find a drugstore and get Perry some medicine."

Zoe fumbled about as if I'd awakened her from a long nap. "What? Where? What do I get?" Sending Zoe to find an all-night drugstore to buy Primatene mist was a risky proposition. She teetered down the street in her stiletto heels in search of a cab. I held Perry's hand.

A boy at the front of the line recognized me. "Julian! We love you." His friends joined him, chanting, "We love you!"

I croaked out, "Bless you, darlings. Have you been out here long?"

"It's never too long to wait for you, Divinity. What are you performing tonight?"

"We're doing a scene from *Whores of Lost Atlantis.*"

The four boys screamed. "That's our favorite. We've seen it six times."

"You really have?" I turned to Perry. "Did you hear that? They've seen it six times."

Perry smiled wanly. I wondered how long it would take Zoe to return. I regretted I hadn't sent one of these sharp-looking fans instead of the vague, childlike Zoe. I leaned over and saw the block-long line down the street. A number of people were waving and smiling at me. Because I wore such heavy makeup and wigs, I was virtually unrecognizable offstage. Only in disguise was I Julian Young. I waved to the queue and shouted, "Bless you, darlings! Hopefully we won't be very long!" The blond one of the four boys in front beamed. "I want you to know, Julian, you have made the eighties worthwhile."

I touched his shoulder. "Oh stop that. You're gonna make me cry, and I'm wearing cheap mascara."

"No, really, I'm serious. We see every show. It's something to look forward to. Something to get excited about."

Then his buddy piped up. "And it's only five dollars! Can we be your official fan club?"

"Really? A fan club? I'd be honored. What should we call it?"

The blond one looked at his friends and then turned back to me. "We've already got a name. We call ourselves the Young Julians."

I didn't know what to say. Perhaps because the experience at Golgotha was so personally affirmative and emotional, I never thought that others could derive such satisfaction from our performances. I had to drop any semblance of a camp mask. I stuttered. "I . . . I . . . I'm really . . . Gosh . . . thank you."

A black stretch limo pulled up. The chauffeur stepped out, came around to the other side, and opened the passenger door. The large crowd and myself were holding our collective breath in anticipation of who would alight. A long, slender, high-heeled leg appeared and a pouf of white fur and a flash of rhinestones. It was Mannequin St. Claire. The crowd burst into laughter and applause. Mannequin was another spectacular drag cult star and beloved. Over six feet tall and reed thin, she was the living embodiment of an early 1960s fashion illustration. She never appeared at Golgotha but ruled several blocks away at the Rectangle Room. She specialized in lip-synching to recordings of stars like Dolores Gray and Lisa Kirk. In fact, no fan had ever heard Mannequin's actual speaking voice. I had long admired Mannequin from a distance, but we'd never met. The chauffeur escorted her to the door while she expanded an enormous open-mouthed smile and waved majestically to the crowd. I whispered to Perry, "Do you want to go in now?" He shook his head and gestured, indicating he could breathe easier outside.

The leader of the Young Julians whispered in my ear, "Don't worry, honey, we'll watch out for him."

I held the door open for Mannequin and followed her inside. Once inside, Mannequin threw down her fur and groaned, "Where the hell am I? A gay bar in Machu Picchu?" She'd hit the nail on the head. The latest theme at Golgotha was a tribute to the ancient Incan culture. Mannequin turned to me. "You're Julian Young, aren't you?" I nodded. She exclaimed, "I've seen about six of your shows here. You're fantastic. How can you throw 'em together so fast?"

"I've got a talented group. We're all in sympathy with each other. How come I've never seen you here?"

"Honeychile, I ain't gonna come in costume. Nothing like trying to steal focus unlike many of our sisters, hmmmmmm?"

"Oh puh-lease, our first night here, that creature that calls herself Thirteen arrived with a pink wedding cake on her head. I hope I'm not stepping on friends."

Mannequin let out a cackle. "Thirteen, the evilest queen in this territory. I wouldn't put anything past that one."

I put my finger to my lips and whispered, "She's in the next room. She's the emcee, you know."

Mannequin sighed. "Then it's gonna be a long evening, girl." It was difficult getting used to hearing Mannequin's speaking voice. I had only seen him onstage lip-synching. His actual voice was that of an adolescent boy with a thick as molasses Southern accent.

I had to ask, "Where the hell are you from, Mannequin?"

"I'm swamp trash from Jackson, Mississippi, and, sweetheart, please call me Stephen."

"Julian!" Roxie hollered my name. She, Mamacita, and Mudge were schlepping four shopping bags apiece. "What is going on here? I smell trouble."

To which Mamacita added, "If it's wet paint you smell, these garments are staying put."

I filled them in on the Camille-Joel-Kiko-Buster-Thirteen and Perry situations. Roxie wasn't shaken. "We've been apprised of the Perry situation. Sam drove us over in his car, and we saw Zoe hobbling down Avenue A. Sam's picking up the Primatene mist."

"But where is Zoe now?"

"Outside. Performing the 'quality of mercy' speech to some very perplexed fans."

At this point Roxie and Mannequin/Stephen recognized each other. "Roxie Flood! I worship you. You're Eve Arden, you're Joan Blondell, you're Roz Russell!"

"What can I say? Isn't it fabulous? Gay men have made me what I am, and God bless every one of 'em." I couldn't help but be amused by Roxie's delusions of grandeur. We all suffered from them. Although by day she was still a corporate librarian and I was a . . . cleaning lady, telephone solicitor, receptionist, envelope stuffer, how could we not get caught up in the illusion that we were as glamorous as MGM deities, especially with bright young men organizing fan clubs? Now it was Roxie's turn to grovel at the shrine of Mannequin. "But you! You! You with the legs of death, the poise, the allure, you with the figure of a Veruschka, a Suzy Parker, a Dovima." Her voice lowered to a whisper. She leaned in to him conspiratorially. "You see how thin I am. I know I look fabulous, but I'm starving. I exist on one mango a day and a few scattered snow peas. It's an illness. Call me sick, but I stand by these words, no woman over thirty can eat normally and look good." Roxie's personality was so intense, it was virtually impossible to compete with her and not come off like a Road Runner cartoon. Beneath Mannequin's inch-thick makeup, I could see the intimidated Stephen staring at her in both awe and dismay.

After an eternity of sound and light checks and drag queens wailing when their mermaid costume zippers jammed, the show finally began. There had to be at least forty performers jammed into the cramped backstage area. It was like being in a rush hour–packed subway car with all the inhabitants wearing enormous Mardi Gras costumes. After Mamacita caught one *diseuse en travesti* slyly stuffing Zoe's bustier in her bag, he decided not to watch from out front with Mudge but stand guard. He hissed, "Vipers! nest of vipers!" to anyone who as much as looked at one of our costumes.

The new Golgotha was overflowing. The hundred people filling the folding chairs were only a fraction of the mass of humanity sweating in that old garage. There was no aisle to exit. Surrounding the chairs were kids sitting on the floor, standing by the walls, leaning heavily against the paintings, perched on top of the ice machine, sitting on the rungs of the ladders up to the nearly swaying packed balcony. The hallway leading into the main room was packed with standees, most of whom couldn't possibly see anything but at least could say they were there. Later I was told two people fainted in the crush and a child was conceived.

Kiko and Thirteen made an interesting pair of emcees. Thirteen was given to lengthy rambling, sporadically amusing introductions always geared to how the performer related to him and always peppered with the words "cock," "cunt," "kooky," and "fab." Kiko's introductions took the form of haikus, majestic and inscrutable. Sam had returned with the Primatene mist, and Perry was able to pull himself together. That is, until he and I heard Kiko onstage explaining how she'd brought theatre to Golgotha and how dismayed she was that commercialism had taken over and art vanished. She prayed that the new Golgotha would not pander to easy laughs and camp. Perry and I were fuming in our campy Atlantean chiffons and glitter-bedecked wigs. I glared at Joel steely-eyed. "She has gone too far."

Joel grabbed me by the shoulders. "If you cause a scene here and make me look like an amateur, I'll be finished with this whole thing." I'm sorry, but Joel's Christian ethos of turning the other cheek didn't wash with performance artists on Avenue C.

Mannequin wowed the people with her miming to Mimi Hines's recording of "Once in a Lifetime." The "Samantha auf Naxos" section of the *Bewitched* opera was a success, but the dry-land underwater ballet was an arid bore. The Uncut Dicks desperately needed cutting and left the stage awash in spilled milk, smashed watermelon, and jelly beans. The East Village audience gave them a rousing ovation, although Roxie watching in the wings gave a dismissive "Mildly diverting."

After an endless intermission to clean up the mess from which amazingly no patron defected, Kiko introduced our company. Indeed, she introduced us not as Julian Young and the Imitation of Life Theatre but simply as the Imitation of Theatre. I shot a look at Joel, who raised his finger in warning. Perry nudged me so I'd be aware of Kiko watching glint-eyed from the right wing. At the very last minute, Joel had decided to change the blocking in our scene and instructed me to enter from the left instead of the right. He would instead enter from the right wing. I appeared to a huge ovation. We had to hold for a long time. It was absolutely thrilling. Before I uttered a word, someone yelled out, "We love you!" I turned my head in profile to

end the applause and caught Roxie's eye. She jauntily winked at me, bringing me temporarily back to earth. We began the scene, and although we'd
had hysterically responsive audiences before, this was somehow even more
extreme. If one of us onstage asked a question, someone in the audience
would bellow out the character's response. They seemed to know the dialogue better than we did. I checked out the right wing to see Kiko's response to our reception, but she was gone. It seemed, however, that there
was a puddle of water on the floor. Then Joel appeared in the wing oblivious, in his long imperial robes. I could also see Mamacita's anxious moon
face trying futilely to grab Joel's attention. With a loud fanfare of trumpets
Joel entered, slipped, and took a flying pratfall flat on his ass, water splashing about him. The audience screamed with laughter, but I could see Joel's
face bright red with embarrassment. I helped him up.

Under the audience's laughter, Joel whispered to me, "It's pee. Someone
peed in the wing."

Perry, at attention near us, whispered, "It was Kiko. That's an old Lupe
Velez stage trick to trip someone."

The whole back of Joel's costume was soaked in urine. Mamacita was in
the wing wincing painfully. My mind was ablaze with thoughts of murder. I
immediately realized the plot was intended for yours truly. I was more offended to see Joel robbed of his dignity. I wanted a gun. I wanted a machine
gun. Somehow I managed to speak my next line, but when it was Joel's cue,
he was still so flummoxed, he went totally blank. The poor guy resorted to
the one ad-lib he could summon up. Grabbing Perry by the collar, he stam-
mered, "I hate you, you . . . you nut! I could kill you!" It didn't matter what
play, what historical period, what character, it was the same ad-lib. I closed
my eyes in shame for us all.

Still, we pressed on, and nothing we could do was wrong. My rage subsided, and I warmed to the affection of the crowd. An inner voice told me,
"Remember this moment. This is wonderful. Be happy." Atlantis sank into
the ocean as Roxie and I ran off to jump into our lifeboat. The scene was
over and the applause deafening.

Kiko had insisted that, for expediency's sake, no act should get an individual curtain call. Our group stood backstage listening to the stomping,
and cheering, both becoming insistent and rhythmic. We looked at one another, mouths open in amazement. Later, we all agreed that at that moment we felt like the Beatles. There were many cries of "Brava diva!"
Mamacita, still standing sentry over our shopping bags, yelled, "For Chris-
sakes, take a fucking bow, so we can get out of here." Joel shook his head.
Kiko, believing in some demented way that the shouts of "diva" were for
her, glided onstage. The shouting and stomping continued but also contained the clarifying word "Julian!"

Kiko tried to quiet the throng, and even Thirteen, swaying slightly from
whatever substance he was abusing, entered to restore order. Finally Mannequin grabbed my hand, saying, "I can't take any more of this," and

dragged me onstage. I in turn grabbed Roxie's hand, she took hold of Zoe's who took hold of Perry's who latched on to Guy who roped in Buster who at last lassoed Joel. Mannequin nearly pushed Kiko and Thirteen offstage as he led us on. We all remained holding hands for what seemed an eternity. Madness overtook me, and I began silencing the audience. I could hear Joel mutter to Buster, "He's not making a curtain speech."

I sure did. I was rolling with the punch, riding the crest of the wave, and nothing and no one could stop me. In retrospect, I'd say I created a tour de force of self-aggrandizement and monstrous ego, but at that moment I had 'em in the palm of my hand.

"Bless you, darlings! You can't imagine what this means to us. You've made us feel so . . . so special." There were shouts of "Julian, you are special! We love you!"

"And I love you, darlings. We're just so thrilled to be a part of Golgotha and to see it grow. We've plans for a whole slew of new plays. Marie Antoinette! The Salem Witch trials. If you'll sign our mailing list in the front as you exit, you can be the first on your block to be in the know. At this moment, I really think we should give a hand to our marvelous emcees, Kiko and Thirteen!"

Roxie stepped forward to lead the applause and said patronizingly, "Weren't they great? So poised, so effortless. Bless their little hearts."

I took over. "This is as good a time as ever for me to thank them both for all of their encouragement and help since we started performing at Golgotha. Especially Thirteen. Darlings, it's not every established performer who would be so generous to a younger generation. Is that a face? Gorgeous, but a little leathery. One time I saw him sitting backstage, and I accidentally threw a luggage tag around his neck. And that Kiko. A genius! Such a brilliant use of nudity. You know, med students are among her biggest fans. Oh yeah, they see her act and can skip their first semester in gynecology."

Joel stepped forward and shouted, "Good night! Thank you!" which got the applause going again and signaled our exit.

The performance, which we later always referred to as "the USO show," was over. Once backstage, we were surrounded by the other acts, all applauding my dishing of our emcees. Both Kiko and Thirteen had gone out front and were seen haranguing Rupert and Ruby. Buster gave me a huge hug and croaked, "Honey, you really plucked their nerves."

Mamacita was helping Joel remove his pee-soaked robe. I asked him, "You mad at me?"

Joel had to laugh. "I forgive you, but you've just declared war. You know they're going to retaliate."

Buster swaggered. "Fuck 'em! Miss We-created-this-fucking-theatre Kiko and her hairy armpits."

Zoe put her hands to her ears. "Buster, please."

Guy, who already had on his serenity earphones, added benignly, "Joel's right. We only hurt ourselves when we relate through anger."

Buster was all worked up, like an overexcited sheepdog. "Really, fuck 'em. I saw Kiko squatting in the wing. She could've fucking broken your neck, Joel. I've got friends, you know, oh yeah, I've got friends who can take care of them."

Camille, inhaling a few desperate drags off Buster's cigarette, added, "Hell, I can call my ex-husband. He can put a contract out on both of 'em." I loved it when Camille got cheap.

An hour later, Joel and I joined Roxie and Sam at the all-night Kiev coffee shop for blintzes. It was sweet watching Roxie cuddle next to Sam in the booth. Roxie had a rather kaleidoscopic persona and changes of wardrobe to go with each personality. There was her Wall Street librarian, garbed austerely in a dark blue suit, devoid of jewelry. She then switched into her queen of the avant-garde character, who wore loose, rough-hewn jumpers with black leggings, and dangling barbaric earrings swaying in the East Village breeze. Tonight, she assumed the persona of the young suburban matron, in a conservative knit dress and simple pearl earrings. She barely said a word, merely nodding in agreement with Sam's every utterance.

"Boys, I'm from a different generation. If I hadn't met this beautiful creature next to me, I would never find myself in a joint like that." He put down his coffee cup. "I'm certainly not an expert on show business. But what I do have is a feel for what goes and a sense of timing. I think you kids have got it. I don't know what you've got but you've got something, and it's my opinion that you shouldn't settle."

I thought I understood what he was driving at, but I wanted to hear more. "What do you mean, settle?"

"Well . . . . I'm sure this kind of craziness at a place like Golgotha, I'm sure it must be wonderful. But I think other people might go for it as well. People like me, who aren't going to sit on folding chairs on Avenue C."

Joel looked Sam square in the eye. "You think our show could be a commercial success?"

"I wasn't going to use that word. It seems to offend young people nowadays, but since you said it, yes, commercial. It's fun, it seems like it's dirty and it is, but then it's not. I'm not a critic, but it's a feeling I get. You're better than you think you are."

Sam was speaking words that we were all feeling but afraid to voice. I didn't want to admit that what we were doing for fun could be done for profit. "But I wrote *Whores of Lost Atlantis* in five hours between phone calls at a switchboard. It's not very good."

"Julian, don't look a gift horse in the mouth. Careers are built on just that kind of fluke. You heard that crowd out there. Some of them were nuts, that's true, but not all of them. You guys have something special going on between you. A love, a gaiety, and it's infectious. That's just my opinion, what do I know?"

Joel put down his fork. "But, Sam, producing a show even off-Broadway is a very complicated affair. Even the lowest budget might be a hundred thousand dollars. I don't know where we'd begin."

"You find a good lawyer who knows from the theatre and he advises you. My brother-in-law's partner is a theatrical lawyer. Remind me to give you Mort's number. And then you raise the money. That's the way you start any business. It's the way I started mine. Find people who've got a little extra cash who believe in you. But, guys, you got to believe in yourselves first. Do you think you've got what it takes?"

A low, strong voice emerged from me. "We sure do, Sam. But most of all, I believe in Joel."

Roxie lifted her water glass in a toast. "So do I."

When we left the Kiev, Sam drove Roxie home, but Joel and I decided to walk back to the West Village. We passed by the lovely and somewhat decrepit Saint Mark's church. I felt so strong and secure being with Joel. What a great stroke of fortune that Joel was my friend and that we now shared a common dream and passion. When I met him in college, he had been a gangly, eccentric boy from Indiana. I looked at him now as we walked through the dark Village streets, and he was a completely different person, physically bigger and emotionally solid and mature. I was so proud I knew him and he liked me.

"Joel, we never talk this way, tough, brittle, show biz types that we are, but I absolutely adore you." I could see he was slightly taken aback. I was merciless. "I love you, Joel, I really love you."

"And I . . . I've always thought you were very special." I started to laugh. Joel was trying very hard to match my theatrical emotionalism, but his upper-class WASP background made it nigh impossible.

"I know you love me, Joel. You don't have to say it. I have this marvelous feeling that together you and I can accomplish great things. I couldn't do it without you. If you weren't around, I could be dragging my ass around this country for another decade with that damn one-man show and still not earn a living."

"You're a great talent, Julian. It's inevitable that great things will happen for you."

"I don't know. It's true I'll never give up trying, but it's your brains and creative management that's going to give me a real career."

We continued walking west, and though we spoke quite intimately, we looked resolutely ahead.

"You don't regret giving up law school, do you?"

"Oh no. I never really wanted to be a lawyer. I just . . . Oh, I just want my parents to be proud of me."

I paused a moment. Aunt Jennie had taught me early on to never criticize anyone's family. Still, I felt compelled to say, "You know, Joel, your parents are so rigid in their values, I don't know if you could ever truly please them . . . unless you moved back to Indiana and joined your father's law firm and married his partner's daughter and had a couple of brats."

Joel nodded in agreement. We stopped to wait for the traffic light to change. I looked to see if there were any potential fag bashers around because I felt an urge to take Joel's hand. I made my move. "Joel, I'm in a wildly emotional mood, but my sentiments are cool as a cucumber. I just have this wonderful premonition that you're going to be a great man, a great man of the theatre. And not merely a successful director or producer but a great gentleman that people will talk about for generations." Even in the dark night, I could see Joel was blushing.

"Julian, I'm . . . I don't know what to say . . ."

"Well, don't say anything, just press on!" And with that I made a sweeping gesture that elicited a "faggot!" from a speeding car. Rather than being upset or even indignant, we both doubled over with laughter.

Joel wiped his eyes. "You know, Julian, everyone at Golgotha thinks you and I are lovers."

"I know. Ruby made some strange comment the other night calling you my significant other. Joel, I don't really care what people think. I wouldn't be ashamed of being your lover. The only thing that sticks in my craw is that now that you've been seeing Buster, I'm afraid people will think I'm being cuckolded and sort of 'the last to know.' That could be a trifle humiliating."

"I don't know what's going on between Buster and me. I suppose I should never have played the role of Mr. Ziegfeld dipping into the chorus line, but I'm just mad about him. That's all I can say. . . . I'm mad about him."

"But, darling, couldn't you have fallen for someone a bit more stable? Buster's a little boy who drinks too much and lives purely by his emotions."

"I guess that's what I'm attracted to. He needs me. He pushes me away and says I'm smothering him, but he really does love me. The other night, I spent the night at his place, and in the middle of the night, he woke me up and started punching me. I was terrified. I thought there were burglars in the apartment. I tried to fight him off and calm him down. I don't know whether he was coming out of a nightmare or what, but then he burst into tears. I don't think I've ever seen anyone sob like that. He grabbed hold of me so tightly, I still have marks on my shoulders. He kept saying over and over, 'Don't ever leave me. Don't ever leave me.' It was horrible, but I won't ever leave him. I really mean that, Julian."

I was shocked by the neurotic violence of the story but also oddly pleased that Joel was experiencing such passionate emotions.

"Julian, you and I rarely talk about things like this. Are you still involved with Camille?"

"No, I never really was romantically involved with Camille. I thought I was. I wanted to be. I love Camille and she loves me, but it was all kind of an improv. We got carried away." It occurred to me while walking with Joel that there was a direct link between my playwriting skills and my problem with Camille. "Joel, you know how well I've been tailoring the roles to everyone in the cast? Sometimes I'm not even aware of it, but I seem to latch on to some weird psychological truth about the kids in the company and I use it to define the characters they play."

Joel laughed. "You've got Perry playing nothing but psychopathic little girls and schizophrenic ballet dancers. You're telling him something. Am I really an effete dictator? Don't answer that."

We stopped walking to wait for the light to change.

"Joel, I don't do it to be mean. It's sort of the same thing with Camille. We were acting. I enjoyed playing house with her. Ma, Pa, and kid. Little did I know she'd always had her eye on my gene pool." I paused for a second. "Or maybe deep down I did."

Joel pulled up the collar to his overcoat. It was the first genuinely cold night of the fall. "Julian, you need to have a good talk with her."

I had tried to approach Camille earlier in the week. We were rehearsing at Golgotha. I entered the unisex rest room and found her at the mirror brushing on mascara. As usual, there had been a scheduling conflict, and a rock band named Sludge was just starting a long sound check. This was a good time to sit Camille down for a heart-to-heart. I would apologize, I would be contrite. I would admit to being in cahoots with the Walker spy family. Anything to smooth things over with her. She continued with her maquillage.

"I love watching you put on makeup, Camille. You're so meticulous."

She put down the applicator and stiffened her small shoulders. "What's that supposed to mean?" She looked at me fiercely in the mirror. "Are you saying I'm anal?"

How does one answer that question? Camille proceeded to brush on the mascara with such ferocity that I feared for her cornea. She continued to speak in a tight, shaky voice. "You guys are so completely self-absorbed and unsympathetic. Here I've been chain-smoking since the age of seven and I'm finally going off 'em cold turkey and I don't get a fucking smidgen of support." She jammed the applicator into the tube. "I know you all think I'm a bitch. Well, I'm doing the fucking best I can." She grabbed her bag and spun out of the rest room like a five-foot cyclone. This was not going to be easy.

"Joel, Camille knows she's being a bitch. She's got a lot going on in her head. Anyway, I'm glad you and I are taking the time to communicate."

"Buster is positive that you're having a wild, passionate affair, and not with Camille."

Buster was amazing. He ran the gamut from almost moronic to extremely astute. I wondered how he sensed that I was seeing Don Caspar at least once a week and that I'd never felt so sexual and uninhibited. Don made me forget my artistic egomania. In the deep, dark recesses of my boudoir, I was his puppet, to experience whatever he chose for me to learn. I needed a confidant. I feared Joel wasn't the best casting for that sympathetic role. He tended to view life in such black and white moral terms. His world was peopled with heroes and villains, and I wasn't sure which category Don would fit into. Joel definitely wouldn't admire Don's infidelity to his socialite wife. It never occurred to Don to feel the slightest bit of guilt. What she didn't know wouldn't hurt her. Joel's conservative attitude about what constituted good sex would never embrace Don and my hypnotic sexual theatrics. However, I did need a confidant. Someone had to hear this story. Dipping my foot into the water, I asked Joel, "Where does Buster get this idea that I'm having a wild, passionate affair?"

"He says you have the glow of someone who's being . . . How did he put it so delicately? 'Fucked right and left.' "

I thought I'd hidden that damn glow under five pounds of stage makeup. But if there was one thing Buster Campbell knew about, it was the aftereffects of hot sex.

"Well, Joel, Buster can be very—" I had a sudden vision of Don Caspar's enormous hands, with the black hair on their knuckles and their odd round nails. Those giant hands were tightly grasping both sides of my head like a nutcracker.

"Joel, I don't want to talk about this."

A group of rowdy and very drunk teenage boys were at the end of the block. I pulled Joel to the other side of the street to avoid any contact with them. There was no use walking into trouble. That was a survival technique curiously absent from my romantic life.

CHAPTER
22

Damn my ministers and high priests with their impotent advice. I shall replenish the coffers of this kingdom, and it won't be through a bake sale.

Milena, *Whores of Lost Atlantis*
Act Two, Scene One

All of us were now single-minded in our pursuit of moving off-Broadway for a commercial run. That would mean we would actually be paid! We would be earning our living in the professional theatre! From our extensive repertoire, we chose as our commercial debut *Whores of Lost Atlantis*. It was our biggest success at Golgotha and certainly had a catchy title.

Sam's brother-in-law's law partner, Mort, wasn't available, but he led us to Myron Passman, a sixtyish shingle who drank straight whiskey out of a Styrofoam cup in his office. Joel was entranced by his brusque film noir manner, although I would have preferred an attorney more in the *Masterpiece Theatre* vein. Despite his lack of soigné charm, Mr. Passman turned out to be a straight shooter and a canny adviser. He helped Joel devise a budget and a plan of attack. We had to raise a hundred and fifty thousand dollars. That figure would become the most important phrase in our vocabulary. It would be split up into units of three thousand dollars each. We started ahead of the game when Sam bought three units totaling ninety-three hundred dollars. We had no idea where to find the rest. Most producers have a group of potential investors who can drop twenty or thirty grand into a show at the drop of a hat. Most of our acquaintances didn't have the scratch for a sub-way token.

I dialed every phone number in my address book and in any old address book I could dig up. When I wasn't calling old flames to put the pinch on, I was on the street handing out fliers. The fliers weren't advertising our up-coming production. They were announcing the opening of a new gym, and Perry and I were paid five dollars an hour for our labors. We compared our fund-raising efforts.

"Perry, do you remember the professor that I was sleeping with in col-lege?"

"I didn't go to college with you."

There were times Perry could be frustratingly dense. "I know, dear, but I'm sure I told you about him."

"Psychology?"

"Philosophy. He was a great love of mine. Anyway, I called him in Chi-cago, and he's buying a unit." Our arms were getting sore from passing out the fliers.

"Julian, have you tried calling that rich lady who used to hire you to per-form at her garden parties?"

"She was the first on my list. I wish I had a dime for every time she said, 'Darling, you are so brilliant. If I can ever help you, please let me know.' Well, I told her this is it, if it's ever gonna happen for me, it's now. You would have thought I'd put a gun to her head. 'Oh, darling, I've just bought a new co-op and with taxes coming up and I've just invested in my son's girlfriend's restaurant, blah, blah, blah.' P.S., she ain't buying."

"My shrink's buying half a unit. He oughta. I've been paying him top dol-lar for twelve years. Oh, and my mother is buying a unit."

"That's wonderful, Perry."

"I figured she would. She'll do anything to help me. I mean, after all, when I was twenty and wanted a new face, all I had to do was ask."

"I wish you'd asked for a better surgeon." Perry and I often talked about his face in a coldly objective way.

"My mother's intentions are good, but she isn't what you call a detail person." When Perry was twenty he was abjectly miserable, nearly suicidal. His mother was desperate for a remedy for his unhappiness. When he asked for extensive plastic surgery, she immediately ran for the yellow pages. She chose a plastic surgeon who worked out of a hotel room and whose nurse had an American flag tattooed on her chest. The results were fascinating. Whereas before he resembled Lotte Lenya, now he looked like a young Mar-tha Graham. He shrugged.

"I like my face. It just bugs me the way some of these critics describe it." We had begun to be reviewed in downtown papers, and one rave review described Perry's comic style like this: "Perry Cole plays the hermaphrodite with a sinister comic flair. The role suits him perfectly. Indeed, his mouth looks as though the lower half of his face has been slashed from ear to ear."

"Oh, Julian, I didn't tell you. Sam's helping me find my birth mother."

Sam was rapidly taking on Zeusian dimensions. He forced us to see our own destiny, invested hard, cold cash in our show, and was now helping Perry locate his true parentage.

Perry explained further. "You know Sam is a Holocaust survivor, and he became active in trying to connect other survivors to relatives they thought had died. Well, this got him involved in other groups that locate people. There's one called SEARCH. I forget what the letters stand for, but they help adopted kids find their parents. I went in for an interview last Monday. They said it's gonna be tough 'cause I know so little about her, but they're going to try."

"What's your mother think of all this?" Mae Cole may have bungled the plastic surgery, but Lord knows she tried. A powerhouse personality, she'd let a Mack truck roll over her for the sake of her kids.

"My mother's all for it. Julian, if she'd pay for my new face, twelve years of therapy, twenty years of acting classes, EST, transcendental meditation, as well as investing in our show, she'll support my search for Sally Riddle. Yeah, that's her name, Riddle. Perfect, huh?"

We heard a high-pitched squeal, and two young guys descended upon us—or rather upon Perry. The black one of the two said breathlessly, "You're Folio, the hermaphrodite! We love you. You've got the most fabulous face!" Perry was about to introduce me, but I signaled for him to desist. I didn't want these guys seeing the diva reduced to passing out fliers to a Vic Tanny Salon. The black queen's chubby, red-haired sidekick said, "We've heard a rumor you guys are moving off-Broadway. Is it true?" Perry explained we were in the process of raising the money. The two boys were thrilled. The black one snapped his fingers. "Well, girl, we're gonna be there opening night. We are major fans. That Julian girl. Whoa, we love that mess." I was standing right beside them, and they had no idea that the skinny guy with the brown hair was the "mess" in question.

The next morning, the phone woke me up. It was Zoe.

"Hello, is this Julian Young?"

"Zoe, I live alone. Of course it's me."

"Your voice sounded different. I don't know, so masculine."

"Zoe, what's up?"

"Lissen, Julian, I'm in a terrible pickle. Guy asked me to assist him in a show today, but my apartment flooded and I have to be here to let in the plumber. I can't even reach him. I'm supposed to meet him at the Golden Wok restaurant on the Upper West Side."

"What can I do to help?"

"Could you do the show for me?"

"Oh, honey, Guy needs a female assistant for those magic shows. I can't fit into the levitating equipment."

"No, this is different. It's not a magic show. You have to be Judy Garland."

I was very confused. "I know it sounds odd, but Guy didn't explain it very well to me either. He said . . . let's see, I've got it written down here. It says, 'Put together a costume like Judy Garland.' It's for some kind of birthday party. Do you think it could be a gay party?"

"It sounds kind of gay to me." I thought about it for a moment. As usual, I could use the honorarium. "I suppose I could be Judy Garland as well as the next guy. But, Zoe, is there really no way to reach Guy to warn him?"

"Julian, I've been trying all morning. His answering machine must be on the blink."

It's not all that difficult rustling together a Garlandesque outfit. I just happened to have in my drag box a simple black knee-length sheath, a beaded jacket, black pumps, and a short, tousled brown wig. I was in business.

Chinese restaurants don't have dressing rooms, so it was easier to arrive in costume. The 1962 Judy is remarkably undated. While I was flagging down a cab on Hudson Street, no one paid me a second thought except for a good-looking fellow walking a weimaraner who hollered, "Sing 'em all and we'll stay all *night*!"

I alighted from the cab on Sixty-fifth Street and entered the Golden Wok. The dignified Chinese maître d' informed me that the birthday party was being held in a private dining room downstairs. I thought the theatrical touch would be to enter singing. I handed the maître d' a cassette of Judy at Carnegie Hall and asked him to put it through the sound system at the cut I had chosen. A short while later, I heard the opening vamp of my number, straightened my seams, and entered the party lip-synching "For Me and My Gal." Gosh, I was terrific. One arm across my chest steadying my other arm while I gestured wildly, lower lip trembling vulnerably, I stalked to the beat of the music, my eyes blazing with the spirit of MGM and Benzedrine. The room gasped at my appearance.

In return I gasped when I saw them. The bulk of the audience was seven years old. Thirty wide-eyed youngsters, their socialite parents gathered to one side stiff with horror. Mingling among them were actors costumed as the Cowardly Lion, the Tin Man, Glinda, the Wicked Witch, and Guy as the Scarecrow with his mouth wide open in shock. Damn Perry and damn me for not figuring out that this was a *Wizard of Oz* theme party. Being a professional, naturally I continued lip-synching. I lifted the side of my skirt as I vamped my way among the tables, one hand frenetically brushing hair away from my forehead. Garland's voice exhorted the crowd to "sing along with me, please!" No one did. One little girl held on to her mother crying, "She scares me!" Several of the fathers were red-faced mad and focused their wrath on a young woman, evidently the professional party giver. I was sure I could win them over with my big finish. Judy did, after all, appeal to young and old.

For once Guy lost his New Age cool and was sweating so profusely, his face took on the sheen of a plastic Halloween mask. I heard him explaining to several parents, "I had nothing to do with this! It's some kind of crazy mix-up. I promise you he won't be at Hillary's birthday next week."

Now I was angry. I may not have been Dorothy, but I was still Judy. So what if I was twenty-five years too late! I belted out the final bars of "For Me and My Gal." Thank God the number was over. Oh dear, I forgot, this was her MGM medley, and off I was into "The Trolley Song." But then I was terminated. Someone pulled the plug, the worst fear of the lip-syncher other than a power blackout.

A few minutes later I was out on the street hollering, "Wait a minute! Wait a minute! Give me my tape back!"

The height of humiliation is to be booted out of a Chinese restaurant in full Judy Garland drag. A dozen parents followed me outside shouting obscenities.

Guy pulled me over to the street corner, a sweating scarecrow berating a latter-day Judy. "What could have possessed you? Are you crazy?"

"Zoe gave me the wrong information."

"No, this is another one of your perverse jokes at my expense, just like when you were my magic assistant and pretended you couldn't unlock the trunk and get me out, so you could do a rotten comedy monologue."

"Oh, so we're back at that again, are we? I wouldn't waste my breath making you my stooge." A number of passersby were gawking at us and laughing. I shouted at them, "Okay, yes, I'm supposed to be her, have a good laugh!"

Guy still wasn't finished. "You once told me you think of all your day jobs like being in a sitcom. It's all a big joke to you. My magic shows are very important to me. It's my livelihood. All of these parents are going to tell their friends. They're all going to blame Guy the Magician. So thank you very much, I hope this will be a great anecdote for you to dine on."

The surreal quality of the moment was getting to me. For a few seconds, I felt like I was Judy being told off by some nasty club promoter. "Guy, I'm getting out of here. But I just want you to know, rationally and calmly, you are an asshole. Taxi!" It was rush hour and impossible to find a cab on upper Broadway. Shelly the party giver came out, and gave me an "if looks could kill" sneer, and ordered Guy to come inside. I was standing in the middle of the street trying to hail a cab.

Guy hissed at me, "Julian, I'm worried about you. I think you have really taken this drag thing too far."

"Oh, give me a break, Guy, or are you channeling Dr. Freud?"

"I don't know who you're channeling, the ghost of Gloria Swanson or Greta Garbo." The silly boy didn't even know at that time Garbo was still alive and kicking on East Fifty-second Street. His tirade grew in intensity. "I can't tell anymore if you're one of your characters or yourself. You talk exactly like the hard-boiled dames you play. I bet you don't even know the difference."

I gathered my dignity about me like a silver fox stole. "I know I find this conversation rather tedious."

"That's what I mean. You're always 'on.' I'm really worried. The way you're going, soon you're going to be living in drag all the time, like those old Warhol stars. You've become obsessed with this whole 'diva' act. Just think about it, will ya?" He turned away and went back inside the restaurant.

I shouted after him, "I should think about finding a new leading man!"

There were absolutely no cabs. A Mercedes was parked in front of the restaurant, and in the driver's seat was a very dignified middle-aged man. He called out, "Are you Julian Young?" I was in no mood to speak to anyone but a bartender carrying a tray of martinis.

"Yeah, what's it to you?" Oh dear, I *did* sound like a hard-boiled dame. Guy had a point, I hated to admit. If I found the line of demarcation between reality and role fuzzy, why shouldn't those around me? Hadn't Perry accused me of this failing months before?

The gentleman in the Mercedes called out to me again. "I'm a big fan. You look rather lost."

I crossed over to the car. "You could say that again. This is a helluva way to get a cab in rush hour."

"It would be a pleasure to drop you off somewhere."

It's not my habit to jump into strange cars, but under the circumstances I took a good look at him. He certainly seemed like the essence of respectability, a bank president, the head of a foundation. I searched for a twitch or tic that would reveal the dark soul of a serial killer. I had a sudden vision of myself lying in an alley with my dress hiked up around my waist and my wig stuffed in my mouth.

He smiled benignly. "My name's Bob Livingston. My daughter June brought my wife and I to see you at, um, what was it called, that strange place, oh yes, Golgotha. We had a terrific time. I don't think you're going to have much luck finding a taxi."

"You've got yourself a fare." I hopped in. He shook my hand.

"I'm sure I'm one of your more offbeat fans. I really didn't know what to expect. My daughter is an aspiring actress, and she enjoys trying to shock her old man."

"Were you shocked?"

"There were a few times I thought my wife would have a stroke, but I reminded her it was like an old burlesque show. I found it charming." He told me he was a vice-president at a large advertising agency. My anger fading, I realized I was seated beside a potential investor. I turned on the vivacity. I told Bob about our plans to produce *Whores of Lost Atlantis* off-Broadway and our need for investors, and he appeared interested. Ninth Avenue was bumper to bumper with traffic. I had enough time to sell him the Golden Wok. Even though he was seated, I could tell Bob Livingston was a big guy, over six feet tall, balding with a gray fringe, a big hawk nose, and on the verge of getting very jowly.

"I must tell you, my wife was envious of your gams."

"Well, I like to quote Dietrich. 'The legs are so-so, it's what I do with them.' "

"Then you must be the master or mistress of illusion. They look great. What size shoe do you wear?" That didn't seem like the obvious next question. It was a bit personal.

"Oh, size eight and half men's, size ten women's."

He reflected on that bit of privileged information. "Quite small, all things considered. What sort of shoe are you wearing right now?" I had that vision of myself with my wig in my mouth again. On the other hand, I really wanted to present Joel with a couple of sold units. I lifted my leg onto the car seat. My black dress raised up, exposing a lot of thigh. I hadn't meant to be so provocative. We were stopped at a light, and his eyes didn't wander up my leg but stayed transfixed on my black satin pump. In a calm, steady voice, he asked, "May I see it? Your shoe?"

"Sure." I took off the shoe and handed it to him. He held it as gingerly as if it were a diamond tiara from Cartier. Gently he caressed the interior of the shoe. I said, "I hope I wasn't sweating in it."

The light changed. He returned the shoe to me and resumed driving. He smiled. "A lady doesn't sweat."

"Are you a connoisseur of ladies' shoes?" That seemed like the genteel way of asking him if he was a foot fetishist.

"I love women's shoes. I love them."

My conversational skills weren't up to this turn in the scene. We drove in silence. Without looking at me, Bob said in a matter-of-fact tone, "There aren't too many people I can confide this to. I shouldn't think you'd be judgmental."

I wasn't sure I wanted to hear his confession. I noticed an odd side effect of my career as a female impersonator was that it seemed to release the inhibitions of those around me. Strangers and acquaintances felt secure to tell me their most personal secrets. They seemed to feel that I had to be the most sexually confident of people, that I was free to be whatever I wished. I think they felt that by being near me, they'd absorb by osmosis some of my positive egotism. On countless occasions, strange men would shyly take out of their wallets snapshots of themselves in drag. They were usually studies of the grotesque, but their bearers found it comforting when I'd coo, "Oh, you look so pretty . . . so real." Bob Livingston didn't take out any photos, but I'd hit the nail on the head in the confession department.

"Julian, I have this dream . . . not a dream really. I guess you'd call it a fantasy. I've never told anyone this before. I hope you won't laugh."

I couldn't believe I was playing shrink to this high-powered executive in a Mercedes-Benz. I wanted so much to present Joel with Bob's investment in the show. I told Bob, "Of course, I won't laugh. Who am I to judge?" We trudged along in the traffic.

"Well . . . I've always thought it would be sort of crazy fun to dress myself up in a frilly maid's uniform, a French maid. Do you know what I'm talking about?"

"Oh yes. A little short black dress with dozens of stiff petticoats and a cute little white lace collar and cuffs."

"What would the cap be like?"

I was disappointed that Bob's fantasy was so generic, so mundane. I wished it could have been more baroque, like desiring to dress up like Nell Gwyn, Isadora Duncan, even Winnie Mandela. Something, you know, different. I tried to throw myself into his fantasy. "Hmmm, let's see. The cap. What about kind of a Breton cap, with little white lace wings coming out on the sides and two long pink ribbons trailing down your back?"

"What would my hair be like?" He had no hair, he was bald.

"Um, I think you'd look lovely with a light brown, not blond but a very natural light brown wig with kind of, maybe a slight twenties feel, sort of a marcel wave." I wondered how I could steer the conversation back to my show.

Bob twisted his mouth in deep thought. "I imagine in this city, one could find just about any kind of costume. I should get an outfit like that."

"Why not? I'm really looking forward to getting all new costumes for my show. It's not a major part of the budget but—"

"My dream . . . my fantasy is to dress up as a lady's maid and serve a beautiful transvestite mistress. Do you think that's terribly bizarre?"

Hardly. In the world of kinkiness, it was about as offbeat as a child wanting to be a fireman. I was frankly let down by Bob's imagination. "I find nothing bizarre in such a desire. It makes sense that a man in a position of authority would feel a need to shake off that heavy mantle and fantasize that he could at last be vulnerable and, well, powerless. I don't think it's odd at all."

Now I know that I'm going to lose sympathy here. I'm apt to appear calculating, opportunistic, and manipulative, but my mind was full of images of my filthy apartment. I could clearly see the dust balls gathering in every corner, the linoleum floor in the kitchen turning a deep gray when it was formerly ecru. It also occurred to me that if I indulged Bob Livingston's fantasy, he might reciprocate and invest in our show.

"Bob, do you really want to live out this fantasy?"

He nodded thoughtfully, still not losing an ounce of dignity. "Yes, I should experience this. I see no harm in it. What I propose is that I come by for a few hours perhaps twice a week and straighten things up."

I lifted my leg up on the car seat again in a Dietrich-like pose. I wanted to show that I meant business. "No, Bob, I think I'd want you to do more than just straighten up."

"You would?"

"Uh huh. I'm an actress, not an heiress, and I maintain only a staff of one.

Any maid in my employ must be prepared for a wide range of duties." I could feel both of us blushing in our new roles.

Bob looked straight ahead at the road. "What would you expect of your girl?"

"Oh, dusting, vacuuming, mopping the kitchen floor, and I mean really scrubbing it. I loathe laziness, and I see no reason why such lax behavior should not be punished." I tried to remember Genet's play *The Maids*. I hadn't read it since college, and it failed me now. I was left to my own inspiration. I was doing well. Bob had broken out into a sweat, and the car was air-conditioned. "Would you really keep the apartment clean, or would I be forced to complain to the agency?" I regretted that last line. I sounded less like a pampered demimondaine than a Long Island hausfrau.

Bob didn't seem to care. "The place would be *spot*less. I'm something of a perfectionist."

I decided to venture into the more rococo elements of domination. "Would my toilet be spotless as well?"

Bob's beady eyes widened, then closed for a second. I feared for his driving. "Oh yes, the . . . the toilet. Spotless. All I ask in return is that you be dressed as a woman in a beautiful negligee and that you order me around . . . humiliate me."

I knew those last two words were difficult for him to utter. "I have a lovely negligee, full length, peach silk, princess collar." The humiliation angle could be a problem. Domination has never been a big interest of mine. I'd cross that bridge when we got to it.

He stopped the car in front of my building. For the first time in a while he looked directly at me, his basset hound face deadly serious. "You don't know how much this means to me. Let me give you my card."

I looked at the card. "Robert Livingston, V.P. of Creative Affairs." Creative indeed. I struggled out of the car. My black Judy sheath was a bit too tight for comfort. "Well, Bob, the sooner you start the better. Bring a bottle of Top Job and I'll reimburse you."

He reached over and grabbed my hand. "Madama, please call me *Wilma*."

CHAPTER
23

Imperial Empress, you are teetering on the edge of a fiery abyss in a pair of spike-heeled mules.

Folio, *Whores of Lost Atlantis*
Act Two, Scene Two

During these salad days, it was a point of honor to me never to accept permanent employment. I had a deep fear that once I was permanently entombed nine to five, I would lose my theatrical ambitions and never be heard of again. However, to make a semiliving wage, I sometimes had up to five different jobs a week and worked longer hours than the most permanently employed slavey. Forgive me for patting myself on the back, but I also turned out a new play every three weeks. The big secret to my prolific turnout were the receptionist jobs. As I did with *Whores of Lost Atlantis*, I'd sit for hours behind the reception desk, typing, typing, typing. All the while, I was impressing the other office workers with my diligence and commitment to their company. I just thanked God no one ever looked over my shoulder and read the titles of my plays, such as my spoof of the Bette Davis movie *The Old Maid*, which I renamed *The Old Cunt*.

Occasionally I took a day off. One afternoon, I escorted Aunt Jennie to the Morgan Library to view an exhibit of letters and documents from the life of Marie Antoinette. We walked very slowly to the library, which was down the street from her apartment building. It disturbed me to see Aunt Jennie so fragile. She was such an indomitable figure in my life, I sometimes confused her with God. Like the Lord, Aunt Jennie was all-knowing, wise, took responsibility for everyone, all-powerful, but judgmental and unforgiving. It was awful seeing God diminished and faltering. She made an effort to look vigorous by wearing the campy rhinestone star pins I'd bought her in the sixties and a bright red slash of lipstick.

"Julian, I was so freaked out this morning." Aunt Jen still employed the slang I'd taught her circa 1969. "I think my memory's starting to go. For the life of me I couldn't remember the name of Audrey Hepburn's first American film. It took me all morning to come up with *Roman Holiday*." Aunt Jen, like myself, was something of a movie trivia queen. "Test me, Julian."

I thought hard. "Give the names of all four Lennon Sisters and their correct ages."

"Don't be an asshole, Julian. Even their own mother couldn't answer that one."

There were very few people in the library that afternoon. We could hear our footsteps tapping along the marble floors. The exhibit was displayed in glass cases throughout the library. Aunt Jennie held my arm, and we peered at the letters of Marie Antoinette. Some were in French, and others, including those to her mother, Maria Theresa of Austria, were in German. Aunt Jennie had taught herself both languages during the past twenty years and was able to translate for me in her crackling Midwestern accent. Our mutual fascination with Marie Antoinette had less to do with any sustained interest in French history than our admiration for Norma Shearer in the 1938 MGM biographical extravaganza. In the ensuing years I've read quite a bit on the tragic French queen, but I still can't get the image of Norma Shearer and those Adrian gowns out of my mind.

We wended our way through the exhibit. Aunt Jennie would translate the letter in an excruciatingly slow, halting manner. To be fair, eighteenth-century penmanship is not the easiest to decipher. I'd then explain to her the historic circumstances surrounding the epistle. This was one of our favorite activities, stemming back to when I was a child visiting her on the weekends. Aunt Jennie loved when I'd teach her something. Starting from when I could first speak, I'd teach her songs, tell her stories, relate history to her that I gleaned from historically themed movies. In return, she wrote most of my school papers and led me through the labyrinthian tunnel system that lies beneath midtown Manhattan. Most native New Yorkers don't even know that on a rainy day one can walk nearly a mile without feeling a drop through a series of tunnels, office buildings, and department stores. In the dark days of my childhood, Aunt Jen's midtown excursions were pure magic.

At the Morgan Library I was telling Aunt Jennie the awful facts about Marie Antoinette's trial that were left out of the Metro picture. When the revolutionary tribunal could find no political reason to execute her, they trumped up a charge that she'd committed incest with her ten-year-old son. I was going into all sorts of heart-tugging detail on this subject and didn't even notice the small crowd of old ladies and gentlemen listening rapt to my spontaneous lecture. It wasn't until one plump little white-haired woman tut-tutted "How horrible for her" that I became aware of my audience.

Aunt Jennie was in her element. She addressed the group. "My boy is so in love with Marie Antoinette. He really knows everything about her." I was in agony. I am hardly an expert. My knowledge on that subject is largely romantic or sexual. I'm totally ignorant of the Jacobins or the fourth estate, but I can tell you a thing or two about Louis XVI's medical problems with his foreskin. Aunt Jennie didn't care. She was very proud. "When Julian was eleven years old, we went to Paris, and he insisted that we walk all the way from the Conciergerie, where the queen was imprisoned, to the Place de la Concorde, where she was guillotined. He was only eleven years old, and no one could believe he knew so much." My elderly audience were shaking their heads in admiring amazement. I wanted to flee. The worst thing about being embarrassed is the embarrassment of being so pretentious as to be embarrassed in the first place. I shouldn't have minded my aunt's pride in my peculiar knowledge of royalist trivia. But at the moment, I wanted to strangle her.

We left the library to get a bite to eat. There is a profuse variety of charming restaurants in my aunt's neighborhood, and she insisted we go to one that has great coleslaw. It turned out to be a generic and very tired Greek coffee shop. Swatting flies away from my cheeseburger, I questioned her choice of venue. "Aunt Jennie, wouldn't you like to have lunched at some elegant little café full of ambience and charm?"

"What's wrong with this place? You can get an excellent Reuben sandwich."

I couldn't help but roll my eyes.

She picked up on it. "I saw that. You're very grand, aren't you?"

I delicately brushed away some of the crumbs left by the last patron. "You will agree that this joint is a bit on the sleazy side, *n'est-ce pas*?"

Aunt Jennie straightened her back, every inch the dowager. "Look over there. Some very nice people are eating here. You remind me of when I was a little girl in Cincinnati. We were so poor and I heard one of our neighbors say about us, 'They're so hoity-toity and yet the chickens crap on their table.'"

Aunt Jennie ate only about four bites of her tuna fish sandwich. "Julian, whenever I think about Marie Antoinette, I just can't get Norma Shearer out of my mind. You know, she was in your mother's favorite movie, *Smilin' Through*."

My mother died when I was seven years old, and every year I remember her less and less. "Aunt Jen, I think my most vivid memory of her is sitting in her bedroom and her telling John and me the story of *Smilin' Through*. You know, I always think of her as this very tall woman because I was so little."

"Oh, she was small and very fragile." My mother had been fourteen years younger than my aunt. Consequently, their relationship was very deep and complex, both sisterly and like mother and daughter. Aunt Jennie wiped her lips with her napkin. "I find I think about her all the time, even after all these years. Sometimes I think it was almost a blessing that she died young. I wonder how she would have coped with growing older and just life, being so complicated."

I wondered whether Aunt Jennie was referring to how my mother would have dealt with her son being one of Manhattan's most notorious transvestite performers. It was best not to dwell on it.

Aunt Jennie was in a reflective mood. "I've done the best I could. I'm sure I've made terrible mistakes, but after Uncle Max died, I was so alone and unprotected. I guess there's no point rehashing it all. Oh, Julian, if I could do it all again, I think I'd try to be more social. I think that's one way I failed you."

"What are you talking about? Failed me?"

"Well . . . we lived such a strange life, you and I. Like recluses. No one ever came to the apartment. No wonder your brother fled. It must have been like living with Miss Havisham."

"It was kind of. But what could you have done? We can't change our natures. We are who we are."

"People don't change. I've been shy and afraid since I was born. If I had been born to a different family and hadn't been so poor, I might have done more with my life. I might have been an opera singer." I worked mightily not to roll my eyes again. My aunt is the most tone deaf person I've ever encountered.

She played with the spoon in her coffee. "My problem, Julian, is I never identified with any group or anyone. I was always a loner. That's a terrible thing to be, and I suspect you take after me."

"I know exactly what you mean. That's why my theatre company is so important to me. It's the first time I've ever really felt connected with people, that I shared a point of view with other people, shared a goal."

"Well, that's a wonderful feeling. I've never known that. I think only once in my life did I have a best friend. That was a long, long time ago."

I felt such a twinship with my aunt. It bugged me that she didn't think of me as her best friend. "Aunt Jennie, I feel like we are very connected. I certainly identify with you."

Aunt Jennie was in a strange mood. Most of the time I could predict her reactions. Her attitude was always the opposite of what the norm should be. Today, however, she was sphinxlike in her ambiguity.

She raised her eyes and looked at me in a frighteningly direct way, as if we weren't related at all. "You think you know me so well, Julian, but you don't really. There are parts of my life I've never revealed to anyone, I don't even dare discuss with myself." Aunt Jen adored mystery and intrigue, but at this moment she seemed genuinely enigmatic and rather frightening.

"Aunt Jen . . . no one can know anyone completely, no matter how much you love them. I suppose that's why we become disappointed in people when they reveal aspects of themselves we weren't aware of and don't approve of."

"We can't even know ourselves completely."

"You mean, even when you're pushing eighty, you still are in the process of defining yourself?" She nodded her head in agreement. I sighed. "Well, that is depressing."

"What's depressing?"

"Oh . . . because I just get so confused. Every time I think I've gained all this great insight into myself, I realize I'm still scrambling around trying to invent a new 'me.' "

"Did something prompt this self-reflection?"

We were close friends, but she was also my surrogate parent, and there were areas in my life the size of continents about which we never spoke. She accepted that I was gay but didn't want the details. She preferred to regard my homosexuality as something vaguely important that I shared with Proust and Noël Coward. I could never share with her the dizzying effect Don Caspar was having on my life. If my relationship with Don had been based on mutual interests, commitment, and a financial stake in my play, I would have forced Aunt Jen to open her eyes. As it was, Don would never have considered meeting her. Our affair existed within the confines of my railroad flat, as Don often reminded me. I needed someone to confide in. It didn't seem right telling my almost-eighty-year-old aunt that the night before, Don had buckled me into an elaborate slave harness. I thought I'd die from embarrassment and the heart-pounding thrill. No, she wouldn't have appreciated the zaniness of the moment.

Aunt Jen sipped her coffee. "Something's bugging you, Julian."

Lucky for me, I had an extensive repertoire of anxieties to choose from. "Oh, I had a fight with Guy, an actor in my company. He said I can no longer tell the difference between the hard-boiled characters I play onstage and who I am in real life. Perry said the same thing. I don't know when the play ends. Maybe they're right. Maybe I don't have a real personality. Maybe I'm just some blank screen that other people project images onto."

The waiter slapped the check on the table. Aunt Jennie picked it up. "Oh, Julian, I wouldn't be so depressed. I don't think you're a blank screen at all. You're a very special person." She squinted at the bill. "My God, four ninety-five for a tuna sandwich. You're very special, Julian."

"But who is that person? That's the question. Maybe I am always putting on some character, maybe I'm never my true self."

She threw the check at me. "Julian, you figure out the tip, I don't understand all this. Oh, it's not so confusing. I mean this personality business."

I looked up from my attempt at doubling the tax. "No?"

"Julian, maybe . . . maybe your characters are who you really are and the person you are during the day is the act. Let's get out of here." She rose out of her seat.

Her closing line rattled through my head. Maybe my characters are who I really am and the person I am during the day is the act. Very comforting indeed.

The following afternoon, Guy came over to rehearse a scene from my adaptation of Brecht's *Mother Courage*, with myself naturally in the unglamorous title role. Joel suggested I stretch my range a bit, and *Mother Courage* seemed just the vehicle. I was nervous having to rehearse with Guy alone. We'd barely spoken since the *Wizard of Oz* debacle. I opened the door and let him in. We hugged tentatively, and I led him into the living room. We sat down rather stiffly on the sofa. I fumbled with the scripts and handed him his pages.

"Julian, shouldn't we talk about, you know, the children's party?"

"I guess so."

Guy lined up the pages of his script. "I may have overreacted that day. The parents of that child are big clients of mine and the center of a whole circle of parents that could provide me with a lot of income."

"Guy, I screwed it up. I'm really sincerely sorry, but you must believe me, I didn't do it on purpose. What kind of horrible person would that make me?"

"I'm sure you didn't do it to be vicious. You and I are very close friends, but don't you think you have to take some responsibility for your actions?"

"I've really been disturbed by what you said to me out there on the street. I've been giving it a lot of thought. I do get confused whether I'm creating drama or living my life. But, Guy, I'm a dramatist. I see everything as a story. You're a story, I'm a story. I see everything with a beginning, middle, and end. And because I'm an actor too. Well, sometimes I can't differentiate between my improvising a character and my own personality. My characters come out of me, so they must say something about my inner life. It's not so cut and dried, you know? Guy, I can only imagine if it's confusing to me, it must be baffling to those around me. I promise I'll try to keep a grip on things. The last thing I want to do is alienate my friends."

Guy put his arm around me. I thought the gesture a bit hokey, but Guy did have a tendency to overplay. "It's just that sometimes, Julian, you get these wild ideas and instead of putting them on paper, you insist on acting them out in real life and you involve innocent people. In my case, it usually results in public humiliation."

"Oh, Guy, I feel awful. I'd never want to humiliate you."

"Julian, I know you dismiss New Age thought, but I truly believe we each create a climate around us that causes things to happen. That's what we mean when we say we create our own reality. The reality you create is often a grotesque farce with me as the buffoon."

"You really think that's true? I feel just awful."

"I don't want you to feel awful. I love you, Julian." He kissed me on the cheek. "I don't think you're even aware that you set up these outrageous scenarios. But I think you get a perverse pleasure out of seeing real people react to your invented theatrical situations."

I hadn't thought of myself that way. It made me seem a bit manipulative but rather fascinating. "Guy, I find it all so perplexing, because, you know, more than anything, I worship common sense and a no-nonsense approach to life. Anyway, I promise you, as costar, playwright, and most of all, as friend, I will try to create a climate of peace, tranquillity, and normalcy. Okay?" I kissed him on the cheek. "Oh dear. Guy, I got a little lipstick on you." I tried to wipe it off him.

Guy looked at me suddenly as if for the first time.

"Why are you wearing full drag makeup? And a wig. And you're in a pink negligee. It's only three-thirty in the afternoon."

"That's because the maid's here."

"The maid?"

"Yes, Guy, the maid. She must have been in the bathroom when you arrived. The situation is a bit eccentric, but just remember one thing. This is about her, not me. Hold on to that phrase." I called out, "Wilma! Wilma, could you please come out here?" We heard the heavy tread of her patent leather pumps, and there she was framed in the doorway.

Bob Livingston's transformation into Wilma was extraordinary. Wilma was a living, breathing woman with her own likes, dislikes, prejudices, and humor. There was nothing of the avuncular ad exec in her makeup, so to speak. Wilma was meticulous, caring, motherly, but not averse to being a bit caustic to a pestering phone solicitor. Bob had found himself a perfect maid's uniform, remarkably similar to the one I had described to him. Unfortunately, he chose a somewhat brassy blond wig when I would have preferred something a bit more genteel. After about an hour, I thought he resembled the character actress Mary Wickes. I guess in reality, though, he looked more like Watergate felon John Mitchell playing Hazel.

"Wilma, I'd like you to meet my leading man, Guy Miller." Wilma gave a short curtsey. Guy looked paralyzed. I glanced at the clock and realized it was time for me to pass judgment on Wilma's handiwork. I sincerely didn't want Guy to have to witness this spectacle but, well, call it bad timing.

"Guy, dear"—I spoke in my most silvery tones—"you must excuse us, but it's nearly four o'clock, and that's our time for inspection. You may join us if you wish."

Guy squinted his eyes, trying to figure out where I was coming from. "Julian, you are on one weird trip."

I laughed. "No, Guy, just running an efficient household. Wilma, scoot into the kitchen, we shall begin in there." Wilma scurried away, and when she was out of the room, I whispered out of the side of my mouth to Guy, "Humor her, please, she's cleaning my place for free." Reverting to my Billie Burke persona, I chimed, "Here we are, Wilma dear!"

This was Wilma's second visit. I'd failed miserably during her first. When Bob stated he wanted to be humiliated, he meant humiliated. When I saw the spotless state of my living quarters, all I could do was express my joy and gratitude. I could sense his deep disappointment and aggravation. I was determined this time not to let him down. Slowly, I walked around the room, wiping my little finger on various hard surfaces looking for grime. Hmmmm. Spotless. We returned to the sitting room. I lifted the cushions on the couch to see if he had vacuumed beneath them. He had. He was very good. I wondered if he had left something intentionally dirty for me to find and berate him for. This was becoming a very original game of hide-and-seek. The roles of mistress and slave were mighty fuzzy indeed. If I didn't humiliate Wilma, she'd quit. Has any homemaker ever had such a servant dilemma? I got on my knees and looked underneath the couch. No dust. I lifted every knickknack, and believe me, I have plenty. Dust free. The goddam living room was immaculate. I decided to try the bathroom. Wilma followed me and was in turn followed by Guy, fascinated by the spectacle.

The bathroom glistened like the enchanted castle in Disneyland. Wilma really was making it hard. I was determined to find a flaw. He wouldn't accuse me again of not living up to my end of the arrangement.

Aha! Miss Perfect had left one detail unattended to. I put on quite a performance. My jaw clenched tight, I shuddered. I shook my head in abject dismay. I raised a trembling hand to steady my rage and still could not contain my horror. In a low, breathy voice I uttered the words Wilma/Bob longed to hear. "You call that clean?" I repeated my query. "You call that clean?" I pointed to the toilet, à la Mommie Dearest.

Wilma was hyperventilating. "Bbbbut, Madame, I *have* cleaned your toilet."

I laughed derisively. "Yes, Wilma darling, you have cleaned the interior of my toilet and the front and sides of my toilet, but you fucking asshole! You didn't scrub *behind* it! How many times must I tell you that the area that is not seen must also be spotless? That is a true sign of an elegant household, something a peasant like you wouldn't know about." Guy tried to interrupt my harangue. I stopped him. "No, Guy, don't you dare defend her." I could see Guy was having a hard time following this scene. I was frankly disappointed, but then no one in our troupe was terribly skilled at improvisation.

Wilma piped up, "Madama, I recall your exact words this morning. 'Wilma,' you said, 'it's not necessary for you to clean behind the commode.' "

That was an out-and-out lie. I was getting mad. I was confused whether I was irritated that Bob was testing how far I'd go or whether my character of Madame was pissed off that Wilma was telling a falsehood. Either way, she was gonna get it. "Guy!" I commanded, "hand me that flyswatter."

"Oh, Julian, come on. This is getting silly."

I grabbed the plastic flyswatter off the coffee table and handed it to Guy. I had placed it there for just this purpose.

"Wilma, assume the position!" Wilma crossed to the mantel, turned her back to us, and bent over, her short dress revealing lace panties. I had to suppress my giggles. "Guy, pity me for having such a lazy servant. Now I want you to slap Wilma ten times across her broad derriere. And put some balls in it!"

Guy's face was flushed. "I can't do this."

I gave Guy a fierce look. Bob was having the time of his life, and I wasn't about to let Guy screw it up. Guy raised the flyswatter and gently slapped Wilma's behind.

"Oh, Guy, really!" I stood with my knees apart, my peignoir opening in a rather vulgar manner, and hauled off and swatted Wilma's behind so hard the sound echoed across the room. Wilma let out a dainty squeak. One! Two! Three! Four! Five! Six! Seven! Eight! Nine! Ten!

Wilma straightened up, fluffed up her skirt, and looked at me with a petulant expression. Petulance on a middle-aged basset hound face is not particularly attractive. In my most severe dramatic accents, I spit out, "Don't you ever contradict me again! Now move your fat ass into the kitchen and fetch Guy and me some tea. Lipton for me and herbal for Guy. That will be *all*, Wilma."

Wilma scurried happily into the kitchen, a new spring in her step. I settled grandly on the couch in the living room. Clearly shaken up by this episode, Guy sat dumbstruck in the armchair. "Oh darling"—I groaned—"don't look at me like that. It's all a big charade. She insists that I dress up and insult her. It amounts to her wages. If I don't get rough, she'll vamoose and I'll be back pushing the vacuum cleaner myself, God forbid."

"Where'd you pick up that old queen?"

"She's not a queen. She's not even gay." I was sure of it.

"Oh puh-lease."

"No, she's got three grandchildren and has been happily married for twenty-eight years. This is just sort of his hobby. Ain't I lucky?"

Guy raised his eyebrows. "She can't be straight with all that mincing around and 'Yes, Mum' business."

I could see explaining the dynamics of my business relationship with Wilma was going to prove tiresome. "Take my word, Guy, he's straight. Where did I read that thirty-six percent of all transvestites are heterosexual?"

Guy lowered his brows. "Have you ever met one?"

I thought about it. "Hmmm. No, can't say I have, but then I haven't made a worldwide survey of it either." I smoothed out the silk skirt of my negligee. "Guy, enough with this domestic blather. Let's rehearse. I want to lose myself in drama." I extended a finger toward his script. "Begin with your first speech at the top of the page."

Stimulating work and a job well done. Isn't that the greatest joy in life?

CHAPTER 24

> Milena, you mock my friendship by consorting with mine enemies. At this point, I wouldn't trust you as far as I could throw an urn.
>
> Ultima, *Whores of Lost Atlantis*
> Act Two, Scene Two

Guy and I rehearsed for a few hours, and then he left, still not convinced that my servant problem was perfectly ordinary. Bob left shortly afterward, thanking me profusely for a splendid afternoon. I thanked him. The apartment sparkled. A glance at the clock made me realize that I had to quickly dedrag. Don Caspar was coming over, and I had to be all boy. I scrubbed my face clean, slapped on a pair of tight jeans and a T-shirt, no underwear, thank you. Don had made vague murmurings about dinner, but there was no point in getting dressed up. If he took me out, it would most likely be some dark little joint by the West Side Highway. A deeply conflicted bisexual married corporate executive will not take a boy to Le Cirque.

Don arrived at six-thirty, looking like the quintessence of the tanned veteran movie star. He had a way of looking me up and down in an impersonal, assessing manner that made me weak-kneed. With all my doubts about my identity and gender and illusion versus reality, it was an odd relief being thought of simply as a good-looking guy who was going to be spanked. Don stood very close to me, his head nearly a foot higher than mine. He spoke low and soft. "I worked out at the gym during lunch. Feel this." He placed my hand over his firm pectoral muscle. For a man his age, he was in remarkable shape.

"It feels good." I ran my hand over his crisp white shirt and under his tie. I slipped two fingers between the buttons and could feel some of his chest hair.

"I thought I'd surprise you, Don. I bought a bottle of that Dewar's scotch you like. I bet you'd like a drink." I fixed him a scotch on the rocks, and we sat down on the couch.

He took off his jacket and stretched his long frame. He smiled. "Have I ever told you, Julian, how good it feels being here with you?" I shook my head. "Well, it does feel good. There's something very warm and inviting about your place."

"My friend Perry says it looks like the Batgirl's cave."

He took a sip of his drink. I knew he would miss the reference. His eyes glazed over whenever I made the slightest camp remark. His sexual taste in men continued to baffle me. He obviously didn't want a masculine butch type, yet it really bugged him if I acted at all femme. Don seemed to like me best when I was sort of a tough Huck Finn with an intellectual bent. It was a complicated characterization at best. I asked him if he was hungry and what he wanted to do about dinner.

"Would you be very disappointed if we stayed here and ordered in Mexican food?" I had to admit I was disappointed. I was sort of counting on him buying me a steak somewhere. Refried beans were a fixture of my poverty-stricken diet. Don continued, "We can go out if you'd like, Julian, but it feels so good in here and . . . my wife . . . I frankly can't imagine my wife ever ordering from a Mexican take-out place."

What could I say? He was presenting me with an image of myself as the hip, spontaneous bohemian as opposed to his stiff, patrician wife. I shrugged. "Tacos or tortillas?"

The Mexican food arrived about six minutes after I phoned in the order. We ate dinner in the living room while Don watched the evening news on television. It wasn't terribly romantic, but it was the most relaxed I'd ever seen him. He took his shoes off and loosened his tie. I enjoyed watching him manhandle his chicken tostada while concentrating on the *MacNeil/ Lehrer NewsHour*. What peculiar fate had brought the two of us together? His complex libido had led him to eat lousy guacamole with an ambitious female impersonator in Greenwich Village.

There was a knock on the door. Don nearly dropped his fork.

"Don, I don't think it's the hotel dick. It's probably the old lady down the hall. She's terrified the landlord is trying to evict her, and he should. She's a witch. She put a hex on the girl upstairs and the girl had a miscarriage. If the old lady doesn't like you and thinks you're up to no good, she gives you the *malocchio*, the evil eye."

"Julian, why don't you just open the door and see who it is?"

It was Zoe, in a getup that made her look like a bedraggled Bo Peep.

"Your front door was open, so I didn't buzz," she said breathily.

I let her in. I couldn't have been more surprised if I'd opened the door and it had been J. D. Salinger. I never saw Zoe except at a rehearsal or performance. "Are you all right?"

"Oh yes. I was in the neighborhood and I passed by this beggar selling magazines and I saw this one and I thought you'd like it." She handed me a tattered, rain-damaged copy of Paris *Vogue*. "I remembered you said you desperately needed new clothes."

"Gee, Zoe. Thanks. This will help. I may have to miss the opening of the new collection at the House of Lanvin. No, Zoe, this really was very thoughtful of you. I adore this magazine." I tried to pry apart some of the rain-soaked pages. The smell of the Mexican food wafted over.

"Oh, are you eating dinner?"

"Yes. I have a friend over. We're just having some Mexican food."

Zoe stared at me with a blank smile.

"Would you like some? Have you eaten?"

"That would be lovely, Julian." She spoke in an affectedly gracious manner, as if she'd practiced it fifty times in front of a mirror. I then remembered Roxie saying that she thought Zoe was making a great effort to be more, how shall we say, "normal," to connect to people and be more social. I certainly didn't want to discourage her. I escorted Zoe into the living room to meet Don.

Mr. Caspar and I had always been alone. Our affair was strictly top-secret. When he saw Zoe, he looked like a startled moose. I realized this was a terrible mistake.

"This is Zoe. She's an actress in my theatre company. She happened to be in the neighborhood. She hasn't eaten dinner and I've . . . invited her to . . . have a bite. A quick bite. Zoe, this is—"

Don stood up and smiled. He extended his hand for her to shake. He said, "I've never met any of Julian's friends before. I'm Tony Andriolo."

I did a double take. What hat did he pull that name out of?

Zoe came up to barely over his waist. She giggled and said in her most studied polite manner, "Pleased to meet you, Tony. I'm Zoe Cornell."

Suddenly *she* was sporting a new handle too. I found myself saying, "And I'm the Grand Duchess Anastasia." They both looked at me blankly. "Zoe, forgive me, but last week wasn't your name Zoe Winters?"

"I thought about it, and it's not good billing-wise to have a last name so near the end of the alphabet. Anyway, I like Cornell. Katharine Cornell was a great actress, and she too had dark hair and pale skin."

I could see Don was amused by Zoe. He told her, "I think Zoe Cornell suits you perfectly. I saw Katharine Cornell on the stage when I was very young, and I don't think I ever saw any woman as beautiful."

Zoe sat on the floor with me and helped herself to the food. I was impressed by the supreme effort she was making to be talkative and vivacious.

She told us she loved Mexican food because she was born in Texas. How-ever, when she was six, they moved to outside of Pittsburgh. She was the second of four sisters, and her father was a retired fireman. This was by far the most biographical information I'd ever pulled out of the Garbo of Gol-gotha. She really was quite adorable that night. She laughed at all my jokes and even had a pithy one-liner of her own. When I told how one night I was so exhausted from my day job that I phoned in my performance, Zoe drawled in the tone of a bored drag queen, "Phoned in? Honey, you mailed it in."

Don hardly phoned in his performance that night. He told her not only that his name was Tony Andriolo but that he was divorced, had no children, earned his living as a dealer in antiques, and had met me through a sales-man in an antiques shop. I said nary a word. I knew Don was inventing a new identity, and I had no idea if the past Zoe was presenting was true or not. Between the two of them, it was like watching a double feature simul-taneously.

After dinner, Don and Zoe became immersed in a coffee table book of movie star portraits. Zoe rhapsodized over the beauty of Hedy Lamarr. It was appropriate, since Zoe shared some of the Austrian beauty's deadpan stare. Then, as if someone had placed a tack under her behind, Zoe jumped up from the couch. "Julian, you've been most kind, but I really should be going."

"I've got some chocolate ice cream in the freezer. Wouldn't you like to stay for dessert?"

She was already moving toward the door. "No, no thank you. It's late and I don't want to intrude upon your evening." Within seconds, she was out the door.

I rejoined Don on the couch. "She's a character, ain't she?"

"She's an original. Julian, do you know her very well?"

"I think you know her as well as I. I've been working with her intimately for months now, and I never knew where she was from or anything about her family until tonight. She's so secretive. She never tells you a word about any aspect of her life. Her age is an ongoing mystery among the Imitation of Life Theatre Company. She must have felt very comfortable with you."

"She's like a frightened little sparrow."

"With the ambition of General de Gaulle. Don't let her fool you. She's a great actress. I wish you could come see one of our shows."

"I'm not sure I'm ready to see you as a woman. I'm still getting to know the real you."

"Well, when you know 'him,' tell me all about him. You'd be doing me a favor. And speaking of 'the real thing,' what's the significance of the name Tony Andriolo?"

Don yawned. "Why do you think the name is significant?"

"Well, not everyone I know has an alias. No, I take that back, just about everyone I know has an alias. Mannequin is Stephen, Mamacita is Hugh, Thirteen is Lewis, Voilà is Martin. Gee, what does that say about my world? Why Tony Andriolo?"

Don picked up the movie star portrait book again. Without looking up, he said, "I simply made it up on the spot. It's probably foolish, but it's a small world and it's remotely possible your friend Zoe might meet a friend of one of my children and so on and so forth. Andriolo is the name of my accountant, and Tony? People used to tell me I had hair like Tony Curtis. Sorry for dispelling the mystery."

"You make it sound like I'm investigating you."

Don was immersed in the photographs in the book. "Ann Sheridan. She was a sexy gal." Without looking up, he added, "There's always something going on behind your eyes like you're trying to figure me out. Julian, I'm just a simple old grandfather with a knack for making money."

"You sure don't look like any grandfather I've ever seen." I grabbed the book from him and jumped on his lap. He gasped and laughed. "Oh, you're a big grandbaby."

I could feel the enormous bulge in his pants getting hard. I nestled my face in his thick neck.

He murmured, "I wish I was a pair of these tight jeans so I could be touching your ass at all hours."

I tried to return the compliment. "And I wish I was your wallet."

He did a take. "What's that supposed to mean?"

"I guess that didn't come out right. I meant, I wish I was your wallet so I'd be next to your dick all day. You know, Don, this is the longest you and I have ever spent together."

"I know that. I want to spend the night with you."

"Sure! My bed's a little on the narrow side, but we could pretend we're sleeping in a canoe." Don lifted me up and carried me toward the bedroom. He took one look at my narrow daybed and said, "It's like a sarcophagus."

"We could imagine we're Mr. and Mrs. Tut."

"I'm six foot five. This will not do."

Don said he knew of a place, but we'd have to drive there. I only had time to throw a toothbrush into a plastic bag before he hustled me out of the apartment.

Don drove a large, sleek white Cadillac, not in keeping with his understated WASP image.

"Where are you taking me, if you don't mind me asking?"

"I do mind you asking."

"Is it a hotel? A motel? A trailer park?"

"Shhhh."

We drove in silence. At Thirty-fourth Street and First Avenue, he suddenly pulled over to the corner. He opened the door and said, "Wait here." He got out of the car and went inside a pizza shop. It had a glass front and was fluorescently lit, so I could see clearly inside. Don was talking to a man nearly his size but blond and with a mustache. They were quite jovial with each other, and after less than a minute, they left the pizza shop together. The blond man was carrying a large, wrapped bundle that could have been a painting of some kind. I sat in the front seat, feeling like a dumb bimbo while they put the bundle in the car trunk. They spent some time talking behind the car. I was getting pretty tired of it, and then Don opened the car door and slipped into his seat. The blond man stuck his head in Don's window and smiled broadly, displaying a large gap between his upper front teeth that gave him a jaunty, vaudevillian quality. He spoke in an odd British-German accent. "Hello, I'm Kurt, very pleased to meet you."

I reached across Don and shook his large, meaty hand. He looked at Don and gave a somewhat lascivious wink. I really did feel like a blond tart with big tits. Don wasn't amused and said flatly, "We've got to go. Thanks for your help." Kurt tipped an imaginary hat and laughed. Don floored the gas pedal and pulled the car away from the curb.

"Who was that?"

"A real character. You think he's sexy?"

"Not particularly."

That was the end of that conversation. It didn't take the insight of Sigmund Freud to gather that Don didn't feel like gabbing about this fella. I was just going to ask one more question about what was in the package when Don turned on a cassette of Sinatra singing Cole Porter that put the kibosh on any further dialogue. Don and I never did much talking. Well, I did. I talked a lot. I told Don all about our shows and my aunt and my father and my brother and what it was like struggling to make it in show business. He seemed interested, or rather he didn't seem bored. My disclosures never prompted him to reminisce, though.

We got on the highway, and suddenly I felt terribly lonely. I missed my friends. I wished I was cuddling on the couch with Buster, stroking his bare back or hearing Perry rhapsodize over Virginia Mayo's performance in *She's Working Her Way Through College*. I missed Camille torturing a wig while relating the details of a five-car collision she'd witnessed. I missed Guy massaging my shoulders and discussing the Beatles' marriages with Roxie. I missed watching Zoe run across a room wobbling on her stiltlike heels, and I missed Joel saying that everything was going to be all right.

I turned to Don, who was humming "Night and Day" along with the Chairman of the Board. "How are your kids doing?"

He blinked as if I'd goosed him. "Where the hell did that come from?"

"I don't know. I know you've got two kids and a couple of grandchildren, so I thought I'd ask how they were doing. How are they?"

"They're fine." He smiled but raised his eyebrow in a way that removed any warmth from his grin.

"How often do you see your grandchildren?"

"Not enough. They live in Denver. They're two and three years old. They don't get around much." He turned up the tape.

"Hmmmm. I've played Denver. Your son's kids, right?"

He turned down the volume. "Is this some sort of attempt to get closer to me?"

"Gee, God forbid. Families are an important aspect of people's lives, and we both are rather close to—"

"Our world is just the two of us. Nothing exists when we're together but what we invent." I could think of no immediate response to that fortune cookie remark. I watched him drive. His colossal size and cool arrogance kept me in a constant state of arousal. I felt an overwhelming need to bury myself in his bulk, but I kept my distance. He was sensual but lacked tenderness. His touch was knowledgeable and seductive but aloof. I had a desperate craving to expose some bit of vulnerability in him. Even with the car windows so tightly closed, a loud smelly fart would have been a welcome respite from his chilly perfection.

I wondered if I was doomed to be infatuated with an elusive lover and reject affection that was direct and all mine. Was that my errant father's legacy? I flashed back to a hotel room in Miami when I was nine years old. My father and brother and I drove to Florida from New York a year or so after my mother died. The drive south was fantastic. The three of us were never closer, and we stopped frequently to visit antebellum plantations and any number of historically themed tourist traps.

When we got to Miami, my brother hooked up with a group of rowdy teenagers and my father with a hard-faced blonde named Elaine. One night, my brother was off making trouble with his new friends and my father had gala plans with Elaine. I was terrified to be left alone in that strange hotel suite. I was determined to keep my father entertained so that he wouldn't leave. I put on an elaborate one-child variety show for my father and his astonished date. I recited the complete list of Academy Award–winning best films from 1927 through 1963 and performed impersonations of Brenda Lee, Doris Day, Pat Suzuki, and Ethel Merman, including the entire "Rose's Turn" number from *Gypsy*. My father was wildly appreciative; Elaine looked mildly horrified. I delayed them for over an hour before they ultimately fled into the night. Was I still compelled to dazzle every man I encountered? I seemed to be attracted only to men I had to seduce with my full arsenal of charm, vivacity, and celebrity impersonations. Don was my latest challenge. I was determined to break through his enigmatic facade.

"Don, please tell me one thing about your family that will make them seem real to me, and I promise to stay clear of this subject forever more."

"You don't give up, do you? Well, let's see. We're having some trouble with our youngest, Trish. She's a junior at Bennington and she wants to shack up with her boyfriend."

"You and your wife are upset?"

"You bet I am. That's not what I'm paying for."

"Is she very in love with him?"

"That's not the issue, Julian. She plays by my rules or she pays her own tuition. Enough of this shit, get your cock out."

"What?"

"Take it out. I want to hold it while I drive."

I looked at him askance. "What? Do you miss having a stick shift?" He snapped his fingers, and I unzipped. We drove down the midnight highway with Don's big paw firmly gripping my hard-on.

I lay back with my eyes closed. The situation was humiliating yet bolstering. Don was the only person in my world who responded to my masculinity. Even Camille with whom I had fantasized a heterosexual union found it more satisfying to relate to me as a strong woman. She liked nothing more than to style wigs that would conceal my masculine forehead and soften my neck and jawline. For my birthday, she gave me a beautiful rhinestone choker and in her card inscribed, "To the most beautiful woman in the world who has taught me not to be afraid of being feminine."

Don was teaching me not to be afraid of being masculine. I may have been passive in our sexual acrobatics, but when he'd have his way with me, I'd look down and notice an array of defined stomach muscles I never knew I possessed.

As we were moving toward an exit, Don pulled the car over to the shoulder of the road. He opened the glove compartment and took out a black silk scarf. It smelled of Chanel No. 5, so I suspected it belonged to Mrs. Donald Caspar. He tied it around my head, completely obliterating my vision. I was startled by this turn in the evening. Speechless, I simply lay back against the headrest. If I was self-conscious before, now I felt idiotic, riding in a white Cadillac blindfolded with my pecker hanging out. I decided to play the moment for comedy, a scene out of a frothy sex farce, but frankly, I couldn't imagine Doris Day in this situation.

"Um, Don, why am I blindfolded? Are we rehearsing a magic act? I hope you don't intend to pull a rabbit out of somewhere."

"I'm taking you to a special place, and I wish it to be a surprise."

"I have absolutely no sense of direction and chances are I'm going to fall asleep anyway. I nod off in any moving vehicle. I could get forty winks on a skateboard."

"Shhhh. Just listen to Ol' Blue Eyes."

It seemed like we were driving for an eternity. Vigorous conversation was awkward under any circumstances with Don, and true to my word, I fell fast asleep even with the driver's hand around my dick.

Don nudged me, and I woke up with a start. Waking up blindfolded is a bit disorienting. Don removed the scarf covering my eyes. The car clock read eleven thirty-five. I looked out the window. We were in a stark suburban community. I wondered if we were still in New York State. My captor wasn't providing any answers. Rather wobbly, I stepped out of the car.

There were no streetlamps. Only the moon illuminated the lunarlike landscape. All of the houses were small, identical split-levels, spanking new,
and arranged in a horseshoe. Each had a small front lawn but no trees or
bushes. I could see in the distance a lush cluster of forest surrounding the
development set off in silhouette against the night sky.

"Don, where the hell are we? Why aren't there any trees or shrubbery?
This place is creepy."

"The development was built three years ago but went bankrupt before
they could finish the landscaping. I was able to buy the house for a song at
auction."

"But why? This isn't your style at all."

"It has prospects. I'll hold on to it for a while." Don took out a remote
control wand and opened the automatic garage door. I followed him inside.
The garage was almost completely empty, no rakes or lawn mowers, only
three big trash cans. Don took out of his pocket a large ring of keys and then
looked directly in my eyes. His face was almost obscured in the darkness.
"You will never tell a soul that you've been here."

"No, no, no one."

He smiled and wrapped his arm around my shoulders, hugging me close
to him. "Forgive me for sounding so sinister. If they could afford it, don't
you think everyone would have a private place only they knew of, some special place that they shared with no one? I bought this house as an investment but"—he squeezed the bulge in my jeans—"but you can see where it
can be useful. Let's go inside. You look cold."

Don unlocked a door in the garage and led me into the house. We were in
what was designed as a basement rumpus room. It was as empty as the
garage, with only stacks of unassembled large cardboard packing boxes
leaning against the walls. We climbed a few steps and went through a second door. We were now in the kitchen. Enough light came through the window for me to see that everything was brand-new. There was even masking
tape across the sinks. The doors to the cabinets were open and revealed
empty shelves. Don took my hand and led me through the kitchen's swinging door and up the stairs to what I presumed would be the bedroom. I
turned my head to get a brief glimpse at the living room. As empty as the
playroom and kitchen were, the living room was jam packed with furniture.
The curtains on the bay windows were tightly drawn, but even with minimal
light, I could see that a large antique divan was flush with an elaborate
eighteenth-century secretaire. Chairs were piled onto chairs; tables were
loaded down with boxes. When Don noticed me pausing for a look, he fairly
yanked me up the stairs.

The master bedroom was as crowded as the downstairs. Massive seven-
teenth-century tables and bureaus were again flush against each other.
There was still no light. Don seemed to be avoiding the light switch. As my
eyes became accustomed to the darkness, I could see paintings of all dimensions leaning against the walls. There were stacks of them, all in heavy,

ornate frames. High on top of a magnificently carved armoire, I could make
out the piercing eyes of a Greek icon mosaic. Don turned me around to face
him and held my face in his hands. Softly, he whispered, "You belong here
with my treasures."

"Are you a collector?"

"Of everything beautiful and unique. You're very special to me, Julian."
His warm hands felt good against my cheeks, but the sheer size and power
of them made me aware that with a simple tug, he could probably unscrew
my head from my neck like a bottle top.

"Don, I know you're a private kind of guy and it's none of my business,
but couldn't you tell me just a little something about what's going on
here?"

Don led me to the bed. He had to lead me, the room was so crowded with
furniture and there was only the narrowest of paths. The bed could have
slept an entire slumber party of decadent noblemen. It had four intricately
carved wooden posts supporting a vaulted wooden canopy. The effect was
more claustrophobic than erotic. No doubt some perverse cardinal had indulged himself here in all sorts of Renaissance kinkiness. Don and I sat on
the bed like strangers in a sixteenth-century Venetian motel room.

"Julian, I've always had an interest in collecting antiques. It's inevitable
that a collector eventually gets involved in selling as well as buying. You
trade with other collectors to get what you want. I have very good taste, and
my trading has turned into a rather lucrative business."

"That's terrific."

"Yes and no. The senior partners in my investment firm frown upon what
they call 'diversification of interests.' They feel it takes away from my concentration on the buying and selling of stocks."

"I get your drift."

"You're a smart kid. So I keep this part of my life a big, dark secret. Will
you help me?"

"Of course, Don. This whole night with you is kind of a dream. Perhaps
I've never really been here at all."

Don didn't reply. His face was so lost in shadow, I could only see his
profile in silhouette. He rose from the bed and moved about the cramped
quarters. He found the Art Nouveau lamp he was searching for. He flicked
on the switch, which bathed the room in the soft rosy glow from the Tiffany
shade, and stared at me from across the warehouse of a room. "Take off all
your clothes, including your watch. I want to see you naked among my
things." His command was devoid of emotion, yet I was immensely flattered to be considered in the same class as these priceless antiques.

As I stripped down, I said, "You know, this bed inspires me to write a play
set in the seventeenth century about a decadent cardinal who's obsessed
with a beautiful Spanish noblewoman. I see myself—"

He clasped his hand over my mouth, using his large index finger to force
my jaws open. "I don't want to hear about that."

My ego, which was larger and more demanding than his could ever be, rebelled like a rampaging Kong, and I tried hard to bite him. He jammed his fingers so far back into my jaw that my eyes teared.

"Son, I'm making this clear. When we're alone you're not a drag queen, you're not a writer, you're not your aunt's nephew. You belong to no one else in the world. You're mine. The same as everything else in this room. I value it and cherish it and it's mine."

I tried to catch my breath and plan a snappy riposte that I could spit out the moment he got his damn fingers out of my mouth. Unfortunately, my bank of quips was depleted. There was nothing I could do to break the pretension or silliness of the rather frightening two-character play we were performing. This theatre belonged to him. I would have to play the rest of the act under his direction. I knew from experience if I just let go, I'd enjoy myself.

I woke up first. I reached for my watch on the nightstand and saw it was only six in the morning. Don was asleep on his side, and as gargantuan as the bed was, he filled up the greater part of it. I studied his beautiful profile. His lips were relaxed and slightly parted. I enjoyed hearing his faint snoring and watching the expelled air purse his lips forward. His coarse salt-and-pepper hair was flattened in the back, pushing some tufts up into a comical hayseed's cowlick. I wished he were knocked out cold so I could play with it. Did I really want him rendered harmless? Wasn't I attracted to the danger of cavorting with a Park Avenue mountain lion? My eyes wandered up and down the various hills and valleys of his sheet-covered body. For a man his age, he had a great ass. Stealthily, so as not to wake the giant, I lifted the sheet away from his midsection for a good, uninterrupted view of my prize. It was a big man's butt, solid and muscular. There was a lot of flesh to grab if one dared. The skin was like smooth, dark marble as he had no tan line. A triangle of sparse dark hair at the base of his spine grew darker as it turned into a mysterious black shadow in the crack of his ass. It took great self-control not to dig my finger inside that enigmatic macho stronghold. I contented myself with a chaste kiss on the fleshy cheek. It really was the ass of a much younger man. Considering that most of the bounty in the room was in transit, I wondered if perhaps the ass wasn't also on loan.

I began to shiver from the night cold and slithered back beneath the covers, creating a parallel curve to his fetally curled up body. My genitals were almost touching his gorgeous behind, and I could feel its warmth. I stared at the back of his skull. What was he dreaming? Surely his dreams contained a quality of innocence totally absent from his waking demeanor. It seemed as if the greater part of our time together was spent studying each other like art in an exhibition. I was a fragile bibelot that he enjoyed examining yet took perverse pleasure in degrading. He was a mammoth marble statue that I felt privileged to caress. Perhaps it was in our best interests not to examine each other too closely for flaws. I fell asleep and dreamed that Don and I were at the White House. We were both nude and making love on a roped-off bed in the Lincoln Bedroom with a lively group of tourists watching us. If I recall correctly, among the camera-toting group were Joan Rivers, Katharine Cornell, Simon Wiesenthal, Wilma, Davy Crockett, and myself in drag. Perry always says my dreams are so easy to interpret that they belong in a freshman psychology textbook.

When I woke up again, it was eight-forty. Don was in the shower. When he emerged from the bathroom with his hair wet and a towel draped around his hips, he looked remarkably like the mature but still devastating Gregory Peck. He winked and said, "We should get going, buddy." I showered quickly, and when I left the bathroom I could hear Don on the phone in the kitchen. I dressed and thought it best to wait in the bedroom and give Don some privacy. I looked around the room, now flooded with sunlight. In the corner was a long, marble-topped Baroque table laden with gold-leaf clocks, candelabras, and a sculptured bust of a snooty Roman senator. Lying flat on the table was a beautiful wooden cross, delicately carved and etched in gold. I was about to place my hand on it when Don walked in. He startled me, and my hand flew off the cross as if it were a flame.

Don laughed and said, "Go on and pick it up. Everything should be touched."

I lifted the cross, and moving slightly to the left, I could see my reflection in the mirror. It occurred to me that the Imitation of Life Theatre still hadn't satirized the religious epic. I had a vision of Roxie and me as lepers healed by Christ or better yet as two terminally spunky nuns conning a real estate tycoon into giving them a building for a new school. I could see us perfectly in the traditional black and white habits but wearing enormous movie star false eyelashes.

No matter how hard Don might try to dominate me, my imagination would always make me the stronger. I wasn't intimidated by him, but I could act intimidated if it amused me. Don sensed my strength, and that's what made me a valid opponent. No master wants a willing slave. My creative imagination had always been the force that governed us. How often he had taken his cue from me, even if he didn't realize it. There had been another big bully who tried to put me in my place, my long departed brother, John. I recalled once more the moment when John became aware of my latent strength. It was good not feeling afraid. I wondered how long this bravado would last.

Don came up behind me. The smug look on his face said he was reading my mind. I was curious how accurate he would be.

He said confidently, "Sixteenth-century Portuguese. It's called the Angelica Cross."

I involuntarily smiled. He caught it.

"What's funny?"

"Nothing's funny. It's so lovely, so simple."

Don placed his hands on my shoulders. We both looked in the mirror. I was holding the cross against my chest.

"That's right, Julian. Press it against your heart and make a wish."

"Only one wish? My heart is full of wishes."

"Don't be greedy."

I glanced around at Don's massive collection. Our eyes met again in the mirror, and I raised an eyebrow.

He chuckled and muttered, "Yeah, yeah, yeah." The years slipped away, and I could see him perfectly as an ambitious young go-getter fascinated by beautiful things.

"Julian, make your wish, and only one."

I closed my eyes and wished for good health for all my friends and family and . . . and . . . I couldn't resist it. I wished that we raised all of the money we needed and that our show would open and become a huge hit and rescue me from failure. I opened my eyes. I placed the cross back on the marble-topped table.

Don didn't move but said, "Take it."

"What?"

"Take the Angelica Cross."

I was confused. "You mean keep it?"

"For a while. Maybe it will bring you luck."

This man was certainly unpredictable. I wondered if he was setting me up for a mean joke. I gave him a good, hard look and saw that he was dead serious.

"I don't know, Don. It seems funny for me to have something so valuable."

His voice betrayed no sentiment. "Someday you'll want to own beautiful things. Get used to it. Besides, it doesn't need to be placed at auction immediately. When I want it back, you'll hand it over."

"It's just that my apartment . . . I don't have a doorman. The security stinks. I've never been robbed but—isn't this a bit reckless?"

He smiled, but his eyes remained expressionless. "Why do you seem so much older than I? I want you to have the Angelica Cross. Take it." He seemed oddly adamant. I think he became aware of his own strange intensity and made a sudden effort to lighten the mood.

"Take it, Julian, and place it somewhere special where only you can find it." He took the cross from me and stuck it down my pants. I wasn't wearing underwear, and it hurt. Don then added, "And where I can find it." The balance of power was shifting back and forth at such a quickening pace, I was terribly confused. I took the Angelica Cross and shut up.

CHAPTER
25

Milena, are there no chambers of your heart that have not been corrupted
by this insatiable desire for power?

Andreas, *Whores of Lost Atlantis*
Act Two, Scene Two

A friend of a friend of Buster's periodontist named Dom Mucci got in
touch with us and said he could be extremely helpful in our money-raising
project. Joel and I met with him the following day. Mucci owned a very successful greeting card company. He told us that he could put at least thirty
thousand dollars into the show in exchange for us modeling for a line of
witty greeting cards. I had an exciting vision of myself in wonderful costumes staring out of the racks of cards at the stationery shop on my corner.

Mucci clapped his chubby hands together. "Kids, I've got a number of
terrific concepts. This morning I had my layout people run up some
sketches." He reached under his desk and took out a stack of large draw-
ings. One sketch was of a redheaded drag queen, evidently moi, in a doctor's office with her legs up in stirrups. The doctor was pulling out of her
vagina a telephone receiver. The greeting read, "Reach out and touch." The
pièce de résistance was of the redheaded drag queen and an elegant man,
presumably Joel, sitting at dinner. On my plate was an enormous turd, the
message being "I'm sick of your shit." This didn't quite jell with my romantic vision of myself. Of course, my own plays were often scatological and

certainly full of sexual references, but I liked to think there was a kind of crazy romantic finesse to them and an innocence as well. Still, Mucci was promising thirty thousand dollars toward making our dream a reality.

Joel cleared his throat and said, "Dom, this isn't really our style."

"Whaddyamean it's not your style? Funny is funny."

"Dom," Joel said patiently, "what we're trying to achieve with our shows is a kind of nineteenth-century romantic theatrical style, with Julian as our elegant grande dame leading lady." Mucci stared at Joel with perplexed, heavy, black, knitted brows. I had the feeling he didn't know from the nineteenth-century romantic tradition. When it was clear that neither of us would budge on the concept of the cards, Joel was still trying to save the investment. "Dom, we may not be able to come up with some card designs right now, but wouldn't you still like to invest in our show and see it move off-Broadway?"

Mr. Mucci had a disappointed sneer on his mug. I decided to opt for the more emotional approach. "Dom, I adore your cards and have bought a million of them. It's just, at this moment, I wouldn't feel comfortable being in them. Perhaps when all my relatives die . . . But the main thing, Dom, is to help us get our show off the ground. What's happened to us at Golgotha is a kind of a miracle, really. A bunch of misfits who were at their wits' end, put on a play for thirty-six dollars and it becomes this cult phenomenon. And it's all because we love each other and, well, it's about the love of the theatre." I could feel my eyes welling up with tears and my throat tightening. Just thinking about the events of the past year got me gushingly emotional, and I tried to use it for dramatic effect. "You didn't get to where you are today just because you're a canny businessman. You have imagination. You have a vision. Be a part of our show. It really is a kind of fairy tale, and we need you to give us a happy ending." I could feel that Joel was both nauseated by my maudlin appeal and hopeful that I'd succeed.

Dom Mucci stamped out his cigarette and shrugged. "Kids, all I can say is you jack me off and I'll jack you off." We would have to look elsewhere for our fairy godmother.

Of course, I was the plaything to a wealthy man. You might wonder why I didn't ask Don Caspar to invest. Well, I couldn't. For one thing, our relationship was terribly clandestine. I wanted Don to see me perform so he'd think of me as something more than an unusual trinket on his mantel, but I also knew if he connected me to Roxie, it would be disastrous. It seemed best not to complicate things any more than they were. There were awkward moments when Roxie would arrive for rehearsal after work and be steaming about Don Caspar's latest act of cruelty. Little did she know that immediately following their encounter, he'd hopped into a cab and sped over to my den of passion. I felt terribly guilty about it. In one sense, I loved Roxie a lot more than I loved Don Caspar. I don't think I actually loved Don at all. As a masochistic lady in a gangster film would say, "I was in his thrall." Perhaps out of some guilt for my obsessive commitment to my career, I felt a need to lose my identity by being dominated by this charismatic son of a bitch. Whatever neurotic baggage I was toting, I not only couldn't give him up but could deny him nothing.

We decided to put on one more new show and then take a hiatus so Joel could concentrate on raising the cash to move *Whores of Lost Atlantis*. Among Roxie's and my mutual interests was anything to do with the Nazi era. We both thought if show business didn't pan out, perhaps we could move to Europe and become Nazi hunters. For the time being, we could vent some of our anti-Nazi passion through a play. Roxie and I collaborated on a World War II epic entitled *Fighting Girls Against the Blitzkrieg*. Roxie and I played Elsa and Schatzi Van Allen, an American sister act on tour in Europe in the early days of the war. Elsa, played by Roxie, gets abducted by a kinky Nazi baron, and the loyal Schatzi (me) joins the ragtag partisan army of Gypsies to save her sister. Joel was the impotent baron, Guy the stalwart leader of the partisans, Perry the mad lady scientist with a yen to castrate Allied soldiers and turn them into Rhine maidens, and Zoe a kooky Gypsy girl in love with Buster, a rather prissy Hitler youth.

By this time I had all of us typecast tighter than the star roster at Warners. All the members of our company had such vivid personalities that it was a pleasure to create roles for them. Each successive play clarified an outrageous comic persona that made each of them a cult star. People would pat me on the back for my loyalty to the cast, but I was the lucky one. It's true I presented them with each role as a loving gift, a flattering though zany vision of themselves, but they saved me from facing the dreaded blank page. I had only to imagine their faces and voices and I found constant inspiration.

There were occasional rebellions among the contract players. Joel said it was tough on his self-image to be constantly playing impotent emperors and nellie Nazis. It didn't help when a casting director came to the show and told Joel he was "a young Gale Gordon." Not exactly a hot sex image for a young man. Guy felt he was being held back by always playing the romantic lead. He wanted to be a character actor, but he was the only actor in the company remotely suitable as the leading man. It annoyed him that whenever the critic from a certain gay paper reviewed us, he used a running gag to describe Guy's performance. His Andreas in *Whores of Lost Atlantis* was Joel McCrea after Ex-Lax. His Lt. Walter Gammersfelder in *Murder at the Ballet* was Richard Widmark after Ex-Lax. His Geoffrey in *I Married a Fairy Queen* was Leslie Howard after Ex-Lax. And his Commander Corcoran in *Sex Kittens Go to Outer Space* was described as William Shatner after a Fleet enema.

My most difficult player was the sole graduate of our starlet program, Buster. Buster's chief attribute for the stage was his masculine pulchritude, and believe me, it wasn't easy justifying his getting his clothes ripped off in every play. He was stripped nude in Byzantine torture scenes, his clothes blown off in tornadoes or even evaporated by an outer space molecule destroyer. My imagination and his fabulous physique paid off. At the point of the show when invariably Buster's clothes would fall off, the audience would burst into cheers and applause. It was his trademark.

Buster finally cornered me one day on the subject of his "image." "Julian, I don't wanna sound like I'm ungrateful or like I'm trying to muscle in on your playwriting but . . . you know, I been really working hard on my acting. . . . I mean, I know I really stunk in the beginning, but now I get my laughs and I get my applauds the same as the rest of youse. I think you could give me something a little more dramatic to do. I'll really work on it. I just get tired sometimes of being the big lunk with the tits and the hot ass."

For the longest time I couldn't quite figure out who Buster was in the context of our company being a parody studio star roster. Now it occurred to me. Buster was my Marilyn Monroe, the frustrated sex symbol. Tired of being exploited as the "boy with a shape," he longed for dramatic respectability. With his bulging round muscles and curves and golden smooth skin, he really was the male equivalent of a "tomato."

"Another thing," he explained. "I know people in the audience think I'm only in the group because I'm sleeping with Joel."

"Oh, that's not true."

"Julian, I'm not as dumb as I look. I know when people are laughing at me. I mean, it was even in goddam print."

"What are you talking about?"

"What's that magazine they give away free in the bars? *Gay New York*? The old queen who writes the gossip column said she envied Joel's casting futon. How the fuck did she find out about Joel and me?"

"Darling, there are no secrets in show business."

Buster wasn't appeased. "I should eat like a pig and get so fat that no one will ever treat me like a bimbo again. Do you know how many times guys wait around after the show and want to pay me to have sex with them?"

My curiosity perked up. "Really? How much were they willing to pay?"

"Julian, that's not the point."

"Do you think they'd pay more to sleep with the star?"

"Julian, I'm serious."

"Darling, so am I. The diva's down to her last dime." I realized I was being too glib. "Buster, I don't mean to be so flippant. I really think you're going to like your role in the new play."

Buster balked when he read the script for *Fighting Girls Against the Blitzkrieg*. Naturally, Fräulein Helga (Perry) was going to perform her dastardly medical experiment on him. He read the stage directions with dismay. "Fritz is revealed nude on the rack as Helga prepares his castration." When he showed up at the first rehearsal late and sullen, I knew I'd have to do some rewriting.

"Buster darling, I know how you feel. We all want to be taken seriously. It was insensitive of me not to realize that you'd have the same desire. I tell you what, if you do this nude scene, I promise you, I'll write you a big dramatic scene as well." I perused the script of *Fighting Girls Against the Blitzkrieg* and found an opportunity for Buster to chew up the scenery fully clothed. In the final scene in the Nazi laboratory, after Fritz (Buster) is released from his shackles, instead of merely running off with Christina (Zoe), I had him turn on his tormentors and revile them for their exploitation of his youth and beauty. Then to guarantee Buster's nude posterior for at least another six months, I had a stray bullet hit Zoe and had her die in Buster's arms. Did Marilyn in *Bus Stop* have such dramatic opportunities? Buster was thrilled and terrified. I coached him for hours in my apartment, employing every technique I could think of to produce the heightened emotion the scene required. I even resorted to emotional recall, the legendary "method" endorsed by the Actors' Studio.

"Buster darling, to make this moment real, I want you to think of an analogy, a situation where you were in similar circumstances, and I want you to remember exactly how you felt emotionally and physically."

"Like what?"

"Well, surely there was some time in your life when you finally let someone have it after keeping that anger boiled up deep inside you. As far as Christina's death, that may be hard, but did you ever have to nurse anyone when they were very ill?"

Buster gazed out the window and then looked down at his folded hands. "Julian, before I met you, there were these three guys who lived in the apartment below mine. Two of them, Paul and Jimmy, were lovers. The third guy, Steven, was a great artist. The four of us became very close. It was kind of like we were all living in a duplex 'cause we spent so much time in each other's apartments. Over a matter of six months, all three of them came down with AIDS, and I ended up taking care of all of them. None of them had any other family but me. All three of them died in my arms."

When we rehearsed with the rest of the company, Buster skirted through his big dramatic scene, screwing up his lines, cracking up laughing, trying to make Zoe giggle, which was hardly a difficult feat.

Joel whispered to me, "I think we may have to cut the scene. You got carried away with this one."

The show was going to look great. Mamacita was able to borrow most of the costumes from productions of *The Sound of Music* and *The Student Prince*. Mamacita himself was causing us worry. He didn't look at all well. He had lost weight, not a major cause for alarm in an overweight giant. However, he had lost the dynamic glow that made him seem like the perfect genie in an Arabian Nights extravaganza. His skin looked sallow, and he had developed a persistent cough.

All of us suspected the worst and didn't have the nerve to voice it out loud, except Buster. "Youse guys may want to live in a fool's paradise, but I know AIDS and Mamacita has it. I bet you anything he's coming down with pneumonia. Believe me, honey, I know all the signs."

Zoe looked at Buster wide-eyed. "But he says he went to the doctor and they told him he just had a weird strain of the flu."

Buster puffed away at his cigarette. "Darling, he never went to no doctor. He's going through what they call denial."

Except for that one discussion, we all experienced what they call denial. We never again voiced our concerns about Mamacita. He made it easy because other than slowing down to cough, Mamacita was his usual caustic and sweet self. As if to ward off the encroaching end of his immune system, he threw himself into a mad frenzy of work. He not only concocted the costumes for *Fighting Girls Against the Blitzkrieg* but did day work sewing alterations on a Robert De Niro film. He also dredged up the energy to participate in an East Village fashion show at the Pyramid Club, employing our company as runway models. *Details* magazine described his efforts as "Voodoo gods and goddesses gowned by Adrian."

His clothes for *Fighting Girls* were equally surprising, but nothing could compare with the surprise of Buster's opening night performance. Buster as Fritz broke from his shackles in the Nazi lab and turned on Joel with such fury, I feared Joel would blank and resort to his usual "I hate you, I could kill you, you nut" improvisation. Usually Buster bounced through our shows with the cool bravado of Merman at her peak. He didn't know enough to be nervous. That night I saw sweat breaking out on his brow and his lips trembling. His line readings, which always had an endearingly amateurish singsong, were terse and shockingly authentic. I forgot I was acting in the scene and stood there watching. Perry played the mad lesbian scientist, Fräulein Helga, who was shot and thought dead. With her dying breath she crawled like a snake, reached for the gun, and shot Christina (Zoe). This is where Buster really devastated us. He cradled Zoe in his arms and spoke my campy movie parody lines with such tenderness and true grief, the play was transformed into something quite wonderful. I could see in my peripheral vision Mamacita, Roxie, and Guy watching from the wings. Tears were actually streaming down Buster's cheeks as he held Zoe tightly to his chest. When the performance was over, we swarmed around Buster, praising his acting as if he were the new Olivier. He was thrilled yet at a loss to explain what had happened. His face deathly pale, he whispered to me, "Don't expect it ever to be that way again."

When Roxie and I got out of drag, we searched for Sam. He had attended the show and was going to give me his signed partnership papers for his investment in *Whores of Lost Atlantis* along with his check. Despite the cold weather, we found him outside the club, leaning against a lamppost. Roxie kissed him on the lips and took his arm.

She said, "Could you believe Buster's performance at the end of the play? Where the hell did that come from?"

I answered, "My dear, Buster has been a private student under my tutelage these past five months. His performance was merely a promise fulfilled."

We gabbed and camped until we realized Sam hadn't said a word. He pulled his arm away from Roxie and said, "Children, it's a very late night. I think I've got to go."

Roxie studied his face. "Darling, what's wrong?"

"You have no idea?"

"Sam, did I say something that offended you?" He looked at her chillingly. He repeated, "You have no idea." He looked at me. "Neither of you has any idea."

He was right. I didn't have a clue. I said, "Sam, I guess we have been rattling on a bit. It's our narcissistic syndrome."

"Is that what it is?" He shook his head. "I . . . I don't think I can even discuss this." He started to leave. Roxie ran after him. I wasn't sure whether I should leave them alone or join them. Since he'd included me in his rebuff, I reluctantly walked down the street toward them. Roxie was saying, "Sam, would ja please . . . Sam, don't turn your back on me. Tell me what's going on here."

After a pause, Sam turned around to face us, his eyes red with tears: "I'd like you both to tell me what this play was about."

Roxie looked at me, the playwright, to explain.

"It's a spoof of anti-Nazi war movies of the forties." As I spoke the word "Nazi," it stuck in my throat.

Sam hissed at us. "For God's sake, I'm a survivor!" The anger and hurt in his voice felt like a stinging slap across both of our faces. Roxie's chin trembled. She reached out to touch Sam's arm. "Darling . . ."

Sam looked around wildly before turning on us in fury. "You invite me here, to see this? You thought I would find this funny? What, are you crazy people?"

I was overwhelmed with the sinking nausea of my own insensitivity. As Roxie's beau, we expected him to attend every new play. How could we have been so unbelievably stupid not to connect the play to his past? I fumbled around for some lame excuse for our blunder.

"Sam, you're right. We were so self-absorbed. We—"

Sam cut me off. "Julian, don't say anything. It's easy now to come up with something to soothe the old man's feelings. I don't want to hear it." His eyes were filled with such bitterness. No one had ever looked at me before with contempt. He continued his diatribe. "No, I sat there and watched your friends stomping around in S.S. uniforms and I listened to that awful audience hooting and hollering at the atrocities of these monsters. Can't you kids understand? My entire family is dead."

People were drifting away from Golgotha and passed us by wondering why this cuddly-looking older man was glowering with rage. The charge of insensitivity tore through me like a bullet. Was my obsession with my talents and goals distorting all of my relationships? If Roxie, standing ashen beside me, only knew that I was sleeping with her worst enemy just to gratify some warped self-image. It was all too complicated. I hated thinking about these things. I wanted the world to be like those perfect moments onstage when I was in control of the scene and everyone was spouting my dialogue and I could bask in the affection of an audience who found me absolutely adorable. I didn't know what to say to Sam. He had been so kind to us, and it was awful seeing him look wounded and bitter. I fumbled around like a dog who's been swatted for peeing on the rug.

"Sam, we should have warned you. We weren't thinking. Please believe me. My intention was to satirize the movies that I love, not to make light of the Holocaust."

Sam shook his head. "No, no, I cannot accept that. You are trivializing an event of such evil. I . . . I really can't discuss this."

Roxie pulled her coat up around her. "Sam, Julian is apologizing. We are both apologetic. We were wrong. We were insensitive. We were oblivious. Can we get over this?"

Sam fixed her with a withering stare. "No, I cannot get over this. There is something innately wrong with people who can make fun of something so horrible." His eyes were red with tears. "I try so hard to be encouraging to you kids. I was so enthusiastic. I thought we were in sympathy about your show, everything. But I don't know you at all. Maybe it's your generation to make fun of everything. Nothing is sacred. I'm too old for this." He turned away from us.

Roxie wasn't about to let him go. "Sam, you're full of shit." I was shocked. I was completely on Sam's side and had already assumed full guilt for everything and wished I'd never conceived of the hateful play. Roxie, however, was going after a different angle. "Sam, that is such an easy accusation. If we ever have any problem, you say it's generational. I am not representative of my generation. I am a unique individual. And so are you."

He led her into a doorway, and I followed. "Roxie, you listen to this and listen well. Anyone who survived what I survived is more than an individual. I do represent something bigger. I stand for my family, for everyone I loved."

Roxie countered with "Sam, you cannot define yourself this way forever. Where do I fit in?"

"I . . . I . . . I guess you just don't fit in."

Two of the Young Julians walked by and not realizing the seriousness of the scene, began exclaiming how much they loved the show. "Oh, Julian, that was hysterical when the Nazis tried to turn you into a lampshade."

Sam interrupted them. "You will excuse me. I didn't mean to ruin your opening night." He took an envelope out of his pocket and threw it at me.

"Julian, here's my investment in your show. Take it, do well." He walked away from us.

Roxie called after him, "Sam, you're not going to say good-bye to me?"

"No, Roxie, I'm not saying good-bye. I'm not saying anything."

"I'll call you tomorrow."

"Don't call me." He continued to walk up Ninth Street. The stoop of his shoulders seen from the back made him appear very old and worn out. One of the Young Julians tried to say something to Roxie, but whether she heard him or not, she ran back into the club.

Alan, the tallest of the Young Julians, grimaced, and said, "What was that about? A lovers' spat?"

"We hurt a very dear friend of ours, I feel awful."

"You look like your whole world has collapsed. Come on. It's your opening night. Cheer up!" Alan brightened. "Hey, we've got someone for you to meet. He saw the show tonight, and he's dying to meet you."

"Who?"

"Tolan Savage." Tolan Savage was a very famous fashion designer, a household name for three decades. Most fashion designers aren't familiar faces to the general public, but Savage marketed himself as much as his dresses. It turned out his photographs weren't as retouched as I'd thought. It was his face that was retouched. Though he was only in his fifties, his skin was pulled as tight as Saran Wrap over a refrigerated salad. His eyes still were lined with magenta-colored scars from a recent eye lift. However, it was a friendly face, full of energy and determined to stay contemporary. He shook my hand vigorously. "You were terrific! So accurate to those old star ladies, and believe me, I know all the mannerisms. I've dressed most of the old girls that are still alive and kicking." He spoke with a slight New England accent and grinned so intensely, I feared for his stitches. He stepped back. "Let me get a good look at you. My God! I never would have recognized you out of drag. Never! You're a very good-looking young man."

"Thank you. Most people assume that out of drag, I must resemble a more wizened Clifton Webb."

"The same here, dear heart. The mere words 'fashion designer' conjure forth images of some effete creature nipped and tucked to oblivion." He asked me what we were doing next, so I told him that we were raising money to move Whores of Lost Atlantis. I didn't want him to think I was putting the screws on him, but in truth, that was what was occupying my mind these days. I'd have been lying if I didn't admit I hoped he'd snap up the bait and offer to write a check on the spot for a hundred grand.

Instead I got a heartfelt "Good luck, Julian." I was about to bid my adieus when Tolan had a very theatrical brainstorm. "Julian, you're looking for investors. I know exactly what you should do. I've been invited Monday night to a dinner party that will be full of moneyed old dowagers. Come be my date and charm them all into emptying out their pocketbooks. If nothing else, you'll get plenty of fodder for a drawing-room comedy."

With Sam's check burning in my palm, I felt like a heartless courtesan. Catching my second wind, I knew I had to go to that dinner party. There was still a lot of money to be raised for Whores of Lost Atlantis, and that was all that mattered from now on. Self-absorbed yet unsure who that self was, I had to forge straight ahead and line up those investors.

CHAPTER 26

Faithful Eunuch, I gaze at my visage in the glass and cannot fathom age ever withering such divine perfection. Bring me my moisturizer, and be quick about it.

Milena, *Whores of Lost Atlantis*
Act Two, Scene Two

I recognized the address where the dinner party was being held as one of the legendary prewar apartment buildings on the Upper East Side. There was a rumor that years before they'd even declined Jacqueline Kennedy's co-op application.

That afternoon, Tolan Savage's secretary had called to explain that Tolan would have to meet me there. I dreaded arriving before he did and not knowing a soul, so I timed my arrival precisely fifteen minutes late. The elevator opened on the ninth floor, revealing only one door. I rang the bell, and I expected to be greeted by a butler. Instead, it was our host, Sims Harley, a robust, white-haired man in his early seventies. His jovial face was decorated with red and purple gin blossoms that foreshadowed a long cocktail hour.

"Aha, you're Julian, Tolan's young friend."

I wondered if he assumed I was sleeping with Tolan. Why not? I would have assumed so. Sims put his drink down on a side table and helped me off with my coat.

"I have bad news, Julian. Tolan rang and said he's been so detained by business that he'll be unable to join us. He tried to ring you, but you'd already left. I'm afraid you'll have to brave the lion's den solo."

I wasn't thrilled, but I was game. He led me into the living room. It was an enormous apartment, as big as Howard Fuller's but in genuinely elegant taste. Sims's money didn't stem from the vulgar royalties of a Broadway show. His old money was most likely built on wheeling and dealing done aboard the *Mayflower*. Seated among the antiques were four human antiques, all men and all on the far side of seventy.

Sims placed a shaky hand on my shoulder to introduce me to the coven. "This is Julian Young, Tolan's friend. Julian is an actor and a playwright." He moved unsteadily toward the fireplace. "Julian, we are all very interested in the theatre. You must tell us what it's like working in the theatre today."

An emaciated, lizardlike creature wearing an ascot and a Brillo pad on his head that was passing as a toupee peered at me and said to Sims, "Tell me his name?"

"Cyril, this is Julian Young."

Cyril pursed his wrinkled lips. "Are you appearing in anything *à ce moment*?"

I sat down on the sofa beside him. "Yes, I perform regularly with my theatre company."

"A theatre company? Do you perform the classics?"

"No. I write plays for the company. We're rather well-known downtown. That's how I met Tolan. He saw one of our shows."

A scary looking old geezer named Norton, whose face seemed to be paralyzed on one side, muttered, "Would we have heard of one of your plays?"

Suddenly, I was the mystery guest on *What's My Line*. "Hmmmm. You might have. Our most successful piece has kind of a flashy title. It's called *Whores of Lost Atlantis*." The four old men laughed into their martinis.

"Oh my, that certainly *is* a title."

"An all-male cast, I presume."

"Not one to bring Mother to."

I was relieved when the spotlight was off me and the conversation centered on maintaining residences in the south of France and collecting botanical prints. The cocktail hour dragged on mercilessly. I was so ravenous, I didn't dare drink, or I would have ended up nude on the piano singing "Bye, bye, Blackbird." Cyril's toupee was beginning to resemble a slice of lasagna.

At long last we moved into the formal dining room. Dinner conversation revolved largely around the collecting of rare first editions. I didn't appreciate it when Cyril remarked he'd heard that Tolan Savage had acquired a rare Trollope and the whole party looked at me and laughed.

A Buddha-like older gentleman named Hilly asked the group, "Has any of you received a telephone call from Donald DeBrier?"

Our host said disdainfully, "Indeed I have, and I've instructed Marie not to take any more of his calls."

Norton asked, "Is this the young man who's writing the biography of poor Max?"

Hilly said, "That is the one. He phoned me at eight-thirty in the morning to ask me the most tasteless, vulgar questions regarding Max's sex life. I hung right up on him."

The cadaverous Cyril fluffed up his ascot and added, "I've heard he wants to interrogate *me*. Let him try. I think it's disgusting."

My ears perked up. This was certainly more intriguing than the question of where one can find a sympathetic urologist on the Côte d'Azur. I turned to a rather thoughtful gentleman named Ellis seated beside me and whispered, "Ellis, who is this Max that they're talking about?"

"The director, Max Milton. He directed the films—"

"Of course I know who Max Milton is. I could give you a list of every film he ever made."

"It hadn't occurred to me, but I suppose all of us were friends with him at one time or another."

I couldn't wait to get back to Perry and Roxie with this one. Max Milton was one of the greatest directors in Hollywood history and very discreet about his homosexuality. He had died only six months before, and already the biographers were swarming about like vultures.

Sims poured himself some more wine and said, "This DeBrier character isn't the only one exhuming Max's secrets. Another so-called film historian wrote requesting an interview. And once again, all he wanted from me was gossip about Max's sex life. It's simply appalling."

Ellis next to me looked philosophical. "I remember Max telling me that no matter how discreet he was, in the end, it would all come out. He was quite resigned to it."

Hilly snorted. "Well, I'm not. It's nobody's business that Max enjoyed sex with hustlers." The alcohol was rapidly loosening the tongues of these old vipers, and I wouldn't have budged from my seat if Jack the Ripper had joined us for coffee. Any discussion of who was gay in Hollywood's golden age leaves me positively wet-lipped with glee.

Cyril purposefully put down his knife and fork. "I suppose they are all dying for us to spill the beans about Max's relationship with the Italian creature."

A pall fell over the table. Sims said quietly, "I don't think Max ever recovered from that one."

Ellis nodded. "He was spectacularly beautiful."

Cyril added, "And lethal."

Hilly joined in. "You know, I was the one who found Max and untied him in his own basement after the Italian creature ransacked the place. Max was totally humiliated. And he had been so generous to the boy, foolishly generous. I wonder whatever happened to him."

Sims shrugged. "Most likely died young. Don't they usually?"

Norton looked thoughtful. "I seem to recall a while back, someone telling me they saw Andriolo and that he was still remarkably handsome and had become this terribly successful entrepreneur."

Cyril wiped his lips. "The whole episode was so distasteful, I've blocked out the hustler's first name."

Hilly reminded him. "Tony, naturally."

Tony Andriolo—that was the name Don Caspar gave Zoe at my apartment! What a funny coincidence, I thought. It couldn't be the same person. I'd have to tell Don. He'd get a kick out of it.

Ellis then remembered, "I think I did hear he'd done well. I believe he married. Some blue-blooded gal with big connections." He shuddered. "I must say, he scared the hell out of me the moment Max introduced him."

I knew so little about Don's present life and nothing about his past. It had to be all a silly coincidence. The cruel young hustler they described couldn't possible have transformed himself into my wealthy, patrician Don Caspar. For the first time in at least an hour, I spoke up. "When did this all happen?"

The gentlemen looked at one another. Sims replied, "Early sixties. Perhaps they met in fifty-six. It was over I'm sure by fifty-nine."

I did some quick math. Twenty-five years, roughly. Don was in his early fifties. He would have been in the prime of studhood in that period. I wondered if they could possibly be the same person. . . . If it were true, what would it matter? It disturbed me that the young man they continued to describe was so heartless, almost evil. Was Don capable of such cruelty? There was an element of sadistic role playing in our sexual relationship, but wasn't that just playacting? I wished they'd all shut up and finish their crème brûlée. The whole notion of Don and the Italian creature being the same person was ridiculous, and I was resolved not to give it another thought.

Hilly leaned in conspiratorially. "Did I ever tell any of you, that while Max was keeping Andriolo, I was his houseguest. One night, I was lying in bed. You remember, the bed Ethel Barrymore used to sleep in, when the Italian creature slithered into my room. Max had evidently informed him of the contents of my stock portfolio, and the next thing I knew, the monster unzipped his pants and hauled out the biggest schlong I'd ever seen outside of Man o' War."

Suddenly, I wasn't so interested in my crème brûlée.

By the time we had finished dinner and after-dinner drinks, it was well past midnight. As the group of us were leaving Sims's building, I hesitated for a moment while I decided which was the nearest subway. Ellis noticed my confusion and offered, "I live on Washington Square. If you're going downtown, I'd be glad to share a cab with you."

I helped him into the taxi. Ellis Farrell was a well-proportioned, fairly tall man, but he moved slowly, as if his bones were brittle. He hadn't spoken much at dinner. He had a detached quality of observing and being amused by his eccentric friends which I found attractive. He was quite old, probably in his eighties. Studying his face in the cab, I could see that he had been handsome in his youth. "Have you all known each other forever?" I asked.

"Forever is too short. Did you find the clan amusing?"

"I have to admit, that dish on Max Milton was pretty fascinating. But rather depressing. Didn't he ever have a real love relationship? Was it always just bought sex with rough trade?"

"Max didn't define himself by his homosexuality. Most of us of our generation don't. It's a part of our lives, but our work and our friends come first. I think you young people make too much fuss about it, all that marching about and sign carrying. Can't they just sleep with who they like, close the door, and shut up about it?"

"Ellis . . . this Tony Andriolo who was so horrible to Max Milton . . . was he really so horrible? I mean, sometimes that sort of cruelty is part of a boy's allure to an older gentleman. Do you think perhaps Max sought that kind of behavior from Tony?"

Ellis reflected on my suggestion. "I have observed that some of the most successful of the 'demimonde' provide the least amount of sex. It's the promise of sex that reaps all the rewards, and often the buyer does enjoy the pursuit more than the act itself. There may have been some of that with Max. He certainly liked a certain kind of macho type."

"But Tony . . . what about Tony?" I worried that my interest in this hustler from the fifties would reveal my secret.

"It was a very long time ago, and one likes to forget that sort of unpleasantness. I do recall he had great charm and a sort of innate elegance. He was presentable, but then out of the blue, he'd reveal an ugly, incredibly vulgar streak. He was reckless. He enjoyed being found out. He seemed genuinely to take pleasure in the moment his treachery was discovered. That was the quality in him that most frightened me." Ellis smiled. "Are you thinking of writing a play about a hustler?"

I thought for a moment. I was tempted to confide in Ellis that I suspected my lover was the mature Tony Andriolo. Would he warn me to end it at once? I decided not to pursue it. "Oh, Ellis, I've always been fascinated by whores. Old whores, young whores, rich whores, poor whores."

The cab was nearly at the end of Fifth Avenue. Ellis said, "I realize it's late, but would you like to come up for a nightcap? My intentions are entirely honorable." I was very intrigued by Ellis. He was so dignified and formal, yet his eyes had a youthful glitter. I was curious to know more about him.

He owned the second floor of a brownstone. It was a handsome, masculine apartment full of wood paneling and Oriental rugs. Henry Higgins would have felt at home here. Ellis poured us both some brandy, and we settled in his sitting room. Over the mantel I was startled to see a famous portrait of Sarah Bernhardt.

"Oh, Ellis, tell me that is indeed the original. I've seen it reproduced in so many Bernhardt biographies."

Ellis gazed at it proudly. "It's the original Clairin. I acquired it about twenty years ago. You have an interest in Sarah?"

I sputtered, "Do I have an interest? It's an obsession! I read everything I can on her. My career—I mean, my life is an attempt to be her!"

He smiled and sipped his brandy. "Well, with your slender frame and curly hair, you look a bit like the young Sarah in one of her trouser roles."

"Do you think so? I've always felt I did."

"I've been fascinated by Bernhardt all my life. I'm something of a collector."

"Please show me whatever you have."

He led me into his den and pulled out of the bookshelf scrapbooks full of original signed photographs of Bernhardt dated from 1886 to her death in 1923. He had letters written to her son, Maurice, and to her last leading man and lover, Lou Tellegen. He had box office receipts, ticket stubs, programs, and her own prompt script for *Gismonda*.

In his bedroom was a glass, velvet-lined display case. Inside were a pair of gauntlets from *L'Aiglon* and a jeweled headdress that she wore as Cleopatra. All this memorabilia made her seem so real and tangible. She was no longer a forbidding icon staring out from a crumbling page but a small, living woman battling to keep a legendary career alive.

We didn't speak. I couldn't. I was breathing in the musty glamour of these theatrical artifacts. I stood transfixed before the crown of Cleopatra.

I was awakened from my reverie when Ellis opened the glass case, lifted the headdress, and gently placed it on my head. The weight of the piece and the magic of the moment nearly made me swoon. I looked at my reflection in the mirror. The headdress was an elaborate metallic weave of Egyptian symbols and Art Nouveau spires encrusted with topazes, marcasites, and barbaric stage jewels. The dim light in Ellis's bedroom created deep shadows around my eyes and gave me the look of someone in a nineteenth-century photograph by Nadar.

I could see Ellis was getting a kick out of watching me admire myself in the mirror. Then a strange thing happened. I burst into tears. I sat down on his large four-poster bed and shook with sobs. I couldn't remember when I'd last cried with such abandon. I'm really not prone to easy tears. Ellis sat down on the bed next to me, and I could feel that he was hesitant to touch me. Then he simply gave in and put his arms around me in the most lovely grandfatherly way. I luxuriated in burying my face in his mossy green cashmere sweater. Ellis was wise enough not to say a word. If he had asked me what was wrong, I couldn't have told him. I didn't have a clue.

My crying jag subsided, and we returned Madame Sarah's headdress to its resting place. As Ellis placed the lid back on the display case, he asked me exactly what kind of play *Whores of Lost Atlantis* was. I explained it was influenced by the melodramas Victorien Sardou wrote for Bernhardt but crossed with elements from *I Love Lucy*. In a semihysterical mood I said, "Ellis, would you like to see *Whores of Lost Atlantis*?"

"I'd love to, but I don't imagine myself journeying to Avenue D."

"Well, you won't have to. I could act out the whole thing for you here."

"Here in the bedroom?"

"Yeah, sure. You sit on that settee, and, well, I'll just use the rest of the room as my stage."

Ellis took his brandy snifter and leaned back on the settee. Although we played *Whores of Lost Atlantis* on an empty stage, I decided to use the heavy antique furniture in the bedroom to my advantage. Indeed, in the palace scenes, I felt as if I were acting in the movie version of the play. I sat imperiously in his large wing chair as if it were a throne. I flung myself across his bed in lusty abandon in the boudoir love scene. It was past one in the morning, but I was having a wild time. I acted out all the roles, imitating Roxie, Joel, Perry, and the others. I described the costumes, I declaimed, I laughed maniacally, I wept bitter tears, I pleaded for my life, rolled on the floor in agony, and pounded the rug in fury. I was in the grip of dramatic inspiration, totally over the top and moving toward hysteria.

Ellis watched with the rapt attention of a child. He laughed at my jokes, gasped at the most outrageous lines, and broke into applause at several points. At the end of the play, after Roxie and my characters escaped to our lifeboat, I transformed back into Joel's character, the emperor, and lay on Ellis's Oriental rug dead with my eyes open as the curtain fell. With effort, Ellis rose to his feet and gave me a standing ovation. I was coming down from my manic high and could barely lift myself off the rug. Ellis helped me to my feet, and after a few steps I collapsed in the armchair.

Ellis sat back on the settee and pronounced, "Julian, it's going to be a hit. I just know it's going to be a hit. I've never seen anything before like it. Can the others in the play perform as well as you?"

"Oh yeah, they're terrific. Roxie's a scream."

"Julian, I'm so touched that you would perform the entire play for me. I'm really terribly honored. I don't think I've ever had an experience like this in eighty-three years. Of course I haven't. How could I?" He asked about our plans for the show, and I explained we were in the process of raising the money to move it for a commercial run. I had to make something very clear.

"Ellis, you must believe me that I didn't do this performance for you tonight as some kind of backer's audition. It was the magic of the moment and because I felt as if you and I were connected through our love of Sarah Bernhardt and because I like you. It would ruin the whole moment if you thought I was trying to sell you something."

"No, no, no. I never thought that for a minute. But still, if I was interested in investing, could you send me a prospectus?"

"Sure! I . . . I could get it to you today."

He rose gingerly from the settee. "It's time we sent you home to bed." I put on my coat, and he led me to the door. I kissed him on the cheek.

"Julian, you've made me feel very special tonight. Thank you."

I left the apartment and practically skipped down the steps, feeling as though I were being led by magic hands. It had begun to snow, and the Village streets were momentarily transformed into a romantic Victorian valentine. I felt so ethereal, I was convinced my feet were leaving no imprint in the sugary snow. I was the one who felt special tonight, as if the world were full of spectacular possibilities that I merely had to sift through and choose.

Joel sent Ellis a prospectus that afternoon. I honestly didn't think Ellis would go through with it once the emotion of our encounter had passed. Sure enough, though, a few days later, his partnership papers returned signed and with them a check for nine thousand dollars. I stared at his spidery signature on the document. I was thrilled that we were that much closer to our goal but also because his signature symbolized that I was bound to a lovely old man, not only financially but affectionately.

CHAPTER 27

You tell me Ultima has the loyalty of the Royal Court. Well, I have the
love of the Army. In their hearts they know I have always been a good
soldier.

Milena, *Whores of Lost Atlantis*
Act Two, Scene Two

We should have kept to our word and taken a break after *Fighting Girls
Against the Blitzkrieg*, but Rupert was fixed on the idea that we do a Christmas
holiday extravaganza at Golgotha. After five months of turning out play
after play, we were exhausted, ill-tempered, and unfunny. The less said
about our production of *Heidi* the better. The *New York Native*'s review hit the
nail on the head when their critic wrote, "Mr. Young's performance in the
title role bore a disturbing and inappropriate resemblance to Martha in *Virginia Woolf*."

Our backstage life wasn't any more upbeat. Roxie was desperately trying
to convince us that she wasn't remotely upset by her breakup with Sam
Fleishman. At one point I innocently asked her, "Roxie, have you heard
from Sam?"

"Sam who?" She feigned ignorance, then proceeded in her most vora-
cious manner, "Oh, you mean Sam, the man I was supposed to marry, who
bought me a Rolex watch and a sapphire ring and told me I was the greatest
thing that ever happened to him in fifty-six years of living. The same man
who now refuses to take my phone calls or answer my letters; the third of

which he finally responded to by sending me a manila envelope full of clippings from the Holocaust survivors' reunion in Israel and accompanied by a note stating simply, 'I survived Auschwitz, I can survive Roxie Flood!' " Her voice incapable of rising to an even higher pitch, she burst into tears and fled the rehearsal room.

On a further update from the romantic front, Joel Finley and Buster Campbell broke up during the run of Heidi. The details are difficult to provide since both parties were secretive about the union from the start, but this is what I've pieced together. Joel, a serious opera buff, took Buster to Boston to see a controversial homoerotic production of Puccini's The Girl of the Golden West. Despite the discussion Joel and I had about the rather operatic elements in their relationship, Joel refused to believe that Buster's drinking constituted a real problem. How could he? Joel was a three-martini-a-day man himself. Joel said the cocktail hour was a WASP tradition stemming back to the signers of the Magna Charta.

On this Boston jaunt, Buster began drinking from the moment they got off Amtrak. By the end of dinner, he was stinko and braying, "Joel, you are so fucking perfect. It makes me sick. Why are you always so fucking happy?" When they returned to their hotel room, he passed out on the bed and couldn't even be revived to see the performance. The empty theatre seat next to Joel finally convinced him Buster was a true alcoholic. He confronted Buster with the problem and told him if he didn't get counseling or go to A.A., they were finished. Buster decided to end the romance.

When they returned to New York, Joel confided in me. "I'll always be in love with him, but I can't destroy myself. What am I going to do? He's just so goddam cute." I felt for Joel. Buster was the only one who could release the child in Joel. Buster's antic silliness allowed Joel to occasionally drop his fatherly, executive manner.

Buster also confided in me. "I love Joel and like I respect him so much. Where would we be without him, you know? But I got real tired of him lecturing at me and trying to play older and wiser 'cause, you know, he's like maybe two years older than me, if that."

I asked him about his drinking.

"Yeah, I drink a lot. So do a lot of people, so do my parents. You're not gonna get me going to one of those boring groups with all those creeps saying, 'My name is Helen Shit and I'm an alcoholic.' Honey, I don't identify with that drama at all."

Joel refused to allow their breakup to color our backstage life, but Buster gave Joel the silent treatment. Only when Joel would be attentive to some pretty young fellow would Buster turn on the charm and flirt with Joel like a muscle-bound minx.

Silence also played a part in my ongoing saga with Camille. We had never discussed the fizzing out of our courtship. Whether it was a coming to terms with her disappointment with me or the end of her painful nicotine withdrawal, Camille was back to her original sweet nature. No longer was she referred to by the company as Caligulette. We didn't socialize outside the theatre, but we could be alone together without the presence of a Pinkerton guard. The purest essence of our friendship was when we'd be in the passionate throes of creating a wig for me. I'd be seated in front of a mirror with Camille bustling around me, snapping gum instead of sucking on a cigarette. Her little ring-covered hands would be molding the red Dynel curls into shape and then spraying them rock hard with lacquer. We were forever debating whether or not she should sacrifice her historically accurate period hairstyles to suit my sometimes bizarre demands for surface cosmetic beauty. Camille thought most of my wigs, whether eighteenth century or 1940s, wound up resembling Zsa Zsa Gabor on *The Red Skelton Show* circa 1965. With Camille's hands full of red synthetic hair and me tossing out suggestions, we were right back to the easy high spirits of the summer. The ghost of our child was as distant as some nearly forgotten performance.

The closing of *Heidi* was a night to remember. Despite its artistic failure, our fans gave us a rousing farewell. I mingled with the audience after the show, still wearing my pinafore and braided wig. In the crowd I saw a strangely familiar face. I couldn't place him right away. My first impression was that he was someone I'd slept with years before. In truth, it *was* someone I'd shared a bedroom with for years—my older brother! I hadn't seen John since he left for New Zealand twelve years before. "John, is that you?" I was dumbstruck.

He advanced toward me slowly. His smiling face became clearer, as if the camera were moving in for a close-up. "Yep, it's me." The situation seemed so bizarre. I could imagine my brother nearly anyplace else in the world—in the rain forest, in an igloo, in a cannibal's stew pot—but not in Golgotha. Was he truly standing before me? Was he a hologram? Like automatons, we stiffly embraced; it seemed the thing to do. During the five seconds of our hug, I felt a quick jolt of passing emotion. This man in my arms was my closest blood relative. We parted.

John eyed me up and down. He was at a loss for words. "You—"

If I'd had my way, I wouldn't have planned this reunion with me garbed in a Swiss Miss costume and wooden clogs. I felt totally inarticulate. "It's . . . it's a career." I tried to collect myself. "John, what . . . what are you doing here? I mean, in New York. How did you find me?"

"We're on our way to Europe. My wife's sister lives in Paris. We've just stopped in New York to sort of . . . I don't know, refuel. This guy I went to college with . . . you wouldn't know him, he said he'd been reading about this Julian Young who does these weird shows. He wondered if there was some relation. Figure out the rest." He smiled and looked around Golgotha, which currently evoked a Christmas crèche decorated by Edvard Munch. John commented, "It is definitely weird."

I was proud that I didn't comment on his comment. "John, did you bring your family?" I asked politely.

"Yeah, I did. Where are they? They were right here," he said, and turned away to find them.

He backed up, and I was able to absorb the physical changes in my brother. He had lost all traces of boyishness. He'd gained weight, and his face had filled out so that it had a completely different shape. He had kept all of his hair and was attractive in a young-daddyish kind of way. I still was feeling a sense of dislocation. Was this really my brother, and was he really in a performance space in the East Village?

So often in my life, situations will remind me of a movie genre, and I find myself adapting my behavior to be true to those films. This was a strange variant of that phenomenon. I felt as if I were in a TV-movie biography of my life. I was playing Julian Young, in the same way Sophia Loren and Shirley MacLaine played themselves on TV. I was acting in some screenwriter's conception of a possible reunion with my brother, and I was now shooting the scene with a likable actor who bore a slight resemblance to John. I was curious to see the actress playing his wife.

I dug my fingers into my palm. This was not a TV movie. This was my life, and I really was about to meet my sister-in-law for the first time. How strange. My aunt and I had only seen one set of photos of her, taken at their wedding in Waikiki nearly a decade before. A woman pushed her way through the throng, laughing with a slight edge of hysteria.

"Here we are," John said, and placed his arm around her. "Helene, this is my brother, Julian."

Helene had a wonderful smile, with lots of big, white teeth and full, pink lips slathered with shiny lip gloss. She was of average height but had the flamboyant quality of a country-western star. I even had the suspicion her mass of crimped blond curls may have been synthetic.

My brother's wife looked like a drag queen! With her ear-to-ear smile, she burbled, "Julian, you were so great. And beautiful. You really look like this photo John has of your mom."

That phrase "your mom" added to the feeling that I was in the TV movie of my life. My mother died when I was seven, so I remember her either as Mommy or in the more objectified version "my mother." I never had a mom.

"Yeah, I look a lot like my mother. And you, Helene, you're so different from what I expected. I'm not sure what I expected—"

Helene lowered her eyelids in a very camp way and drawled, "A house-wife from New Zealand. I should look like Helen Reddy. No, honey. It doesn't work that way." Her female impersonator insouciance was making me giddy. She continued. "Julian, you and I have some major things in common." She paused for dramatic effect. "An obsession with eye makeup. What brand of eyeshadow do you use? It really pops out."

"Christian Dior. I've got a friend who runs the counter at Bloomingdale's who swipes it for me."

Helene began pressing me for details regarding specific names of colors and advice on eye makeup removers. I couldn't believe I was discussing cosmetics with my brother's wife. She was cute, trying to break the ice. I liked her. I glanced over at my brother, who looked a bit uncomfortable—but then he always did. He gave the impression of being someone who woke up in another man's body and was trying to make a go of it. "Relaxed" is not a word I'd use to describe him.

I said, "Helene, I think John's feeling a little left out."

Helene put her arm with its jangly, multicolored bracelets around John's waist. She uttered very simply, "My baby always feels a little left out."

Those words made such an impact on me. She understood him far better than I ever could. In that one moment, I could see their entire marriage. What a marvelous cushion she must be for him in a baffling world. She was sort of vulgar, but, boy, was she smart.

Helene had a sudden panicked expression on her face. "Where's Mara? Where's my daughter?"

We all spun around. Standing by the bar talking to Buster was a little girl with long brown braids. She caught us looking for her and ran toward us, followed by Buster, still in his lederhosen as Goat Peter. John placed his hands on her shoulders.

"This is my daughter, Mara. Meet your Uncle Julian."

She was very small and thin, with reddish brown hair separated into two long braids that reached her waist. She wasn't very pretty. She had inherited her mother's wide mouth and my brother's squinty eyes. However, I could see immediately that her eyes weren't evasive and frightened but rather direct and inquisitive. She looked up at me as if she were trying to penetrate my masklike makeup. "You were so neat. I believed every second. It was so cool."

I had to laugh. "I didn't think kids spoke that way in New Zealand."

John held her close to him. "We live in an area with a lot of Americans."

Mara never removed her eyes from my face. "I'm nine years old. How old were you supposed to be as Heidi?"

"Oh, I don't know. Maybe twelve. It doesn't really matter, does it?"

"No. But sometimes you were a little girl and sometimes you were almost like an old lady and sometimes you were a boy. It was so funny." My nine-year-old niece then launched into a frenzied monologue analyzing the play-within-a-play conceit of the Imitation of Life Theatre. She was not an obnoxious, know-it-all child. She was bright. She knew exactly what we had in mind and had far more perception than most of our deliriously campy audience. I was impressed.

Buster looked dumbfounded. When Mara took a breather from her thesis, I introduced Buster to John and Helene. For all his braying sexual swagger, Buster could be terribly shy. He smiled and nodded and said not a word.

I was feeling a little wobbly, so I appreciated just having him near. I asked John, "Will you be calling Aunt Jen? She'd love to hear from you."

"We leave tomorrow. It's going to be crazy, but I'll try."

I knew he wouldn't. That much of the past he wasn't ready to embrace. Helene's uncharacteristic silence indicated that they'd been through this subject. John wanted to ask me something but seemed unsure how to phrase it.

"So, Julian, do you, um . . . can you earn a living doing this?"

Helene slapped him gently on the wrist. "What kind of question is that?"

I was surprised that it didn't bother me. "Pretty soon I'll be able to. I get by all right. And you? I guess you do fine, huh?"

Helene answered for him. "John got promoted by his company. We've just moved into a new house. Don't I sound hideous? The point is, Julian, we have a guest room at long last. Someday you'll come visit us."

I laughed. "Helene, if I could fly to New Zealand for a long weekend, I'd be there."

John wasn't paying attention to us. He was looking down and straightening his daughter's braids. Helene and Mara were both chattering at the same time. I pretended to listen, but I could only focus on John straightening out those long braids. How ironic that he'd escaped from Aunt Jen and me only to be overshadowed once more by a flamboyant lady and her imaginative child. This family seemed to give him far greater satisfaction. I was genuinely happy for him.

I was also glad to have my big tomato, Buster, standing beside me. Holding forth by the rest room was Roxie, gesticulating more broadly than she had onstage. I could see Perry giving himself a quick spray of his asthma inhaler. Zoe had long fled into the night, but her nutty performance as Heidi's crippled friend, Clara, was still on everyone's mind. I looked across the club and could observe Guy flirting with some well-wishers. He was carrying the case that held his rabbit, Charlie, a bit player in our show. At the end of the bar, Joel was making an emphatic point to Rupert. Camille, downing a beer, was offering her two cents. Rupert was cornered. So much of my world was present within these four walls at this moment. It was a good feeling.

Helene apologized that they really had to get going. I walked with them to the door. John and I still had said very few words to each other.

At the front of the club, my niece latched on to Roxie. As usual, Roxie's voice cut through all others. "Oh my Gawd. Julian's niece. Look at you with the braids."

Mara once more rhapsodized over the show. Roxie had to stop her. "Please, not since Susan Sontag have I heard such an artistic analysis. This child is a wunderkind."

I said quietly to John, "You didn't really get it, did you?" I instantly regretted saying it. It sounded like a put-down. Did I mean it as a put-down? What a dumb thing to say at this very last minute.

John's face retained its usual blank expression. He said without any edge, "Does it really matter?"

The three of us exchanged hugs and good-byes, and then they were gone into the night. I decided on the spot not to tell Aunt Jen that I'd seen them. That was the only fully developed thought I had. I knew there was some significance to John's visit, but it seemed facile to think of it as either a chapter ending or a new beginning. I was just pleased we both had people in our lives who loved and forgave us.

I walked over to where Joel and Camille were ganging up on poor Rupert, delighted to jump into the fray.

CHAPTER
28

Men, *help me send them foreign troops packing, and I promise I'll free all of you galley slaves.*

Milena, *Whores of Lost Atlantis*
Act Two, Scene Three

My brother's question "Can you earn a living doing this?" was a natural one. I couldn't, at that precise moment, but I was sure if we could only raise that damn money my life would turn around. My poverty had one very glamorous element: I had my lady's maid four times a week. Wilma was insistent. She loved her job. Bob Livingston was such an important executive that he could take off as much time as he wanted, and he wanted to play maid to an East Village cult diva. I grew accustomed to having Wilma around and found her presence a comfort.

It was tiresome, though, having to dress up in drag whenever she came to clean. Finally, I had to lay it on the line. "Wilma, if you really want to come over that often, and, I have to admit, the place does look terrific, I appreciate all the little homey touches you've done to class up the joint and you're awfully good company but, well, you'll just have to accept me as both master and mistress. I just can't dress up all the time." Another point had to be made. "Also, Wilma, I find the S and M aspects of our working relationship rather dreary. I just can't quite get into being your dominant mistress, and, besides, I nearly sprained my ankle kicking you last Tuesday."

Wilma was very understanding but asked that I at least allow her to continue dressing up. I said, "Sure, far be it from me to dictate fashion in the workplace. But, Wilma dear, aren't you getting a bit bored with this maid routine?"

Wilma looked at me with a moony smile. "Oh, Madame, it's just so exciting being your servant, meeting such flamboyant, theatrical people and hearing about the fantastic things you do."

I was honestly touched. I tried to view my life through Wilma's eyes. I suppose to her my existence was bohemian, and our search for investors had taken on the frenzy of a scavenger hunt. It stuck in my craw that Wilma didn't offer to write a check herself, but she was such a boon in other ways, I never brought it up.

In time, Wilma was not only my maid but my secretary. She answered the phone, fielded calls, took messages, sorted fan mail, created a file system, and reconciled my pitifully minuscule checkbook, with its typical balance of $10.39.

It was always an awkward moment when, at the end of the day, Wilma would go into the bathroom and transform into old Bob Livingston. Wilma was my confidante, Birdie to my Margo, but I never had much to say to Bob. I didn't dare even mention Wilma to Bob in fear that I would jar something in his subconscious and wreck the spell. From his emergence from the can to his exit two minutes later, our dialogue consisted of a terse "If it's convenient, Julian, I'd like to come on Wednesday."

"That would be great, Bob. You've got the key. Just let yourself in."

"See you Wednesday." The door closed.

There was no temp work to be had, so I sat at the kitchen table making lists: a list of everything I had done professionally during the previous twelve months, a list of every famous person I'd ever glimpsed on the street, a list of who I'd invite to a party if I ever had the cash to throw one, and as my depression grew, a list of the complete films of Lizabeth Scott. Wilma, sensing my melancholia, kept a low profile, restricting herself to light dusting and no vacuuming. She attempted to brighten my mood by baking my favorite chocolate chip cookies. The phone rang. Wilma answered it, covered the receiver with her big paw, and whispered, "Madama, it's Don Caspar."

"Thank you, Wilma. I'll take it in the living room."

Don sounded a bit peeved. "Do you still have that old queen in your apartment?"

"Of course I do. And he's not an old queen. Don't you know that thirty-six percent of all transvestites are heterosexual?"

"You've told me that before. There's something weird about having him in your apartment all the time."

"Wilma works here and I'd be lost without her." I said that for Wilma's benefit because I could sense her listening in the other room. I often had the feeling Wilma was listening in on my conversations, but I didn't care. I knew she found my life outrageously glamorous, and having an audience rather jazzed up my dialogue.

I confided to Don that I was depressed over my financial situation.

He surprised me with a business proposition. "Julian, I could help you make some money."

"You mean, you want me to be your temp receptionist again? I don't know. I think working for you might kill our romance." I didn't mention that I couldn't possibly be in the same office with him and Roxie. I'd need the acting skills of Madame Sarah to pull that off.

"No, Julian, this is something different. Nothing to do with Fletcher, Kimbrough and Moss. It's my other business, the antiques business." I never would have thought Don would dare integrate me into other aspects of his life. Once, in my apartment, he had gone into the bathroom, and I'd peeked inside his pocket address book. I looked for my name. There were no Youngs listed under Y, but under J was my phone number next to the name "Juliana's Cafe." You can imagine I saw this latest idea of his as a slight shift in attitude.

"Julian, before you turn me down, listen to my proposal. Occasionally I need people to move furniture into my truck. I've never mentioned this before because frankly I can't quite picture you doing such labor, but . . . I thought maybe you could organize a group of your actors to help you."

"Is the stuff heavy?"

"Very rarely, and my associate Kurt would take care of that."

"I hate to be vulgar, but how much could you pay us?" I could see Wilma snooping about. I stuck my tongue out at her. She giggled and scooted away.

"If there are less than five of you, I could pay you each fifty dollars a night and ten dollars extra for each item bigger than a chair. How does that sound?"

"Listen, I'm desperate. If you asked me to rob a bank, I'd say hand me some panty hose to pull over my face."

Don didn't react. A sense of humor wasn't at the top of his list of attributes.

"Don, if I can just get through the next few months, I have this feeling I'm going to be on easy street."

Guy wasn't interested. He was making a good living between sawing children in half at their birthday parties and healing the metaphysically lame. Roxie made a fine salary on Wall Street. But Perry, Joel, and Buster agreed to be movers. Camille also joined in, since she was starting an antique doll collection and could use the extra cash. Buster wondered why I didn't call Zoe.

"Buster, she's barely five feet tall. She won't be any help."

"She's really strong. A couple of months ago, I figured out a workout for her, and she's really been pumping. You should feel her biceps."

"She has been looking good," I agreed. More than muscles, Zoe's appearance had taken a turn toward the conservative. The line of her red lipstick had much more to do with the actual shape of her mouth, and she'd stopped tacking on those awful matted falls and had her own dark hair cut in a stylish shoulder-length bob.

"Buster, she seems to open up more to you. What's going on with her?"

"Far be it from me, Julian, to spread gossip, but I think she's in love."

"With whom?"

"She won't tell me anything about him, but I get the idea he's a rich businessman and not some East Village deadbeat. She's really very happy." I was delighted. Zoe was so vulnerable and vague, one wondered how she was able to handle the basic mechanics of living.

"Buster, do you think she might marry him?"

"I asked her, and she said she'll never marry because nothing must interfere with her career." Buster begged me not to mention anything about this to Zoe because he was sworn to secrecy. I promised not to say a word.

I phoned Zoe and asked her if she was interested in making some extra money moving things and if she was free to start Saturday night.

"Oh gosh, Saturday night. I may be . . . Oh . . ." I imagined she was about to say, "I may have a date with my rich lover." Instead she said, "I may have other plans, but I really could use the money. I'm waiting to hear from someone. Can I get back to you?"

I told her of course, but I couldn't get off the phone with her without getting a little tidbit of information regarding her new beau. "Zoe, I don't know if I've told you, but you're looking so beautiful these days. I love what you're doing with your hair and makeup."

She giggled. "I went to Elizabeth Arden's for a 'day of beauty,' and got completely overhauled."

"Elizabeth Arden's. That's rather pricey, isn't it?"

"Yes."

"Did somebody give you a gift certificate as a present?"

"Yes."

I wasn't getting anywhere being subtle, so I decided to go for the kill. "These are all signs that you may have a new beau. Am I correct?"

There was a silence at her end of the line. Then after a beat she replied, "Will Roxie be joining us Saturday night?"

"No." I said flatly. I hung up the phone irritated at her sphinxlike stubbornness and annoyed with myself for being so nosy. Who she was dating was her own affair. Perhaps she was the healthy one, reserving an area of her life that was private and away from the meddling of the company.

As it turned out, Zoe was available, and she, Joel, Perry, Buster, and Camille showed up at my place at nine o'clock Saturday night. Joel sat in the armchair drinking a beer.

"Julian, don't you think it's rather peculiar to be moving furniture on a Saturday night? Do you know these people?"

"Of course I don't. My friend—" I was about to say "Don," but then I remembered it might get back to Roxie and get her on the scent. I thought about saying "Tony," but I didn't want Zoe to connect Don/Tony with the gentleman she'd met in my apartment. I was getting very confused. "My friend, Rick, is an antiques dealer, and these are clients of his. They constantly trade furniture back and forth." I never wanted to lie to Joel, and I wasn't lying now. I wondered if changing someone's name constituted a lie. I explained that Don's clients were a married couple, the McKenzies, and they had a town house around the corner from me on Bank Street. I was to call them at nine-fifteen when everyone had arrived. I was instructed to phone twice. Let it ring once, hang up, then dial again and Mr. McKenzie would pick up. Joel wondered what the point of that little charade was. I shrugged and said, "Maybe since they're such rich collectors, they want to make sure we're really legit movers and not crooks. Oh shit, look, it's nine-seventeen. I've got to call."

The six of us walked around the corner to Bank Street looking for the house. It turned out to be a charming town house that I'd passed a million times on the way to the Laundromat. We had been told to enter through the servants' entrance in the back. A very narrow walkway protected by a gate lay between the McKenzies' house and the adjacent building. I opened the gate, and we walked down the dark, silent path. It was so black we had difficulty finding the door. Perry whispered, "In the book *Death Comes to the Manor Born*, this was where the first murder took place."

Suddenly, an arm jutted out in front of my face and slammed against the side of the building. We all gasped as a blinding flashlight illuminated the rugged face of an extremely large, blond man. He smiled, clearly enjoying the horror movie effect he was creating. "I take it you are the whores of lost Atlantis?" he said with an ambiguous accent, a polyglot of German and English.

We had just encountered Don's associate, Kurt, the guy I had met the night Don took me to his house in the suburbs. He had scared me then, and he gave me a creepy feeling now. He opened the door and let us into the house. Kurt turned on an overhead light in what I assumed was the boiler room. We all looked grotesque in the green light. Kurt was rather good-looking in his oversized, scary way. He had slightly balding reddish blond hair, a mustache, and a wide grin exposing a jaunty gap between his upper front teeth. I remembered that gap. He also had the biggest hands I think I've ever seen outside of a CinemaScope epic. "You I've met before."

My little band stared at me. I'm sure they all wondered how I knew a sinister act like this. "You have a good memory, Kurt. Lovely seeing you again."

He flicked at the space between his teeth with a dirty fingernail.

"Save for the two of you," he said, pointing to Buster and Joel, "the rest of you are midgets. You're not going to be much help to me."

Camille piped up. "We all took the time off to be here, so we get paid."

Kurt looked her up and down and said with a sneering smile, "Ooh, very feisty. You'll get paid, dear." He took another dismissive look at this pathetic troop and said, "You will all follow my instructions and work very quickly with no talking. You understand? Now, we go upstairs."

I looked at Perry. "Bizarre, n'est-ce pas?"

We followed Kurt up some narrow steps and found ourselves in the back of a grand marble-floored foyer. An elegant winding staircase led to an upper landing. Buster nudged me and whispered, "I think I got laid here once." The foyer led to a charming sitting room shimmering with the light of a magnificent crystal chandelier.

I asked Kurt, "Aren't the McKenzies home? He answered the phone when I called a few minutes ago."

"Mr. McKenzie thought it best if he and the missus left for the evening. She is very emotional to be parting with her collection."

Kurt instructed Buster and Joel to move a heavy lacquered cabinet downstairs and into the walkway. He gave Zoe and Camille boxes to fill with the contents of an étagère. Perry and I were told to remove all the dining room chairs. On our third trip back to the dining room, I heard Kurt yell sharply at Camille, "What the hell do you think you're doing?" He grabbed her steno pad away from her.

Camille, who was about half his size, craned her head toward his and fixed him squarely in the eye. "I am taking note of each and every object and/or stick of furniture that is leaving this house."

"And why are you doing that?"

"To ensure that we are paid for our services, since the agreement is that we get ten dollars extra for each piece bigger than a chair. Also to protect us from being accused of stealing anything by you and your partner."

"You have a suspicious mind."

"You're a suspicious character."

Kurt laughed and returned the steno pad to her. We all were thrilled to see Camille face down this thug. I was proud of the generations of petty Mafiosa blood coursing through her veins.

Half an hour later, the front salon and dining room were nearly stripped bare. Kurt left to get the U-Haul from around the block. Without our sergeant watching over us, Perry, Joel, Camille, and I sat on the staircase and watched Buster swing Zoe in a mad waltz beneath the crystal chandelier. Kurt honked the horn, and we began schlepping the stuff from the walkway into the large U-Haul. When we'd finished, Kurt took out of his pocket a big fat roll of bills. He gave us each our fifty dollars, and Camille presented her tally of how much extra he needed to pay us. He laughed and shook his head but paid up the rest. Climbing into the car, he smiled his gap-toothed grin, said, "We'll have to do this again soon, kiddies," and drove off with all of the McKenzies' lovely antiques.

We were exhausted and stumbled back toward my place. Joel pulled me aside and said, quietly, "I never want to do this again."

He made it seem so sinister. "Joel, we were only there a little over an hour. What was so terrible about that?"

"Do you really trust your friend? That Kurt acted like a crook. I think all of that furniture was stolen."

"Joel, I know it looks bad. Kurt was kind of creepy, but my friend is a very successful executive on Wall Street. Believe me, there's nothing criminal about him at all."

"And he's also in the antiques business? How come you've never told me about him? Is he your lover?"

"Joel, he's married and in the closet. That's why I've kept it all a big secret. He knew I was broke, and he thought this was a way of helping me."

"If he's so rich, why isn't he investing in our show? That's the kind of help you really need." I hated all of Joel's questions because I didn't have answers to them.

"All I know, Joel, is I don't think D—To—Rick would do anything that would get me in trouble. For God's sake, he's on the board of the Lincoln Center Film Society."

"Well, your instincts may be right, but I don't want to be included in any of this. And in the future, don't even tell me about it." Joel's attitude was making me feel horribly guilty, and I hadn't done anything. Of course, Joel was dead on target—one could easily imagine Kurt's mug shot—but Joel didn't know Don Caspar. I had worked hard to wipe out my suspicion that Don was the notorious Tony Andriolo. My Don's world was one of benefits for the opera, private islands, Wall Street. He wouldn't be involved in anything that would jeopardize his immaculate image. On the other hand, why was he seeing me?

Several nights later, Don was over at my apartment. We were in the living room, where he could watch the president speak about the economy on TV. For a change, I was clothed, wearing a T-shirt and boxer shorts; Don was completely nude. He sat in the wing chair looking for all the world like Gregory Peck starring in *The Emperor's New Clothes*.

During a commercial break, I said, "Don, some of the kids the other night felt the scene over at the McKenzies' was a little on the shady side."

"Shady?"

"Well, we felt like we were stealing their furniture. Kurt was downright scary. Everything is on the up-and-up, isn't it?"

"You guys really are hooked on those old movies. No, Julian," he said with a tinge of exasperation, "life is not a Hollywood B movie. You've got to learn the difference between what's real and what's not. I'll tell you what's real. My anger. I don't like being insulted and having my integrity questioned."

"I . . . I didn't mean to—"

"This is real life, Julian. I am not Raffles or Cary Grant in *Notorious*."

"You mean *To Catch a Thief*."

Don was speaking in the cutting, derisive tone I'd heard him use on Roxie in his office ages ago. "I *mean*, Julian, I buy and sell old things. No melodrama, no car chases. So you can tell your little friends not to be so jittery. They've got nothing to worry about."

"It's just they don't know you." I was proceeding with extreme caution into unfamiliar territory.

Don looked at me with a total lack of expression on his magnificent face. "Do *you* know me?" His legs were spread, and I found myself mesmerized by the enormous, powerful organ hanging from his dark crotch like some massive steel anchor. He repeated his question with the force of a command. "Do *you* know me?"

I didn't know him and didn't want to know him. I wanted to know more about myself. What guilt was I consumed with that required me to seek punishment from this man? Was it for being ambitious, self-absorbed, narcissistic, for being a rotten son, a lousy brother, gay? My intellect rebelled and consoled me. I was a unique, talented, lovable person. Why did I want him to humiliate me?

Don leaned back in the chair. "You're not much of a sparring partner today."

I sat on the floor staring up at him. He snapped his fingers and pointed to his cock.

"Make it happy. Mr. Reagan's about to speak."

Despite my reassurances, Joel didn't accompany us on any more of our nocturnal activities. During the spring, Buster, Perry, Camille, Zoe, and I did about one or two jobs a week. You couldn't rely on it, but it was nice extra cash. It was also educational. I began leafing through copies of *Architectural Digest* and recognized objets and furniture similar to those we were moving. After a while, Buster and Perry and I could debate the authenticity of a Biedermeier secretaire and discuss the finer distinctions between Flemish and English tapestries. We could toss off an entirely new vocabulary of words, such as girandoles, gueridons, maquettes, and méridiennes. Buster could sashay into an exquisite sitting room and with his index finger flying point out, "repro, repro, repro." I'd say, "Buster, I don't know, that side cabinet looks like the real thing."

"No way, Renee, look at how coarse the ormolu is."

Then Perry would look in the back of the cabinet and remark, "Buster, you're full of shit, it's a signed Topino." All of us could have applied for positions at Sotheby's.

Perry occasionally would question the legality of our actions, expressing his doubts naturally in movie terms. "Julian, I feel like we're in some sort of sixties caper movie, a bunch of misfits planning a heist. Or is it a thirties screwball comedy and we're a bunch of debutantes mixed up with con artists? I hope you're right about this one."

Camille, a tough cookie if there ever was one, added, "You notice I always wear gloves. You won't catch my prints on any of the boodle. A little lesson I picked up from my Uncle Bruno."

I tried to alleviate their concerns. The truth of the matter was I was so under Don Caspar's control, he could have asked me to steal President Reagan's hearing aid and I would have bought the next ticket to the capital. I resented his hold on me and knew it could not go on much longer, but I had to believe that Don was the man he claimed to be.

Camille continued to annoy Kurt by notating everything in her steno pad and refusing to be intimidated by his brusque demeanor. His attitude toward us was always that of the hard-boiled mercenary soldier forced to command a troop of bumbling incompetents. He also didn't trust us. Zoe had a habit of lingering lovingly over some fragile objet d'art, holding the crystal figurine into the light or posing with a candelabra before the mirror as if in preparation for her Lady Macbeth. I'm sure Kurt was convinced Zoe had slippery fingers. He always looked as if he wanted to hold her upside-down and shake her to see if anything would fall out. I definitely wasn't tempted to pocket any trinkets. I had the even more antiquarian Angelica Cross hidden among my tomatoes and peppers. Possessing the Angelica Cross gave me an odd sense of comfort. Often when I'd be anxious and scared about the future, I'd take it out and press it against my heart. I was moved that some little artisan four centuries ago had created the Angelica Cross out of such devotion and purity of spirit. Don told me it could make a wish come true. I'd be testing its power shortly.

CHAPTER 29

I beseech thee, you gals have got to stop this senseless slaughter.

Folio, *Whores of Lost Atlantis*
Act Two, Scene Three

Very early one morning, I was awakened by the phone ringing. It was Joel. "Mamacita's in the hospital. He was rushed to Lenox Hill in the middle of the night. Both of his lungs collapsed. He nearly died."

As soon as Mamacita was able to receive visitors, we gathered at his bedside. Joel and I arrived together. My heart stopped when I saw attached to his door a list of AIDS precautions for the staff. I heard voices inside the room. Sure enough, the place was packed. Roxie and Zoe were seated on the bed. Buster was crouched on the floor. Perry was in one chair by the window, and in the far corner was Mudge, seated, dressed all in white like some fragile Chinese priest, silently beading a large piece of black velvet. I was relieved to see Mamacita boldly gesturing and holding court.

"Darlings, I have the nurses jumping through *hoops*. They are terrified of this big black Mama. I don't know why. I am the most harmless creature on the planet." There was something so magical and genielike about Mamacita, one could easily envision nurses' aides and IV equipment flying about the air at his command. He gathered us all near him on the bed. He ran his fingers along the top sheet as if trying to press it without an iron.

"*Mes chères,* as you may have figured out, your Mamacita nearly cooled over the weekend. When your fingernails turn a sour shade of periwinkle blue, you know your number's up. I'll say it out in the open. Open the window, let the public hear. I've got it. AIDS. There, I've said it. I can't take it back."

We all sat on the bed silent. That awful four-letter word blanketed us.

"I shall recover from the pneumonia. Although both my lungs collapsed like circus tents, they're getting all puffed up again. It seems I don't have as bad a case of PCP as some of our sisters get. I may actually get sprung from here in two weeks." His constantly moving fingers betrayed his fear, but his voice was firm and precise as a governess's. "So, Joel, if you harbor even the slightest, and I say the slightest notion of replacing me as costume designer on *Whores of Lost Atlantis,* you will know no peace from my vindictive use of island voodoo."

Joel took Mamacita's hand and said kindly, "Hugh, you will not be replaced. We will not do the show until you're ready to do the costumes."

Zoe sniffled into her handkerchief. Mamacita would have none of it. "Zoe Whatever-your-last-name-is-this-week, we are not playing Beth's death scene from *Little Women,* so you stop that caterwauling this minute. When I really am dying, then I'd like all of you to weep like the Trojan women and Mudge will provide the beaded handkerchiefs—but not at this moment." He tempered his tough words by sitting up and pressing little Zoe close to him. "I'm being very MGM brave, and I won't have you stealing focus, baby. Now I must have a cigarette."

Buster leaped up and said, "Mamacita girl, you're really gonna have to change your ways. No cigarettes are gonna touch them lips and no drinking and no reefer. You don't think I know it, but you've always been a pothead. You're really gonna have to cool it now."

Mamacita gasped at the indignity of Buster's lecture. "How dare you speak to me in that manner! Mudge! Escort him out!"

Mudge merely nodded and continued to bead.

Buster wouldn't relent. "Look, Mamacita, I am quite the expert on your little illness. Oh yes. Like I have personally nursed several friends to their untimely demise. Like okay? So if you want to try and last long enough till they find a cure, you better mend your decadent ways." Buster lifted the various medications that were sitting on the nightstand. "Bactrim, AZT, pentamadine. Oh yeah, I know these real well. My friends who died were assholes. They didn't lift a finger to learn anything about their disease. The only way to live with AIDS is to become an expert on it. You've got to investigate every experimental drug that comes out of China or France. And you've got to question everything your doctors say."

Roxie, whose eyes were red and swollen, still showed some of her old sizzle. "Darling, I will personally handle the investigation. Your illness and survival will be my personal mission."

Mamacita sank back among his pillows. "I see my condition is going to bring out the obnoxious in people. Buster, I resign myself to your ministrations. Et *pourquoi pas*? Guy was here this morning threatening to cure me through emotional catharsis, healing massage, herbal enemas, and that dreary entity who never shuts up." He picked up a hand mirror and gazed at his reflection. "What I really need are a few hours at Georgette Klinger. My pores are as clogged up as the Suez Canal."

Shortly afterward, Mamacita wanted to take a nap and eighty-sixed us from the premises. Mudge led us out of the room. Mudge, who rarely uttered a syllable, stood among us outside the room and said, "You are our family. We have no one else. Everyone on the island disowned us, you know."

I told him, "Mudge darling, whatever happens, you belong to us."

Joel asked, "What can we do for you now?"

To which Mudge replied, "Go to Sheru's on Thirty-eighth Street and buy me a pound of black jet beads."

Joel convinced Mudge to get a bite to eat at the coffee shop around the block, and Perry and Buster joined them. Roxie had to return to work. I was heading back downtown, and Camille said she'd join me. Before we left, I had one last errand to do. I scooted back into Mamacita's room.

Without opening his eyes, Mamacita murmured, "Julian, what did you forget?"

I sat on the bed, and he wearily opened his big, fishlike eyes. "Mama, I brought you something, but I didn't want the others to see it."

"A joint?"

"Cool it. I have in my possession a rare religious relic from the sixteenth century."

"Oh dear, not some poor saint's big toe, is it?"

"No." I opened my knapsack and took out the Angelica Cross.

Mamacita's eyes widened as big as majolica serving plates. He had an extensive background in art history and instantly knew the value of what I held in my hand. "Oh honey, tell me you didn't rob the Metropolitan Museum of Art."

"No, someone gave it to me—or rather lent it to me. It has a blessing attached to it. It's supposed to grant you a wish." I placed it in his hands. Mamacita dropped his glib facade and closed his eyes while he pressed the cross to his breast. I closed my eyes too and made a prayer. I prayed that death would stay clear of us and allow Mamacita to enjoy the conclusion of our fairy-tale adventure. I opened my eyes and saw Mamacita watching me pray.

Quietly, he said, "Do you say your prayers every night?"

"Well, not formally. I mean, like I don't have any words memorized, but I do lie in bed and make wishes for those I love. I always include you in my prayers, Hugh."

"Thank you. You're a nice boy." He looked at the Angelica Cross with an appraising eye. "Julian, this is the genuine article. I'm no fool. What are you doing with this?"

"It's a long story. A sexy story but a long story. Let this be our secret. I'm going to lend it to you until you're feeling in the pink, okay? Then I want it back. It doesn't really belong to me. And don't let one of the nurses get their mitts on it. We'll never see it again. All right?"

"Well, I've got to get better. Buster is handling the scientific end, Guy is handling the cosmic, but I never expected you to handle the spiritual."

"Darling, we female impersonators even have our own goddess," I said à la Lana Turner in *The Prodigal*.

"Go on."

"It's true. Venus Castina, the goddess of transvestism. She's a mighty strong lady. I pray to her every night before I go onstage. When I forget, I almost always lose a false eyelash. Go figure."

I left Mamacita clutching the Angelica Cross and walked down the hall. In each room, I could see emaciated, ashen, bald figures watching television or talking to friends.

Camille was waiting for me at the end of the corridor. Her eyes were red, and she was rummaging through her bag for another Kleenex. "Oh, Julian, it's just awful. We've been so lucky. There's been so much dying around us, but I always felt like there was this magic circle protecting us. I thought we'd be spared. You really did test negative, didn't you?"

I put my arm around her. "I really did. I'm fine. I'm getting bunions from my high heels, but other than that, I've never felt better. Hey, do you have to go back to work?"

"No, I'm taking the rest of the day off."

"Camille, come back to my place and I'll make some tea. Wilma's not around, and we can have the place to ourselves."

"We haven't been alone together in about six months."

"I'm not afraid, are you?"

She giggled and wiped her nose.

As we were walking toward the elevator, we saw Zoe stumbling out of the phone booth. Her change purse had slipped, and nickels and dimes were spilling in every direction over the floor. Camille and I helped her collect her rolling change. This latest catastrophe was the final straw and released a floodgate of tears from Zoe. When we'd picked up the last penny, we sat her down on a bank of chairs.

Zoe wept. "Why Mamacita? It's so unfair. I'm going to nurse him. I'll move in with him. I'll be with him every second." Camille and I looked at each other. We were both thinking that if Zoe tried to pull that off, Mamacita would put a contract out on her. Zoe took a compact and her flame red lipstick out of her purse. Her hand shaking wildly, she drew on an enormous brave mouth.

I knew she'd never accept, but I asked her if she'd like to join Camille and me for tea. She blinked and darted her eyes furtively. "Oh no, no. I just called my friend. I, um . . . but thank you, sweetie."

Camille took out a Kleenex and wiped a bit of Zoe's excess lipstick off. "Zoe, I know you're a very private person, but I'm just so happy you've found somebody. What's he like?"

I was sure Zoe would flee at that direct question, but perhaps because of the emotional nature of the moment, she replied, "He's a very complicated man. He's a businessman, very busy. He's . . . well . . . he's very handsome."

Camille asked, "Is it serious?"

Zoe gave a little nod. "Very serious. That's one of the reasons I don't talk about it. I don't want to spoil it by turning this relationship into gossip. That does seem to be the primary offstage activity of this company. This relationship is very precious to me. I've never been with a man like him before."

There was something so quicksilver and elusive about Zoe. I was afraid any bold question would have the effect of a gunshot on a frightened deer. I asked her, "Do you think you might marry him?"

"He hasn't asked me, Julian, but if he did, maybe I would. Many actresses marry executives and make a success of it." Her dark eyes grew serious, and she leaned in to us. "You know, I only plan to marry once. I don't believe in divorce."

Her sudden mood changes unnerved me both onstage and off. "I had no idea, Zoe, that it was so serious."

She shifted colors again like a kaleidoscope. She sat up very straight, her eyes blazing. "What do you mean? What have you heard? Are people talking about me?"

Flustered, I said, "No, no, no. Nobody's talking. Well, I mean, Buster saw you walking with a very handsome man and, yes, he told us. We're all so thrilled for you. Sincerely thrilled."

That appeared to calm her down. She looked down at her folded hands and said demurely, "I love him very much."

Camille and I left Zoe and subwayed down to my apartment. I found a couple of tea bags I had saved from my last Chinese take-out order and dunked them into boiling water. Though it was only three o'clock, the sky was threateningly black. We were in for a torrential downpour. Batgirl's cave seemed awfully warm and cozy. Camille and I curled up at either end of my pillow-strewn sofa.

Camille played with a small, round damask pillow.

"It's been a long time since I've been here."

She looked like a little girl lost in the cornucopia of tassels, velvets, and fringe. I really did miss her.

"It's been way too long."

Camille sipped her tea and sat very still while she collected her thoughts. There was only one question she could ask. "Why did you stop calling?"

After all these months, I still didn't know how to answer. This time there was no excuse.

"I was scared."

"I pushed you too hard, didn't I?"

She was generously setting me up for an easy out. I couldn't accept it. "Camille, we were both pushing it. It was so much fun, but it was just playacting. I wish you hadn't taken it so seriously."

"Didn't you ever really want it? Not even for a second?" Camille looked unbearably plaintive.

"Maybe for a second. I guess I like the idea of 'family.' I like the idea of you being a part of my family. And I've got an overly developed imagination. I think I got you all tangled up in the machinery. Do you know what I mean?"

Camille nodded. This was a difficult conversation for her. She looked embarrassed by her gullibility.

"Camille, don't feel foolish. I . . . I thought it was the most beautiful fantasy. It would have been nice to have someone to love like that."

Camille exhaled a deep breath. "Suddenly I was forty-one years old. Oh, Julian, I would have been a great mom. I really would have."

I felt very bad for her. I'd never had a door to a dream completely closed. The chances that she'd have a child were very slim indeed. The rain started hitting the air conditioner like fingers on a typewriter.

"Camille, I'm so sorry I cut you off. I'm so sorry. I don't know what my problem was. You got me all horny, and then you got me confused. Confused and horny. That's a rotten combination."

I was pleased that I had her laughing.

"Gee, I'm so sexy, I can even get a gay man all hot and bothered."

"You did. You really did. And I was so entrenched as the queen of drag queens. I didn't know which way to turn, so I just kind of turned you off. I really didn't mean to be so cruel."

Camille fluffed her hair away from her face. "All right, all right, all right. You apologized. I accept. No more whipping ourselves. I'm not mad at you anymore. I really was mad for a while, but not anymore. Do you know why?"

"I don't have a clue."

Camille began straightening out the wrinkles of the velvet throw on the sofa. She was preparing me for a good story.

"Well, you know that Sam was involved in this agency to help adopted children find their biological parents. Right?"

"Yeah, and Perry was going to get them to help him."

"Well, they located his mother."

I was dumbfounded. Why hadn't anyone told me? "When was this?"

"About a month ago. Don't get worked up. Nobody knows. I wouldn't have told you, but I need to explain why I've acted the way I have. She lives in Baltimore. You know how Perry gets. He was a wreck. So he asked me to go with him to see her."

"You went to Baltimore?" I couldn't believe all this drama went on and I had been so oblivious.

"We took the train on a Monday. His mother was very apprehensive to meet him. She canceled twice and, you know, if the birth mother doesn't want to be identified, they won't give you her whereabouts. She was like twenty years old when she got pregnant with Perry. His father was just some fling. She had no intention of marrying him, and she was Catholic so she had the baby and gave him up for adoption. She married a couple of years later and has, I think, three grown children."

"What was the house like? What happened when they first saw each other? Does she look like him?"

"Her new last name is Hurley. Sally Hurley. They live in this very dreary suburb of Baltimore, just on the border of middle class. Actually, the house wasn't that different from the house where I grew up in Brooklyn. The same idea. Her husband let us in. He's kind of an Archie Bunker type, fat face and belly, beady, suspicious little eyes. He looked at us like we were plotting to run off with his bowling trophies. I think they have three daughters, and he kept eyeing Perry up and down. I thought he was wondering if he'd had a son with Sally if the boy would have been like Perry."

"I'm just curious. A month ago, how blond was Perry?"

"He dunked his head in a vat of black dye just before we left. He didn't want to scare her." Now I recalled the rehearsal when Perry'd shown up with hair as black as Cochise's. Camille continued her story. "His mother was seated sort of stiffly in her living room. I wondered how long she'd been sitting there dreading and anticipating this day."

"Does she look like him?"

"I couldn't see it. She has dark eyes, and her hair is dyed a sort of ashy blond."

"So that's where he gets it."

"Perry sat with her on the sofa, and they were very polite, like they were meeting in a dentist's waiting room. She asked him what he did for a living and he told her he was an actor. That struck a spark in her. She asked him if he was ever on a soap opera and he said no. She asked him if he knew anyone on a soap opera and he said his former roommate had an under five on *One Life to Live* and that perked her up more than anything else the entire day."

"I'm sure their reuniting was a bit more emotional than that."

"It was pretty cool. They had nothing in common. He told her about his allergies and asthma and she said her brother had the same problem and she asked him if he and I were engaged and we said no. When her husband left the room, she got fidgety and very concisely told Perry the circumstances surrounding the adoption, that she'd never seen the baby and so it was much easier to give him up. We were there about an hour, tops. She took out a family photo album and showed him pictures of her parents and brothers and sisters. She had a brother who never married named Joseph, kind of the black sheep. He lived in Greenwich Village and died very young, sometime in the mid-sixties. Sure enough, in the photo album, he had Perry's same kind of Martha Graham face. She gave him a snapshot of her family from the fifties which I thought was a sweet gesture and they invited us for dinner but we decided not to stay."

"After all that. You only stayed an hour?"

"They had said everything. And, really, I don't think the Hurleys sincerely wanted us to stay."

"Was Perry terribly upset the way it turned out?"

"Yes and no. I think he was disappointed that she wasn't June Cleaver and Betty Grable rolled into one but I think he was relieved that the search was over and that she wasn't going to complicate his life, like she's not a needy bag lady who's going to move in and start a drug ring. I think meeting her was a comfort to him. He doesn't feel so alone. He knows there's someone in the world that he has some connection to. It's calmed him down. Actually, I was the one who was upset by the whole thing."

"Why was that?"

"All the way back to New York on the train, I kept thinking that just because you have a child it doesn't mean he has to love you. Maybe you won't like each other at all. Hell, I hate my father, maybe my kid would hate me."

"I don't think so."

"The point is, having a kid won't make you complete. It's as simple as that. I still have to figure out another way of feeling like a whole person." She looked wistfully out the window. "I have my doll collection. They love me. Promise me you won't tell Perry I told you about this."

"I promise."

I freshened our tea, and then Camille asked me if I had met someone during our period of estrangement. I stared at her for a moment while holding the tea tray. My relationship with Don Caspar was the only secret I'd ever kept. Desperate as I was for a confidante, I'd finally accepted that Don's identity was for me and only me to know. Camille challenged me with her direct question. If anyone had a right to demand an answer, it was she. She repeated it but this time as a statement. "There was somebody else."

"Yes. I'm still seeing him. He's a mysterious sort of person. An older man. Very charismatic. A big guy, very tall and handsome and dignified and a little too complicated for me. He's married and even has two young grandchildren."

Camille took her teacup from the tray. "What is it with all of you and these older men? You, Zoe, and Roxie. No one under fifty can apply."

"I don't know how much longer it can go on. He doesn't really make me happy. He just makes me—"

Camille interrupted me. "That's all right, honey. I get the idea. I certainly couldn't fight that."

The Chinese tea tasted good on this dank day. "Camille, he's very sexy, but if he dumped me tomorrow, I wouldn't go crazy. Maybe I would for a week but I'd recover."

"Julian, let me tell ya, you are one tough cookie. You make my old Mafia buddies from Rego Park look like wimps."

For once, she didn't make toughness seem like an attribute.

Camille picked up the phone to call her answering service, but something disturbed her.

"Your phone sounds weird."

She handed me the receiver, and I listened. I heard a slight clicking, muf-fled sound. "It's sounded like that for about a week. Oh, you know the phone company. They must be digging around somewhere."

"I don't know, Julian. This sounds like my Uncle Vinnie's phone when it was being tapped."

"Uncle Vinnie. Was he the one who was executed in the barber chair?"

"No, that was my cousin Sal."

"I can't imagine why my phone would be tapped. As far as I know, there's nothing criminal about wearing a wig onstage. Otherwise Carol Channing would be on death row."

Camille wrinkled up her nose in thought. "Do you know anyone who might be under investigation by the government?"

"No, but I've signed all sorts of strange petitions on Christopher Street. Sometimes I don't even read them."

"You really shouldn't do that."

After feeling all warm and toasty, now I was slightly nauseated. "Oh God, Camille, I wonder what I could have signed. This is how people got black-listed during the fifties. You really think my phone is being tapped?"

Camille started clearing the tea things. "I can't be positive. Maybe it's just trouble on the line."

I had the sinking feeling I was in trouble. My only comfort was the knowl-edge you didn't need a license to perform in drag in this town. Nobody could take that away.

CHAPTER
30

Which one of you vipers poisoned my eunuch's iced tea?

Milena, *Whores of Lost Atlantis*
Act Two, Scene Four

A few days later, I received a surprise visit from Roxie. I was busy doctoring up some canned spaghetti. I buzzed her in and opened the door, awaiting her entrance. It was an entrance worth waiting for. She stood in the doorway, hands grasping the frame for support, her face drained of color.

I dropped a spoon. I could only gasp. "Roxie, he's dead." I was sure Mamacita was gone.

She looked at me confused, realized my assumption, and shook her head. "Mamacita's fine. The medication's working, but *me*! I have been *terminated*!" At that, her face crumbled like a building that's been hit with a wrecking ball. Tears tumbled down her cheeks. I'd never seen her weep like this. She was convulsed with hoarse sobbing.

I made her sit down at the kitchen table. "Oh, honey, what happened?"

She tried to speak but failed. She took a deep breath and attempted to compose herself. I ran to the bathroom, ripped off a large wad of toilet paper, and gave it to her.

"I'm in shock, Julian. I am literally in shock. You could stick a pin in my thigh and I wouldn't feel it."

"What happened?"

She dabbed at her swollen eyes. "I have been terminated from F, K and M. I go into work this morning and I go to the coffee urn and Roseanne says Don Caspar wants to see me immediately. What a way to start the morning."

What a way to start the story. I really didn't want to hear anything about Don Caspar. It was always difficult for me to pretend that I didn't know him save for having been his temp for a day.

"So I go into his office and he's got this sickening smirk on his face. He says, 'Well, Ms. Flood, you've done it this time.' 'Done what?' I say and he goes, 'The police were our guests yesterday after you left.' I decided to play it flip and retorted, 'What did you do, Mr. Caspar, run over an old lady with your Cadillac?' 'Not that I can recall,' he says. 'They were investigating a certain fag hag named Ms. Roxie Flood. They really seemed to mean business. They insisted on speaking to Walter himself.' Walter Kimbrough is the senior partner in the firm. He's always been so kind to me, almost paternal. He was even going to invest in our show. I was surprised. He's so conservative. Old, old, old money. His wife is related to . . ."

Roxie was off on a tangent and would have chronicled Mrs. Kimbrough's entire family tree if I didn't steer her back on course. "But, Roxie, what do the coppers have on you?"

"I don't know. No one will say. Caspar seemed to know, but he just kept smirking. He said, 'Roxie, my girl, you better clear out your desk. You're washed up on Wall Street. It's time for you to call Jacoby and Meyers.' "

I could hear Don saying those nasty words—not that he'd ever spoken to me in that snide tone, but I had heard him reading people's beads on the telephone.

"Julian, I couldn't even respond to that asshole, so I marched right over to Walter Kimbrough's office. His secretary Edith's an old-time dyke. Once I found her putting clothespins on her girlfriend's nipples in the storage room. Well, she tries to stop me, but I pushed her aside and walked right in. I said, 'Mr. Kimbrough, something is going on here and I have a right to know why I'm being fired.' He looked very pained and says, 'Roxie, dear, sit down.' And he explains ad nauseam all about the conservative, delicate nature of the company, the old tradition, and that they can't be involved in anything with even the hint of scandal. I said, 'But what did I do? I've told you all about my theatre company and I've tried very hard not to let it interfere with my work here. I thought you approved.' I figured maybe somebody told him I flash my tits onstage or maybe he heard about the blow job scene in *Fighting Girls*. He says, 'I don't believe it has anything to do with your theatrical endeavors, but then perhaps it does. You'd be the best judge of that.' And he looks at me strangely, like they had discovered a dead baby in my desk drawer. He says, 'The police were here yesterday questioning me as per your activities and your involvement with our client base. I said, 'Didn't you tell them I was just your corporate librarian?' 'I did, and they found it very intriguing that you were privy to our most confidential information. Now, they are in the process of subpoenaing all of our financial records. This we cannot allow. It is not in the best interests of F, K and M to have anything more to do with you.' As a final blow, he added, 'I realize I said something about investing in your play but, well, under the circumstances—' I walked out of there like Nixon in the final days. No one would even look up from their terminals as I walked that last mile past the water-cooler."

Roxie got a demented gleam in her eye. "It's drugs. You know, it must be drugs." I wasn't following her drift at all. She ranted, "I ran into Rupert over the weekend, and he told me Kiko had been hauled into the police station and questioned about something."

"If there's any justice in this world, they'll deport her ass back to Hiro-shima," I quipped, still irked by the memory of Kiko peeing on stage right.

"You don't understand, Julian. She's fingered me." It was a distasteful image. "Julian, whatever squalid trip she's into, she intends to drag me along into it."

I found that hard to believe. Roxie and Kiko had had almost no contact with each other except for one brief shining moment at a screening of *Shoah* when they spat at each other across the aisle. But it was possible that Kiko was smuggling contraband in her turbans. . . .

Roxie covered her face with her hands and moaned, "It's all so sordid. Drugs, performance artists sticking yams up their twats. Here I am a divor-cée with one ovary trying to remake my life and I get mixed up with all this decadence."

I tried to offer solace. "Roxie, on the positive side, I know you were ago-nizing whether or not you'd quit your job once we opened off-Broadway. Now you won't have to make that decision."

"Julian, I can't live the way you do." She made a sweeping gesture around my apartment. "The show could fold in a week, and then where will I be? A thirtyish fag hag who needs a chin implant. When I got hired by F, K and M, I was recently divorced, flat broke. I was sleeping on the floor of my girl-friend Roz's apartment in Jackson Heights. In the middle of the night, her cat would vomit on me. I was a failed comedienne. Can you comprehend the gravity of those words, 'failed comedienne'? Is there any role in life more degrading? F, K and M gave me an identity, a dignity. They allowed me to rebuild my ego."

I didn't tell her she'd rebuilt her ego a few stories too high. I really did feel bad for her. "Well, Roxie, you're just going to have to rebuild yourself again. I'm beginning to suspect we rebuild ourselves continuously until the day we die."

Roxie chipped away at her nail polish. "You're very comforting, dear," she said, not buying it.

"Roxie, you are a very funny lady, and you're starring in an off-Broadway show. Think of how many dames out there would kill to be in your shoes. I think it's a blessing they canned you from that dreary place."

"Julian, there's more to life than the stage."

I brushed that thought off immediately. "Some girls do marry. Is Sam totally out of the picture?"

"He considers me on a par with Rudolf Hess and Goebbels. Julian, hear me now. I am definitely over the allure of the pampered, tormented Jewish male." She stuck out her lower lip defiantly. "From now on, I am going to be the pampered, tormented Jewish male."

I hated seeing Roxie and Sam split up. Their union had seemed so perfect, as if I'd conjured it up in one of my plays. I wanted to sentimentalize their comic May-December romance. He seemed like the perfect man to handle her hyperenergetic, chameleonlike personality. She seemed like the perfect girl to bring fun and spontaneity into his well-ordered life. Their breakup highlighted my obvious lack of insight into the nature of love. Roxie's eyes had a slight glaze over them. I knew that she was in her own reverie and that she'd share it with me.

"Julian, I doubt I'll ever marry. My mother was right. I'm a career girl. A bachelorette. Alone in a well-tailored suit, listening to my messages on the answering machine. Maybe I'll go dyke. It's a life-style." She nodded her head as if considering which supermarket in which to buy her supper. "Oh yeah, I'll probably end up a leathery, chain-smoking lesbian with one breast. Oh yeah, I'll have cancer. I've accepted it."

I usually reveled in her bullet train of thought fantasies, but this time I thought it best to contradict. "Miracles do happen, Roxie. Look at Zoe. She's madly in love with a wealthy man. I think he wants to marry her." I knew gossip was the only way to get her out of her morbid self-pity. She leaned in to deliver her scoop.

"Julian, Buster told me Zoe's mystery man has even given her a diamond engagement ring. I forget the carats. Buster knows. But, please, don't tell him I told you what she told him."

After Roxie left, I began scrubbing out the pot in which I'd incinerated my spaghetti Juliano. An odd notion floated into my head that perhaps there was some bizarre connection between Roxie getting the sack and Camille's suspicion that my phone was being tapped. It was a horrible thought, but as I dug the Brillo pad deeper into the blackened pot, all sorts of paranoid visions sprang to the surface. Could Kiko and Thirteen be plotting some elaborately malevolent revenge? Would they go so far as to incriminate us in criminal activity? I felt trapped in a web of intrigue and deceit, yet I didn't feel defiant like Susan Hayward or even Jane Greer. I felt pathetic and scared. How far would my enemies go in trying to discredit me? Would they resort to violence? I looked around, imagining myself trapped in an apartment engulfed in flames. I saw myself standing by an open window and being shot by a paid assassin or disfigured by acid thrown at me from a speeding car. Roxie was right. We were mired in a world of sordid ugliness. I couldn't wait till we opened our show off-Broadway and could say farewell forever to Golgotha and the loathsome East Village.

I was thrilled when the phone rang. Anything to get me off this paranoic treadmill. It was Don Caspar. As Roxie would say, I was feeling "less than enchanted" with my charming demon lover after his treatment of my friend. I was fed up with myself for associating with someone who could be so cruel. I found myself acting very cool to him.

However, it wasn't my coolness that he picked up on. "Julian, is there something wrong with your phone?"

"Oh, ever since Ma Bell split up, my service has been lousy."

"Don't you hear that strange clicking sound?"

I did, but I pretended not to. "No, I don't hear a thing but your dulcet tones."

"What's wrong? Are you in a bad mood?"

"Well, to be . . ." What could I say? The whole situation was so convoluted, I didn't even know where to start. "Don, it's just been one of those days. What's up?"

"Something is definitely wrong with your phone. Call me back from the pay phone across the street. I'm at the office."

Before I could protest, he'd hung up. This was ridiculous. Why should I have to drag myself across the street to call him back? I was in a foul mood. I put on my bedroom slippers and threw on a coat and crossed the street to the pay phone. I called F, K and M, but now it seemed that Mr. Caspar was on an international conference call. This was becoming truly irritating. I leaned against a lamppost while two other people used the pay phone. A messenger stayed on the phone a good fifteen minutes. When he finished, I dialed F, K and M again. This time I got through to Don.

"Julian, what took you so long?" Before I could deliver an appropriately acid retort, he plowed on. "In the mood to make some cash tonight? I've got a job for you and the gang."

I had no plans for the evening, but the last thing I wanted to do was help him out. Still, we were heading toward the end of the month, and it would soon be time to pay the bills. I sighed. "Sure, go ahead."

Buster, Camille, and Perry were available, but Zoe had a date with her mystery beau. I offered the job to Roxie. She was delighted to make the extra cash, since it was strictly off the books and wouldn't interfere with her unemployment checks. Honestly, it wasn't until I hung up the phone that the irony occurred to me that Roxie was now being employed by the same man who'd taken such glee in her being fired.

We gathered at a brownstone in the east nineties. As usual, the sardonic jester, Kurt, let us in. Efficiently, we went about our business of packing things up and carrying them into the U-Haul.

Perry and I carefully moved a beautifully japanned and gilt table. Perry exclaimed, "Julian, I bet you anything this is a signed piece by Lannuier."

"Definitely, 1815, I'd say."

Roxie was astonished at our knowledge of antiques and nearly toppled over when Buster, in his skin-tight jeans and Chelsea Gym sweatshirt said, "Roxie, open the door while I carry out this fauteuil à la Reine."

Roxie sputtered, "What's a fucking fauteuil?" We all looked at her with the patience accorded a child.

Camille replied, "It's the small chair, Roxie."

"Which chair?" To which the three of us nearly in unison said, "The one with the boulle marquetry."

Roxie found it impossible to concentrate on the job and was compelled to snoop around the town house, checking out the bookshelves and medicine cabinets. She surmised that the couple in question were experimenting with anal sex to enliven their marriage. She came to this conclusion based on the copy of *The Joy of Sex* lying under the bed and the tubes of K-Y jelly and Preparation H in the medicine cabinet.

As she regaled us with her findings, Kurt suddenly shouted at her in a frighteningly violent tone, "Shut the fuck up!"

We stopped dead in our tracks. Roxie was stunned. I could see Camille was about to give him hell, but I beat her to it. "Kurt, don't you ever speak to any of us like that again. We're not your flunkies."

He said nothing and left the room. None of us spoke another word, but we worked quickly in silence, like concentration camp inmates toiling under a vicious capo. While I was packing up an exquisite girandole (a sconce, to the uninformed), I made up my mind never to do this again. I never wanted to see Kurt again, and I had come to the conclusion I had finally had quite enough of his boss.

During one of my trips outside, I noticed a broken window in the basement laundry room. I took a sheet of stationery from a Georgian rolltop desk that Buster was carrying out and penned a short note to the owners of the house.

"Dear Mr. and Mrs. Phelps, I discovered a broken window in your laundry room. You really should get it repaired before someone uses it to break in. Also, I must compliment you on your wonderful collection of Louis Quinze. Sincerely, Julian." I left the note on the table in the breakfast nook.

Shortly afterward, Don offered to take me to lunch. Naturally, it wasn't at a well-populated midtown eatery but at a rather squalid coffee shop in my neighborhood. It was just as well. I had decided to tell Don I wasn't going to see him anymore. It seemed better to have such a hunger-destroying scene over a cheeseburger than to waste an expensive filet mignon.

After the waitress took our order of one cheeseburger and one Slenderella, Mr. Caspar got down to business. "Julian, I'm afraid there'll be no more work for you. The antiques business like most has a season and that season has come to an end."

"I'm glad you're telling me this, Don. Kurt was abusive to one of my friends, and none of us want to deal with him again."

"Oh, Kurt is harmless. He just has a surplus of energy. He's a big guy—he laughs big, he shouts big." Don ordered a glass of ginger ale from the waitress. "So, Julian, my friend, I hate to leave you without an income."

"Oh, I'll get by. I always do. I guess it's back to the temp pool."

"Don't you think it's time you settled down and found a real job?"

I wondered who he thought he was talking to. "A *real* job? My real job is acting and writing. I take part-time work so that it won't interfere with my real job." I couldn't believe after all this time I still had to explain this to him.

The waitress served him his drink, and between sips he said, "When your 'real job' doesn't pay you anything, you may want to rethink the direction of your life. You know, I think you're cute as hell, but, my friend, you are pushing thirty."

He was taunting me with this conversation, and I couldn't figure out why. I tried not to express my anger. "Don, although I've never asked you to invest, we have been quite successful raising the money to move our show off-Broadway. We're really almost there."

"How many times I have heard that one? In my life, I've known many aspiring show people, and the money is always 'almost there.' "

"All I can say, Don, is I have great faith in my partner, Joel. Perhaps we shouldn't be discussing this."

Don slowly sipped his drink, and I could see the wheels of his mind turning while he toyed with my emotions. This discussion wasn't meant to advise me but was a sort of sadistic exercise to dominate me just when he sensed he was losing me. "Julian, suppose you do get all the money, do you really imagine this little skit of yours is going to be a success? Sometimes we become infatuated with a fantasy that's best discarded."

With every bit of acting ability I possessed, I was determined not to let my voice quiver and shake. "I agree with you, Don. Sometimes it is best to discard a fantasy when it's lost its meaning. I'm glad you suggested we get together today, because I wanted to tell you I don't think we should see each other anymore."

He chuckled and sipped some more soda. "You're lying. That idea popped into your head this very minute. I've dashed your dreams and hurt your feelings. You know I'm just concerned, Julian."

"You've always been terribly concerned about me," I said sarcastically.

Don made a painful grimace. "Oh, Julian, don't disappoint me by being so conventional. Don't play the wounded mistress. But then maybe you're

taking your cue from one of your movie actresses. Who are you now? Bette
Davis or Joan Crawford?"

Surprisingly, my anger was subsiding, and the detached playwright in me
was studying Don as a subject for later use. "Don, why are you trying to hurt
me?"

"I'm not trying to hurt you. I'd like to fuck you."

This bizarre curve in the conversation forced me to laugh. Don laughed
too. "That's my boy. So what do you say? Should I pay the check and we go
up to your place?"

He was so remarkably handsome, yet the cruel sneer of his mouth reminded me of Dorian Gray's portrait after the first murder. He was undeni-
ably fascinating, and I wondered if he was more desirable today or when
he'd been known as Tony Andriolo and brutalized poor Max Milton, the director. I had no intention of revealing my knowledge of his past, but the
words tumbled out of me. "You're Tony Andriolo." For the first time since
we'd met, he had a simple, unambiguous expression on his face—that of
sheer surprise. "What?"

The voice that emerged from me sounded only vaguely like my own.
"Tony Andriolo. You knew Max Milton."

His large, sculpted face was now blank. He reminded me of Disneyland's
mechanical Abraham Lincoln without the juice on. "Why are you saying
that?"

"Because . . . I know who you were or rather who you are because you are
the same person. You would like to hurt me the way you hurt him." I was
aware of the melodrama of my speech, but there was no way to avoid it.

"Who told you this?"

"I've known for a long time. You're a scary guy, aren't you?"

He lifted his glass in a mock toast. "From one monster to another," he
said, and drained it. He leaned back in the booth and said, "You know, I
see a little of myself in you. Not the most interesting part, but the selfish-
ness. You're so wrapped up in your little movie star fantasies, there ain't
much place for anyone else, is there? That's okay by me, kid. Whaddyasay
we tip this joint? That's an old movie line for you." He locked his eyes
into mine, and it became a contest over who would break the stare. I
prayed the waitress would come by and interrupt this ridiculous contest.
Without shifting his gaze, Don lifted his empty glass and seductively
raised it to his lips.

At that moment I both wanted to rip his face off and have him fuck me
right across the coffee shop table. I very nearly whispered, "Pay the check
and come upstairs" when he placed the rim of the tumbler in his mouth
and bit down on it. The glass didn't shatter but left a perfect fragment on
his tongue. As if it were the most normal behavior in the world, he removed
the piece of glass from his mouth and had an expression on his face that
said, "Now?"

I pulled myself out of the booth. I didn't dare look at him. He exuded such power in his very stillness. I was so shaken I felt that if I caught his eye I'd turn into—well, if not a pillar of salt, at least the greasy salt shaker on the table. I steadied myself with one hand on top of the banquette and exited the restaurant. Wonderfully alone.

CHAPTER
31

Hey, *did you feel that strange rumble? Nah, I shouldn't have had that last Sambuca.*

Ultima, *Whores of Lost Atlantis*
Act Two, Scene Four

Harold Alpern is a celebrated Broadway producer known for producing prestigious, star-laden vehicles with literary pretensions that tend not to run very long. As a side line he also books shows into the rather run-down but legendary Washington Square Theatre. Joel and I were suitably in awe when we entered his suite of offices. Posters of his well-pedigreed succès d'estimes lined the walls.

Harold was a vigorous, large man in his sixties, sitting behind his desk in his shirtsleeves with his tie loosened.

"Come in, sit down. Talk to me." He asked us how we were progressing with our money-raising.

Joel, looking very impressive in his gray Brooks Brothers suit, said, "We have nearly our entire capitalization. We're missing twenty-five thousand dollars, but we have several possible investors we haven't spoken to."

He meant my aunt. One of Aunt Jennie's favorite lines of dialogue comes from *Annie Get Your Gun* when Sitting Bull says, "Don't drink, don't smoke, don't put money in show business." Joel refused to admit that it would be easier to move my aunt to a reservation and turn her into a chain-smoking lush. But to Harold Alpern, I nodded my head enthusiastically.

Harold clapped his hands together and bellowed, "I think we should do it. Mind you, I've got two other shows dying to get into the theatre, but I'm not so sure about them. I've got a good feeling about you guys. You know, I'm usually leery about these campy shows that spring out of a bar."

Joel sat up even straighter than usual and replied, "I can certainly understand that, Mr. Alpern, but Julian and I were more like tourists to the Lower East Side. Our background is very much in the commercial theatre. We're not kooks."

I was still reeling from my closing scene with Don as well as sinking into a quicksand of depression over my suspicion that my phone was being tapped and that I had implacable enemies out to destroy me. Joel may have been a presentable, theatre professional, but I was definitely feeling like a kook. We hadn't performed at Golgotha for several months, and I was losing a sense of my own cult fame. Once again I felt like a marginal figure in society filled with impossible ambitions.

Harold looked out of his window that had once revealed the Great White Way but now exposed a Lego landscape of construction sites. "Boys, I think if you promote the hell out of this thing and keep your costs down, you could have another *Rocky Horror Show*. And I think you've got yourself a potential star in this one." He pointed to me, and my mouth dropped open.

I stuttered, "B-b-b-but you haven't seen the show."

"Sure I have. I saw your closing night at that dive."

Joel was as surprised as I. "I had no idea."

"Sure, I keep a lookout for properties. My son told me about it. Yeah, I can't believe I schlepped down to that lousy neighborhood at great personal risk, but I enjoyed it. Julian, you reminded me of Charlotte Greenwood or Fanny Brice. You've got it, kid."

We signed the contract and handed over a check for a month's deposit on the theatre. Perhaps it was foolish putting down this money when we still hadn't raised the entire capitalization, but we were determined that we'd be opened by June 28, less than two months away.

As we stepped into the subway station, Joel turned to me and said, "It's time you hit up Aunt Jen."

I decided to throw a dinner party. I thought if I could pry my reclusive Aunt Jennie from her Park Avenue sanctuary, her disorientation might work to my advantage. I also hoped she'd be touched by my attempt to cook dinner, since my lack of culinary prowess bordered on the legendary. Dinner would be an intimate affair—Aunt Jennie, Joel, and myself. The menu for the evening: spaghetti with meat sauce and by this I mean fresh pasta boiled and not from a can, a simple salad, and garlic bread. Wilma came over that afternoon and worked like a domestic cyclone. The two of us got on our hands and knees and scrubbed the kitchen floor till it glistened like a designer igloo.

It was late afternoon, and my guests would be arriving at seven o'clock. I was in the kitchen rinsing out lettuce and waiting for Wilma to vamoose. At a quarter to five, she was still puttering around.

"Wilma darling, the place looks swell. You better go before you hit rush hour."

"Madame, the more I think about it, I really should stay and help you with dinner."

I was horrified. That was all I needed, a six-foot grandfather in a maid's uniform dishing out spaghetti. "Wilma dear, that's awfully sweet of you, but my aunt, well, she's pretty hip but um . . . she may not understand how I . . . how I could afford a maid. That may not go over well particularly when I'm about to ask her for money." I wondered if I could apply for a day job as a diplomat at the United Nations.

"Madame, can't you say I'm a fan who enjoys serving you?"

"No, that would not do. I really think you should go home."

Wilma put down her Dustbuster. "I don't know. Throwing a dinner party even for three is far from simple. Timing is all. And you'll be nervous and distracted. You need me. You really do."

This was getting extremely tiresome. I knew eventually Wilma/Bob would flip, but what a night to have to call Bellevue. I would have to be firm. "Wilma, sit down. We need to talk." Wilma fluffed out her skirt and sat down in an exaggeratedly ladylike manner. "First of all, I'm going to call you Bob." Wilma showed no reaction. "Bob, I've become so fond of you and, um, Wilma. I honestly forget who's real and who's not. I absolutely adore Wilma, but tonight we must have a firm grip on reality. This dinner is very important. I must instill in my aunt a sense of confidence and security so she'll invest in my show. Wilma may be real to us, but Aunt Jen may not get it. Wilma's kind of an acquired taste . . . like anchovies. Don't you think it would be better if we saved the fantasy for just the two of us?"

Bob/Wilma pursed his/her lips thoughtfully and replied in a masculine though tender voice, "Julian, I understand." I breathed easier. Bob then said, "However, I still think you need me. We've never done this before, but I think Wilma can still be present in Bob's body." I was very confused. He continued to explain this new concept. "Wilma can prepare and serve dinner and clean up afterward and you will know she's present but your guests will think it's Bob. Trust me, it will be perfect."

Joel arrived at a quarter to six looking rather jittery. His jitters turned to hysteria when he took a gander at Wilma, I mean Wilma-hiding-within-Bob's-body placing garnishes on a tray of hors d'oeuvres.

Bob/Wilma chirped, "Good evening, Joel."

If it's possible for one to smile grimly, that's what Joel did. "Hello, Wilma."

At that, Bob/Wilma looked at me smugly and said, "You see, dear, Joel knows I'm Wilma even if I am dressed as Bob."

Joel took my upper arm and said stiffly, "Julian, we need to plan our strategy for the evening." He led me into the living room, where Wilma had set up the card table and created in an astoundingly short time a lovely dining room complete with origami napkin holders.

"Joel, didn't Wilma do a fabulous job?"

"You are crazy, aren't you?"

"Why? Do you think it's too cutesy?"

"What is Wilma doing here?"

"I couldn't get rid of her. She's stuck to me like space-age eyelash glue. But look at this spread. She's turned my pitiful spaghetti dinner into a gourmet feast. We're having fusilli puttanesca. That's Italian for screws whore style. No wisecracks."

Joel paced the room. "I can't believe you'd risk this investment on a schizophrenic drag queen with a serving fetish."

I was afraid Wilma would hear him. "Shhh, she's very vulnerable. Believe me, everything will be hunky-dory. Wilma is posing as a man tonight."

"So do we call him Bob?"

"No, we call him Toby. It's all very complicated, but Wilma can't use Bob as a cover because Bob is real, so she needed another self . . . Oh, just forget about it. All you have to know is Toby is a neighbor in my building who is helping me out tonight. Don't worry, Aunt Jen will think it's camp."

Aunt Jennie arrived a little after seven. When she buzzed the intercom, I sent Joel to help her up the stairs. I was still rummaging through my drawers in search of a shirt without a rip or stain on it. Getting Aunt Jen up the three flights of stairs took the same amount of time as boiling a vat of water. She emerged at the door looking absolutely adorable though panting. She was swathed in an odd collection of scarves and beads. Her jewelry that night included a valuable antique jade necklace and love beads I'd strung for her in the sixties. Joel carried her shopping bag.

"Julian, I can't believe you made me schlepp all this shit up here." I kissed her on the cheek. Everything she wore and everything she touched was permeated with the same wonderful, exotic fragrance, a turn-of-the-century perfume that she had found on a trip to France in the fifties. She'd been able to locate an eccentric *parfumier* in Brooklyn who could duplicate the scent and who'd been her supplier ever since.

"Aunt Jen, were you able to find any of the stuff I asked for?"

"I don't know. See for yourself. I've got so much crap in my apartment." We needed some hard-to-find props for our show, and I had a feeling Aunt Jen could dig them up in her memorabilia shop of a home. She shook her head in theatrical dismay and told Joel, "It's dreadful. I keep collecting more and more junk and Julian won't let me give anything away." She turned to me. "You're going to be in trouble when I kick the bucket and you have to dispose of everything."

She looked around. "I haven't been down here in years. I forgot how nice and big your kitchen is. It's a pity the walls are collapsing." She took Joel's arm and lifted her face coquettishly toward his. "Joel, I'm going to embarrass you again. You have grown so handsome. I just love your looks. You were good-looking before, but now you've got such dignity. You remind me of my husband." She looked at me and sighed. "Oh, Julian, I wish you would stand up straight like Joel. But I give up. I just hope I'm gone when you've got dowager's hump and are hobbled over with arthritis."

She walked through the apartment toward the living room. Bob aka Wilma aka Toby was lighting the dinner candles. Aunt Jen looked surprised to see a man Bob's age in my home.

"Um, Toby, I'd like you to meet my Aunt Jennie, Mrs. Holman. Toby . . . Wilmer. I was having a terrible time getting this dinner together. Toby's my neighbor. He's been so generous helping me out."

"It's very nice meeting you, Mrs. Holman. Julian's told me so much about you."

"I'm sure he has. He tells everyone I'm a kook." Her 1930s chiffon dress certainly helped maintain that image.

My servant in disguise was doing very well in his imitation of normalcy. "Mrs. Holman, Julian has told me wonderful stories of his growing up with you."

"Well, it's just the two of us. And his brother—but we haven't seen much of him lately." She shook off that unpleasant topic and exclaimed, "This table setting is magnificent. But I only see three places."

Wilma smiled benignly. "No, I'm the caterer. I'll be busy in the kitchen."

Aunt Jennie wouldn't accept that. "That's silly, there's plenty of room at the table. You've done such a beautiful job."

I thought I detected a glint in Wilma's eye that she might accept my aunt's invitation. I had to nip this in the bud. "You don't understand, Aunt Jen. Toby and I have a deal. I'm doing some artwork for his catering company for free in exchange for his services tonight. We've got it all worked out."

Aunt Jen looked skeptical and murmured, "It's all rather silly." She turned her attention to the contents of her shopping bag. "Look through this stuff and see if you want any of it." I had asked her to help me find some things that could resemble a royal seal, an antique dagger, and a sinister-looking vial for poison. She didn't disappoint. Out of the shopping bag came a selection of four paper cutters, any of which would make a splendid dagger, a variety of small vials, and several peculiar objects that she thought could double as a royal seal. I was amazed. Anything could be found in her apartment.

Bob Livingston, who'd been doing such a bang-up job sublimating Wilma, picked up a jeweled paper cutter and cooed. "Ooh, pretty." A visible jolt went through him when he heard Wilma's voice emerge.

Joel took a large swig of his martini.

Bob decided to make a hasty exit and in his best vice-presidential voice excused himself with "Pardon me, Mrs. Holman, I must go to the powder room."

When he left, Joel and I looked stricken and Aunt Jen queried out of the side of her mouth, "Is he for real?"

I was already exhausted and improvised wearily. "He lives next door with his wife and two daughters. I guess it rubs off. Let's eat."

We sat down to dinner, and, say what you will about my servant, Wilma the mysterious had produced a magnificent repast. We began with a pungent Caesar salad, which led to a full-bodied fusilli puttanesca woven with a dazzling variety of tastes and textures and accompanied by lusty Tuscan garlic bread.

Aunt Jen wouldn't accept Toby as merely a servant. She felt compelled to engage him in conversation on his every entrance. "Toby, are you also in the theatre? You have such a wonderful speaking voice."

"Aunt Jen, I told you Toby has a catering business."

"I know, Julian, but many actors have another business on the side." I wondered if she was about to go off on that tedious tract again.

Wilma laughed and said, "No, I've never been on the stage, but I certainly can understand its allure. It's fun occasionally to pretend to be someone you're not."

I didn't appreciate that remark. Wilma was toying with my nerves.

Aunt Jen digested his statement. "I can identify with that. When I was a little girl in Cincinnati, we were so poor. I often pretended I was a princess from Ireland or India. For a long time, I convinced my schoolmates I had a talking cat in my basement. I still have fantasies of being a great opera singer."

I found Aunt Jen's speech about expressing one's fantasies truly dangerous. Wilma's frilly uniform was in the closet in the very next room. Bob's mind could snap any minute and on would go his fishnet hose.

My rambunctious maid picked up Aunt Jen's thread. "Imagination can be wonderful and also a problem. I hope Julian can control *his* imagination. He has a gift for dramatizing life's situations, and that could make him easily manipulated." Joel and my eyes met; neither of us had a clue to what Wilma was talking about. I wished I had a little bell at the table to order him from the room. Or the flyswatter.

I could see Aunt Jen scrutinizing Wilma in her most Miss Marple manner. She chose her words carefully. "I know Julian can be distracted. It runs in our family. But I think he's basically very stable and has good values." She shifted her gaze to me and asked, "I'm right, aren't I?"

"You bet." I reached for my fork and knocked my entire plate of salad into my lap. Wilma rushed into the kitchen to grab some paper towels. As soon as he was gone, Aunt Jen made a grimace indicating she thought he was a nut. All I could do was anxiously shrug.

Aunt Jen swallowed her last piece of meticulously al dente pasta and decided to call a spade a spade. "All right, you two, I know you didn't invite me here just to give the old bag a night on the town."

Joel coughed up an olive. I dabbed my napkin to the corners of my mouth. "Of course, Aunt Jen, it's in the worst possible taste for you to expose my deception."

"Some deception. You must really think I'm a babe in the woods. You're looking for money for your show."

"We have almost all of it, but we're just a little short. I didn't want to involve you, but we're really down to the wire. Besides, I honestly think it's going to be a hit. I mean, if people will line up for hours to see us on Avenue C, why shouldn't they come in droves when we're in a lovely theatre in a safe neighborhood?"

"Julian, Uncle Max loved that line from *Annie Get Your Gun* where Sitting Bull says, 'Secret of long life. Don't drink, don't smoke, don't put money in show business.' "

"Yeah, yeah, yeah, but Sitting Bull didn't have a nephew who's been struggling and working his ass off for nearly ten years."

"How much do you want from me?"

"Six thousand dollars."

I turned the floor over to Joel, who had been silently downing martinis all evening to steady his Wilma-frayed nerves. Now he had to compose himself and present a responsible image for Aunt Jen. With only a slight slur to his British-inflected diction, Joel explained the nature of a limited partnership, how the play's profits would be distributed, the risks involved, and the joys of participating in a theatrical gamble.

I could see Aunt Jen didn't understand most of what he was saying. She knew the only question she needed answered, and she waited till he finished his long discourse. "Joel, I'm very impressed. You know, I think you're a, well, a superior person, but I just want to know, how much is your family putting in? I don't want to feel like a stooge."

"Mrs. Holman, my parents bought two units for sixty-two hundred dollars, and my grandmother and Aunt Mary are splitting a unit."

Aunt Jen was trapped. "Oh well, then I suppose I must. Put me down for two. This is something I swore I'd never do but . . . you know, Joel, I have this theory." Aunt Jen had studied Kant, Buber, and Kierkegaard and out of her studies had distilled her own philosophy. "I have this theory that the world is divided into two categories: assholes and shitheads. An asshole is someone who does terrible things but doesn't know why, and a shithead does terrible things with full knowledge and self-awareness. I give everyone a rating from one to ten, ten being the worst. This is all a way of saying that I suppose if I don't invest, I'd be a number nine shithead."

Joel looked a bit confused, but I was extremely touched. We got up from the table with Aunt Jen sighing, "Boy, this was the most expensive dinner I ever had. At sixty-two hundred dollars, I figure I just spent seventy-five bucks per fusilli."

Joel, spent from the ordeal and fairly smashed, bid us farewell. "Good night, Mrs. Holman. I'll drop off the partnership papers tomorrow. Forgive me for being a bit tipsy. I find these dinners difficult, you know, asking for money. I suppose that makes me a number six shithead and a number four asshole."

Aunt Jen pondered that for a second. "No, no, Joel, you were more conscious than unconscious when you chose to drink so that would make you a number eight asshole but only a number two shithead." She was getting her own theory screwed up.

"No, Aunt Jen, he's more of a shithead than an asshole because you see—" Before I could finish my statement, Joel had stumbled out the door.

I brought Aunt Jen into my bedroom to show her a collage I'd made of photographs of nineteenth-century stage stars cut from a magazine.

"Oh, Julian, I love it. You have such a creative eye. I do wish you'd take up painting again. I just know you could be a famous artist." She looked around the red-painted room. "This is some bedroom. I can't decide if it resembles Sarah Bernhardt's boudoir or a steak house."

"Face it, it looks like your apartment."

"It does not."

We sat on the bed shoulder to shoulder like a comedy act waiting to go on. "Anyway, Aunt Jennie, I just want to thank you for coming through. I know it's a lot of money, but I think if it's ever going to happen for me, well, this is it. This is my chance."

"Julian, I know I give you a hard time. But I just felt it would be wrong for me to make it too easy for you."

"Well, you sure haven't."

"Look, I came to New York in 1932 with twenty-five dollars in my purse. I didn't have a rich aunt. But, Julian, I don't think anyone could have worked harder than you these past years." Her eyes widened in a childlike manner. "You're obsessed!" She took hold of my hand and patted it. "Julian, you're okay in my book." We sat for a moment lost in our own thoughts. Then she checked to see if the coast was clear. She saw that Wilma was washing the dishes in the kitchen. She whispered, "That man gives me the willies."

"Do you think he's the type that would dress up in a French maid's uniform or something?"

"I don't know about that, but it's like he's studying us, like he's a spy. I'd stay clear of him. You hear all sorts of stories about neighbors getting perverted fixations about people."

"Oh, he's harmless. He just likes to talk. He doesn't mean anything. He's just an asshole," I said, dismissing the subject.

Aunt Jen checked once more whether he could hear us. "No, Julian, he knew exactly what he was saying. He's a shithead, and I'd say a number ten."

Andreas, look at the strange glow along the horizon. The entire ancient city is suffused with light. Why am I so frightened?

Milena, *Whores of Lost Atlantis*
Act Two, Scene Four

We were now only ten thousand dollars short of our goal. At this point, the wheels of the production could truly begin to roll. Sets had been designed and were being built, and lights were being ordered. Camille and I sketched pages of new wigs and began visiting our usual Korean haunts for wigs, wiglets, and switches. Joel worked out a rehearsal schedule, and when I saw on paper the day-to-day process of putting on the show from read-through to dress rehearsal to first preview to opening night, the enormity of the situation finally hit me. I was about to face the entire battery of New York critics for the first time with a skit I'd written in five hours between phone calls! In a sweating panic, I furiously began rewriting *Whores of Lost Atlantis* in a mad attempt to give it more depth and at least a patina of literary style. I succeeded in transforming a lighthearted romp into a pretentious bore. Joel read the rewritten script, went to bed, and had a nightmare of epic proportions. His dream was filled with irate theatregoers charging down to the footlights shaking their fists in fury. "This isn't the show we paid for! Call Actors' Equity! Write your senators! Hang 'em high!"

The following morning, Joel pleaded with me to accept that this New York debut might not be everything we might have dreamed of but that we had stumbled onto something unique and shouldn't tempt the fates. I took out the "improvements."

Mamacita recovered from his bout of pneumonia. He surprised me by crediting his speedy recovery most of all to Guy's metaphysical ministrations.

"Mamacita, are you on the level?"

He put down the brightly patterned fabric he was using to create himself a new caftan. "Julian darling, Guy may be an arrogant son of a bitch with expensive tastes in home furnishings, but, baby, he's got what it takes when it comes to healing."

"What did he do to you?"

"It's hard for me to tell and perhaps I shouldn't even try. The voodoo masters on my island always told us to keep word of their magic to ourselves. Let me just say that our Guy is a different person when he's on his healing trip. There's a peaceful calm that comes over him, and it moves over to you. Now you know, darling one, that I'm the most skeptical bitch in the world. When he saw me the first time, I had a chip on my shoulder the size of Mount Fuji. But he just sort of held me and breathed along with me. I found myself telling secrets that I never discuss with myself, and not even with my beloved Mudge. Your Mamacita has had a very rough life." Mamacita gathered the exotic fabric up to his clownlike face. "Julian, don't judge me, but I felt as if Guy and I weren't alone. I felt as if we were joined by all the spirits of my dead loved ones. They all wanted me to be well." He dropped the fabric into his lap. "Julian, my temperature dropped three degrees in one hour."

"But you were on massive doses of medication."

"Bitch, don't rain on my cosmic parade."

Guy and I rarely socialized outside the theatre, but after hearing Mamacita's testimonial, I felt compelled to ask him to lunch. We ate at the same coffee shop where I'd played out my last scene with Don.

"Mamacita speaks of you now with the reverence accorded to the founders of the world's great religions."

"I'm glad he thought I was helpful."

Employing every vocal and facial tool I possessed to express sincerity, I said, "I want to thank you for helping him. I know I've been flippant and sarcastic about this side of your life, and that was wrong. I don't want to be a judgmental person. Will you forgive me if I ever offended you?"

My intensity clearly perplexed Guy. "Julian, are you all right?"

I nervously brushed my hair off my forehead, a Judyesque gesture I hoped didn't remind Guy of the children's birthday party fiasco. "I *am* a bit on edge these days, you know, with the show opening so soon." That was an understatement; I was jumping on an emotional trampoline. "I imagine you must be pretty frenetic yourself, Guy, between your magic shows and the healing."

"It's been wild. The spring is always my busy season for children's parties, but the healing work I'm doing is taking up more and more of my time. It's so fulfilling to me. I can't believe sometimes I'm involved in all these people's lives. Julian, you'd be amazed at the incredible things I'm seeing."

"So I hear. Everyone's talking about it. Camille, Perry. They tell me crutches are flying out your window, tumors are shrinking, the mute speak, dyslexics are typing up a storm."

"You're being facetious again."

"I don't mean to. I write and speak in comedy rhythms. I can't help it. It's just that I've known you since you were nineteen. I suppose this spiritual side of you was always there, but I was never really aware of it until the past year."

"Neither was I. It's like I'm three different people, your leading man, the children's entertainer, and this person who works with sick people. It's hard sometimes to reconcile that all this comes out of the same body."

"Welcome to the club." I had ordered Don's usual fare, the Slenderella—hamburger, lettuce, fruit, and cottage cheese—and couldn't more than pick at my cottage cheese. "It's funny, Guy. Just about everyone I know is sort of a split personality. Or is it that they lead so many different lives and have a specific persona to wear with each?" I counted them on my fingers. "Let's see, there's Perry, who is clinically manic-depressive. He's either trembling with enthusiasm or morbidly silent. Buster, who is the most adorable, cuddly little boy but when he drinks becomes an abrasive bore. Roxie is a walking cast of thousands. I don't even know how she keeps her wardrobe straight. Joel is a young man from Indiana who's transformed himself into the perfect English gentleman. Zoe changes her name every week. Camille changes her life every five years from Mafia child-wife to secretary to disco champion to drag wig stylist. I have a maid who's really an ad exec. My aunt is both an elegant Park Avenue widow and a tough-talking dame."

"And you?"

"Me?" I laughed with an edge of hysteria that surprised us both.

"Me? I win the door prize, Guy. I'm a man, I'm a woman, I'm a boy. I'm a clown who wants to be taken seriously and an actor who wants to be a leading lady. I don't know. I thought I had some sense of myself, but I give up. I don't have a fucking clue. Maybe it doesn't matter." My oration was exhausting me, and I released a long sigh. "I don't know, Guy. Do I even believe what I'm saying, or am I just bullshitting? Am I trying to impress you with how deep I am? I'm ambivalent about even that. Hey, if Zoe can change her name all the time, maybe I should change mine to Ambivalena. That's a good drag name." I speared a chunk of melon, then rejected it.

"Why the hell did I order this? I don't even like honeydew melon. My aunt's the one who likes this." My hand was shaking so wildly, I had to put my fork down. I placed my palm over my mouth to steady it and shut myself up.

Guy let a few seconds elapse before he spoke.

"Julian, did you ask me out because you want to work with me, the way I work with Mamacita? Would you like to try that?"

I chewed on my nail while I thought. "Do I want that? I suppose the idea crossed my mind but I couldn't. I probably should but I won't. You see, I may not know me very well but I'm afraid, my darling friend, that I know you too well." That line had a certain zing to it but at that moment I had the feeling that I didn't know anyone in the world very well.

Mamacita didn't discuss his illness anymore for he was now plunged into the maelstrom of designing and building a completely new set of costumes. This time he had a budget considerably larger than the price of a one-way bus ticket to Atlantic City. The costume studio where he worked allocated him a large corner, and he drew on favors from all his buddies in the costume business. Whereas before he and Mudge were the lone seamstresses sometimes hot-gluing us into a flimsy improvised costume as we ran onstage, now Mamacita had a team of volunteers creating sumptuous costumes that befit the royal courtesans of Atlantis.

The cast all visited the studio for costume fittings except Zoe. No one had been able to reach her.

Mamacita was beside himself. "Where is that crazy child? She stood me up for her fitting. I've left at least ten messages on her answering machine and she never returns my calls." Joel had tried to reach her as well, to no avail. He had to hand in the program information to *Playbill* magazine, and we had no idea what last name she wanted to be billed under. During our final engagement at Golgotha, she called herself Zoe Anonymous. We had the feeling she was running out of ideas.

I had to return to the costume studio for my second fitting. I took the elevator up to the large industrial loft where Mamacita plied his trade. I always looked forward to visiting the studio. It had the ambience of a decadent Santa's toy factory. At every worktable, artists were gluing the hair on a giant ape's head or dying large bolts of fabric or placing the last rhinestone on a sugarplum fairy's tiara. Patti Page was singing on the tape deck, and Mamacita was on his knees fitting Buster for his new and improved G-string. The boys and girls at the studio put down their projects to gaze upon Buster's physical gorgeousness. It was the most glittering, bejeweled G-string imaginable. Buster flexed his muscles and studied himself in the full-length mirror. After impressing us with his masculine posturing, he lifted an enormous Follies show girl headdress off a nearby table and placed it on his head, then paraded around the studio like a muscled peacock. Mamacita barked, "All right, Pavlova, get those bunnies over here Speaking of which, it's time you laid off the candy bars."

Buster stopped dead in his tracks. It was true, he had gained a touch of weight during our hiatus and none of us had the nerve to tell him.

"Mamacita, you have truly plucked my nerves. There isn't a man in any gay bar in this town who wouldn't buy me a *cock*tail." He sashayed grandly back to Mamacita's worktable.

I hastened to note, "Honey, it looks like there's a few too many tomatoes in that can."

Buster lifted his nose in the air, dismissing his critics. They resumed the fitting. Buster tugged at his crotch. "Mamacita, you got to make it tighter under here." He pointed to the area between his legs. "I am blessed with a lavishly endowed scrotal sac, and we don't want me to fall out of this G-string in front of *The New York Times*, now do we?"

Mamacita removed several straight pins from his mouth. "My dear, if something's going to be altered, it'll be your scrotal sac. I always thought you had a bit too much testosterone for your own good."

I spied something in the corner. Draped on a dress dummy was new my Act Two gown. Extravagantly dripping with glittering beads and gilded lace, the gown and headdress evoked images of both a Byzantine empress and a carnival cootch dancer. I tore off my clothes, and Mamacita helped me into the costume. He then fastened a heavy, jeweled choker around my neck. The entire costume was akin to wearing a beaded chiffon snakeskin, with the long train swinging cobralike behind me. I practiced walking about the room, allowing the train to fan out and raising my arms to create a bat-wing effect with the lace attached to my wrists. It was more fantastic than I could have dreamed possible. I just looked at Mamacita. Words couldn't convey my gratitude. Even Buster kept his mouth shut while I explored my new diva poses in the spectacular gown. Once more Mamacita's eyes met mine. We were both welling with tears. Could it have been that we were both thrilled with the effect of his brilliance and heartsick that an early death would preclude him from reaching the zenith of his creativity? It was so unfair.

CHAPTER 33

Venus Castina! The Temple is falling!

Milena, *Whores of Lost Atlantis*
Act Two, Scene Four

Sunday, June 21, was Gay Pride Day, and Joel thought it would be invaluable publicity for us to have a float in the Gay Pride Parade. On a less crass note, it was also a way of thanking our gay audience for their support during the past year. The cast gathered at my apartment—that is, everyone but Zoe, who was still unreachable. We were starting to think about having to replace her. Mamacita had gained back a good deal of his lost weight and wore one of his most idiosyncratic outfits. That morning he sported a voluminous peasant shirt from Afghanistan and turquoise spandex biker shorts that on him resembled a long-line panty girdle. He topped it off with a large plumed hat pulled from a stock production of *The Three Musketeers*.

His creations for us were no less flamboyant but a lot skimpier. We looked like figures from the Arabian Nights as performed by the cast of Minsky's Burlesque circa 1942. Guy, Buster, and Perry were garbed in very abbreviated loincloths and body glitter. Every few minutes they'd be on the floor doing push-ups in a last-ditch effort to pump up. Joel had brought over a pitcher of Manhattans, and he, Camille, and Roxie were feeling quite giddy and festive. Roxie was rigged up in an erotic creation. The most singular feature was two gold snakes that coiled over her bare breasts and whose snarling jeweled heads covered her nipples. She wore one of Camille's largest wigs, a flowing blond monstrosity that divided on top into two three-foot cones.

My own costume consisted mostly of number-fifteen sunscreen. A sequined G-string, a flimsy piece of glittery tulle tied around my hips, the usual spike heels, a waist-length red wig, and most of Aunt Jennie's costume jewelry composed my fashion ensemble that June morning. Still, Mamacita felt something was missing.

"Yeah," quipped I, "panties. It ain't dignified for a dame in my position to be so scantily clad."

Mamacita fussed over the placement of my beads. "Just keep your knees together 'cause, dearie, one false move and there goes any illusion of pussy." Mamacita eyed me up and down in dissatisfaction; then a look of rapture overtook his eggplant face. He rummaged through his bag and came forth with my old friend, the Angelica Cross.

"Julian, I want to return this to you. It worked. Look at me, glowing with false hope." Mamacita was perversely enjoying the effect of his gallows humor on all his loved ones. "But sincerely, Julian, and this is very difficult for me since my middle name is Glib and my confirmation name is Flippant, I really did appreciate having this in my hospital room. Frankly, I can't even express my true feelings because they are embarrassingly profound." He handed me the cross.

"Mama, you can keep it longer."

"No, no, I'll put it away somewhere, and then I'll die and be on the local to heaven, and some strange health-care volunteer will riffle through my goods and stick it in her bag. Better take it now and . . . aaaaad . . ." He stretched that small word into at least eight syllables. "Aaaaaaad wear it today in the parade."

"Where?"

"Turn around, baby. Right here!" I protested but did what I was told. With his genius for improvisation, he attached the priceless Angelica Cross to a two-dollar gold chain around my hips. The cross dangled right over the crack of my ass.

"Oh, I'm astonished at you, Mama. That's downright sacrilegious."

He pooh-poohed me. "No, it's not. Nuns have been wearing them as accessories for years."

We had to be up near Lincoln Center by twelve-thirty to hop aboard the float. Buster had brought his camera and wanted photos of us leaving my building in our stripper costumes. Joel and Camille insisted that we hurry, but Roxie, somewhat blotto on Manhattans, was adamant on taking just one more photo.

Before we could stop her, Roxie mounted the hood of a car parked in front of my building. She struck a series of sexy Vargas-like calendar girl poses while Buster clicked away. We were all so amused by her antics, none of us noticed the teenage boys on the roof of the building across the street. It was a shock to us all when one! two! three! Roxie was struck with eggs. Her body was flung about like a rag doll, and when the attack was over, egg yolk was dripping down the side of her face, on her lovely breasts, and coagulated in her wig.

When the shock of the violence subsided, she began screaming like a banshee. She raised her fists and hollered at the hysterically laughing kids in the ugliest fishwife voice I'd ever heard. "You motherfucking, cocksucking assholes! Your mothers suck dick, your sisters . . ." That was before she really cut loose. Joel climbed onto the car hood and dragged her off, her face a welter of smashed egg and blinding tears.

Back inside my apartment, Mamacita and Camille cleaned her up as her rage grew to Godzilla-like proportions.

"I have been assassinated! Assassinated! I know exactly how JFK felt!"

Perry, desperately trying to suppress his laughter, said, "Oh come now."

Roxie glared at him. "Perry, I have known the assassin's bullet! This was an exact re-creation of the events in Dealey Plaza on November 22, 1963. I was hit once in the throat, once in the back of my head, and once in the breast."

I was compelled to disagree. "JFK was not hit in the breast."

Roxie would have none of my quibbling. "Julian, do not make light of my ordeal."

"Roxie, next you'll be saying there was more than one egg thrower."

"But there was! One person could not have thrown three eggs simultaneously."

The laughter left Perry, and he looked at us all with an expression of horror. "What if it was a conspiracy? What if those kids were put up to this by—"

I finished his sentence: "Kiko and Thirteen." This was the final blow to Roxie, who sank to her knees in defeat.

Fortunately, the parade was late getting started. We taxied uptown and found our flower-bedecked float. The words JULIAN YOUNG AND THE IMITATION OF LIFE THEATRE were emblazoned across the back of the float, as well as the logo for *Whores of Lost Atlantis*. At the center was a pyramid of wooden boxes painted to resemble old-fashioned steamer trunks. The company sat on the various boxes, and I was perched on the highest level.

With a great lurch, the car to which we were hooked took off. It felt like the height of vulnerability to be placed so high on top of a large moving float, yet it also was incredibly heady to the ego. I felt like Cleopatra making her entrance in Rome. The float made its slow progress down Central Park West and through Columbus Circle. The streets were packed with smiling gay people and fascinated straights. All of us on the float were open-mouthed with astonishment at the overwhelming affection of the crowd. I was amazed to see so many young men shouting, "We love you, Julian," and raising their thumbs in support. More people had seen us at Golgotha during this past year than we'd realized. Camille, Mamacita, and Joel marched alongside the float with a number of other parade marshals handing out fliers advertising our upcoming show. After about six blocks, Mamacita's energy began to flag, and he decided to go home and rest. Mudge was planning a special dinner for us after the parade. Buster stood in the front of the float, arms akimbo like some golden-skinned masthead. His beauty inspired a continuous barrage of catcalls and hooting and hollering from the masses.

I leaned down and said to Roxie, "What a pity Zoe isn't here. She would have loved this."

The mystery of her disappearance was solved somewhat when we stopped for a long light at Twenty-third and Fifth Avenue. Three of the Young Julians burst out of the crowd and raced over to us. Eric, the blond one, grabbed my outstretched hand. "Julian, you look gorgeous." That was debatable. In the afternoon sun, I feared my makeup was sweating off and by the time I reached Christopher Street I'd resemble nothing less than Ernest Borgnine in a fright wig. The Young Julians were chattering enthusiastically until Lyle, the overweight, dark-haired one, said, "Poor Zoe." Roxie asked what he meant by that, and he uttered gravely, "Well, you know, she's like off the deep end."

Lyle filled us in quickly before the light changed. "Oh, honey, I ran into Zoe in a hardware store in midtown." The story was already bizarre. The sheer thought of Zoe in a hardware store strained credibility. "I almost didn't recognize her 'cause she was wearing this weird blond wig. I mean, it wasn't combed or styled or anything. And her face was all swollen like she'd been crying for days. So I asked her if she was okay, and she gives me this sort of demented smile, kind of like the way she does in *Whores* when she's about to jump into the pit of piranhas. And she says, 'Where do you think they display their guns?' I told her hardware stores don't usually carry firearms, and she looked very confused, kind of like she did in your ballet mystery when she hid the severed head." I was flattered by the references to my oeuvre, but they were slowing down his revelations. "I tell her maybe she should sit down, and I offered to buy her a cup of tea somewhere. I took her to the Galaxy and I know how private she is but she like spilled her guts out to me. It was horrible. This rich man she was in love with promised to marry her. I think they were even going to elope and then out of the blue, he dumped her. He told her he was married and you know how Catholic she is. Did you know she once planned on being a nun and had gone as far as shaved her head?" None of us knew that. In fact, none of us knew much of anything about her after more than a year of working together. The light had changed, and Lyle's companions were dragging him away before they were run over by the Philadelphia group Dykes on Bikes.

Lyle's parting words chilled us. "The last thing she told me was she was rereading something by this guy named Christopher Marlowe, and she said, 'Vengeance shall be mine!' Anyway, you guys look fabulous. Happy Gay

Pride Day!" Our driver stepped on the gas, and off we sped.

Our dismay over Zoe's misfortune was interrupted when, around Eighteenth Street, Buster shouted, "Look to the right!"

Marching on the side of our float were none other than Kiko and Thirteen costumed as Siamese twin show girls. They wore matching black Louise Brooks–style dutch bob wigs and were attached across their middle by a wide strip of red spandex that ended just below their crotches, revealing their fishnet-stockinged legs. The crowd was amused by their appearance, and they pranced around our car trying to steal focus. Our driver was afraid of hitting them and repeatedly honked his horn. I looked around for a parade marshal to get the deadbeats out of our path. Then Thirteen in the midst of a high kick got his heel caught on a manhole cover and stumbled to the pavement, dragging Kiko along with him. The diabolical twins' struggle directly in front of our car brought the entire parade to a standstill. Behind us a boisterous contingent, Grandparents for Gays, were bellowing for us to move our asses. To my eternal astonishment, Joel decided to take his Christian ethic of turning the other cheek too, too far and offered a lift to Kiko and Thirteen. All of us on the float were shocked at this conciliatory gesture. It took four marshals to lift the Siamese twins onto our float, after which they rudely pushed Buster out of his key front position. Triumphant, Kiko and Thirteen linked arms while we sat behind them like helpless parakeets on a swing. However, when the parade began moving again, our float took off with another sudden lurch, sending our new arrivals sprawling across the floor. This time none of us lifted a finger to help them. They managed with great effort to crawl toward the center of the platform. Ever the benevolent star, I motioned Roxie to share my spot on top and allow the trespassers to settle their dusty haunches on her steamer trunk.

The float was inching past Washington Square, which was packed with NYU students and wild-eyed street people screaming encouragements. Kiko looked up at Roxie and queried with false concern, "Darling, what's all over your face? You look like someone was making crepe suzettes on you."

Roxie extended her long neck in an elegant fashion and cooed, "Kiko, I had an experience we could share. Having egg on my face or should I say in your case, on your twat."

Kiko dropped her facade of gentility with a thud. "Face or twat—both look the same on you."

This was the final straw for Roxie, who was still convinced Kiko was behind her banishment from Wall Street. She growled, "You ugly bitch," and lunged for Kiko's throat. The two women clawed and latched on to each other like mad dogs. They toppled from their steamer trunks and rolled across the floor of the float, Kiko dragging her attached twin, Thirteen, beside her. Perry sprang to Roxie's defense and joined in the fray. The crowd cheered them on with crazed enthusiasm. Buster and Guy tried to wrench them apart. I, however, continued to wave to the crowd like a beauty queen from hell.

In the distance, I heard a police siren. By now Camille had climbed onto the float and was trying to salvage Roxie's wig. Buster noticed a large, ugly Kiko-induced red scratch across Perry's bare buttocks, and bellowed, "Rabies alert!" The siren grew closer, and now it seemed as though there were a number of sirens blaring in concert. Blinding orange lights began swirling around us. I wondered if there had been a traffic accident nearby or a violent protest against the parade. I thought perhaps this police action was merely to stop the melee that was destroying my once beautiful float.

I looked up and was amazed to see we had stopped almost directly in front of Ellis Farrell's town house on Washington Square. Indeed, Ellis and a few of his ancient cronies were watching the parade from his terrace. He recognized me and waved. I was about to wave back when Joel began shouting something at me. The police sirens were so cacophonous I couldn't understand a word he was saying. A horde of policemen broke through the crowd and descended upon us. I could see Joel in an agitated discussion with several of them. A sea of blue-uniformed cops swept over the float, dragging off my friends and finally separating the battling parties. I remained on my high steamer trunk until a burly cop leveled a finger at me. At once, three of his colleagues stormed the float and snatched me like Marie Antoinette off my throne. Washington Square reminded me of the Place de la Révolution, with its hysterical mob thirsty for blood.

A large black paddy wagon right out of a thirties gangster picture was pulled up beside the float, and an array of squad cars screeched to a halt at every diagonal. I watched everything around me as if it were a Cinerama movie. I was dumbstruck as Roxie was dragged screaming toward the paddy wagon. She looked hideous: her wig had been yanked off, and her face resembled an abstract painting of smeared black eye makeup and dried egg yolk. Her long Olive Oyl legs kicked wildly like a frenetic marionette as she was tossed into the Black Maria along with Kiko and Thirteen. Joel was in some sort of negotiation with the cops until he was unceremoniously thrust into a squad car along with Camille. My former betrothed, a born cop hater, was all jutting elbows and gun moll bravado as they slammed the car door behind her.

In the madness, while the police were busy rounding up Guy, Perry, and Buster, the attention was off me. The Warner Bros. spirit overtook me, and I was one of the prisoners in a chain gang. I brushed my wig away from my eyes and took it on the lam. My spike heels served me better than track shoes as I ran for it. I sprinted about thirty feet to where the crowd was cordoned off. Disregarding the vulgarity of my action, I threw a naked leg over the police barricade and tried to push my way through the crowd. Seemingly dozens of outstretched hands were pawing my G-stringed flesh. I was pleading with them to let me pass, but their own mirthful cries of "We love you" drowned me out. One hand grabbed my shoulder with such force, I spun my head around, to find myself face-to-face with a brawny flatfoot.

"Julian Young, I've got a warrant for your arrest."

Breathless, I could only muster, "You're kidding."

He wasn't. "Girlie, you're goin' for a ride."

While being roughly handcuffed, I looked up again at Ellis Farrell's terrace. He was leaning over the balcony desperately trying to make something clear to me. All I could do was holler back, "Call my aunt! Mrs. Jennie Holman! She's in the book!"

Two cops, a man and a woman, climbed into the paddy wagon with us. Dialogue familiar from a slew of movies and TV shows was hurled at us. "You have the right to remain silent. Anything you say can and will be used against you in a court of law."

The image of Marie Antoinette remained with me. The long ride in the paddy wagon wasn't far removed from that of the tragic French queen in the tumbril. With her as a role model, I tried to retain a regal dignity despite my humiliation. It was made difficult by the endless catfighting of Roxie, Perry, Kiko, and Thirteen.

They were preferable to Guy, who glared at me beady eyed. "Guy, please don't look at me like that."

With his lips as tight as a ventriloquist's, he spat out, "I never want to speak to you again. Every time you involve me in one of your fucking schemes, it ends in disaster. This time, whatever it is you've done, I may end up with a criminal record." I tried to soothe his nerves. He would have none of it. "Don't you understand what you've done to me? I am a children's entertainer. You have ruined me. I have responsibilities. I have a mortgage to pay." I tried to defend myself as a caring, sensible person. "Julian, you are an evil, manipulating, controlling, amoral—" The male officer leveled a finger at Guy. "Enough out of you, Romeo." In complete frustration, Guy pulled his headphones out of his bag and plugged into the reassuring voice of his beloved entity.

Roxie smoothed back her matted hair and asked Kiko, "Perhaps you have an inkling as to what is happening to us. Perhaps you and your seedy cohort have been rather careless in your drug dealing."

Kiko responded in a less than grande dame manner. "Cuntface, speak to my lawyers."

Her seedy cohort, Thirteen, responded by sneaking a small vial of pills out of his décolletage and, when the cops weren't looking, swallowed every last one of them. One eye closing involuntarily, Thirteen sneered at me. "No-talent whore. I'm a bigger star than you'll ever be. Class tells." He threw his head back in a drugged stupor and farted uncontrollably.

Buster beside me was strangely silent. I wondered if he'd been through this before.

"Buster, you don't hate me, do you?"

He put his large muscled arm around my shoulders. "No, honey, I love you."

I lay my head down on his lap, and he gently stroked my bare back as we continued our bumpy ride to destiny.

The paddy wagon pulled up in front of a large municipal building. Buster's eyes bugged out. "Oh shit, we're at the Tombs." The sinisterly named monolithic Art Deco building was Manhattan's infamous courthouse and jail facility. We were herded out of the vehicle and into a dreary anteroom. We sat on two benches facing each other, the eerie fluorescent lighting making us look in our ravaged makeup and sweaty wigs quite repulsive indeed. A terrified silence overtook us, and suddenly I was aware of my near total nudity. Ineffectively, I rearranged my flowing Dynel tresses to give me the most coverage.

A pleasant-looking woman in her forties, a sort of butch TV mom, came out, accompanied by the two policemen who'd ridden with us. She introduced herself as Detective Rhonda Feeney, and she informed us that we were being indicted on eleven counts of robbery and conspiracy.

All at once, our voices, shaking with hysteria began pleading, "Robbery and conspiracy? What does that mean?" Detective Feeney explained that a Donald Caspar had been indicted and arrested along with one Kurt Andresen in the early morning at their residences. The police had evidence that Caspar was the leader of an international antiques thieving ring and we were co-conspirators in their criminal enterprise.

My fellow detainees looked at me in shock. Every muscle in my face lost control, and I feared I was about to have a major stroke. I would have welcomed it. Could they imprison a totally paralyzed ex–female impersonator?

Roxie seized my arm. "Don Caspar? Who I worked with?"

I nodded.

"You know him?"

I nodded.

"We were working for him?"

I nodded.

She peered at me intently. "Were you sleeping with him?"

I nodded.

"This man who was my sworn enemy? And you've never told me?" Buster tried to restrain Roxie, but she pushed him away and grabbed the arm of Detective Feeney. With her other arm, she pointed to me in the grandest of gestures. "Bring me to judgment! *Bring me to judgment*! I will denounce this man before the highest court!"

A small, reedy voice emerged from my throat. "Is Don . . . is he here?" Detective Feeney answered, "He's in custody on Riker's Island. He was arraigned this morning." At once, we began pleading, "I'm innocent! I knew nothing! I'm a hopeless dupe!" Detective Feeney and her backup cops led us to a holding pen. Kiko was defiant. Thirteen wobbled stoned out of his mind. Roxie was wailing uncontrollably. Buster was tragically resigned. Guy gave me one last vindictive look of hatred. Perry whispered in my ear like a broken record, "I told you, I told you, I told you—"

"Told me what?"

"I don't know, but I bet I did."

After we were deposited in the holding pen and left alone, my fellow prisoners turned on me like harpies, all demanding answers. I had no answers. I retreated into mute despondency, oblivious to the shrill voices around me.

A few minutes later, a phalanx of officers came into the room and announced we were all to be separated and interrogated. As the ringleader, I was to be transported to Riker's Island. That news regained me a bit of my old popularity. For a brief moment, I thought my good companions would hold the cops at bay like wild animals protecting their young. However, the presence of those blue uniforms, badges, and nightsticks made them cower and whimper. I gave my friends and enemies one last fragile wave and was escorted between the two policemen down a long, wide corridor. I must have cut a pathetic figure in my matted long red wig, G-string, and cha-cha heels. I felt something scratching my lower back and remembered that I had the very valuable and very hot Angelica Cross swinging over my ass. I thought it best under the circumstances to say nothing.

Abandoned in a small, windowless former classroom, I was convulsing with terror at the thought of being taken to Riker's Island—a prison! I heard a rattling smoker's cough and saw that I wasn't alone in the room. There was another person in detention, a grizzled-looking Hispanic fellow in his thirties, balding with an unkempt mustache and heavily tattooed arms. He gave me the once-over and said in a thick accent, "Your first time, my friend?"

I could barely nod my head. I had to hold on to my sanity until Aunt Jennie arrived with our lawyer. Aunt Jennie would clear this up. She had worked miracles throughout my life. Hadn't she saved me from being sent to a foster home? Hadn't she gotten me into a first-rate college despite mediocre grades? Surely, she could work one more miracle in her old age.

And yet I was guilty. Images of the past few months rushed back at me like a tidal wave. I saw myself writhing nude on that damned cardinal's bed in Don's antiques warehouse of a love nest. I was mortified at my own stupidity, my vanity, my gullibility. Only a complete fool could have fallen for Don's line. Moving furniture indeed. Now it seemed so hopelessly obvious. Kurt was nothing but a thug, a henchman. But hadn't the others fallen for it too? No, they had fallen for my line. They had trusted me, and I'd failed them. I thought of Guy's accusation that I created theatrical situations in life so I could see them played out. Weren't the sheer facts of my life unusual and I merely went with the flow? Maybe in my heart I always knew Don was a thief. If I did, how could I live with this guilt?

My grizzled companion extended his hand. "Jorge."

Weakly, I shook it and inaudibly murmured my name.

"They book you for cross dressing?"

I was in no mood to discuss my legal problems with Jorge. "No, they did not. It's very complicated and a very big mistake."

"Hey, man, don't be mad. I respect you. My brother's a drag queen." Jorge whispered to me in a confidential manner, "Lemme give you some advice, man. Before they ship you off to Riker's, tell 'em you're a faggot. I know some drag queens say they're straight, but say you're a faggot so's they put you in the sex tank with the gay boys. You don't wanna be in the regular prison population. Man, I hate to think what they'd do to that cute little butt of yours."

Jorge brought out my most hoity-toity Dina Merrill behavior. "I appreciate your advice, Jorge, but I sincerely doubt I'll be going to Riker's. I'm expecting my lawyer any minute, and he'll clear up this ridiculous error."

Jorge shrugged and began humming a familiar seventies disco tune while cleaning his teeth with a toothpick.

Shortly thereafter, two cops came in to escort me to another room for interrogation. To think that Don Caspar had told me that life wasn't a B movie. Who was he kidding? Personally, I'd always seen my life as a prestige picture, a top-notch MGM star vehicle directed by Cukor. At this moment, I was relegated to the dismal production values of a Monogram cheapie.

I was led into a small, gray, windowless room, lit by a bare light bulb. The chamber reeked of stale coffee, cigarettes, and the perspiration of generations of the accused. Two cops guarded the door. My interrogators were Det. Rhonda Feeney, Det. Frank Gattuso, a heavyset Paul Sorvino type, and the assistant D.A., Bernard Rauch. Mr. Rauch had the comforting air of a Nazi scientist, whippet thin with pitted skin and piercing eyes. They sat me down while they remained standing. Detective Feeney offered me a cup of coffee. I declined. I was so wound up, the last thing I needed was a nerve stimulant. I felt like I had a satellite dish stuck in my wig.

Detective Gattuso patted my bare shoulder. "I'm sure, Julian, this is the worst thing that's ever happened to you."

"It's certainly up there."

"These are serious charges, so we need some serious answers. Understand me?"

"I'll do my best to answer anything you want to know. I'm completely innocent, so I don't know if I can help you too much."

"I'm sure you can. You can start by telling us all about you and Don Caspar."

My first impulse was to spill everything. It was a fabulous story, full of sex, betrayal, and a great final renunciation scene. I wanted to disarm them with my vulnerability. Then I remembered those words spoken to us in the paddy wagon: "Anything you say can be used against you." I cleared my throat. "I want to be cooperative and I certainly will but I think I should wait until my lawyer arrives."

Mr. Rauch chuckled malevolently. Detective Feeney looked down at her sensible shoes.

Detective Gattuso patted my shoulder harder. "I don't think you get it. This is deep shit. We're talking about millions of dollars in stolen property."

I remembered that house in the unknown suburb filled to the rafters with gorgeous antiques. Obviously, that was where Don stored the booty. And I'd thought he was simply mad for clutter. "I'm sorry. I'd like to wait till my lawyer gets here."

Gattuso suddenly banged his fist against the desk, making me jump a few feet in the air. "Cut the crap!" His face turned a violent shade of purple. I'd heard Duse could blush at will. I wondered if her countryman, Detective Gattuso, could do the same. Surely, he couldn't be that angry with me. He grabbed me roughly by the jaw. "Kid, you're in big fucking trouble. You're looking at twenty to thirty years at Attica!"

"Attica?" I shrieked.

He let me go. The snakelike assistant D.A. spoke softly. "Julian, talk to us. I can see you're not a criminal. You're a sensitive young man or should I say, a sensitive young lady." I was confused. He continued in this vein. "Do you prefer to be called 'Miss'? I have a great deal of experience working with cross dressers and transsexuals. You're one of the prettiest I've seen. Wouldn't you say so, Rhonda?"

"Oh yes, she's very pretty. I wish I had legs like that."

I didn't understand why suddenly Feeney and Rauch were coming on to me like cosmeticians at Max Factor. Then I realized they thought I was a full-time drag queen. "I think you've got me pegged wrong. I'm neither a cross dresser nor a transsexual. I'm an actor. This is just a costume. As a matter of fact, if you have some men's clothes, I'm not picky, I'd love to—"

Once more Gattuso slammed his fist down on the desk. "Fuck you! Fuck you!" he repeated.

I recalled from millions of TV shows that there's always the good cop and the bad cop in these interrogation scenes. Gattuso and Rauch were playing their roles to the hilt. I thought only show people took their behavior from pop culture. If they wanted to improvise a scene, I'd certainly join them. My sincerity was getting me nowhere. I welcomed the opportunity to lose myself in a role, because I was frankly terrified. My burlesque queen costume and 1940s pompadour-styled wig certainly aided my characterization. "Look here, fellas, you ain't gonna get me singin' to the coppers till my shingle arrives. So you can belt me, you can kiss me, but I ain't hittin' no high C's."

My performance left my costars momentarily stunned. We were acting in different styles. They were in a 1980s TV cop show, and I was evoking Stanwyck in her mid-forties Warner Bros. period.

Detective Gattuso snickered. "If we can't get anything out of him, let's ship him off to Riker's. He can wait for his 'shingle' over there."

My tough-as-nails Stanwyck character vanished. "Please don't send me there!" I recalled Jorge's advice. "I guess you can tell I'm gay. I'll be ravished over there. Is there a special area that's safe for gay people?"

An ugly smile swept over Gattuso's swarthy face. "Yeah, we have that. There's a special place for homos right here in the Tombs."

I breathed a sigh of relief. Unable to get me to squeal, they opened the door, and the two policemen guarding it walked me to my new place of detention, the ring of hell reserved for gay felons.

We walked endlessly through a maze of hallways, down an elevator, and down another flight of stairs to a subbasement. We were now on a floor that looked exactly like a prison, with a row of cells with doors that each had only a small window with bars across it. The officer unlocked one and indicated that I go inside. I hesitated, and he gave me a sharp shove. Once inside, I heard the door close with a thud and a series of heavy locks fall into place. Here I was, a college graduate, a recognized solo performer, a sensational cult figure, tossed in the slammer like some common criminal.

I was relieved the cell was empty, and I lay down on the lower berth of a bunk bed. I had a splitting migraine and wondered how much more of this torture I'd have to endure. Then I heard someone humming in the room. The tune was familiar—a seventies disco song. The humming was coming from the bunk above me.

I looked up and saw Jorge leaning over the edge of his bunk, grinning broadly, revealing three chipped gold teeth.

"Hey there, little buddy. You under protection now."

"Are you gay, Jorge?"

"I go both ways. Variety is the spice of life, hey man?" With simian prowess, he swung off the upper bunk and landed on the floor, squatting beside my bed.

I decided to revive my Stanwyck characterization. "Jorge, if you've got something to say, then say it. Otherwise cut the chin music and go back to your tree house."

He moved his face closer to mine. "Ooh, you a pretty she-male."

"Thank you, Jorge, but compliments will get you nowhere. Now, if you'll excuse me, I'd like to take a nap." Jorge took out his toothpick and began chipping at his receding gums again. I snapped with the tough hauteur of Crawford in *Female on the Beach*, "I prefer not to have the remains of your enchiladas suizas in my face."

He laughed and tossed aside the toothpick. "I'll do anything you want, princess." He began running his fingers up my bare leg.

I pushed them away. "Would you fucking cool it? I'm gonna call the guard."

"No you won't, pretty thing, they ain't gonna bother us. Why'd you think I got you here? We gonna party."

"This party's over!" I pushed him away, and scared now, scrambled out of the bed.

He unzipped his work pants. "C'mon, baby, you gonna like this. I got three little warts on my pee-pee that the ladies say feels like they's bein' fucked with a French tickler."

I pushed my face against the window and yelled for the guard. Jorge kept laughing and pressed himself against me, trying to stick his wart-dotted pee-pee up my naked ass. I kept screaming for the guard, but then I heard Jorge make a strange choking sound and saw him quickly move away from me. I looked back at my attacker. His eyes were bulging and he was fervently crossing himself as he stared, transfixed by my behind. I was momentarily perplexed.

Ah, the power of the Angelica Cross! I held myself proudly and intoned, "Behold the Angelica Cross, sinner. My body is a sacred sanctuary, and those who invade it are eternally damned." The role of High Priestess definitely had a zing to it. I'd have to remember this moment for a future theatrical endeavor.

The guard returned, and when he saw Jorge cowering in the corner of the cell, he thought it best to move me elsewhere. "Elsewhere," as I quickly learned, was solitary confinement! Dark, dank, and deathly still, the tiny room was the perfect representation of loneliness. I sat on the cot, a stiff, prematurely aged husk of a female impersonator, without past, devoid of future. The abyss of solitary confinement seemed to be a metaphor for the terror I lived with: the fear of invisibility. This was the ultimate state of anonymity. The only way I could retain a sense of self was to assume a role. My identification with the ill-fated French queen, Marie Antoinette, became complete. I was no longer in the Tombs on Centre Street but imprisoned in the Conciergerie in the year 1793. If I strained to listen, I could almost hear the bloodthirsty rabble at the Place de la Révolution. No doubt on the other side of the locked door I would find the head of my confidante, the Princesse de Lamballe, stuck on a pike for the mob to jeer. In my morbid fantasy, the princess didn't have much chin and had dried egg yolk on her face.

I have no idea how many hours I languished in solitary. Time was no longer measured in minutes but in fleeting fears and dreams.

Finally the heavy door was unlocked, and I was told it was time for my arraignment. Humiliated, filthy, and in rags, I would show them all what a queen could be. Didn't Marie Antoinette write in her last letter to her children that it is only in adversity that we become what we truly are?

I straightened my G-string and left my cell with regal grace.

CHAPTER
34

> *The imperial palace is crumbling about our heads, the city in flames, my beloved emperor dead. My dancing girls are all drowned, their lovely ponytails floating above the mire. What have we done to deserve this?*
>
> Ultima, *Whores of Lost Atlantis*
> Act Two, Scene Four

My eyes, accustomed to the darkness of my cell, were momentarily blinded as I was led into a brightly lit courtroom. All the tables were filled with people. Only the judge was missing. In my exhaustion, I failed immediately to recognize all the players in the scene. Joel and Camille were seated at one table, with a very distinguished lawyer who I imagine had been recommended by Joel's father in Indiana. Someone had notified Sam Fleishman, and I was pleased that he had been able to shake off his disappointment in us and rush down to the courthouse. When Roxie saw him standing in the back of the room, her first reaction was horror at being seen looking so hideous. Her next was to fall sobbing into his arms. "Oh Sam," she wept, "how could this happen to me?"

He stroked her matted hair. "My darling girl, the only question you should ask is 'How do I survive this with a sense of humor?' I'm still trying to learn that one myself."

Guy, Buster, and Perry sat at a table in the back. In their parade costumes they looked like extras who had stumbled into the wrong picture—they'd been hired for a gladiator epic and wound up in a courtroom drama. Ellis

Farrell was seated at a table with Aunt Jennie and her lawyer, Dan O'Hara. Aunt Jennie took one look at me in my skimpy drag costume and groaned. "I don't believe this." Dan helped her out of her chair, and she hugged me tightly. Dan, who has guided Aunt Jennie through numerous tribulations over the years, comforted me in his thick-as-stew Gaelic voice. "Don't you worry, son, we'll be clearing this up shortly."

I told them all, "I'm such an idiot. I had no idea he was a crook. I thought we were working for an antiques dealer."

Aunt Jennie motioned me to sit down beside her. Ellis handed me his overcoat. "The least they could have done was to give you a change of clothes." He placed his coat over my shoulders, and then I noticed another familiar face.

Smoking a cigarette and chatting with a couple of policemen was Wilma! I shouted, "Wilma . . . I mean, Bob, what are you doing here?"

Aunt Jennie stopped me. "He's a detective."

"He's a what?"

Joel, seated in front of us, turned around, his cheeks flushed.

"Yes, a detective, Julian. He's the one who arranged this whole merry adventure."

Wilma/Bob sauntered over to us. "Well, Julian, I hope they haven't been too rough on you."

"How could you do this to me? I trusted you. I befriended you. Was everything an act?"

"I'm afraid it was. I was placed undercover in your apartment. My job's to report what I hear and see."

At that point, I lost all self-control and slapped my former servant so hard his jowls shook.

He twisted my arm. "Sit down before you get yourself in even more hot water," he said coldly.

I was shaking with fury. Under my breath I muttered, "Imagine my own maid ratting on me."

Joel turned around again and whispered angrily, "He wasn't your maid, he was a plant."

"Whaddyamean he was a plant? He *watered* the plants!" I shouted across the room to the squealer, "Hey, Wilma, you left your cookie tin at my place, you son of a bitch!"

Aunt Jennie's lawyer shook his finger at me. "Control yourself, Julian. You're going to make things worse."

Judge Newton Wong entered the courtroom. We rose. I could have sworn Judge Wong did a double take when he took a gander at my outfit, or lack of one. The clerk called the court to order. I noticed the court reporter already taking everything down. He'd have plenty from me. I would expose Wilma as a hypocritical sexual fetishist before this entire court of law.

The case was explained to the judge by the prosecutor, a dowdy, mean-faced brunette with a bad perm. Judge Wong spoke with a slight accent, reiterating that we'd all been indicted on eleven counts by the Grand Jury of New York County. "Mr. Young, how do you plead?"

Indignant in my flame-red tresses, I bellowed, "Absolutely not guilty, of course. Even the notion that I was in any way—"

Dan O'Hara dug his fingers into my arm, forcing me to clam up. My fellow conspirators also pleaded not guilty, though for a second, Buster looked as if he wasn't quite sure.

The prosecutor, Mrs. Jaronik, motioned to excuse two suspects who, it was learned, were indeed "innocent bystanders" at the time of arrest. That was the only time the word "innocence" was applied to those two dames.

Thus Kiko and Thirteen were quickly sprung, having unfortunately been in the wrong place at the wrong time. That would teach them to horn in on somebody else's float. Kiko didn't take her false arrest lightly. She left the courtroom in a blaze of performance-art fury, vowing revenge for her ancestors and invoking the names of several powerful Japanese industrial magnates who, she threatened, would sue the pants off the NYPD. Thirteen, stoned out of his mind, was simply relieved to be off the hook for once. He had evidently more petty arrests in his past than gowns in his closet. And so, exit the red herrings.

Mrs. Jaronik claimed to have two witnesses who could establish the severity of the crime and how these defendants (my raffish crew) figured in. Her witnesses would support her contention that we be held without bail. I couldn't imagine who they could be.

Escorted into the courtroom wearing a stringy blond wig and ripped trenchcoat was none other than our wayward ingenue, Zoe Gomez. I knew she was a kook, but was she a stoolie? Could she really be a witness for the prosecution? Zoe now had the power to send us all up the river. The judge asked her her name, and we all gritted our teeth in anticipation of her response.

She didn't disappoint. "Zoe Monroe, Your Honor."

The young officer beside her gave the judge an amused look and said, "Zoe Gomez, sir." Zoe, it seemed, wasn't in trouble at all. In fact, in the eyes of the law, she was an all-American heroine. She was asked to explain her activities during the previous twelve hours. Zoe fidgeted and twitched and in her breathy little-girl voice explained how she was responsible for Don Caspar's arrest.

"Your Honor, this is very difficult for me because, you know, I firmly believe an actress owes the public only her best performance. Her private life belongs to herself. My emotional life is what I draw on to make my performances profound."

Judge Wong had clearly never come across a character like her before. With great patience he said, "Miss Gomez, we appreciate your sensitivities, but could you please tell us what happened?"

"Well, Your Honor, I am but another victim of Mr. Anthony Andriolo, known to most of the world as Donald Caspar." I then recalled that Zoe had

met Don briefly in my apartment months before. Zoe's monologue un-
folded like a badly edited children's book, with too many illustrations and
not enough captions. "Tony told me he was an antiques dealer, and he was
most helpful to me. When I moved into my new apartment on First Street,
he lent me several exquisite Biedermeier pieces. Swedish, Your Honor, not
Viennese." Zoe had learned her lessons well. "I was very much in love with
him. He promised to protect me and manage my career. He promised to
produce a film based on the early life of Eleanora Duse to star me and to be
shot this fall on location throughout Italy and at Cinecittà Studios in
Rome." Zoe lowered her eyes in sorrow and disappointment. "He promised
to marry me. We were planning to elope to Maryland. You see, my father
has very strict principles and he objected to my marrying a man so many
years my senior despite his vast wealth and holdings. But, Your Honor, you
must believe me, it was not his fortune I was after. I was so very much in
love with the man."

I looked around the courtroom, and Zoe's audience was riveted by her
bizarre, movie-inspired performance. And once more I was in awe of Don's
astonishing duplicity. The man was addicted to intrigue. Not only was he
married to a distinguished socialite but he was having a gay affair with his
corporate librarian's best friend and also sleeping with her female costar.
How many other liaisons did he have? My vanity was shattered that I wasn't
the only femme fatale in his life, yet I was tempted to applaud the dexterity
of his sexual juggling act.

Zoe took a deep breath, her large eyes welling with tears. "Last Wednesday night, I had my bags packed for Maryland. When Tony arrived at my
apartment, I could smell liquor on his breath. He took one look at my
matching Samsonite luggage and burst out laughing. I asked him what he
found so amusing and he informed me in the most humiliating manner
that he never seriously considered marrying me—that he couldn't possibly
marry a weird, trashy East Village actress." Her voice began to shake wildly
and came out in fits and starts. "He told me . . . I was borderline psychotic
. . . and it was inevitable . . . inevitable that one day soon I'd . . . I'd wind up
in an insane asylum." She quickly threw her hands up to her face, trying to
block us from seeing her tears.

Of all Don's crimes, I detested him most for deliberately hurting this fragile, helpless kitten. Zoe tried to compose herself. "You see, I have had periods in my life when things have not always been easy for me . . . I have tried
. . ." She strained to catch her breath. We had never heard her speak so
intimately, and now to witness her exposing herself before all these strangers was too much to bear. We had gossiped and conjectured so much
about her past, and now that she was laying it out before us, I felt revolt-
ingly voyeuristic. "I once entertained thoughts of suicide, but due to my
faith, I could not go through with it. But when Tony told me . . . when he
revealed that he . . ." She looked up at the judge as if he were an all-wise
father. "Oh, Judge, he told me he was already married. And he laughed as

he told me that. He took pleasure in telling me. He enjoyed watching me discover the truth about him. He laughed . . ." Zoe dissolved into tears and there was no way she could continue her narrative. She was excused from the stand.

The prosecutor called Officer Keith Muchowsky to the witness box. This was the young cop who had escorted Zoe into the courtroom. Muchowsky—we just have to say it—was a pretty devastating hunk. He looked tenderly at Zoe, who was still sobbing uncontrollably into her handkerchief.

"Miss Gomez at this point purchased a blond wig and followed Caspar for two days. Our own surveillance team noticed her, and her visibility helped us keep track of Caspar. However, we lost her early yesterday. Six o'clock in the evening Miss Gomez rented a car and followed Caspar as he left his Wall Street office and drove to his home in Westchester." The most amazing part of the story thus far was that Zoe could drive. "She parked the car a block away from the house and waited several hours. Your Honor, what has delayed our arrest of Caspar has been our inability to locate where he had hidden the stolen furnishings. Miss Gomez was able to track him down. At approximately one in the morning, she decided to confront Caspar in the house on Eastway." As the police officer described her activities, Zoe sat expressionless, her face a tearstained porcelain Pierrot mask. "She saw an open window on the second floor and climbed the drain pipe in an attempt to break in. A neighbor walking her dog saw Miss Gomez dangling from the drain pipe and called the police to report a burglary. A squad car arrived, and that, Your Honor, is how we recovered millions of dollars of stolen property."

While Zoe was about to be awarded the keys to the city, the rest of us were still suspected of robbery and conspiracy. The prosecutor then introduced her second witness, who, she claimed in a raspy voice, "will tie all the ugly strands of this tawdry tale together." Her witness was Detective Floyd Cashman. Wilma!

My former maid presented the judge with a two-inch-thick dossier of information he'd collected while in my employ.

Wilma now spoke in a low butch voice which I'd never heard before, not even when he was posing as Bob Livingston. The virtuosity of his performance these past months had been truly dazzling. Still, I loathed and despised him. I felt raped. I had honestly thought Wilma loved me. "Your Honor, Donald Caspar is a man of many identities."

I murmured sotto voce to Aunt Jen, but for the benefit of the entire courtroom, "He should talk."

Wilma/Cashman continued. "Among his aliases are Anthony Andriolo, Patrick Minton, Frederik Rogers, and Neil Fraser. It's perfectly fitting that he chose as his accomplices a troupe of actors."

Perry yelled out, "I never even met the creep." The judge banged his gavel, ordering Perry to keep silent. Wilma wove the most extraordinary tale fabricated from bits of truth. He told how I was introduced to Caspar by

Roxie Flood, who worked in Caspar's office. Roxie was a financial wizard whom Caspar was training to swindle the clients of F, K and M. It was suspected that Ms. Flood was another of his kinky sex partners.

That allegation was too much for Ms. Flood, whose distinctive voice rang through the courtroom. "Shame, Wilma, *shame!*"

Once again Judge Wong was forced to bring down his gavel. Wilma told the court that he saw me struggle to pay my bills each month and had Xeroxes of my checkbook. He saw me fall under the spell of Donald Caspar, becoming his willing sex slave and partner in crime. During this same period, I was engaged in raising funds to produce a pornographic stage show. I convinced my theatrical business partner, Joel Finley, that he could skim some of the proceeds of the antiques thefts to finance our stage venture.

Now he had gone too far. It was one thing to accuse me of skulduggery, but I couldn't bear him dragging Joel into this sordid fantasy. I leaped out of my seat. "That's a goddam lie, Wilma, and you know it!"

Judge Wong brought down his gavel again and berated me. "Mr. Young, if you do not cease and desist, I'll hold you in contempt of this court."

Wilma went further in describing our weekly robberies. He included all sorts of bizarre violent details that he'd mistakenly picked up from my phone calls where I had been describing our current play. When he began implying that I was part of a neo-Fascist cult (undoubtedly culled from conversations he'd heard regarding *Fighting Girls Against the Blitzkrieg*), I found myself running over to the judge's bench. I grabbed hold of the front of his desk as I'd seen defendants do in dozens of movies.

"Don't listen to him, Judge," I cried. "He's a nut. He's got some weird ax to grind."

Judge Wong was banging his gavel so hard and so often, Aunt Jen had to put her hands over her ears. Nothing could stop me.

"You've got to believe me, Judge Wong. He posed undercover in my apartment as my maid in drag. He called himself Wilma and made me spank him and hand-washed my underwear and baked éclairs and don't tell me that was all in the line of duty."

Two cops tried to pull me away from the judge's bench. Roxie, Perry, Buster, Guy, and Camille all were standing shouting, "Listen to him, Judge!"

Ellis rose from his chair and raised his hand. Judge Wong recognized him immediately. "Judge Farrell, my old colleague and predecessor on this bench. I had no idea you were here. Please forgive me."

"That's quite all right, Judge Wong. I must make clear to you that this is all a grievous mistake. I know this young man very well, and I am an investor in his theatrical enterprise, which is far from the pornographic show that has been described."

Feigning amusement, Wilma told the judge that he had nothing further to add and stepped off the stand. Ellis asked the judge for permission to present two witnesses in our defense. I looked around the room to see who the first would be. It was me! I took my place on the witness stand and promised to tell the whole truth and nothing but and to respect the conventions of the court procedures. I realized my hysteria had done nothing for my credibility. My appearance in a waist-length fright wig, glittered G-string, and spike heels wasn't helping matters either.

I tried to speak calmly. "Your Honor, please forgive my appearance. We were arrested while appearing on a float in a parade. I met Don Caspar while working as a temp receptionist in his office. It's very painful for me to admit this in front of my aunt, who raised me, but I fell completely under this man's spell. Something about him clued into whatever was weak in me and I could deny him nothing. My worst crime was that I forced myself to believe he was a man of conviction and that the work we were being paid for was strictly on the level. I can never forgive myself for involving my dearest friends in my foolishness." I might have been overplaying a bit when I added, lower lip trembling becomingly, "I only hope my friends forgive me with far greater grace than I can ever forgive myself."

I've got perfect 20/20 vision, and I saw Perry in the back of the courtroom rolling his eyes over that one. I also saw Wilma, née Floyd Cashman, looking smug and whispering to a cop in the corner of the room.

I switched gears and went from sorrowful regret to righteous anger.

"Judge, the one you ought to be investigating is this Cashman character. There's something funny about a detective getting so into his undercover role. I bet you anything he's got on those red lace panties and the brassiere I bought him right now. This guy's a psychopath, and he's framing me out of some strange fixation of wanting to be me, a famous cult figure. I'm his Magnificent Obsession. And since he can't be me, he now seeks to destroy me. That's the truth, Judge, pure and simple."

Before I could go any further in my denunciation of the evil Wilma, Ellis cut me off. I thanked the judge and returned to my seat. I thought I'd done pretty well until Aunt Jen rolled her eyes and whispered to me, "You didn't get this way from me, did you?"

Former Judge Ellis Farrell's second witness was Camille Falluci. She swore to tell the truth, yet her opening statement was something of a falsehood.

"Your Honor, my name is Camille Falluci and I am engaged to marry Julian Young." Nothing could keep me from checking out the reaction of the audience. I was gratified that no one present was stifling a laugh. All were aware that at this moment, we were playing for drama and not for comedy. Even Roxie remained poker-faced. Camille handed her trusty steno pad to the judge.

"This is a complete record of what we were paid for our services. It was agreed that we were to be paid fifty dollars a night and ten dollars extra for every piece bigger than a chair. Something seemed fishy about this whole deal, and I know that my fiancé isn't what you call a detail person. I felt he needed to be protected from his own innocence, so I accompanied him and the others in the troupe even though I make a good living as a word processor. When I work independently and not through a temp service, I can net thirty dollars an hour. I wish I didn't have to word-process because my first love is designing wigs for Julian. What he has on his head right now is a horrible mess, but believe me, the way I originally conceived it . . ."

I adored my faux fiancée, but she never knew where to draw the line, whether it was dishing out too much information or teasing a coiffure too high.

Ellis had to cut her off before she began handing out her card, which read,

CAMILLE FALLUCI
WORD PROCESSING CONSULTANT
DRAG WIG STYLIST

The years seemed to drop away from Ellis as he made his final remarks. One could easily envision him in his flowing judicial robes. "Judge Wong, I place my entire reputation and word upon this young man's character. He has been cleverly manipulated by a master con artist. I strongly urge that all charges against these people be dismissed."

Wilma protested strenuously but lost ground when Buster produced from his wallet a Polaroid of Wilma *en travesti* coyly shining a moon at my birthday party. The prosecutor agreed to the dismissal of charges if we agreed to cooperate in the prosecution of Caspar and Kurt Andresen.

I yelped, "Cooperate? Turn me loose. I'll give you enough evidence to send the son of a bitch to the guillotine!"

Roxie chimed in with even greater force: "Castration first! And I will wield the sword!"

Joel later said that was the point when Mrs. Jaronik began to think we weren't the most reliable of witnesses.

I was feeling very wobbly after my brush with the law and wasn't aided by having worn four-inch heels for the past ten hours. The whole gang, most of us nearly nude, crowded around Ellis and thanked him. He refused to take credit, saying he believed in the system and that our innocence was most evident.

I enjoyed seeing him and Aunt Jennie together. They had acquired a sort of twinship in my mind, my two saviors, and I fantasized about them going off together. Of course, the only snags were that he was gay and she was an eccentric recluse and they were both around eighty. Still, they made a lovely couple. He held her hand and said, "Mrs. Holman, I can see where your boy receives his inspiration." Aunt Jennie replied, "We owe you so much."

"Would you allow me to take you and Julian to dinner sometime?"

"I'd like that very much. Of course, I'm not sure if Julian will be able to join us. I may have murdered him by then." I was greatly relieved she decided not to expound on her asshole/shithead thesis.

Aunt Jennie took my left arm and Camille my right. As we left the courtroom, we heard a high-pitched commotion. An elegantly groomed dowager was being led down the hall by an attentive policewoman. She was in a highly agitated state. I could decipher only fragments of her conversation.

"It's priceless, I tell you . . . when I heard Andriolo had been apprehended . . . they must find it . . . I will pay anything for its return . . . It's more then a mere possession."

The old woman took a look at my androgynous stripper's attire and shuddered. When I walked past her, she evidently took one last look at my exposed derriere and unleashed a bloodcurdling scream. All eyes were on my ass.

The old lady cried out, "There it is! The Angelica Cross!" and fainted.

CHAPTER 35

CURTAIN CALL

Girl, grab your emeralds and get your ass into that rowboat.

Milena, *Whores of Lost Atlantis*
Act Two, Scene Four

The old lady was Mrs. August Lenehan, and she was so grateful for the return of the Angelica Cross that she rewarded me with ten thousand dollars. I invested it in the show—our capitalization was complete!

For the next week I was still rattled by my brush with the law and near incarceration. I was also mortified by my complete gullibility and how I had implicated my closest friends in this folly. It says something about their sweet natures that they forgave me so readily.

To Perry it all seemed so movielike that it shook him out of an oncoming depression and made him consider writing a courtroom mystery novel. Perry announced to me one day, "My therapist says that at some crucial point in your life, Julian, you turned yourself into a fictional character."

"Oh, Perry, that's so simplistic. I'm real; it's the world that's a three-act play." I wasn't sure what I meant, but it sounded good.

Guy retreated into his New Age philosophy and accepted that in a previous life he must have inflicted some awful wrong on me and was now doomed in this life to pay for it. He forgave me, poor kid. Joel found solace in the teachings of Christ and in the pages of *Variety*. Buster searched for a

literary quotation that would express his feelings toward my foolishness
and came up with a rehash from *Othello*. Something to the effect of "It's
better, Sweetie, to have loved too much than to be a dried up old prune
who's never been laid." I appreciated the sentiment. Roxie got over her
anger about my affair with her hated boss because she was desperate to
hear every sexual and romantic detail and knew I'd be tight-lipped unless
she conceded to total forgiveness.

Zoe cornered me one day and said haltingly that she was disturbed over
something regarding Don and her and me. She started and stumbled several times, so I took over. "Zoe darling, please don't feel guilty over having
an affair with my lover. You suffered in some ways far more than I. And
really, I'm in no position to condemn. I was the 'other person' too. His poor
wife is the one with whom we should sympathize. And besides, my relationship with Don was so secretive, how could you have known I wasn't just a
mere acquaintance of his? Please believe me, I bear you no ill will."

I searched her face for a response. Her brow was furrowed in deep
thought.

"No, Julian, I never thought of any of those things. I just want to know,
did Don promise to star you in a film about Eleanora Duse?"

"No, Zoe"—I sighed—"that one was all yours." She smiled beatifically.

I considered dragging myself over to Riker's Island to confront the villain
who had nearly destroyed me. There is a wonderful scene in the movie *Gas-
light* when Ingrid Bergman has her final showdown with a tied-up Charles
Boyer, who's been caught by the police after having attempted to drive her
mad. It was the scene that clinched her first Oscar. I longed to reenact that
moment with Don Caspar, who was even more handsome and sexy than
Boyer, but I realized he'd recognize the movie and laugh in my face.

The bottom line was he may have given me a hard time but now he was
actually doing hard time. It was an open-and-shut case. Kurt Andresen was
deported and sentenced to fifteen years and Caspar to twenty. He's sitting
in stir right now, but knowing Don, he's probably running the joint and his
cell is filled with Louis Quinze and no repros.

It must have been humiliating for Don's family to see his face splashed
across the front pages as the ringleader of an antiques thieving ring. The
press had a field day describing Don Caspar's double life and digging up his
unsavory past as a two-bit Hollywood hustler. Publicity hound that I am,
part of me longed to be revealed in print as the secret love slave of the
elegant gentleman crook. Joel nixed the idea, and our newly hired publi-
cist's first job was to keep our names *out* of the papers.

All thoughts of Don Caspar had to be pushed aside. Suddenly we were in
rehearsal and working twelve-hour days readying *Whores of Lost Atlantis* for its
off-Broadway opening. Zoe Gomez surprised us by being billed under her
real name. "This dreadful scandal has given me a new sense of identity and
my own strength of character." When we had to fill out insurance forms, we

all craned our necks to see what Zoe would put down as her age. She never disappointed. On the line designated for age she wrote "Frightfully young." I was just relieved she hadn't used Frightfully Young as her stage name.

We opened for previews and were heartened to see that our cult following was traveling the few blocks west to our new, higher-profile digs.

Unlike the old days, when the critics attended opening nights and rushed to hand in their reviews to make the early papers, nowadays they attend one of several previews but their review doesn't appear until the morning after the opening night. The critic from *The New York Times* came on a Thursday night, and our official opening wasn't until the following Sunday. Awaiting transportation to Riker's Island was a pip next to the anxiety of waiting for that *Times* review. So much depended on that one man's opinion. We had moved so quickly from that first performance at Golgotha just over a year before. It seemed unfair that this miraculous fairy tale might end with such sadness because of one critic's venom.

Opening night was sold out, and it was, as I've come to learn, a fairly typical opening-night performance. Most of the audience had seen the show before and were just as anxious as the cast. The upshot was that their laughter started off a bit too raucous, reminiscent of the laugh track to *My Favorite Martian*. The performance was as relaxed and effortless as a race at Aqueduct. During the curtain call, I made a brief speech thanking Harold Alpern for having us at his theatre, thanking our investors for their faith, and introducing each member of the company. I introduced Joel last—as actor and director and producer—and I was thrilled at the strength of his ovation.

For our final bow, we all linked arms. Roxie shot me a brief glance, and I could see that she shared my pride in how swell we all looked in our new costumes and the air of confidence we exuded. We weren't solitary figures furtively searching for a place in the world. We were a company.

When the curtain fell, we hurried downstairs to the dressing rooms to get ready for the cast party at a new dance club named simply Red. None of us had the time to pull off a wig before the majority of the audience descended into the green room, and we all left the dressing rooms to mingle with the crush. I was amazed at the sea of familiar faces in the strangest of combinations. I saw Joel's former boss, Howard Fuller, who'd invested a wildly generous two hundred and fifty dollars in the show, chatting with Mrs. Lenehan, the owner of the Angelica Cross. Naturally all four of the Young Julians were present but looking a bit saddened, wondering perhaps if their personal property was now going to be whitewashed for mass consumption. Rupert and Ruby were chattering with good cheer about their financial points in the show to Harold Alpern. They wore the same chic Armani wardrobe they'd modeled in a recent issue of Italian *Vogue*. Mannequin made a grand entrance in a bronze sequined Norman Norell sheath and was engaged in conversation with Keith Muchowsky, the handsome cop who'd been so gentle to Zoe in court. Sam Fleishman was holding up Roxie, who looked spent from the virtuosic mugging she'd done onstage for the past two hours. Only Ellis and Aunt Jen were missing. Ellis had a cold and had to stay home. Up until the last minute Aunt Jen was going to attend. The morning of the opening she phoned contritely. "Julian, if my presence would help you tonight you know I'd be there. But I'm afraid I'll make you nervous, and I think I'd totally freak out." I understood perfectly.

Camille found me and gave me a big hug. I had never seen her look so pretty. While she was stage-managing the show from the lighting booth, she had set her hair in rollers, combed it out, and made up her face. "Julian, you know I want only the best for you. Whatever has happened to us or whatever will happen to us, I want you to know that you're my best friend."

We heard shouting from the back of the room near the door. It was Buster. He had run out of the theatre still in his bathrobe to buy the first edition of *The Times*. He shouted, "It's here! I've got it!" My throat contracted, and I thought I was about to throw up. Buster tore through the crowd waving the newspaper. Silence descended over the party crowd as he approached me with the dreaded object. Buster's childlike face conveyed none of the terror I felt at what lay on that printed page. He handed me the paper, but my hands shook so badly I could only toss it over to Joel. Joel also couldn't bear to read it aloud and stood there in a state of helpless panic.

Sam Fleishman grabbed the paper out of his hands. "I don't think my nerves can take much more." He quickly scanned the opening lines of the review and gulped. "It's good." His voice shaking, he read aloud *The New York Times* review. It was better than good! It was one of the greatest rave reviews I'd ever read. After each line, everyone in the room cheered.

"With its air of charming decadence and innocent sophistication, 'Whores of Lost Atlantis' should become a cult success that could run for years." Everyone connected to the show was mentioned. "Joel Finley, besides playing a perfectly perverse and funny emperor, directs the show with great aplomb. He never misses a comic step and infuses the entire evening with a surprising elegance." Of Roxie, the critic noted, "She is the hysterically funny embodiment of every movie tough dame from Joan Blondell to Eve Arden." Perry was "possessed of a comically mobile face that evokes the great silent film comedians." Guy was no longer merely Joel McCrea after Ex-Lax but "a comic leading man of true sincerity." It was written that Zoe had a "fragile doll-like appearance that splendidly masked her brilliantly raucous comic style," and Buster was mentioned as being "the requisite beefcake who is able to earn his own share of laughs." Camille's wigs were cited as "spectacular," and Mamacita's costumes were "scrumptiously vulgar and oddly splendid. Indeed with all the scene stealing going on, Mr. Normand's outrageous costumes threaten to steal the show."

And what of the star and playwright, you may ask? I'd hate to be like Kiko and quote my own reviews, but if you *must* know: "The audience laughs at every line and even some of the silences. . . . Mr. Young not only provides himself with a great role but is exceedingly generous in providing wonderful roles for his company. . . . Mr. Young is no ordinary female impersonator but an actor of great subtlety and range. He not only possesses the best gams of any current leading lady but emerges at the end of the evening a true star."

When Sam read those words, Camille squeezed my hand. I felt nothing. I was in shock. Sam finished reading the review, and pandemonium reigned at the Washington Square Theatre. People were sobbing and embracing. It was as if the *Titanic* had been raised with the passengers and crew still alive. I just stood mute as seemingly everyone in the room kissed me. I heard someone whisper, "Look at him. He doesn't know what hit him." Oh, but I did. I was overwhelmed by that knowledge. I slipped into my dressing room and closed the door. I sat down, held on to the edge of the dressing table, and indulged myself in a good cry. Ten years of struggle had led up to this moment. Now I had a career. Now I could truly begin. Maybe it was more than ten years—maybe it was more like thirty years. Every event of my entire life seemed to have brought me to this moment. I wanted to remember each second because right now I was completely happy. No movie fantasy could be as perfect as this, no expectation or dream as magical. Not only was I a success but I was able to bring everyone I loved along with me. Everyone had been singled out, no one ignored. The world couldn't be so bad if this could happen to us. I looked in the mirror and knew that it didn't get much better than this.

Gradually the green room emptied out as everyone scurried over to Red. Before I could leave the theatre, I had to make two phone calls.

Aunt Jennie picked up almost before the first ring, and she knew it was me before I could say a word. "The doorman ran upstairs with the paper when he read the review. Is it really true?"

"It is. I'm holding the paper in my hand; I'm looking at it and there it is."

"I'm going to have to see the lawyer tomorrow and change my will to include that critic." Aunt Jennie paused for a moment. "You know, Julian, after I read the review I found myself talking to your mother in heaven. I said, 'Gertie, our boy is on his way. We did a good job.' "

I then called another elderly person unable to attend the performance. Ellis had also already read the review. "A young neighbor of mine ran to the corner newsstand and brought it to me. Good work. You've really done it. Of course, I knew it would be a rave when you performed the play in my bedroom. It just confirms to me the good taste of *The New York Times*. How exciting it will be to see what happens to you now."

I said wearily, "I hope it won't be as exciting as what's happened to me in the last few weeks."

"Grist for the mill, Julian, and eventually the stuff of fiction. I'm sure someday you'll write about it." Ellis was about to bid me good night when as an afterthought he said, "Oh, will you be around in the early part of the day? I'd like to send a messenger over with a little belated opening night present."

The next morning, I was awakened by the front door intercom. Groggily, I stumbled out of bed and asked who it was. It was Ellis's messenger. I opened the door, and the fellow carried in a large square box. With trembling hands, I cut open the packing tape. I didn't dare imagine what could be contained in it, but I had a suspicion.

It was the Bernhardt headdress. My heart stopped. I lifted it out of its newspaper wrappings and carried it like the Holy Grail into the sunny living room. The morning light made the century-old stage jewels sparkle brilliantly. Never had anything been so dazzling. Gently, I placed it on the center of the mantelpiece. The fireplace had been plastered over decades before, but the crown was the real thing. One could quibble and say the jewels were just paste, not real rubies and sapphires. But it was genuine artifice. An actress had created fantastic memories in the minds of everyone who saw her wear it.

My memory of Ellis and his generosity will stay with me forever, as well as the memory of all the eccentric children who fill my world. Brushing my fingers over the crown, I thought perhaps it was time to lay to rest all those impossible-to-resolve questions about identity and how one fits in. Experience is what defines a person. Our lives are cluttered curio cabinets full of experiences transformed into memory like ore into gold. It's those memories of love and friendship and work that make us strong and complete.

This happened five years ago. So as the newscasters say, "Where are they now?" Well, for one thing, *Whores of Lost Atlantis* ended its New York run barely three weeks ago. It racked up 2,024 performances and broke the record of being the longest running nonmusical in the history of off-Broadway. Not bad for something I wrote between phone calls at the receptionist's desk. It's been performed in theatres all over the country, from Cleveland to Tampa to small towns in Maine. Our original company didn't remain in the show for the entire run. We played in it for nearly two years, then we all left to appear in my next play, *Gidget Goes Psychotic*. We played that for a year and then did another year in *Unisex*, a farce about Greenwich Village in the early seventies.

I've done just fine. I count my blessings every day that I'm one of the few people who can honestly say that I earn my living doing what I love. I wouldn't say I'm exactly a household name, but if I wasn't me, I'm sure I'd know me. I'm still hopelessly stage struck, and I've got a million ideas for new plays with wonderful parts for myself. In my next play, I'm going to play a radical role—a man! I'm finally ready to ditch the wigs and gowns for a while. It'll be a strange experience appearing onstage with no makeup— well, I *may* use a touch of base and a little mascara. I'm also in the process of writing a novel based on our days at Golgotha. However, I'm in a terrible quandary over how fictional it should be. I wonder if merely changing everyone's name is enough.

What are the others doing? Joel is living in England, where he is directing and coaching English actors on how to speak with an American accent. Roxie married Sam Fleishman and has achieved local fame as a television spokesperson in a series of funny commercials for Fleishman Fashions. Buster is also associated with a product. His handsome face and form grace the pages of every national gay magazine as the model for a mail-order undergarment called the Butt Enhancer. Joel and Buster never rekindled their romance, but a true friendship developed between them and continues to grow even though they live on opposite sides of the ocean. Guy had a major emotional catharsis and out of his pain began channeling his own entity. He now has a cable TV show run in several markets and makes big money as a New Age guru with his videos, audiocassettes, books, and sold-out seminars. By the way, his entity—over whom he has no control—is a rather grand ancient courtesan who goes by the name of Julia. Hmmmmm. I say he has some explaining to do.

Perry decided to go back to school to get a degree in psychiatry. He has finished writing his first mystery novel. It's about a small theatre company in New York with a drag leading lady. Actors are getting knocked off like flies, and it's finally revealed that the leading lady is the mad killer. Perry, too, has some explaining to do.

Camille decided she'd had it with New York and has moved to New Hope, Pennsylvania, where she has embraced what Roxie calls "the alternative life-style." Yes, she has become a fun-loving lesbian and fills her nights with lesbian square dancing and her weekends white-water rafting with her girlfriends. She confessed to me recently that she always had repressed lesbian desires, and perhaps her crush on me was merely because I was the closest thing to a woman without being one. Camille also has some explaining to do.

Mamacita died two years ago. His health was remarkably good until right after we opened *Unisex*. After that, his decline was swift and devastating.

His illness brought out the best in us. Guy spent hours massaging Mamacita's aching muscles and helped him express his deepest feelings about letting go of this world. Buster cooked Mamacita's favorite foods and served them in the nude. Perry made himself available whenever Mudge needed to take a break, and to lift Mamacita's spirits, bleached the invalid's black hair platinum blond. When Mamacita's eyes began to fail, Joel, Roxie, Camille, and I took turns rereading to him the complete works of Jacqueline Susann. Through it all, the faithful Mudge, always dressed in white, sat quietly in the corner, forever sewing beads. When he finished beading the voluminous black velvet cloth, he used it as an exquisite shroud that was buried with our wonderful designer.

In some ways Zoe was the most devoted among us. There was no task too personal or too distasteful for her to perform. She also provided Mamacita with a satisfaction she denied all others. Shortly before he died, Zoe was alone with him and Mudge. Mudge told me Zoe was about to leave to get a bite to eat when Mamacita motioned her to come closer. Explaining that death was near, he managed to ask Zoe the question we all wanted to know. "How old are you?" She thought for a moment and gallantly whispered her true age in his ear. Then she put on her coat and quipped in a tough voice, "Mamacita, when I get back from that deli, you better be history."

After Mamacita's death, Zoe disappeared. She was always a bit of a mystery, but after several years went by, this time we worried we'd never hear from her again. With his fascination for the mystery genre, Perry was determined to solve her disappearance.

Last week, I received a letter from him from Key West. The weather was great, he had a brief fling with a handsome mortician from Buffalo, and he'd seen a hysterically bad amateur production of *Whores of Lost Atlantis*. Perry included a flier for a show that had played Key West a few weeks earlier. It was a one-woman show about Helen Keller called *In Her Own Words*. It starred an actress with the odd name Angelica Cross.

FOR THE BEST IN PAPERBACKS, LOOK FOR THE

In every corner of the world, on every subject under the sun, Penguin represents quality and variety—the very best in publishing today.

For complete information about books available from Penguin—including Pelicans, Puffins, Peregrines, and Penguin Classics—and how to order them, write to us at the appropriate address below. Please note that for copyright reasons the selection of books varies from country to country.

In the United Kingdom: For a complete list of books available from Penguin in the U.K., please write to *Dept E.P., Penguin Books Ltd, Harmondsworth, Middlesex, UB7 0DA*.

In the United States: For a complete list of books available from Penguin in the U.S., please write to *Consumer Sales, Penguin USA, P.O. Box 999— Dept. 17109, Bergenfield, New Jersey 07621-0120*. VISA and MasterCard holders call 1-800-253-6476 to order all Penguin titles.

In Canada: For a complete list of books available from Penguin in Canada, please write to *Penguin Books Canada Ltd, 10 Alcorn Avenue, Suite 300, Toronto, Ontario, Canada M4V 3B2*.

In Australia: For a complete list of books available from Penguin in Australia, please write to the *Marketing Department, Penguin Books Ltd, P.O. Box 257, Ringwood, Victoria 3134*.

In New Zealand: For a complete list of books available from Penguin in New Zealand, please write to the *Marketing Department, Penguin Books (NZ) Ltd, Private Bag, Takapuna, Auckland 9*.

In India: For a complete list of books available from Penguin, please write to *Penguin Overseas Ltd, 706 Eros Apartments, 56 Nehru Place, New Delhi, 110019*.

In Holland: For a complete list of books available from Penguin in Holland, please write to *Penguin Books Nederland B.V., Postbus 195, NL-1380AD Weesp, Netherlands*.

In Germany: For a complete list of books available from Penguin, please write to *Penguin Books Ltd, Friedrichstrasse 10-12, D-6000 Frankfurt Main I, Federal Republic of Germany*.

In Spain: For a complete list of books available from Penguin in Spain, please write to *Longman, Penguin España, Calle San Nicolas 15, E-28013 Madrid, Spain*.

In Japan: For a complete list of books available from Penguin in Japan, please write to *Longman Penguin Japan Co Ltd, Yamaguchi Building, 2-12-9 Kanda Jimbocho, Chiyoda-Ku, Tokyo 101, Japan*.